THE
HOUSE
OF THE
SOLITARY
MAGGOT

JAMES PURDY

Part Two of the
Continuous Novel
SLEEPERS IN
MOON-CROWNED VALLEYS

THE
HOUSE
OF THE
SOLITARY
MAGGOT

1974
Doubleday & Company, Inc.
Garden City, New York

DESIGN BY RAYMOND DAVIDSON

Library of Congress Cataloging in Publication Data

Purdy, James.
    The house of the solitary maggot.

    The second vol. of the trilogy, Sleepers in moon-crowned valleys, of which
the first vol. is Jeremy's version.
    I. Title.
PZ4.P9853Ho   813'.5'4
ISBN 0-385-04413-5

Library of Congress Catalog Card Number 74–4866

For my Grandmother, Minnie Mae

THE
HOUSE
OF THE
SOLITARY
MAGGOT

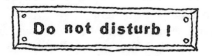

Do not disturb !

reads the plaque over Eneas Harmond's house.

I can see no one, he would call out from behind his shutters. (Eneas Rex Harmond is the complete name.) The town has fallen, how else can I explain it, he began, but in this communiqué style, our town of Prince's Crossing has fallen, Mr. Skegg, its leading citizen has been interred in Lady Bythewaite's rose garden (a few delphiniums are growing there also), with the body not having been inspected by coroner or doctor (there is no coroner or doctor for miles around), and if you ask me Lady Bythewaite and her alleged great-great-nephew are both out of their heads. He has just come home from the war, and is, if not a madman, using a dangerous drug, he is seldom clothed, and they spend their entire afternoons and evenings (their mornings are spent in their hobbling around in a state of undress drinking pot after pot of strong Louisianne style coffee) in listening to a tape recorder into which Lady Bythewaite has been persuaded by this said nephew to pour out the story of her life in Prince's Crossing. Furthermore, I have never heard this alleged nephew say more than four or five words in succession. Actually I have only heard him clearly pronounce only *Yeas* and *Mnnos*. Despite my willingness to believe him an impostor there is a strong family likeness in his face and body to both Lady Bythewaite (she is called Lady by the people of Prince's Crossing, a village as I say which no longer exists, expunged by a merciless state, county, and township authority) and to her common-law husband Mr. Skegg, who has, as I say, recently died (mysteriously) and been perfunctorily buried by order of Nora Bythewaite. The nephew, a stalwart fellow, though of delicate mouth and eyes, buried him, assisted by me as shoveler. There was no ceremony.

But this is only part of the reason I, Eneas Harmond, have put up the Do Not Disturb sign.

My own sanity seemed to be at stake, I who had been her steward, bailiff, caretaker, use any word you like, for so many years.

I stood that morning of the burial my eyes on the delphiniums so that one would suppose I was a judge of them, was studying them, and they were, I know, almost hurting-beautiful in the cool spring air.

"I am happy at last, Eneas," Lady Bythewaite whispered. "Happy . . . at the very last."

"I never knew you had a great-great-nephew. Never knew, actually, anybody had."

"He searched the land for a relative," she explained. "But did you know, oh Eneas," she came back to what was, I gather, her happiness, "did you actually know there were such things as these tape recorders which catch the human voice?" I almost heard *tapeworms*. Here in Prince's Crossing, I cogitated, deaf now to her running words, here we have almost consciously ignored the world. First we were a town in the nineteenth century, a flourishing little place, then we were downgraded to a village, as the twentieth century came blighted into being, and finally in the Great Depression, we fell to *Unincorporated,* and, wait, only lately a huge truck from the county or township or state came and deprived us even of that designation. We are not even a crossroads, perhaps. Prince's Crossing ceases to exist! That is another reason I have left the sign on my house DO NOT, etc.

"Lady Bythewaite is to blame!" I spoke to myself after that rude funeral. Or perhaps the dead man, Mr. Skegg, known as her common-law spouse, was even more blameworthy! But the overriding fact, up and beyond his death and her guilt, remains: a "community," if not a great city, has fallen. (Lady Bythewaite being a staunch individualist eschewed and even loathed the word "community" because it implied using other people's property and talent to loaf and dwindle away on.) And Mr. Skegg who was the living embodiment of this "settlement" (here I avoided the word community, so under her heavy jurisdiction was I, though it was on my tongue's tip to say.)

"My great-great-nephew will be staying with me," she had begun that day of his arrival, ushering me into her study, trying to prepare me for the change in the great house his coming would effectuate. "Do you hear what I am saying to you, Eneas Rex Harmond?" she called out to me like a voice in the county seat registrar's office. "My nephew, be prepared, is like an unwashed . . . , say, horse," she took this animal for a comparison after having had on her tongue to say, I do believe, *horse* in the first place, but almost changing it to goat, not wanting to call him *horse* for a reason that a listener is more apt to understand when he has heard all her words which went into the whirling spools. "There are real nettles, burrs in his hair, I do believe, and Eneas, are you minding? he is alas using some powerful stimulant . . . But when one's town, one's property" (she lifted hands and eyes to the rafters) "are falling on top of one, I am glad to have almost anybody in this house . . . It is most unusual for me at my age (what was her age?) to see a young man at the breakfast table without anything on at all but a neckerchief. I believe my great-great-nephew is good-looking if one washed off all the accumulations of . . . deposit, say dirt . . . Eneas, he is not after my money, I know that. He cares nothing for property. I don't know whether it is the stimulant he uses or what, but he is indifferent to goods, don't you see, indifferent to all that the world has to offer."

Her voice had gone far far down on the scale on these last words, like one still talking while falling to sleep.

"But as we know," she cried coming to with a jump and start, "Mr. Skegg is dead, and his body lies in that room yonder. Pray step in and say a last farewell to him . . ."

But the nephew came in at that moment, and stopped me from paying my respects. We stood looking at one another in strained embarrassment, Lady Bythewaite making no move to introduce us.

"What is your nephew's name?" I began at last.

"What is his name?" she countered, like one who has been deeply insulted.

The nephew replied by roaring out a laugh which caused Lady Bythewaite to put her hand to her temple.

"He is entirely impossible, Eneas, but I am not in need of a *possible* young man."

"To return to Mr. Skegg, my sorrow is greater here than you perhaps will care to admit to yourself, oh hard, judging Eneas. To think he lies dead in my parlor! He had lost everything, owned not a penny, after being the greatest magnate in this part of the country. Penniless! Not a red cent! He came to me. He said, I will go to the poor farm. Never, I countered, not while there is breath in my body. But to no avail! He was obsessed with going to the poor farm. My hospitality was too kind! So there was nothing to do to satisfy him but lend him my horse and buggy to convey him to the poor farm. I had always offered him my home, with free access to all the rooms, at any hour . . ." Here she first observed her nephew was fiddling with the little machine and spools which were to capture the words that will begin to unfold momentarily. "A court reporter, Eneas Rex Harmond!" she exclaimed, more surprised than angry. Occasionally, letting the spool roll without his aid, the nephew would go take a peep at the dead man stretched out on a Victorian ottoman, a beautiful lap robe over his high shoes, his long white freshly shampooed hair down to his shoulders. He was the great magnate, soul of Prince's Crossing, who, without Lady Bythewaite's intervention and friendship, would have known a pauper's grave, had there been such a place in our vicinity, but there being none, he was to be given a plot in the rose garden. Mr. Skegg, whose chief fame other than being a magnate, was that he was the father of the great silent film star MAYNARD EWING, who has undergone a revival, as people tell me.

Lady Bythewaite has never acted more irresponsible in some ways than she does today, that is has never acted more like herself, one might say. She claims the young man is her nephew, but perhaps for reasons best known to her, or to him, she has invented this. Many people think she has invented her entire life. For instance, why do people call her Lady Bythewaite? True, she is English, that is she came from Britain in the last century, but, and here is the important thing, does anybody think that *Lady*, so laughable in this district and part of the world, implies any usurpation of a title? And if he is her great-great-nephew, who was his father, mother, what were his beginnings? She keeps her lips closed on all that.

But the scandal of Mr. Skegg's death! Had any ordinary person been mixed up in all this, he would be visited by the authorities, indeed would be taken into custody. But there are no authorities in Prince's Crossing, except, come to think of it, a sheriff two or three counties away who comes on very unusual occasions to take a look around. And remember, about the time of Mr. Skegg's strange death and burial it had already been decided that Prince's Crossing, which had been a town in 1800, a village in 1902, is today nonexistent, and people have told me they had not even got a glimpse of it when they drove through it even at a slow pace!

Lady Bythewaite always smiled, I thought, when we talked of how Prince's Crossing no longer existed, perhaps because she owns principally all the fine old houses left, and so what was a town, a village, and then unincorporated is, in a way of speaking, her "fief." It is all Lady Bythewaite's private domain. And the people here and about (I was tempted to use the phrase "in this neck of the woods" but she has forbidden the use of this expression in her presence) are not up in arms against her at all, as they may have been years and years ago. They now claim they love Lady Bythewaite, though her great-great-nephew being one of those youngsters (long hair, stimulants) is far from finding favor here. Yet even he, coached no doubt by her, is a favorite-favorite with the few people who have run up against him. We are going fast! we Prince's Crossing people. Mr. Skegg's death was so serious! He who had been one of the richest men in the country died a pauper. In fact, he had debts which Lady Bythewaite paid.

There is a long-standing rumor that Lady Bythewaite was the mother of Owen Haskins, Mr. Skegg's younger son, and that she may even have been the mother of the famous silent-film star MAYNARD EWING, who appeared in the silent screen classics *The Eagle's Nest* and *Eye of the Storm*. Then before I began to listen to her in earnest, to hear the spools as they flew with her talk, my own sense of the succession of events was confused, clouded, for there was Mr. Skegg laid out in the parlor, and then there was the frightful accident of the "funeral" itself. I came home ready to burst with horror. For a horse and wagon were racing about the streets and roads, and suddenly the driver stopped, and out from his coffin Mr. Skegg fell to the pavement. His mouth opened showing he had his own teeth and, unlike many ancient persons', they were very very white . . .

But she seems almost to welcome this dissolution of the country, the losing of our railroads, the general confusion and disrepair. For what other woman of her antecedents would have taken in this boy, avowed nephew? He's not right, I cogitated, once Mr. Skegg was gathered up again, put in his coffin, and we had buried him. Look at his eyes, hair, mouth. He's under the influence of some strange powder or plant, who knows?

Am I, too, along with her and him, taking advantage of the fact that Prince's Crossing is no longer under any immediate jurisdiction of federal, state, or local government? In the confusion of the present day when even the weed-grown-over sign *Unincorporated* has at last disappeared . . .

"He was spared a pauper's grave, remember, Eneas!" She had bent over me as I sat there in my blackest depression. "Do not reproach yourself, I say. He was laid to rest by friends."

Lady Bythewaite kept her eyes fastened on me as she spoke into the whirling spools of the nephew's recorder, while my glance rested on him. He had received some sort of eye damage in the war, and used spectacles which he had purchased at the dime store, but which he put on only when he adjusted the spools or looked over old papers or photographs.

Unused to recordings I interrupted with "You mean to tell me you have buried a man without the proper authorities being apprised of this fact, or of his death, indeed?" Later I was to realize all these "uncalled for" remarks of mine went down on the record of the spools, but the nephew did not seem to mind.

"What do you expect me to do, give him over to the crows, buzzards, field rats?"

Lady Bythewaite always used three or even four examples to back up her defense where one would have done, that is why didn't she just say *leave his body to the crows.*

Her digression expanded: "The doctors all left here ages ago. There is no coroner because there is no local government, and you of all men know this, Eneas!"

Yes, she was bright as a button—the rumor she is mad is unfounded.

But the great-great-nephew, I pondered. What *isn't* wrong with him? She refuses to blame his war experiences for his condition, however. She merely says he has always been an unusual boy. Besides, the present generation, Lady Bythewaite informs me, is most remarkable.

The word remarkable, like many words used by her, seems obscure in meaning to me. Did she mean worthy of remark, terrible (which to her often meant unendurable but satisfying), wonderful (good), or what?

"Imagine my telling him of my life, Eneas," she again addressed me instead of the spools. "Imagine, if you can, a young person who wishes to know everything about me. That is what is remarkable, that and that alone, don't you see?" She was laughing uproariously, and I now saw that she was smoking the same pestiferous drug he used.

I did not answer her, I did not accuse her either. She was al-

ways ready for the new provided she could have her own way
with it.

"He has brought me back from the state Mr. Skegg was in
. . . Before my great-great-nephew came, I had nearly lost my
memory . . . You recall, how once when you were away, Eneas,
I hired the old man down the road, Mr. Cruikshank, to come
in twice a week and catechize me as follows: What day of the
week is it? what season are we in? what are the principal con-
stellations when I look up at the heavens? hour of sunrise, sunset? Finally," she added, watching me grin, "what is my name,
and who do they say I am about the county?"

"Our Lady Bythewaite always makes a joke of everything," I
addressed the nephew.

"Cousin Harmond," she used my *county* name now, "sit quiet,
please, as I speak." There was only the kitchen stool which
pleased me to sit on, and I had been squirming a good deal even
on it.

"Get your sprawling farmer's body quiet . . . My great-great-
nephew has fallen hopelessly in love with me. Rather, in love
with my period. I have seldom known such happiness. To be
heard out, I mean. To speak into the little whirling reel and
hear it but a moment later come back, a bit coffined it's true in
sound and volume, with my—as he calls it—*voix d'or*, for our
nephew has traveled. Eneas, he loves the story of Mr. Skegg
. . . And the bravery of the boy to bury him. He buried my . . ."

"Lady Bythewaite, since you have thrown all caution to the
winds," I started up, "why don't you use the word for *him*
Prince's Crossing always used?"

"My *paramour*," she responded immediately, a softening of
the lines about her mouth, "or in common parlance, lover,
common-law husband." She laughed like a young woman.

I had been upstairs. I had seen to my considerable surprise.
(I am beyond terror, I was in the "other war," there is no horror
that I have not sat down to. I once held a man's eyeballs in my
hand, I was buried in another man's bowels for two days, I have

been subjected to intolerable physical abuse, atrocity by the enemy, and so on, but this is not my story, the world is tired of heroes, though I am one.) I saw the imprint of two heads in the giant feather bed. Great-great-nephew and great-great-aunt were sleeping together at night, for the twofold purpose, one that he did not wish to miss anything she might think of in the night (the recorder and spools were kept at the foot of the bed), and two, because owing to his war experiences he sometimes became hysterical at night, and then while he shouted and cried she smoothed his hair, and heated for him a special calmative to drink.

"You are responsible for me." Lady Bythewaite was shaking me gently, bending over me. Ah, yes, the terms of her will. She had named me executor of her estate when Mr. Skegg had died, and was buried, after falling out of the buggy . . .

"Doesn't your great-great-nephew ever speak?" I, Eneas Harmond, inquired at various times of Lady Bythewaite.

"I hear him talking in the bathroom at night, but that's after he's had his pipe," she replied after a great deal of hesitation for her.

"Ah, so," I said, trying to act as if I found his mum nature not really remarkable.

"And, Lady Bythewaite," I began after even more hesitation than she had shown when her nephew's constitutional silence was broached, "is it perhaps true, as I have thought at times, that all these spools of your speech . . ." However, I stopped.

"Go on, for God's sake!" She counterfeited impatience and anger here.

"Is it true the spools will see the light of day? I mean, will they be printed?"

"Printed!" I saw that she was almost horrified. The thought of her voice on the spools finding print had indeed hit her hard. I was afraid it would spoil everything, indeed, that she would stop, that the nephew would be banished perhaps, and I, restricted to the humdrum necessary chores, never spoken to again except when some particular task was ordered me.

"Light of day, print, the public." She was going on about my even thinking such a thing, let alone saying it out loud. She stared at me as if I were berserk. "After the years you have served me, Eneas, it is a pity for me to see how ill you know me. You don't think I'd share my life with a public, do you? It could never read and today, poor socketless thing, perceives reality only through its major muscles! Share myself with the great public! Eneas, you astound me . . . Go home."

"But is your nephew . . ."

"He's normal. He's taken a vow of silence."

"At his age?"

"He won't speak—he has managed to convey this much to me, Eneas—because of the crimes of the country, you see. But he is willing to hear me speak. I will speak for him. He doesn't approve of me, but he will hear me out. That's our arrangement."

Once Mr. Skegg was interred, and they, or rather I, had dismissed the maids, the cleaning women, the other bailiff, all their tasks now fell to "trustworthy" me.

I proffered to do all this because I, again, and not they, did not want anybody in our fallen village to know that a great-aunt slept with her great-nephew. Explain it that there was only now this one great bed, a feather bed, in the house, that it was not a sexual passion between them . . . Still, there was love there, unholy, preternatural, older than time.

One day she spoke: "He complains, Eneas, of the feather bed, says he is sinking into it, that he can find no *footing* . . . Have we anything else?"

I fetched from the barn two sumptuous Victorian divans, carried them, to their admiration, on my back. He commented on my strength two to three times, though I wondered a bit how he could see my "feat" owing to his being "blinded by the dandelions" (which is how he referred to his semi-blindness).

But though the Victorian sofas were placed side by side, and fitted with bedclothes, they, in the end, preferred the feather bed, and went on sleeping together there.

"I am going back in time now, dear Eneas." She held on to my hand as people did long ago from the window of a fast-train which is already beginning to move. "He has willed it, and I cannot begrudge him any favor, in view of . . . You have been a faithful and dear servant, but you do not need me, Eneas, as much as he does . . . He will die if I do not re-create for him the story of our life, my family and his . . . He has told me this in the dead of night . . ."

I wanted to blurt out that he was an impostor, but as I looked at his waiting face I saw all too clearly he was indeed her nephew, the great luminous, if going-blind, eyes, the mouth of so hungry lips, the delicate complexion, the brown-black hair, ending in curls, and the long lashes disguising the dying eyesight.

And so I protected them. He was, for all I know, a dangerous criminal, certainly he used a "dangerous" drug, which I now occasionally shared, they had buried a man without the knowledge of the law or authorities, and I had done nothing to inform anybody they had done so, they were living in sin, though a century apart, and I went along with this, abetted them, their accessory, a court of law would claim. And like them, all I wanted to hear about was Prince's Crossing, and the silent films. Something too lacking and unreal in the present epoch, something base and wrong had riven us backwards and backwards. I shook my head, wiped my own eyes of a mist, as if I too had looked too long at the yellow of the dandelions.

"We are ready to begin, Eneas Harmond. Ready!" Her golden voice!

The winter was passing, had passed, though it would still cover Mr. Skegg's grave (we had dug him over eight feet deep) with some occasional frost, a snowflake or two, but the golden voice was bringing him into the room, and with him the three sons, one a bastard, one a castaway, one a great star of the silent screen.

But she was not quite ready for the past and, interrupting herself, exclaimed, repeating herself:

"For the first time in my life I am free! You have been faithful to me, Eneas, but recollect this well, when Mr. Skegg my only foundation and hope fell, and the earth was ready and opening also to receive me, as from nowhere, from out the ether, came this great-great-nephew (he stood up as she said this with one of the spools in his left hand), having only his army clothes on his back, a pipe, and his recorder. He lifted me up from the grave, he restored me to speech, he buried my husband on the day our town had fallen. I am not only alive again, I am young!"

She was speaking a truth. If one half-shut his eyes Lady Bythewaite resembled a young girl as she gamboled about the garden, and went up the steps two by two. What had the great-great-nephew given her! Indeed at times he looked older than she did. And they did little but talk into those spools! Like her, he wished to go back in time, to her time, he wished to be, I could only suppose, in the age of the silent screen.

I fetched down an old upright piano from the attic, an idea entirely my own, and planked it down before him. He banged on it for a while. Then he returned to the spools.

One day just before they settled down in earnest to talking into the spools, he had rushed out into the meadow, and then came back holding his eyes.

"The yellow of the dandelions has killed my sight!" At least this is what she thought he had said. But she was not sure they were his exact words, he spoke so seldom, but he brought back a dandelion wet from the dew. The beautiful yellow of it had hurt his retina. She soothed his head as he lay on the sofa, and talked:

"I will tell you everything. I have been a terrible woman they all agree and that will calm you knowing I have been so. You and I are free because we judge nobody. You accept all things, dear young nephew, and I accept you . . ."

I, Eneas Harmond, overheard it all. They excluded me, and I let them, for what they did not realize was that I was more eager to be a witness than *he* to hear or *she* to tell . . . But because of the strain of my devotion, well, sometimes I wilted before them, yes that is the right word, my head fell over from my sitting posture, and then in pity of that devotion, they handed me the pipe, and I smoked with them, sitting finally away from them on the floor, while she went on with her golden voice telling and telling and while he held his eyes from the pain of the dandelions.

"I fear, Eneas, he will lose his sight." She took me aside while he fiddled with the spools. "Perhaps you could go to the dime store in some nearby village and get him stronger specs."

I raised and lowered my head. I knew it was useless to mention a doctor, they would not allow one to set foot in the house, and then there wasn't one for fifty miles in any case.

I noticed Lady Bythewaite was making clothes for him, for he had only his army fatigues to cover his spare sinewy form. I will not say that then the scales fell from my eyes, but I realized with each new "meeting" with them that all we have learned about women is false, maybe they taught it to us false to hide from us who they are, but this naked robin of a great-great-nephew had brought back from the long ago a woman I did not know, the same woman whose story was being recited into the whirling spools. I don't know which I observed more, the alleged nephew with his glaucous eyes "spoiled by the effulgence of the dandelions" ("He went blind from looking at these harmless meadow weeds," she kept whispering to me), or the dew-fresh aunt who slept with him, ate with him, was never out of his presence, and though he almost never opened his mouth to say a word, employing a grunt now and then when he wished her to stop talking long enough for him to change a spool of the recorder so that we could go on with the glories of Maynard

Ewing, and the old magnate, Mr. Skegg, or "maggot" as they pronounced the word magnate in Prince's Crossing.

Touching on Mr. Skegg, she said: "He refused to pity me when I told him I was pregnant by him!" "Pregnant by me, my child," he had stormed, "when hardly a night passes while I'm out driving I don't see you in some ditch with a farmer's son . . . Take those pathetic tales back to England with you . . . She shipped you here because she knew your trade, and I disremember ever so much as having exchanged a kiss with you . . ."

"Yet," Lady Bythewaite told the spools, "he was the only man I had been intimate with for those few years, during which my three sons were born . . ."

There, I felt, a fact had come through at last, and then out of her mouth, like pebbles falling, I heard the numbers

1900,   1902,   1909.

Were these the years her bastard sons were born? And did she speak the truth they were by Mr. Skegg, the old maggot (magnate)?

No one had ever known any solid fact pertaining to her in Prince's Crossing.

Nonetheless, when the great-great-nephew heard the year 1900, his strange dim orbs lit up, he cupped his ears as if hearing the tick-ticking of enormous clocks. Lady Bythewaite suddenly looked very ancient, instead of as a few moments before when she had been gamboling about the room like a farm girl. The sound of numbers had restored us to reality, which Lady Bythewaite once said was another name for death.

1900, 1902, 1909 the tape recorder wheezed and sighed through its bone-like apertures which recalled for me the rotting corpse of Mr. Skegg in the rose garden.

She has buried her seducer, her common-law husband among the choice flowers, the thought drifted again and again across my mind.

Then I heard their combined attack on me.

Lummox, big strapping thing, rustic boor, clout, wake up!

But they knew I was faithful, and would not call the authorities, and wasn't I an accomplice? A kind of indefined series of crimes had long ago settled over the old house, the mansion, but our chiefest dereliction was we were going backwards in time instead of like all mortals forward to death.

Actually (I go back to the burial now) Mr. Skegg is laid to rest more in the cornfield than in the rose garden, that is, the sweet corn has sort of gone wild and encroached upon the rose garden, so that in fact he is buried a little within both, his head rests under the roses, his feet and thighs under the corn.

As I came through the kitchen door today I heard Lady Bythewaite saying: "We haven't been allowed to own gold since 1933, the Republic fell about a year or so afterwards, there has been nothing but world-wide carnage since . . ."

The tape recorder had stopped. The nephew wheeled it on only when she was talking about Mr. Skegg, the sons, or her shame as an unwed mother.

She gave her short speech then against the Federal Government, and the criminal record of the Presidents.

Then we were back again to 1900 or so. She said . . .

It was not too hard for her to say great-great-nephew, but gradually he permitted her to say *Corliss Vallant*, his baptismal name. I think he forced her to use both his names together for suddenly now she addressed him, instead of *greatgreatnephew*, as Corlissvallant.

She said: "*Corlissvallant* has got me almost to the place where I met Mr. Skegg for the first time. He had retired from Wall Street young, you know . . ."

They looked at me benignly now and again, as one would at a stray bull which is permitted, once they are sure it will not butt or gore, to move about in the pasture land. Corliss Vallant let me know by gesture and a certain kind of nodding he was aware of my once and still residual great strength, an idea which calmed him.

"You should have known Eneas Harmond when he was

young," she told him. "I saw him lift a steer onto his shoulders. He also, at a county fair, raised aloft a tree . . ."

I sat down tired at the thought of my diminishing muscles, strength, marrow. I was preparing for death at a quicker rate than she was. Not speedier than he was, though. I felt the angel's wings about him from the moment he arrived. I heard wings in the revolving tape recorder.

"My heart is not too good." My voice once rose against the whirring of the tape recorder. "The doc some while back said I am a powerfully built man yet, but my heart is tired."

Lady Bythewaite nodded as if she had heard something set forth which was an accomplishment.

"You served your country, Eneas. You are above reproach. Sometime you might show Corliss Vallant where they bayoneted you. Yes, now."

I had never stripped before people since "service," and a few weeks ago had anybody said I would remove my shirt before the old dame, I would have told him where to go and would have forgot it.

I realized how damaged the nephew's eyes were now, for he had to come clear up to me to be sure of the bayonet wound. And Lady Bythewaite, see what stuff she was made of after all. Only now was I beginning to know her complete. The wound from the bayonet looked almost as fresh on me as the day it had been plunged into my abdomen and chest. The sight of it had made even some doctors wince. But she was quiet.

"But your arms are as strong as a young man's," Lady Bythewaite commented.

She and I both paused in any speech we might have made, for Corliss Vallant had put his hand into the still remaining hollow of my wound, and kept it there until my face grew scarlet.

"We have all been through a great deal," Lady Bythewaite spoke, almost near embarrassment, or was it compassion for Corliss Vallant's understanding of my flesh's own memory.

"Eneas is in a draft," she cautioned her great-great-nephew, and handed me my shirt.

I believe though that in the silence which followed we were all thinking of the plastic unstable unprotectable death-meant quality of the human body. How had the human race, considering its fragility, come so far, especially in view of the fondness we have for total error.

Eneas Harmond must have fallen asleep on the front porch, in the old green swing. I speak of myself at times in the third person, at times if anybody should peruse this, in the first; that is because sometimes I seem still *I,* sometimes I belong to the entire past-past along with Mr. Skegg, his three bastard sons, and the woman who was their mother, who, by some concatenation of events, sits here almost as dawn-fresh, if cut down, as her great-great-nephew.

I say then that I, or he, Eneas, was sleeping on the green porch swing, when I felt a kind of fanning of air come over my face, too sweet-smelling in an almost artificial way to be from the lake or the river. I did not open my eyes. Eneas Harmond did not open his eyes. "What is it?" I said with my eyes shut, knowing it was human breath on my face, knowing too, I think, who it was.

"Do you know where you are?" I put my second question. There was no answer, but the breathing seemed to stop.

"If I could have some of the marrow like from your bones, do you think I could get through the rest of it . . . my life?"

I think that was the first complete sentence the great-great-nephew spoke in this house, though of course we were, to be accurate, on the porch; perhaps the porch gave him the background for a sentence, as the house maybe did not. The house was too grand, I sometimes thought, for speech, with its thirty-foot ceilings, its cornices, its gold filigree work.

"You have your own marrow, plenty of it."

"Echo that," he retorted.

Eneas Harmond opened his eyes.

The nephew did seem to see better in the dark. His eyes looked quite clear to me.

"They have scooped it all out of me," he said, and sat down at my feet.

I think I was forming my mouth to say No when a long white figure appeared in the doorway.

"There is nothing more alarming to hear than whispering in the dead of night," she said. "I might have known you would put your two heads together against me." She sat down on the porch swing beside me.

Then we, she and I, both looked at the great-great-nephew. He had gone fast asleep against my boots. Even when we shook him, he did not awaken.

"It must be the first time he's slept since he came . . . home."

"Ah, so," I replied, and Lady Bythewaite smiled to hear this peculiar Prince's Crossing expression.

"So you have somewhere about your person the real poppy juice," she spoke loudly. Corliss Vallant did not awake.

My eyes went out over the little hills and the tiny mountains that were our landscape. There were roads there, no mistake. But one could wait an hour before he saw headlights from a car. Had one the eyes of eagles he could see from here the unused, rusted, derailed paths the trains had taken. We were pretty much cut off then from the world of travelers. We had buried a dead man, and we had perhaps some kind of deserter under our roof—I caught myself saying "our." Well, she would not have taken offense had she heard me say "our." She had no interest in property. About once in four years she went over all her possessions kept enumerated in a huge ledger. When she had read all she was worth she would grin. She was the one person I have known (I have not known many, though, so what is this worth?) who understood almost exactly what the Preacher was talking about when he wrote about Vanity. Yet she was not immune to it. She had fallen in love with her nephew, after several times in the past having declared herself enamored of my own person. Older than the hills, she should have been in some ill-marked grave, but here she sat in the pre-dawn light, swinging back and forth with me in gentle drowsy cadence, while the nephew snored like some young farm beast, saliva and drivel coming out from his mouth and nose.

"I believe sleep interests me the most now of any human activity," she said, or I thought she said.

I was about to ask her about her statement when she gave me her sign I was to keep silent—this was done with a certain movement with her wedding finger, though she had never been married, which movement meant *you heard exactly what I said, you understood it, and so silence!*

"There are certain things, Eneas, one does not tell other people, but I am telling this boy all of them. You see, there must be destiny. Just when we think we cannot go on another day, someone comes, or death comes. Instead of death he came. And you do not begrudge me my happiness, Eneas. It is all more than I hoped for. But to be able to tell all that one thought one would never tell even to oneself! My fortune is too good. This destiny I call it which brought him to me must be jealous it has given me too much. Nobody gets too much in this existence, the planners above see to that . . . Now, Eneas, you must carry him up to our bed."

She sat grinning admiration as I slung him over my back and took him above.

When people ask me if I knew Clarence Skegg, I realize despite the frequency of the question being put that a blank look must come over my face. Even when he was a young chap he was already Maynard Ewing. He played theater, or "show," from the time before he went to school. With no acknowledged mother, Clarence came to accept the gossip of the townspeople that his father had driven that poor woman off to the city where she had died, and when he questioned Mr. Skegg, he changed the subject back to his only abiding topic of interest, property. Even then Mr. Skegg had been always scowling, though he did not need glasses, and even then was beginning to go white in his leonine shock of hair, and too tall to pore over ledgers, he was a bit stooped in all his great height, and his hazel eyes saw through everything but human beings.

"Pay no mind to Mr. Skegg," Lady Bythewaite's voice reached young Clarence, cut off as they were from one another by Mr. Skegg's decree that the boy had no living mother, "you will be on the stage, Clarence, or better yet, in the movies . . . Mark my words, my boy . . ."

"Mr. Skegg was to blame me for all of it," Lady Bythewaite was speaking now into the spools. "At the time I pretended to be guiltless, wronged, even noble, but now that he lies dead in my rose garden, I can see that he was right. In death all dreams come true—where does that sentence come from? In death all . . . We had quarrel after quarrel, Mr. Skegg and I. Our whole life was quarrel. I was, nonetheless, the *acknowledged* mother of his second bastard son, Owen Haskins. Haskins had been my mother's name. Oh, at the very end Mr. Skegg had made some offer to marry me . . . But I wanted my son for my own, my very own. Besides I had seen what he had done to Clarence, amend that to Maynard Ewing. And these two boys, called by the townsfolk half brothers, became playmates, but Clarence always tyrannized over Owen, and in the end was the shaper perhaps of his destiny, in malevolence, in a kind of love that too frequently wore the mask of hate, and when he was unable to love himself, which was about as infrequent as the cessation of ticking from our grandfather clock, when the mirror no longer threw back such fetching pictures of his good looks, he turned to his 'half brother.' But I never knew what went on in the soul of my own boy, Owen Haskins, so eclipsed was he by the greatness of Clarence, of Maynard Ewing, star of the silent films and silver screen, and yet even then, without my having a vestige of suspicion, under the power and influence of a much greater 'hero' . . ."

The great-great-nephew lay with his head in her lap, for the reel had only just been set in motion. The spring day was cloudless, the robins, song sparrows, and little flitting wrens made their woodsy background for this so-long solo she was singing.

"I was dusting the banister in my big house where the maid had shirked her duty," Lady Bythewaite spoke, and she looked toward the same banister some fifty years later unchanged, saw the orange band of sunlight revealing the myriad dancing motes of dust like countless stellar worlds.

"And when I go to New York, Owen, you will die of grief for not seeing me, you know that." Maynard's or Clarence's voice was coming again from the inner room, where they had played at all kinds of games together, and where their quarrel went on continuously.

"But won't I follow you to wherever you go, Clarence . . . ?"

"Never, poor Owen, never . . . You know you belong here . . . You're meant for small towns, and countryside. We're from different stock, after all. You favor our father more than I, I must favor my poor mother who was a whore, I'm told . . . Ha, I thought that would make you start, Owen! No, Owen, I will not even miss you, for my own path is to be glory, you know that, I've heard you confess it to me . . . But when I am successful I will let you visit me . . . There, don't cry so . . . You'll forget me too, Owen, for you know the country is everything to you . . ."

"You shan't crush the poor boy like this!" Lady Bythewaite entered the room where the two boys were closeted. "You have broken poor Owen's heart." She took Owen's head and held it to her breast. "Clarence, you are very cruel. You love only yourself, but the day will come, the cold day they all refer to here in Prince's Crossing when you'll give anything in the world to have the affection, admiration, and trust of your little brother . . . You'll find when you go out to conquer the world, what stuff it is made of!"

"Does that come from the horse's mouth, Lady Bythewaite, or did you read that somewhere in a book. I would like to remind you, apropos of reading, that it is hard on beauty and you seem to be losing yours."

"I should slap your face for that, Clarence."

"I know just the same that when I am gone, you'll have nobody to complain about, be shocked over, nobody to criticize, except of course Mr. Skegg."

He called his father Mr. Skegg as we all did, as one would speak of a building, monument, or park. There was little father and son relationship there, and they were separated not only by the chasm of age, but by such an all-all difference.

"And when I achieve the great reputation which I know I will," Clarence orated while Owen and Lady Bythewaite almost huddled together like persons unexpectedly caught in a blast of freezing wind, "you'll all remember how you laughed at my ambition, derided my hopes and aspirations . . ."

"Oh, stop it, Clarence . . . You know I've encouraged you in all your dreams. Haven't I gone to your father again and again, and interceded . . . And hasn't he at least listened, hasn't he sometimes softened a little . . ."

He bit his lip.

"You needn't intercede again," Clarence Skegg said, "for I'm leaving tonight on the Big Four express . . ."

I, Eneas Harmond, felt the weight of that name, the Big Four express, as if it were capable of bearing someone away from this planet.

"Have you told your father, Clarence?"

"No, Lady Bythewaite, I have not told my father . . . Do you reckon he'll send the authorities after me, with a little nudging from you?"

"But how will you live, Clarence! . . . Certainly not on your good looks . . ."

He gave Lady Bythewaite a look of royal disdain.

Then perhaps to the surprise of all present, he took his brother in his arms, kissed him, hugged Lady Bythewaite, covered her with kisses, and was gone forever from Prince's Crossing as Clarence Skegg. For even when he was to return, when destiny had tired of him as the great silent-film star, he returned even in that chilled changed aspect not as our Clarence but as Maynard Ewing.

And so he died to us, and poor Owen nearly died. Hero worship is one of life's miserable calamities, especially when the hero, as nearly always the case, is steeped in cruelty.

"No, Owen, my precious, you won't get over Clarence leaving you for a while yet, for I know what a large place he occupied in your heart . . ." Lady Bythewaite thus comforted her illegitimate son, just as she had in his last lonely insane years comforted "the old maggot," Mr. Skegg. She went on: "I know it must seem he has blotted out the rest of life for you, and that is why . . ." But Owen was not listening, or she thought because of the motionlessness of his eyes and mouth he was not listening, but she went on anyhow: "When you love somebody, as you loved your brother, you think nobody else will come to fill the void. But my dear son," she put her hand ever so gingerly on his coat sleeve, "if you keep yourself open to life, somebody else will come, somebody, I know already wants to fill his place." Owen turned away, and a kind of snort came from his nostrils, and moving he dislodged her hand from his sleeve, but she went on. "We never get over any grief, Owen, you will discover, no wound ever really heals . . . But there are distractions, you see until . . ." Owen had stood up, his eyes flashing, she faltered, she saw she was then no longer talking to a boy, and for the first time she felt fear in his presence.

The great-great-nephew and Eneas started up at that look on her face. An expression of terror had wandered into her voice with her last words.

"Until what, Lady Bythewaite?" Eneas exclaimed.

Then as if the spool had been put on properly again, her voice continued: "I comforted Owen Haskins, but he did not want comfort. He was hopelessly attached to his brother. The world was a wilderness without Clarence . . . But I could never send this half-formed young man of barely fifteen to the wilds of a metropolis, for I knew Clarence would not properly guide or protect him, would in his old self-loving and offhand way push him in some wrong direction . . . Perhaps I was wrong. Owen was, however, so much more handsome and manly looking than Clarence. But of course he did not know it, and Mr. Skegg and Clarence and Prince's Crossing, and I, too, had all hurt him, not because we all reminded him he was a bastard by our very existence and proximity—people hardly knew he was, and they were afraid of me and my buggy whip, afraid of my money which I had dragged from the bowels of this system by sharp investment, no, I think now Owen came scarred from his Maker . . . Had he been born of royal and married parents, and I believe sometimes he was, he would have come with a damaged destiny . . . Whether I loved him or hurt him, whether his brother loved him or corrupted and neglected him, my son, my only acknowledged son was damaged . . . I could only stand and watch him drown, I was tied to a window far above where he struggled in the waters of the lake . . . I called until my voice was a shred, a scratch like a nail pulled over a slate: Owen, Owen, Owen, don't let him hurt you, don't give yourself over to suffering . . . Don't go to New York. He'll kill you, Owen . . . He's made of different stuff, he's only your half brother in truth, if not in fact."

As if sensing some danger, that the dead Clarence was about to enter and claim her dead son Owen, she had commanded me, Eneas, to go to the front of the "great property" and set up the seldom-closed gates, of which there were three principal pairs, never used, a heavy gate which closed the estate from the road, and a few rods nearer the house another gate, not used in many years, which groaned and resisted and squeaked as I shut it, and finally an enormous iron bar of a thing which could be brought against the palatial white door, but which until now I had forgotten ever existed.

"We must not be disturbed." She *smiled*. I must say that Lady Bythewaite almost never smiled. She saw that I was aware of this as soon as her lips had softened at me, and she looked up abruptly then, as if she already had thought better of wasting such an expression on me. I should say that the muscles around her mouth, though she still had her own teeth, seemed to be incapable of anything but speech and commands, the lips, that is, were lifted only in utterance, never in expression, and her voice itself, which in England had been called true gold, had a distant and expressionless but extremely meaningful cadence, but was all the same a voice coming from an incalculable distance, and, I always thought, beyond sadness.

"We must never be disturbed again by the outside, Eneas," she said so low that I wondered if I had not put the words in her mouth, in my own imaginings, I mean.

"There must be some other boy your own age you can know, Owen, now that he has abandoned us for New York . . . Someone who can go horseback riding with you . . ."

But her mind was on Clarence almost more than on Owen. She could not believe that a young man like Clarence, of such powerful influence on the lives of all of them, a boy of such boundless energy, who turned any gathering into great animation and hilarity, who, she once had quipped, had he walked through a cemetery would have evoked from the tombs some sort of whispering half response. Without him, the great house was full of echoes, the countryside, the pasture behind the house still and peevish, the sunrise, sundown more pallid, and Owen dumbfounded, stunned, almost imbecilic.

"Clarence has gone to attempt the most difficult thing in the wide world," she told her son. "A raw country boy going to New York to be on the stage, or . . ."

"The movies," Owen corrected his mother.

"More difficult yet . . . You see, Owen," and here a rush of hope came over her, "he'll be back by Christmas! An apple never rolls very far from where it falls. Your brother will be back, and settle down, and we'll all be happy again . . . You mark my words."

"This is your doing!" A crypt-like voice had come into the room, as she had sat at her spinet desk, in that long-ago, following with sore eyes a huge column of figures. She had trained herself, in fear of men, to be brilliant with mathematics, and in fear of ruin, the poorhouse, being parted from Owen, she had outstripped her male competitors, and, some said, herself.

"You have the raw nerve entering my house unannounced!" She spoke with a contempt which would have cut down anybody but the person who had entered her home, Mr. Skegg.

Mr. Skegg was believed to have never been worsted by any adversary in his life. Lady Bythewaite had been no exception. But she defied, some would have said *defined*, his assaults on her. He had tried every stratagem and ruse to beat her to her knees. He had, as mad people are said to do, plotted hourly against her, digging if not her grave, a pit into which once fallen she would only emerge with his help and then face prison for life, prison in his custody.

"From the beginning," Mr. Skegg went on, while seating himself at a small marble-topped table on which sat a winged figure of some god, and which he touched gingerly as if with ineffable loathing, "you've filled Clarence's head with stardust . . . I believe his expulsion from West Point was owing entirely to the kind of letters which you habitually wrote to him. Letters that would unman any boy. You've always acted not only like his mother but his sweetheart. And now you've driven him away . . . But he will fail, Lady Bythewaite, and will return and follow the path that I have with so much pains cut out for him . . ."

A bit cowed by his fury, stung even more that he spoke about Clarence's coming failure almost in her words, she paused longer than she was accustomed to in the course of their battles, and then cried:

"No path Clarence follows could bring him to more wretchedness than the one you have cut out for yourself. There is not a comfortable hour in your day or night. Your only friends are bankers, and they loathe you, being after all men . . . As to my having plotted to drive your son from you . . ."

At this moment in the fray, Owen Haskins entered the room.

Mr. Skegg deliberately now rose, so in contrast with his usual etiquette with respect to Lady Bythewaite's son. "The very fellow I've been hunting all over for! Owen, Owen, I never thought I would have the good fortune to find *you* in. You're always scouring the countryside on your horse, I observe, always in and out of doors, and of late, I notice, in close company with Aiken Cusworth . . ."

Here Lady Bythewaite looked straight at Owen with a hard interrogatory light in her eye.

"I'll be brief with you, my boy," Mr. Skegg almost shouted. "I've come to take you home with me . . ."

Lady Bythewaite's splendid laughter rushed through the room, the house indeed, and in effect rendered his speech, his invitation, something never uttered, and Mr. Skegg as somebody who had not only never called today, but never existed.

"Do you hear, Owen?" Mr. Skegg shouted still louder, nettled and turning red at her derision.

"Give Mr. Skegg your answer, Owen," Lady Bythewaite emitted one of her great whispers.

"I am to leave . . . Mother?" the boy got out after a long, painful—for her—intermission.

"You would not be leaving her, Owen. That would not be possible in any real sense. You would be coming with me to learn the business . . . I have been deserted, abandoned by my former son."

Even Lady Bythewaite's physiognomy moved a bit under the phrasing of his last sentence.

"I believe," Owen began babbling, "that is, I don't believe . . . Oh, no, sir, no!" he suddenly got out, and rushed past Mr. Skegg to the shelter of the dormer window, and stood looking out at the pasture land there.

"Do you hear that *No*, Mr. Skegg?" Lady Bythewaite had

risen, having made her *No* thunder so much louder than Owen's.

"You ruined one son, Mr. Skegg," she continued, going up to within a few inches of the old maggot. "And once he escaped your clutches, you come immediately skulking about for mine . . ." And now her laughter knew no control, and might have known no cessation until she began violently to cough, and Owen springing from the dormer window helped her to the ottoman, looking down on her, both with great relief, doubtless at her having rescued him from Mr. Skegg, and with great deepening worry at her paroxysm.

Mr. Skegg had picked up his hat, and had begun his progress through the long expanse of the drawing room, but at the very end of his journey there, her coughing having subsided enough for the sound of a voice to be heard, he looked back at the pair and shouted: "You'll change your mind one day, Owen, for you're not after all as mad as Lady Bythewaite! Meanwhile the doors of my house and business are open to you!"

"I want you to tell me that he is not my father," Owen began after Mr. Skegg had slammed the two huge front doors, causing all the windowpanes to clatter and the great clock in the hallway to wheeze and tinkle. Lady Bythewaite had picked up a Swiss paperweight, whose miniature snowstorm beginning to rage within its glass confines by her touch, she professed to study.

"Swear to me," he intoned, taking her right hand, "that as you are my mother, he is not my father. I will not have him be my father!"

"Oh, Owen, precious, we have been over this before. You are growing into a man. Soon other unwelcome knowledge will have to be yours. You are going to find out, sweetheart, that the world is based on a great foundation of horror. He is your father. I am sure you are not going to blame me all over again. And I'm sorry I cannot pick out a father that is more suitable to your very exacting tastes. I don't know where your sensitivity, your highly developed aesthetic inclinations come from. I stand in amazement of you, Owen. Perhaps when you think how you hate your father, you can think of how much you love your brother, Clarence, and Clarence means less kindly toward you than Mr. Skegg. I wish you would reflect on this from time to time."

Owen let loose of her hand, and bit his lip vehemently. She put her hand to his mouth, and shook her head.

"Don't refuse benefits when they are kindly meant," she advised him. "That has been one of my faults."

"I'm grateful to you nonetheless for not having married my father," Owen said with truthfulness. "I am also a little vain of the reputation it has brought me in Prince's Crossing. But I would be freer still if . . ."

"If you would only give up your brother!" She let the sentence

come in a voice so much like Owen's that an observer might
have thought it had issued from the boy's lips.

"There you're at that again!" he turned suddenly on her but
without as much of his former violence.

"I only meant, Owen, you mustn't let your whole world be
wrapped up in a . . . Clarence . . . He's a very cruel, selfish,
and I'm afraid ungovernable boy, who . . ."

To his considerable surprise some tears came down her cheek.

"I do believe," she went on, after taking a kind of deep swallow, and hesitating again while he put his hand now to her lips,
whether as an angry caress, or a warning not to go on with her
line of thought, "I do believe, Owen, that he would willingly
sacrifice all our lives to have his fame and glory be known to
the world . . . Oh, my dearest, pray try to forget him. You are
so much finer than he is, more capable, with a better brain. You
are even better looking than he if you only . . ."

". . . only what?"

"Well, if you, say, looked the part."

They both laughed.

"I mean," she went on, "if you believed in your own gifts,
didn't look apologetic at the world . . ."

Owen caught a glimpse of himself in the huge hall mirror.

"I know I will lose you because you will grow up, are already
growing up. But, Owen, I don't want to lose you to him. Don't
you see, though he loves you as much as he can, he loves himself so much more, loves his own image. He can't give you what
you need, and he might give you something you'll never be rid
of . . ."

"Why, Mother, you talk as if he was the devil with horns,
pitchfork, tail, and so forth . . ."

"I wish he was as harmless!" Lady Bythewaite stood up, and
folded her arms. "And I know I'm doing all the wrong things
by warning you, telling you not to. Well, I never did anything,
I don't suppose, right. Who does? But I know Clarence. Know
him as if he were as legally mine as Mr. Skegg's. Know him

better because, thank God, I don't have to blame myself anymore for him . . . Maybe I've even helped him!"

"Well, he loves you the most," Owen said bitterly.

"He thinks he does," she corrected him. "When he finds somebody in New York more to his definition of grandeur, do you think he'll remember me or . . ." She stopped short.

"All right, all right," Owen retorted. "I'll stay and be a farmer, and pitch manure along with Aiken Cusworth! . . . And here to end our confab is somebody coming up the walk for you, Lady Bythewaite . . ." He spoke in the play-acting tones of Clarence Skegg, who treated his mother with the royal etiquette he supposed was conferred on crowned heads.

At church, at the general store, at the post office, and in front of the bandstand where a group of elderly musicians played hymns and musical comedy favorites, Mr. Skegg told everybody he had lost his boy through Lady Bythewaite's turning his head "by reason and example of her own days in the theater." Clarence had run off without a cent in his pocket, or a realizable dime to his name, etc., and Mr. Skegg would see him dead before he helped him. He then lengthily listed to whoever would bend an ear the boy's misdemeanors, his having been expelled from West Point, the long private terrible letter from Clarence's captain in that wonderful institution (Clarence's uniform still hung in camphor squares in Mr. Skegg's own private closet bedroom), his drinking, etc.

Still stung by his being rejected by Owen, Mr. Skegg had gone home to issue a "summons" to the real source of his "rejection," Lady Bythewaite.

Indeed the person coming up the walk who had interrupted Lady Bythewaite and her own illegitimate son's confab was, in the terminology of Prince's Crossing, the "bread boy," Aiken Cusworth, who, though it is true, he delivered a few loaves of bread for a few isolated farmers, from his horse and cart, was primarily Lady Bythewaite's "horsetender" and "groom," being in daily attendance on and care of the twenty or so splendid horses in her pasture land; along with the delivery of bread from his cart, he was known to fetch messages, usually, as was the case today, from Mr. Skegg, who depended on Aiken almost as much as did Lady Bythewaite. Aiken held in his thick, heavy, but well-formed fingers one of those sealed great envelopes immediately recognized by all inhabitants of Prince's Crossing as a "summons" from the old maggot. How many farmers and small businessmen had felt their hearts sink when they were handed a "document" emanating from Mr. Skegg. It meant foreclosure, revocation of a loan, or something equally catastrophic.

"Aiken, you will wait a moment please," Lady Bythewaite addressed the "bread boy," receiving from his brown and stained hands the document. "There may be an answer wanted to this. We all know of course who it is from . . ."

Only she defied the maggot. Only she could have opened the letter from a man who owned county after county surrounding them of farms, and great houses, pasture land, lakes and mountains.

She read aloud perhaps not only to show she was fearless and had nought but contempt for Mr. Skegg, but to make his message to her contemptible and picayune.

> It is you and you alone who have taken Clarence from me. I have therefore decided that unless you can persuade him to return immediately, a certain note which I hold with your signature, and which is past due will be presented for payment . . .
>
> Mr. Skegg

"There is no such note!" In saying this, she crumpled the letter, or document, and pressed it into the hand of a somewhat astonished Aiken Cusworth, who was not accustomed to have Lady Bythewaite touch his person owing to his being, as she herself had once said within his earshot, forever covered with the stains of earth and animal manure, but whilst Lady Bythewaite ranted and raved, her eyes were actually for the first time resting in full earnest on the "bread boy" and she suddenly realized that he was much too attractive and dignified to be a "menial." Furthermore, it was on this occasion that she saw for the first time that she had underestimated his intelligence, for he showed by his smiles and suppressed chuckles that he had found something humorous both in her dramatic reading of the letter and in the maggot's peremptory wording of his "decree" or "edict," which things he had read about in World History.

"My reply, Aiken, will be as follows," Lady Bythewaite had begun.

"Mother, must you dictate a private message like this before others!" Owen implored her. He had blushed a deep scarlet, looking from Aiken to his mother, but on hearing his words, Aiken Cusworth too colored, and gave Owen a look of flashing indignation.

But Lady Bythewaite appeared not to have even heard Owen or to be aware of his not wanting Aiken to be privy to their secrets. She was walking up and down the big parlor, and the "bread boy" had taken out a small ledger from his hip pocket, and a stump of a pencil, waiting for her answer:

"Owen, if you are ashamed of your mother, and you have every reason, I suppose, to be, leave the room until Aiken has marched off with his reply, for he is not ashamed of me . . . Aiken is not *others,* as you call him! Remember that! Say this, Aiken:

> If I have inspired anyone to be free, and to do as his own talent bids him do, I plead guilty. Let those who have failed as fathers and men and husbands sit alone in their counting houses and meditate on their own shortcomings and especially on the fact that no one will willingly attend their approaching funeral.
>
> Lady Bythewaite"

Aiken Cusworth gave a kind of grunt of satisfaction on getting this down on his ledger, and hurried off with his "reply," fearful perhaps that she might change her mind, as she had in times past, and recall him, substituting a dilute rejoinder for this more acerbic one.

"Confiding your secrets to the bread boy," Owen said, shaking his head.

"As if you had not confided quite a few secrets to him yourself!" Lady Bythewaite, stung, retorted. Then by something she saw on her son's face which bespoke some trouble she did not quite fathom, she went on: "There are no secrets in Prince's Crossing. I've found, as a woman of my peculiar position, that it is much better to say it all in public oneself, and you strip everybody of the sh-sh of later gossip. I am what I am, have declared my faults for all to hear, and nobody has been led to believe I am anything but myself. Let the preacher's wife and the superintendent of the Sunday School tremble under the bedclothes at what the town will discover later on. I have been whipped and branded, but can walk the pavements with my head up. And thank God, Clarence has escaped . . ."

A kind of sob escaped from her, and she took Owen's hands in hers. "But oh, do you think he will be able to stay there?" she wondered as if alone. "For he's a mere boy himself, and imagine him going on the stage or into the movies."

Then the thought of Clarence's peril was so overwhelming, she dropped Owen's hands, and sat down on the ottoman with a heavy plop. In her distress she almost felt she could hear the sound of his bones being crunched, his skull laid open, his limbs severed and bleeding.

"Only I know what he will be going through," she mumbled. "I went through it all myself. But in some ways a woman is better prepared for the world than a boy . . ."

Owen could only study his mother's face in a kind of admiring confusion.

A few days later she was polishing her silverware in a kind of desperate diligent manner under the imperfect illumination of an ancient floorlamp, and Owen, his knees covered with caked mud and his face and brow scratched from where he had been climbing the hills and brush of the neighboring countryside, sat in one of his characteristic dejected poses, his fingers covering his eyelids gently. Lady Bythewaite smiled bitterly, tossing a great gleaming fork aside, noting that Owen's habit of touching his eyelids was also that of Mr. Skegg, his natural father. So there is something in heredity, she opined, since the two never spent more than an hour together.

A crumpled letter lay near the pile of polished silverware. She had crumpled it, for it was from Clarence, begging her to allow Owen to follow him.

If you go, Owen, she had warned him, *I will send the sheriff after you.*

Stirred by this impudent letter, in her vehemence, she rose from her task of polishing, she seized hold of Owen, and slapped him vigorously.

This slap roused Owen for almost the first time from the deep sleep-like expression which he almost always wore. He looked about him brightly, like the one who sees for the first time where he has been absent-mindedly dwelling.

"You feel very strong about this, Mother."

"Don't call me Mother. I am nobody's Mother . . . Do you know that your brother Clarence tried to make love to me!"

"Well, must you go on about it!" he flashed back at her.

She shook him now again. "Clarence never had any mercy on me!" She had turned away from Owen and spoke again as if by herself in her own room. "He wanted to complete my shame, I have a mind . . ."

"And did you allow him to do so?" Owen had suddenly leaped up, and his moody menace almost cowed her a little.

"He will use you to ease his loneliness, Clarence will," she went on, "in order to feel he has not lost all the scenes from familiar life and gentle affection. And then when he towers in glory, for, Owen, he will be successful, I am sure of this now, you will be destroyed by him. He nourishes only poison for all of us . . ."

At the same time, despite her outcries, there was an unspoken understanding that Owen would go, that he was expected to go, that it was in the cards and so no one could prevent it, that Mr.

Skegg and Lady Bythewaite had already been apprised of his coming journey, and merely read from hastily written "parts" their perfunctory, if angry, objections. For consider the background, these two boys, one a bastard, the other an heir, had never been separated. They had quarreled viciously, even injuring one another, but their lives were certainly knit together in some unfathomable way.

The suggestion, the "news" that Clarence had made love to his mother did not change Owen's feelings toward either Lady Bythewaite or his brother in any fundamental way, though he mooned over it now—if indeed she had told the truth! What was a physical act in any case between Clarence and a mere woman, compared to the obsession the boys had with one another, their quaking fear of loneliness if the other one was absent, or not writing letters. And how many times in the past had not Aiken Cusworth carried letters from Owen to his brother when the latter was ill with some real or imaginary ailment, and kept to his princely bedroom.

Now, genuinely separated, they wrote one another daily, Owen walking five miles in the mud to see the letter went out on the Big Four train, which now in the midst of these meditations of his and at this precise moment let out its iron wail of grief and crazy beckoning invitation.

And so Lady Bythewaite began "going over" all his clothes, having his shoes resoled and reheeled, mending his shirts, and purchased him some new cravats from a mail-order house.

"The City is terrible," she would go on speaking to him from under the floorlamp in the succeeding evenings. "London is a horror, and New York will surely be worse. Everyone goes wrong, Owen, when he is away from his roots . . . You have everything here," she spoke with furious patriotism, and added almost whispering the conclusion, "except of course a father . . ."

"Well, let him go and be damned!" she cried to herself later in her bedroom. She saw him already dead, in his coffin. Her hand trembled, her eye could not see the needle she held in her shaking fingers. She must let Owen go, or expire herself.

"Clarence's whole hankering after the theater has one and only one source: you!" Mr. Skegg had begun his "Process" against Lady Bythewaite, a few weeks after Clarence's departure, in his cathedral-huge study, where he had summoned her peremptorily. Actually, she had ignored this summons, and had gone to his mammoth study solely on a mission of her own: to intercede with Mr. Skegg to prevent Owen from following after his brother, and she had come only to find that Mr. Skegg had decided all on his own to send the younger boy after his actor-brother in order to "fetch the runaway home"!

"You'd throw one person into the quicksand headfirst to bring up another who is settling toward the bottom!" she opined, forgetting in her anger the bad picture she was painting of Clarence's plight. "And why, may I ask, do you have this sudden impetus to send Owen after Clarence, when it is I, according to you, who am so subject to brainstorms? You must be in receipt of special news . . . You know something I don't know!" She finished, nettled that this should be so, for she had always prided herself on knowing everything about her sons, while Mr. Skegg remained in some outer sphere, where only incidental intelligence was accorded him. And from as far back as she could remember, she had always wanted Mr. Skegg to know nothing about the two boys until she was prepared to let such information "go."

"Would you have the kindness to read this newspaper account . . ." Mr. Skegg proffered her a cutting.

She blushed. She could not read the newspaper without her glasses, always mislaid, for she had long tried to pretend she did not need glasses, loathed having to wear them because they spoiled her good looks, and so now, without them, she began peering and straining at the little black characters of print.

"Very well . . ." Mr. Skegg smiled with superior satisfaction. "I will read what it says, proud darling . . ." He proceeded with:

"Mr. Clarence Skegg, who made such a sensational debut in the Broadway play *Cyclone* has just signed up to take the juvenile lead in the high-budget film *Out of the West.* He will begin at that time to use the name Maynard Ewing. A splendid career is seen for the young actor, who has already won a huge following."

Mr. Skegg went on reading from the newspaper, though he was now into other information not directly connected with his son, when suddenly looking up he saw more to his incredulity than concern that Lady Bythewaite had slumped down in the chair, as if she might slip any moment to the floor. He summoned the maid, and they brought her "to," with whiskey and bathing her temples with cold compresses.

"Go ahead with that damned newspaper," she got out after a somewhat puzzled look about her.

He put away the cutting in his breast pocket.

"You have never deceived me, Lady Bythewaite, as much as you pride yourself on thinking."

"Very well, then, I am jealous." She took now a mere drop from the glass of whiskey and let her head fall back against the chair.

"Jealous! I never heard of anybody fainting from jealousy." Mr. Skegg stared at her. He had assumed his most magisterial bearing, and she could only bring to mind that among his other callings there had been that of an attorney. "Long ago," his severe tone now reached her, "you had the thought that your two sons would never leave you, that they would be satisfied with you and you alone about them and near them, and so on and so forth. Why underline the obvious . . . But one has left, and the other will follow unless the first is not brought back!"

"And so you wish to run the risk of losing both of them by sending Owen after Clarence!"

"That is my plan," he had to admit, though she had spoiled the effect he had hoped to make by a more gradual approach to his secret—sending Owen.

Lady Bythewaite stood up, and put down the whiskey not even half consumed. She tucked back a large hairpin in her raven hair.

"Owen as a messenger, or policeman, truant officer for Clarence Skegg! Good God Almighty, Mr. Skegg!" She laughed, and it was her kind of laugh that always set his teeth on edge. Anger had brought back the color to her cheeks. She picked up the newspaper from which the cutting had been excised, and almost clawed at it, giving it an accusatory look of its having ruined her.

But Mr. Skegg had been talking, or as she now began to listen, raving! "He will either use his own name, or I will disinherit him. I will allow him to be in the films, but he must use his own name."

Yes, even Lady Bythewaite was astounded.

"You once told me that you had a better estimation of a common pickpocket or pimp than a motion picture actor . . . Now you demand that he use your name . . . Don't you think he may have changed his name to spare you?"

"When did he ever spare me?" Mr. Skegg wondered.

She paced up and down the room. It was he now who looked ashen and faint.

"I refuse to allow Owen to go," she said. "And I think your son Clarence absolutely right in changing his name . . ."

"He will fail," the old man was almost muttering. "He will be home. When he is ruined there, as he will be—don't you know I know how weak he is—he will be back. But if he comes back he will come as a beggar and then he will have to use his new name, for I will have disinherited him . . . I will give Owen a thousand dollars to go to New York, enough to set him up in his own business here when he is a man in a few years. Clarence, besides, will listen to Owen . . ."

"You must have taken entire leave of your senses. You can do so well in figures, Mr. Skegg, but you are the complete idiot when you deal with the first element of human nature . . ."

Nora Bythewaite who had been looking at the westering sun scarcely blinked all the time Mr. Skegg was telling her that Owen would follow Clarence, but when she had got out into the soft April twilight she could barely see—indeed what was the point of seeing, she thought. She who had passed for worldly wise, sensible, sharp, clever, a match for any man, brave, indomitable, fierce, man-like in her strength, persevering—and one could fill up her ledger with the praise a hating world had bestowed upon her. There were thus two women, a Lady Bythewaite who answered to the above description, and Nora Bythewaite who loved only her sons, and who in her dream of life had never thought they would leave, or that she would grow old. It had seemed to her from the day Clarence kneeled in front of her and took her hand and pressed it against his cheek, and the time that Owen as a small boy had begged her never to desert him and go back to London, she had fallen, like any silly Prince's Crossing farm girl into an illusion which she mistook for genuine coin. She broke off a branch of a tree, and tapped her way home. In those days hardly a car passed one on the road, there were a few buggies, almost no pedestrians, but Aiken Cusworth, who was going homeward in his "bread van," spotted her, and stopped his horse.

"Lady Bythewaite, what's amiss . . . ?"

"You can ask that again till your mouth is dry." She looked into the direction from where the voice came. "I think the Lord has stricken me at last, Aiken . . ." She pointed to her eyes.

He helped her into his cart.

"And when are *you* leaving home?" she addressed the young horsetender savagely, so that he came near to dropping the reins.

"Answer me," she pursued her question, her eyesight beginning to come back now as they drove past sycamores and elms and fresh black fields that would be corn.

"And where would one like me go to, Lady Bythewaite?" he mumbled in reply.

"Clarence has gone," she sobbed angrily, "and now Owen has been hired to follow him, by orders of that gilded . . ." And here

Lady Bythewaite employed a word so obscene, though Aiken had never heard the word before, but like many words it was imprinted on his soul so that hearing it for the first time he knew its full meaning, knew that no lady would say it unless driven to distraction and lunacy, and the reins fell to his feet . . .

"Won't you stop him, though?" he wondered, regaining the reins and driving on again now.

"With what will I stop him? My rifle?"

Fully clear-eyed now, she jumped from the van before it had properly stopped.

"I'll be very surprised, Aiken, if I don't hear you're leaving within the week! These leave-takings are contagious, you know." She cried goodbye to him.

He watched her run and disappear. He spat to the other side of the road as he said *geeup*.

But Lady Bythewaite had turned back to watch the horse-tender's van turn presently into the road that led to Wolf Stretch. She stood a long time watching after the disappeared wagon.

So she was just like any other woman after all, so went her cogitations, except that like many smart people she was in the end easier to trip, and fell harder when she did fall. So she was a fool, the way God was said to mean women to be, and her own circumstances were common as dirt, for like all women from the dawn of time she was thinking of one or ones who had gone away, would never be back, or if they did come back would have only so much of their time or person to tantalize one sick with again, making the second coming more a sickness than their going away in the first place, and the screams of the Big Four which tormented all the landscape now for miles round and about tore at her like some steel claw. Waiting for its demon voice to subside, she held on to the stone post which marked the boundary of her "estate," then sidled past it, and turning to the great high gate closed it viciously, hearing it bang shut against the road, and against, it seemed, all other human habitations.

But she stood by the gate, the words from her monologue being fed back to her again. Since the beginning of time, the words went on, there have always been journeys of young men to cities of destruction, while someone waited helpless and wrung her hands—it was never *his* hands, she felt sure. She had thought up till now she was different, and would be able to rearrange the ancient pattern. She had never doubted this, and now her eyes smarted from some disease she feared she had had from her father, and let out great thick tears like pieces of rock salt.

Then a slight ray of hope and pathetic optimism broke to shine for her. She could count on Owen's hating to get up in the morning, and thus missing the train, which left at 4 A.M. from a desolate junction ten miles west of here. She would see that he never made that train, no matter how many mornings dog-faithful Aiken Cusworth stopped to pick him up in his van.

"And what will they say, Owen, when they see you in New York?" she spoke to the moving shadows of the coming night. "That you look like you had just left the plough?"

Each morning, then, Aiken and his van came to fetch Owen and take him to the junction, I say *each* morning because do what they would, they could not wake him between three and four of a morning. They slapped his cheeks, rumpled his hair, pulled his toes, to no avail, he slept on, driveling and whining faintly in his slumber like a newborn.

"Oh, let us give up, Aiken!" Lady Bythewaite announced in triumph on the last attempt, a frosty bitter morning for April.

Aiken, to her considerable regret, suggested that Owen and she and himself stay up all night, that the boy never approach his bed or take off his clothes, but sit by the grandfather clock which wheezing in its extreme antiquity would keep the heaviest slumberer conscious.

Flashing a look of malevolence at the "bread boy" for this inspiration, Lady Bythewaite could only say "she would see," and turned her attention to Owen, who that day had received an unusually peremptory letter from his brother Clarence, which Lady Bythewaite had stolen a peek at, and which said merely

> If you don't come within the week, your place will be filled by somebody more devoted, and I will be through with you forever. Your formerly loving
>
> *Clarence*

"He and the Pope!" Lady Bythewaite snorted. "Well, Owen," she began, glowering, however, in the direction of Aiken, "you've heard what resourceful bright Mr. Cusworth has thought up for you, and as I have nothing to do tonight but go through some old ledgers, we will sit up all together, and then if the improbable should come to pass, you and I and Aiken will go catch you the fast train . . ."

Owen gulped and nodded. She looked away. This time she would not be herself, would allow him to depart. She would be, that is, somebody who never was. Well, in any case, Owen would be back, and she began to whistle, which startled the two young men. She had not whistled since London.

A night of pure heavenly beauty with every star and planet revealing their splendor was above them, as the van drove up, and mother and son seated themselves inside. At the very last, she pushed a luncheon basket into Owen's hands, ample enough in its provisions to feed four men. Even at this late moment, in their parting, she had hoped against hope that as the trainman swung his red lantern, Owen, who had never been on a train before, would lose heart, and that the ferocity of the great wheels, the steam, the unearthly cries heard now directly from the iron monster, the black smoke and stench would strike it into his mind forever that he belonged with his boots here in the mud, and if not with Clarence, and her eye roved then toward the horsetender, yes, with Aiken Cusworth.

But Owen had got on the train. And then she saw him waving his blue handkerchief to her, and then she knew nothing until Aiken was rubbing her wrists with one hand, and holding the smelling bottle to her nostrils with the other. She was indeed lying in Aiken's own ramshackle house, presided over by an elderly housekeeper, who watched her and Aiken with helpless awe from a great rocking chair.

"He'll never be back," Lady Bythewaite was saying, "and if he does come back, he'll . . ."

But from her nose came a thin stream of blood which restored her brain to clarity. She offered to stand up, but both Aiken and the old woman, who had left her chair, commanded her to be still in combined voices so stern and emphatic, she was carried back to many years before in England and her mother's sorrow over her own disobedient heart.

Then from the back of her throat she uttered one solitary incomprehensible word in a voice like that of a raven. Then silence. Strive as he would Aiken Cusworth could not get her to pronounce the word again.

"What is this I hear that Lady Bythewaite has suffered a 'mild stroke'?" Mr. Skegg was cross-examining Aiken, who had entered the great front room of the old maggot's mansion, without properly wiping his feet, for he had been "summoned" like so many countless others before him, and being summoned he had come with not only his feet in a filthy condition, but his trousers and shirt put on in such haste, he stood squirming before his interlocutor like one caught in a variety of compromising positions.

"Yes, I do believe she has had one!" Aiken managed to get out this number of words, in response to Mr. Skegg's renewed demand for information.

The maggot was walking fast about the room, very much like a trapped—well, Aiken could not remember now in his mental confusion what the animal had been he had trapped some years ago, for he was not only in a state of confusion owing to Mr. Skegg's cross-examining of him about Lady Bythewaite's stroke (her copious nosebleed had saved her from death, the doctor, finally summoned with the greatest difficulty from twenty-five miles away, had said), he was thinking endlessly of the words she had used to describe the person of Mr. Skegg.

"I suppose she continues to blame me for having sent away her son Owen . . ."

"Your son too," Aiken muttered inaudibly, whilst placing his hand on the back of his trousers and attempting to adjust their falling condition.

"Now, then," Mr. Skegg was about to go on when he saw Aiken adjusting his clothing. The old man looked away confounded, then his usual magisterial pomposity went on, "Has her stroke, I say, impaired any of her many faculties?"

Mr. Skegg had put this question with the anger, irritation,

and extremely short patience of a man who wants to know the damage a recent cyclone has caused to his outbuildings.

"As she lay so sick and still, she spoke one word, a word that sounded like whippoorwill," Aiken almost without being aware he did so spoke aloud. He had hardly gotten this statement out and seen the effect of it on the astounded countenance of the old man, when his trousers fell with the rapidity of a curtain to his big soiled boots.

"Aiken, do you mean to tell me you have come here dead drunk, when I summoned you."

Aiken was too astounded to pick up his trousers, but stood as immobilized as one caught in an unusually ingenious net.

"Will you dress yourself, sir!" Mr. Skegg's anger began to take precedence over his slight horror and distaste.

"This lack of attention," the old man went on, having turned his back on the horsetender while the latter brought up his trousers, "must be endemic to country folk . . ."

"Between your hasty summons, sir," Aiken's voice rushed against Mr. Skegg's back, "and Lady Bythewaite's need for care and attention, I have been running hither and yon . . ."

"And so she used a strange expression with you!" the old man now faced a properly clothed Aiken Cusworth.

"Ah, so," Aiken closed his eyes, and nodded. "Just after she had her stroke, she did indeed use a very strange word which I have never heard anywhere before . . ."

To the horsetender's astonishment, the old man showed a decisive and lively interest in all this, resembling an attorney who having long since given up any hope of finding a shred of evidence to convict the person he is prosecuting is unexpectedly handed from nowhere a damning bit of irrefutable and concrete information.

"Sit down right here, why don't you, Aiken . . . That's all right. The maid will clean up the floor from your boots, and . . . your soiled trousers, after you've gone . . . What did she say, now? What did Lady Bythewaite say?" And lowering his voice:

"Do you think she was in her right mind, by chance, also, when she said it."

"I had never heard this word before." Aiken spoke bashfully, sitting on the chair in the manner of one who settles down into broken glass.

The old man's eyes had brightened.

"You may tell me the word, Aiken. We are alone here, my boy." The old maggot came near to bending over his witness, and watched the color come and go in the young man's face.

"I have, sir, been trying to recall it ever since she said it." Aiken was always too truthful to be doubted. His truthfulness was only equaled by his skill as a horseman. "But for the life of me, I can't recall the word . . ."

"Can you think of maybe what it might have sounded *like?*" Mr. Skegg was most patient. He patted Aiken's grimy knee.

"Ah, well, sir," Aiken spoke averting his eyes from his questioner, "it did sort of sound like *whippoorwill.*"

This statement did not please Mr. Skegg at all.

"The word," the old man began after furrowing his brows, and digging his hands into his trouser pockets, jingling what sounded like silver dollars there, "the word which you have so conveniently forgotten—must surely be connected with whatever caused her to her stroke, if stroke indeed it is. She has no control over her emotions!" Going back, however, to his curious preoccupation with the word, and which Aiken wished a thousand times then and later he had never mentioned, "I mean this unknown word is probably the key to her worry . . ."

"I believe it is a bad word, sir," Aiken replied to this, looking into a crack in the molding of the wall. "I do think it was."

Mr. Skegg looked dumbfounded at this suspicion of the horse-tender.

"A bad one, you say?" the old maggot spoke in silkily soft tones for fear, doubtless, he might frighten Aiken from unburdening himself of the truth.

Aiken colored violently and backing down almost completely begged Mr. Skegg to consider the possibility he had not understood the word aright from the outset, and had probably not even heard it correctly.

"A word which sounds like whippoorwill," the old man went on with his cogitating, and walking over to the great bay window, he turned his back to his witness.

"A bad word that sounds like whippoorwill," he went on muttering and shaking his head.

Then to Aiken's complete astonishment, confusion, and even fear, Mr. Skegg, wheeling about without warning, and also without any preparation began rattling off one unprintable and indelicate word after another, many of which the horsetender himself had only barely heard pronounced in his twenty-some years of life.

"Not one of those words, eh?" Mr. Skegg finally cried after his catalogue of scurrility, and only his own intense hankering for the divulging of the word itself made him fail to notice the deep shame and embarrassment his spieling off so many obscenities had given to the horsetender.

Deeply disappointed, with his energy and enthusiasm for discovery spent, Mr. Skegg could only mumble: "Then you must have been mistaken, Aiken, my boy." The old man was severe. "If she did not use one of those words which I have pronounced here before you, then it is clear that what she said was not obscene, that is to say, dirty, don't you see . . . Also, bear in mind, she was in the aftermath of a stroke . . . Now I know *you* wouldn't deceive me, Aiken. Deceit is not in your nature. But you are after all, dear fellow, a farmer and horsetender to boot, and you may be unaware owing to your calling that there is no word in our language, no bad word which sounds like whippoorwill, although I want you to think about it, as I will of course . . . Now, Aiken, here's a silver dollar for your trouble . . . No, no, you must accept it . . . And go out the rear door as you leave . . . Don't mind the mud you have deposited on carpet and floor, it's quite all right, and will be tended to . . . And don't breathe a word of this to anyone else, if you don't mind . . . Good day, Aiken, and much obliged to you . . ."

To the considerable astonishment of the farmers of the neighboring counties, Mr. Skegg was now paying them unexpected visits. They assumed the maggot had come to purchase their farms, or try one of his many underhand tricks to dispossess them. The rumor, however, soon spread around that he had come to talk about "words," and more specifically to ask them all and sundry if they knew of a particular word which they would not allow themselves to say in front of their womenfolk, but went sounding something like *whippoorwill*.

Mr. Skegg is said to have called on something like forty farmers. This was the beginning of a serious change in his reputation. Hitherto he had been known as one of the greatest speculators in real estate throughout this part of the nation, and still in these people's reckoning a youngish man. But from the start of his coming merely to inquire about a word (which nobody had ever heard pronounced, let alone mentioned or discussed) dated the true beginning of his being known as the maggot, the lonely maggot, who was no longer thought to be of sound business practice, and beyond the shadow of a doubt showing the signs of old age and his hermitic years of isolation.

Sounding like whippoorwill.

Where his researches would have ended nobody can guess had not a somewhat serious thing happened to the maggot. At night now, farmers and tradesmen heard, passing, heartsore, terrible muffled moans and cries coming from his great house. Too stingy to sit up wasting light much past bedtime, he usually kept his mansion an inky battlement after sundown, but now during the period his moans and cries punctuated the night, his entire lower chambers were as blazingly illuminated as if some sumptuous banquet were in progress.

Though people seemed to have forgotten that Lady Bythewaite was once human enough to have been intimate with the maggot and become the mother of sons by him, a kind of memory of some connection between the two caused a particularly intrepid farmer to stop at her house, and report through an only half-opened door that cries and moans were constantly coming from the old speculator's mansion.

"Yes, yes," she cried, speaking in reply through a mere crack of the mammoth portal, "*I* have heard them, and *they* have heard them certainly to the ocean's shore! Yes, I am alarmed. I live in a state of alarm . . ."

Then as the farmer began to retreat down her interminable front path over her interminable yard, Lady Bythewaite coming out from the shelter of the portal cried out to him, and the words of this cry were soon reported in many other farmhouses:

"I hope God is about to see reason and take him! Perhaps," she coughed out into the night, alarming birds in their nests, and disturbing other wildlife which prowled about her acres, "perhaps there may be a God indeed, and He is punishing him at last for all he has done to me and my boys!"

She saw, she fancied she saw the farmer looking back at her from his wagon, and then she heard his whip and wheels and he was gone with her words to tell all whom he met.

Then there stood before her the inevitable Aiken Cusworth, his horse and buggy waiting outside.

Nora Bythewaite threw on her heavy cloak, arranged a flowered hat over her dark hair, and without even bothering to inquire of Aiken why he had come or where they were off to, she followed him to the buggy and they drove the short distance to the house of the maggot.

"Yes, you're bad, Mr. Skegg . . ." Lady Bythewaite lay her hand on the forehead of the sick man. "I doubt indeed you'll recover, but of course we can do our best for you." She shook her head dolefully, and began taking his pulse.

"What is this you've been saying to my horsetender about whippoorwills?" the sick man exclaimed, rising up in his bed, his mane of white hair sticking up at all angles as if lightning were passing through it.

At her first astonishment at these words, Lady Bythewaite looked nowhere in particular, and then her gaze settled down on the impassive face of Aiken. That faithful young person was ready, she saw by his downcast eyes, to receive her accusation of revealing secrets—how many had she not crammed him with against his wishes?—but Lady Bythewaite only said, "Our patient is delirious, Aiken," and the horsetender breathed a sigh of relief.

"Now where do you hurt, Mr. Skegg?" She lifted the patient up suddenly, and felt of him with rough professional reconnoitering.

Mr. Skegg, after giving her a wild look which may have conveyed his fear she had come to murder him, could get out no words in reply, and pointed instead to one of his back teeth.

"Fetch the little lamp from over there, Aiken."

Mr. Skegg was reclining on the same kind of ottoman which he was later to lie dead on so many many years afterwards, but minus the lap robe . . .

While Aiken held the kerosene lamp over the suffering man, Lady Bythewaite looked cruelly and long into his mouth, which was not, as one might suppose, cavernous, and his lips drawn back showed now somewhat small and mean, as one might expect. He was in possession of all his teeth, she soon saw, despite the fact that owing to his extreme stinginess or perhaps because of his suspicion of all other human beings, he had never paid a call to a dentist.

Waving back Aiken with the lamp, Lady Bythewaite cried in vociferous triumph: "You have an abscessed tooth, Mr. Skegg."

"Won't it correct itself, Nora?" the old man asked casually, and began fastening one of his gold cufflinks which had become undone.

"Never. It's quite full of pus, and the poison is coursing through your entire system . . . Hence your delirium, and your irrational speech."

"I beg your pardon, Nora, my dear," the old man spoke respectfully, "I know perfectly well what I am saying, and know furthermore to whom I am speaking."

"You have been talking of birds," she exclaimed with such anger and authority he was silent, and looked away from her to Aiken for some comfort, to whom he now delivered a speech quite commonly given in Prince's Crossing by nearly all its few inhabitants concerning the anomaly that there was no doctor, or dentist, or other medical assistance for miles and miles about.

"You want me to pull this tooth of course!" Lady Bythewaite spoke in loud ferocity like one addressing both a deaf man and an idiot at the same time. She had, without waiting for his assent, begun to roll up her sleeves, but had forgotten she was wearing her hat, until Aiken indicated she might wish to remove it.

Then preparatory to any surgery she took out with great slowness and caution a small bottle from the deepest recesses of her dress. Mr. Skegg's eyes fastened on the vial in the manner of one who had been waiting for it and it alone on all those nights he had howled, those howls which together with his interrogations concerning an unknown word had destroyed in effect his reputation.

"Now, Mr. Skegg, this is quite strong," she cautioned him in a wearied angry and highly edifying tone. "It is opium."

Where Lady Bythewaite had learned medicine nobody knew and indeed nobody cared anymore. But all could recall who were still among the quick and still of sound wit that she had set broken legs and arms, delivered babies, in those contingencies (common) when nobody else could be fetched. And she had pulled many a desperate person's aching teeth.

But the kind of instruments she now assembled from a little satchel, which even Aiken had not noticed she had fetched with her, and which she made no motion to purify with flame or alcohol, looked even to Mr. Skegg settling down under the strong sip of opium, yes, a little large for a human mouth, a little dull and brown with age in the flickering kerosene light.

People talked of the screams and moans coming from the great house that night for many a revolving year to come, and if the hearers were alive now they would be talking still of it. Some of the listeners even thought that the wolves might have come down from the north again, as they occasionally did, so barely human were those cries.

When she had only half-yanked his tooth out, and a swelling rivulet of pus and foul-smelling gouts of blood had, so it seemed to Aiken, unnecessarily stained the maggot's fine cambric shirt, both the horsetender and Mr. Skegg heard a voice coming from an ill-defined place, not recognizable as a woman's or indeed human being's:

"Mr. Skegg, you are to call Owen home . . ."

The voice paused, while the owner of the voice pressed the knife close to her patient's swelling jugular.

Then, closing his eyes, Mr. Skegg nodded in agreement to that voice.

"In writing, Mr. Skegg." The patient waited, eyes still closed, then he nodded even more energetically in assent. Then she put in the forceps, there was a suffocating scream, the tooth was jerked out.

"They have had the doctor to set his jaw, which was badly dislocated, if not broken," Aiken spoke, his eyes fixed on a short thick notebook so that he appeared to be reading a text to his employer, some few days after the incident of the toothpulling.

"And where under the running sun was a doctor fetched from?" Lady Bythewaite wondered. Though she had three, perhaps four servants in constant if almost invisible attendance on her needs, Aiken had found her shelling peas in the parlor. He consulted his notebook of accounts again. His delay in reading the wanted information caused her to raise her eyes; she recognized the notebook as nothing less than the ledger in which he kept his bread accounts, the cost of the oats and other feed for the horses, etc.

"A doctor was fetched from round the vicinity of Stotfold, ma'am."

"You come to me with reports of a wayward old man's having

dislocated his jaw when I am sick to death with apprehension because there is no word from New York . . . Or is there? for you in your ceaseless rounds in your buggy see and know more than the sun in flight!"

"There is no word of Owen Haskins, ma'am."

The sound of her son's name brought her up short. Two weeks had passed before she had received his first postcard with the words:

I'M HERE. OWEN

Over a month had passed since and there had been no additional word.

She had not been able even to give her boy a legal name, she was musing, while Aiken stood as mute and insensible-seeming as a caryatid. Owen's name was, so to speak, invented. She had, she went on thinking, for she felt alone, invented Owen's life. She had dimly deeply cherished his bastardy. She had not been able to do anything for him. And she had allowed a coarse, cunning, really insane man (*maggot* also you see meant *peculiar* person in the lingo of Prince's Crossing) to send her boy away. Why hadn't she stopped the train that night, yanked Owen off it, and then gone over and burnt the maggot's house to the ground with him in it.

"He dislocated his own jaw, Aiken!" Lady Bythewaite made this sudden outburst, catching Aiken unprepared for it, causing him to stammer and flush. "He dislocated it because he wouldn't keep his mouth shut and bear the pain with calm like a man . . . It's the easiest thing in the world to dislocate one's jaw by talking too much. Remember that. And his screams! Can he, do you think, face me again, after his whimperings, squaw-like yells, and ki-yi wolfhowls! A mourning dove can stand pain better than he . . . When pain's to be endured, go study women and boys, for these strong men we have nowadays turn into mewling infants on seeing blood drawn."

But Aiken Cusworth paid no more immediate attention to her sudden unexpected cries, her tempests in which she broke expensive furniture and china than he did to the peremptory commands of the maggot, or in the more recent past, the imperious injunctions of Clarence Skegg, now Maynard Ewing.

"Mr. Skegg has no intention of bringing back Owen, despite his pledges!" Lady Bythewaite was going on.

Mr. Skegg had become aware of the fact that he had dislocated his jaw not after her brutal pulling of his back tooth but on the day he had got word that two of his finest farm properties had, during his illness and inattention, been purchased by Lady Bythewaite. He had let out a great cry of vexation, and his jaw had slipped down, causing intolerable pain, or perhaps at that precise moment the opium had worn off, and his jaw, dislocated during the "operation," now informed its owner of its true condition.

At any rate, he did not need this fierce physical pain to remind him of the way things were changing, or preventing him from seeing the handwriting on the wall, or on the barn door. He had an implacable enemy in the woman whom at first he had refused to marry and who herself, later, had refused to marry him. She had maimed him while he lay helpless, and while she was tearing out his back tooth with the fury of a savage chief, at that very moment, by bold if not underhand means, she was in the process of depriving him of some of the finest farm lands in the nation.

A few days later Mr. Skegg came to her. His jaw was bandaged, and he had lost weight, a great deal of weight. Studying his flat stomach, and where his jowls had been, she calculated he had parted with twenty-five pounds. The loss of weight did not become him because she knew nothing became him. From looking like a bull he had changed in appearance to resembling a mangy stag.

He removed his hat, and held it over his heart, a gesture which infuriated her.

"You're not in a mortuary. Put on your headgear, you'll catch cold in here . . ."

Despite the approach of summer, it was almost freezing in her house, always poorly heated, probably owing to her custom of stomping and stamping about so much that she needed little if any heat except that coming from her own body.

Mr. Skegg was in the act of explaining how he had tried to locate Owen Haskins in New York.

"I've telegraphed and even gone to the town of Stotfold to try to telephone for information . . . There is no trace, my dear Lady Bythewaite, of Owen Haskins . . . I have spoken with Clarence through the very unsatisfactory operation of long-distance telephoning. He denied however there is such a person as Clarence Skegg, though he condescended to speak with me under the name of Maynard Ewing . . ."

The hurt of his one legally recognized son's changing his name, she saw, was genuine. His voice trembled. But Nora Bythewaite was implacable. She looked about wildly, in search, perhaps, of some chisel or pair of pliers to remove more of his white teeth.

"We will, nonetheless, continue the search for him," Mr. Skegg raised his voice now to catch her wandering attention, though the effort to increase the volume of his speech must have hurt him, for he clapped his hand to his swollen jaw.

Aiken, at a peremptory movement of Lady Bythewaite's eyes, opened the door for Mr. Skegg to take his departure.

"Don't come again, Mr. Skegg, until you have something to report! Your sorrow over having robbed me of my son is not convincing . . . And as to your jaw, beware of the contingency of blood poisoning! You are not out of the woods at all, by any measure of means."

But he had been gone only a few moments when she rushed out the door after him, and pursued him down the long path to where he was seated in his new automobile, and almost pulling him away from the steering wheel, she shouted:

"Do you have any conception of how old Owen Haskins is?"

He gazed at her, used though he was to her carrying on, with a marvel of complete disbelief in what he saw in her face.

"Tell me how old Owen Haskins is, will you?" she vociferated.

He tried to start the motor of his car, but her hand pulled his arm toward her. "He's barely fifteen!" she informed him. "And if he lies in a New York mortuary, I'll charge you with murder . . ."

"Clarence is fonder of Owen than of anyone else in the world, for he only half-loves me, I sometimes think." Lady Bythewaite was speaking in a voice which carried easily to the lake nearby her property. "But his love for Owen is destructive . . . He is quite capable . . ." At that moment she saw for the first time as if his face had been handed to her for appraisal, perhaps sale, like a farm, the countenance of Aiken Cusworth. A shiver ran through her body. She felt as embarrassed as if she had come upon him stripped. He lowered his eyes, but it was too late, he had given up his secret. He loved not only her, but all of them, she saw, even—she feared—Mr. Skegg. But certainly, oh certainly Owen Haskins, his special pride. Because, she supposed, there was nobody else to love. There is only us, she thought, and so he loves us. She had always thought, echoing Mr. Skegg, in part, that Aiken was just a clodhopper, but she saw suffused over his face, along with his crude roughly chiseled good looks and perfect health, something deep and intuitive. She must be careful, she must not hurt him too.

"I will not send *you* to New York," Lady Bythewaite thundered. "We will lose no more boys."

"If you change your mind, you know where to find me, Lady Bythewaite."

"Don't tempt me, Aiken. Don't ever tempt me." Then with real fury she added: "Clarence has always wanted to kill Owen because he is perfect . . ."

Looking up a moment later she saw that the horsetender had left the room.

Rushing out to the front gate, she called his name after him, called it with the deep feeling of one who understood the meaning of his name at last: *Aiken, Aiken!*

She looked after the retreating horse and carriage, finally calling his name only in a silent moving of her lips. Up until now she had thought the horsetender was only a boy, and here he was more of a man than the whole rest of the pack, and she had not known it. She had another son on her hands, she feared, another son to worry about, to fret over . . . But as she pronounced the word *son*, a kind of whirlwind overtook her, and in the whirlwind she saw the features of this Aiken for the first time, saw them with blinding clarity. *No, it could not be*, she spoke to herself. *Aiken could not be her . . . lost . . . boy . . .*

The next day came and went, and Aiken had gone. She took to her bed. In the middle of the night following the day of his departure, she lay under the heavy embroidered sheet, which suddenly looking like graveclothes, she tore with a sweeping decisiveness as if she had cut it with a great sword. Rising, she was about to go down the hall on her way she knew not where when she heard footsteps approaching. It was Mr. Skegg.

"Yes, I admit I am ill, but I doubt there is a name for it." Having said this she fell against him. He led her back to her four-poster where she had lain tossing and turning for so many years celibate and burning. He kissed her forehead and she cried out like one who had been touched with hot coals: "I will never bear you more sons, Mr. Skegg . . . Don't touch me . . ."

After dozing awhile she looked up at him, still there. The expression on his face chilled her. In the mild darkness of the room he was unrecognizable, or perhaps he was recognizable as himself at last. Faces are always changing in meaning, as the mystery and deceit of light plays upon them, until, she thought, death, freeing the soul, renders all faces indecipherable forever.

"How did you know I was ill, Mr. Skegg?"

"You left all the lights on downstairs."

"I hope I am dying," she smoothed the quilt under her thin veined hands, "for I have discovered something I had long feared to discover . . . How can anyone fear death," she went on, seeming to wander, "oh, perhaps the pain a little, but how can one fear to part with something which never lets us be ourselves, always traveling, never arriving, always footsore, never rested, always the future, never the goal."

"Aiken will find him," Mr. Skegg said after a silence.

"I believe if anybody can, he might," she replied, and she motioned for Mr. Skegg to reach her her medicine.

Then just as the spring morning was lighting up the waters of the lake, the van drove up, Aiken alighted, helped a young man down with two pieces of new luggage, the two young men exchanged a firm handclasp, and Aiken had leaped into the seat of his van again, and whipped up the reins, when they heard the great front gate open, and Nora Bythewaite came running down the long path and presently stood beside the horse.

"Come down, Aiken. Come in."

But who was it he had helped alight from the van? For a split second she did not know him. That is, she knew him only because who else was there whom Aiken would fetch and deposit?

Aiken hesitated to come down, and then she was imperious, though she avoided his eyes.

Inside the house they all sat down at a great many-leafed dining table, and the hired girl brought in a pot of coffee, steaming rolls, oatmeal, and then went out into the kitchen to prepare something more substantial yet.

The best thing for Lady Bythewaite was not to look at him at all, that is, Owen, for his pursed lips and wretched eyes kept pleading with her not to gaze at him. His hair had been cut short, and he wore a suit which must be tailor-made, at any rate it was of shockingly expensive material which her hands longed to touch, the early light caught the silk of his foulard, which set off his pure sea-island cotton shirt, from which emerged scintillating cufflinks, and on his hands which lay folded like those of a drowned person were two gleaming rings, one gold, the other of some semi-precious or, who knows, precious gem.

She almost felt she heard a voice from heaven, not a voice of gold, but one of harsh ear-splitting trumpets, reminding her of how she should have clothed and brought up her only acknowledged son. He had been found, identified, and sent home to her as a lesson, a corrective of her own many failings toward the boy.

"But it wouldn't have done for him to wear good clothes here in the country, and you know it!" she suddenly spoke in reply to this imaginary trumpet voice, but her eyes as she spoke fell on those of Aiken, who looked at her with moved consternation.

Her strange incoherence restored the two young men to life, for up to now they had sat munching the rolls and sipping the hot strong coffee in acute embarrassment.

A thousand questions rose, questions which she saw she would have to put to Aiken, for she felt that Owen had been tampered with, and would not speak the truth, that is, he had been bribed, she felt. Where, for instance, had Aiken found him, and had he gone all the way to New York for him in his van? And finally, would Owen remain with her, or would he go back where they had touched him with grandeur.

And so she wept. The great Lady Bythewaite, whose reputation for hardness, cunning, indomitable will, who was, as everybody in Prince's Crossing knew, working night and day to overthrow Mr. Skegg and herself become the "maggot" of the crossroads, there she sat, ridiculous and rather ugly, certainly red and creased from her grief and recent illness, making a miserable homecoming for the runaway, who might indeed never have been heard of again in these parts without Aiken's bravery and resourcefulness.

"And so this is all Clarence's doing!" she let out these words with a banshee scream, looking for some "reason" and happening to fix her eyes on Aiken, who immediately disgorged a large mouthful of oatmeal onto his plate, and choked on what he had swallowed the wrong way.

"Here I thought Clarence was penniless!" She rose, and her dress trailing pulled a fine plate to the floor with a bang, but being of the same stuff as its owner it did not break. The hired girl came in, picked it up, and walked off with it to the kitchen.

"And where then did he get the money to robe you in this

finery!" She turned her fury at last upon Owen. "How dare you come back, how dare he send you back to shame me like this! How could he clothe you so, Owen, when he's been disinherited? I said *disinherited*. And he's changed his name like any common forger, bankrupt, or crook. How dare he clothe you like this!" And she went up to Owen and roughly handled the material.

"Oh, I'm not going to tear your garments!" She let go the lapel of his suit as if she had touched slime. "But you'll find little use for such raiment here among folk like me and Aiken!"

Owen turned his full gaze wonderingly, if appreciatively, now on Aiken Cusworth, who bowed his head. Then Owen blurted out:

"He is a great star, no question about that, Clarence is." Then he subsided into a moony silence, his pupils narrowed, his heavy lids closed for a moment seemingly to contrast this breakfast scene with those days in New York.

"And when are you returning to this great star, pray tell? . . . You've come home only to settle your affairs before you join forces with him permanently?"

"Oh, I can never go back, Mother," Owen spoke still gazing intently at Aiken, indeed studying the countenance of the horse-tender. "I've disgraced him, you see. He can never have me back. I'm not presentable enough, not the conversationalist he requires to please his advanced circle."

"But this raiment!" she returned to the subject of his clothes, and not able to keep her hands from his jacket again, her nervous fingers with admiring loathing feeling out the hand-sewn edges of the pockets, the skillful setting of the elaborate buttons, and the beauty of the lining.

Aiken had excused himself, dried his lips, was about to retire, when Lady Bythewaite motioned for him to follow her into the long hallway, where so many private, desperate, and serious conversations had taken place for over a hundred years.

"No, I cannot accept it!" Aiken's voice drifted back to Owen, who holding a solid silver spoon in his hand looked out into the soft purling water of the little lake. "That is all over," Owen sighed, speaking aloud to himself. "I was a paid messenger, and I failed to fetch him back."

He looked up out of his reverie to see his mother eyeing him narrowly.

"You'll never be satisfied here again, Owen Haskins, even if I were to give up my life for you."

She leant over the breakfast table, and peremptorily put an entire hot biscuit into her mouth, chewing hungrily, like a woman who had performed many chores without a morsel to sustain her since daybreak.

He had forgotten how coarse she sometimes was.

Mr. Skegg was scolding Aiken—it was just after dawn—for constantly refusing to give up his "bread route" with the van when he might just as well be his steady hired man, and this very usual complaint was followed by the peroration on Money, which went something like this: When man realized God was a myth, he came to know the comfort—not the worship, mind you—the comfort, deep meaning, and purposeful morality of money, which was the key to the modern world, which had made our country the greatest under the sun and our people the most self-resourceful, high-minded, and successful which the world had ever seen.

Aiken Cusworth was attempting meanwhile to adjust his sleeves, they were a bit too short for him, as the shirt he had on was not his, it was Owen's, that is, Owen had received it when in New York City, and had given it to Aiken, as, one supposed, a kind of reward.

"You steadfastly refuse then to be my permanent hired man?" Mr. Skegg inquired, staring with a look of deep personal humiliation at Aiken's improperly elongated cuffs.

"And can't your confounded housekeeper sew better than she does!" Mr. Skegg finally blurted out. "I refer to your sleeve length . . ."

"I did see your son," Aiken finally responded, after a lengthy stare direct into Mr. Skegg's eyes, for he took it that all his long peroration about Money and God and America, and his peevish complaining about his sleeves was a mere pretense to get him to turn and tell about his trip.

Mr. Skegg now shook like the maple tree in a summer thunderstorm. The more he attempted to stop his trembling the more pronounced it became. He finally, Aiken felt, resembled a fish that had been pulled to land, and his convulsive breathing could be heard outside the house.

"For a bread delivery boy and horsetender, you are deuced clever," the old maggot was finally capable of saying. "One would think you were a policeman! Finding lost persons so easily, and what's more persuading him to return.

"But you couldn't persuade Clarence to come back, could you?" The old man's anger supplied the force which now stopped his trembling. He was still as a sheet as he said this. "Didn't you tell him I had disinherited him . . . Didn't you tell him what I think of movie stars, actors, and the rest of the bilge?"

"He knows it by now, Mr. Skegg. There was no point in my telling him what he knew already to a T and committed to heart."

"Are you sassing me, Aiken Cusworth? . . . By God, you are!"

Leaning over the floor, where he thought he saw an army of pismires marching out toward the kitchen, but which turned out to be, when he had put on his spectacles, small lumps of dried mud from Aiken's feet, he began one of his interminable "memory" speeches: "At the time of Lady Bythewaite's first arrival here, she had had the bad taste to still do some of her theatrical presentations. This ruined both boys. They are both, as a result, stage-struck. Owen has been too browbeaten by his alleged mother and his supposed half brother," here Mr. Skegg became very nervous again, as if having stepped in over his head, "I venture to think, to ever be anything but a wonderstruck fool, at home only in country landscape . . . Aiken, she is entirely to blame for all our wretchedness! I wish I could merely call her a whore, as some do, but she's so far far worse. She is a temptress of some other kind. A whore, after all, only tempts men's bodies. She will only settle for their souls. She has also outstripped me in a land deal!"

Aiken had sat down, Aiken had stood up, and sat down again. The bread was waiting in his van outside to be delivered—late.

"I say, what did you see!" Mr. Skegg's voice reached him quite close because the maggot in point of fact was standing right by him, having been roused to ire by the youth's inattention to come directly to his side.

"Why, I went to the movie studio, sir," he began like one talking in his sleep, but saw at once with a start he had made a mistake and that this piece of information had failed to please. "I found him before those blinding lights, wearing, well," he went on in spite of himself, and he studied Mr. Skegg's mouth, "a sort of kimono and little else, and made up with rouge and lipstick which Clarence explained is necessary in the pictures . . ."

Mr. Skegg hobbled off back to his rigid easy chair.

"Later," Aiken went on hesitantly, swallowing again and again, "we went to grand places, where there was nothing but chandeliers and big tables with flowers. A gentleman with a monocle took us all 'in tow,' which is the way Clarence expressed it . . . I mean Maynard Ewing . . ."

"His disinherited name, Aiken," Mr. Skegg cried out lightly, in the tone of one who is explaining a text which is being falteringly read by an immature reader.

"His motion picture name, sir." Aiken spoke with thorough assuredness.

"I have disinherited my son," Mr. Skegg acted again as prompter. "But go on, go on, your delivery route is waiting . . ."

"Yes, I must be up and out, Mr. Skegg. I really have overstayed . . ." He looked out at the position of the sun.

The old man, however, looked so crestfallen that Aiken, though he dimly realized that what he was about to say might not please any better than what he had already said, went on with, "But coming back to where Clarence, or Maynard Ewing, lives was quite a comedown . . . He lives in a room no bigger than a shoe box. It has a sort of large closet, and in this closet are all his motion picture clothes, for he dresses like a . . . a . . . prince . . ."

"And the studio supplies this wealthy wardrobe?" Mr. Skegg wondered in a faraway voice.

"I have no idea, sir."

"Well, what in blue hell do you judge, if you have no idea! After all you were there, were you not! You profess to have been there!"

Aiken, however, had had enough, excused himself, and was on his way out, but Mr. Skegg followed close at his heels.

"Do you remember the name of the place with the chandeliers, by any chance?" he called after the horsetender. "After all, Aiken, I was once in New York, that is, went to Wall Street rather frequently."

Aiken gazed from the bread van in the direction of the maggot. Then somewhat weakly, almost languidly for so husky a fellow, with irresolute moving of his hand, he waved a goodbye as his only answer to his interlocutor, and drove off.

"I walk in without knocking or announcing myself," Lady Bythewaite told Mr. Skegg, "because neither you nor your hired girl ever hears me when I do knock . . . Here's your money!" She spoke more disdainfully than ever, and threw an envelope on the marble-topped table at which the old maggot was seated, eating breakfast.

"So he refused my peace offering?" Mr. Skegg snorted.

"First you disinherit him, I refer to Clarence, although you have already disinherited your other son. And then you . . ."

"Owen Haskins is not my son. How many times have I told you that? How many times have you tried to make yourself believe he is my son?"

"The day will come, Mr. Skegg, when you look closely at the boy, now he is approaching manhood, and you will see there some of your few better qualities . . . But to go back to the point we are discussing. First you disinherit Clarence, then you send him his brother with money asking him to come back to the fold."

"I see nothing irrational in that . . . When he comes home, and gives up his depraved career, he can be reinstated. Not as fully as before, but to some extent . . ."

Lady Bythewaite was lost in thought. She would have laughed at the word *depraved* a few weeks ago, for, having been an actress herself, she knew how false most of the "tales" about acting folk were. But she knew nothing about motion pictures. All she knew was that something quite fundamental had happened to her son Owen as a result of his visit to his brother.

"He is not himself!" She heard herself speaking without any prior wish to divulge her apprehension to Mr. Skegg's oversuspicious mind.

"Who is not himself, Nora Bythewaite?" the old man demanded, putting down his coffee pot. "You were never *yourself,* some people have opined! I say, who is not himself?"

"Owen of course . . . Owen." Her reply was barely audible.

Mr. Skegg sat bent, gazing at the money. The one thing he could not fathom in all this was how Clarence could turn down money. Was a beginning motion picture star so rich?

"*I* always felt most unlike *myself* when I went to New York," the old maggot began to speak now more cautiously, more pleasantly as he saw the turmoil through which she was passing, a turmoil he had not seen in her for twenty years.

"What is worst of all," she went on, having moved to seat herself at the marble-topped table, and to his mild surprise, unbidden had begun to eat some of his muffins, helping herself to the gooseberry preserves, using his own knife to spread the sweet, "what is inexplicable is he wears those clothes which his brother—I assume it was his brother—gave him, in all his rambles about the countryside. Why, he has quite startled everybody who knew him only in his gadabouts and glad rags. I myself did not recognize him the other day when I was driving past Fieldstone Acres. There he sat on top of the hill looking like he had dropped from the sky."

Mr. Skegg rose, the coffee trickling down his chin.

"What do you mean by *he has clothed him?*"

"I have already told you he did so . . . He came back with at least five new suits of clothes, all preposterous, shirts of an expensiveness which makes my head swim, cravats of a width and elegance no one has worn since Edward VII."

"Why, then, they're wardrobe castoffs, I reckon!" he spoke, relieved.

"No such things . . . They're gifts!"

"Gifts, thunderation. They're bribes, and we both know it." He went over to where she was eating, eating not through hunger but desperation.

"Don't you see, Nora," his voice was almost "petting," "Clarence means to use your Owen to bring both of us to our knees . . ."

"I am too muddle-headed to know anything about that, but I know one thing," and now she rose, and looked straight at him, and his hand took the bread knife, and put it in its leather sheath, "he will be asking Owen to come back for future visits unless you do the one thing that will stop him . . ."

He was at a complete loss to know what she meant, and his staring at her with mouth open gave her more assuredness as she went on:

"You must recognize Owen legally. You must make him one of your heirs. If you've disinherited your only elder son, you can inherit your illegitimate son."

"The only way to do that to the law's satisfaction would be for you to marry me, Nora . . . And we all know that you would not do that years ago when you could . . . You wanted your freedom, didn't you, precious girl, and don't say you don't have it! But Owen has paid the price. Don't talk about strange rich clothes driving your son mad, or a visit to his brother, even if he does wear lipstick before the cameras!"

"Who in God's name told you that?" It was Nora Bythewaite's turn to be dumbfounded. She rose from her second breakfast, her jaw resembling his when dislocated.

"I am not as entirely in the dark as you have always made out," he began. "You've taught the world I am a rustic idiot, but, the world has long since passed you by since the days when you came here as some sort of dethroned queen from London . . . You can marry me, and restore your son to sanity, or you can let him rove the countryside in the company of your favorite clown Aiken Cusworth until his New York brother decides it's time for another dose of high life for him . . . There is after all only one person he really loves, indeed worships. It's not you, or Clarence, but Aiken Cusworth."

One morning Mr. Skegg had come up to his cupola to look out upon the lake with his field glasses when he spied on the top of the little hill which rises and then slopes down to this body of water an extraordinary happening which he could not credit his eyes with seeing. His throat became painfully dry, and his old vertigo came over him so that the field glasses fell from his hands. Gradually his brain cleared and he was able to look again, but only one of the two persons who had been engaged in the struggle which he had thought he saw still remained on the top of the hill, and he was stained with blood, he perceived, as he scrutinized him with the glasses, and furthermore he was now wending his way in the direction of his house. It was Aiken Cusworth, and he carried a buggy whip which his assailant had struck him with again and again, over the face, over the body, ripping his shirt and even his tough cord trousers.

In his confusion, Mr. Skegg had thrown the heavy bolt over the door instead of removing it, so that the attacked man had to hammer again and again before the old maggot could remember to unbolt the door.

"Shall I call Lady Bythewaite?" Mr. Skegg addressed the bleeding man, but the usually gentle Aiken let out a string of *God damns* and *Almighty Christs, "No!"*

"I may not be the surgeon she is, I'd have you know, but there are worse ones about carrying little black bags than me."

Even as he spoke, Aiken had collapsed on the floor, and small rivulets of blood found their way from his torn work-shirt onto the rich carpet of the hallway.

Unable to lift him, Mr. Skegg let him lie for the moment, and went upstairs to fetch blankets, then down again to a medicine cabinet largely stocked with Lady Bythewaite's drugs and nostrums.

But Aiken had come to by the time the maggot reached his side again. He refused the whiskey, the smelling bottle, every token of aid and comfort.

"I'm not hurt bad, Mr. Skegg. More surprised and sick than anything."

Was it an almost animal curiosity, sympathy, or the beginning of some dawn of recognition that made Mr. Skegg so considerate of someone he had called to his face so many times a dirty groom, brute, and simpleton.

"I could not quite see who was giving you this beating," the old man averred, watching his guest with the most complete attention, almost whispering these words lest the volume of his questioning might check a reply.

Aiken Cusworth's great sides heaved as if they would burst their ribcage, drops of sweat stood motionless on him like those seen on freshly churned butter, the veins in his hands and wrists looked ready to burst, his hair which had always looked short now fell easily about his ears. A strong pungent odor like that of horses rose steaming from him. And though he wiped his face and chest with rags dipped in warm water and alcohol, again and again the rivulets of blood came as if from every vein in his body. He seemed to be weeping blood, and yet curiously enough, there was a look of relief, of some strange knowledge on his mouth and in his eyes, like that of a great athlete, who, though within the jaws of death from exhaustion, is assured winner, sole victor.

"I say," Mr. Skegg spoke gently, coaxingly like one who is to be entertained, not entertaining, and himself far from home, "I did not quite see your assailant."

"You saw it all?" Aiken wondered, incredulous, after being perhaps unsure what to do with the word "assailant."

"We don't have this sort of thing around here, as you know," Mr. Skegg philosophized, but without any conviction or emphasis. Then coming out with some impatience, almost anger, and more like himself, speaking just above a whisper: "I'll have to have the details, nonetheless, for it was taking place on my property!"

"I am entirely to blame," Aiken murmured.

To Mr. Skegg's even more considerable astonishment, great snorts of grief more like that, again, from his horses than from a human being came out, quickly suppressed by Aiken's biting his lips, and at this exertion of force, as if from a signal, his wounds opened to give off more running crimson.

"Since you've ruined my furniture and rugs, though you've refused to drink my whiskey or sniff my smelling bottle, by Christ, you owe me the honesty to tell me who gave you such a thoroughgoing horsewhipping . . ."

"I horsewhipped myself, you nosy old skinflint!" Aiken bawled out. "Look at me!" he cried now in maniacal fury, and painfully rising and struggling up to a pier mirror he gazed in disbelief at himself. In his mounting anger, he tore off the few remaining shreds of his shirt. Mr. Skegg drew back, not only at the obscenity of Aiken's appearance, but at the insult he had received from a hired man and stable boy. At the same time, Mr. Skegg looked considerably pleased and animated. The "insult" had caused the blood to rush to his own head, clearing his brain, and he felt spryer, and indeed quite satisfied with life for a change.

"I will not pry, Aiken," the old maggot spoke sweetly. "But you must go upstairs and rest."

"On your lily-white sheets? To hell with you and your hospitality! To cruddy hell with everybody!"

Then plumping himself down on a great chair which he immediately stained, he said in the softest tones: "I've lost him, Mr. Skegg."

Mr. Skegg seated himself now on a stool, which he did not observe until too late was also stained with blood, and so he had ruined his own trousers, possibly, but no matter, seating himself as comfortably as possible, and with one of those angelic masks which criminal lawyers sometimes don just before making the suspect name the time and place of his felony, Mr. Skegg said softer than a spring breeze: "So it was Owen, little Owen who horsewhipped you?"

"So it was, sir, and nobody ever deserved it more."

"But how could he whip someone whom he worships, shall we say, next to, if not above, the former Clarence Skegg?"

"Clarence Skegg be fucked, begging your pardon, sir. God damn it all!" he howled in a volume of fury whose equal Mr. Skegg had to go back years and years to recapture.

All this passion and stench of animal heat and blood had considerably altered the old maggot since the moment Aiken had put his foot within his door. The old man had, one might say, come into his own realm again, after so much work with mortgages and foreclosures, and the ruin rained down by banks, and he was no longer with Aiken Cusworth the horsetender, but with his Scotch ancestors in the highlands a century or so before, and like them an outlaw from justice.

"It's that old whore on the hill who's behind it all, make no mistake about it," Aiken went on, for now that he had stripped himself of all shame, he could speak as himself, even if before this gentility and quality, and after all what more could they do with him than send him to jail.

"Oh, how Owen shamed me, sir . . . He *shamed* me! And 'twas me told him to horsewhip me . . ."

Then as the old maggot leered and almost licked his fingers, the pleasure of Aiken's story being so keen, Aiken went blithely on telling of how Lady Bythewaite, in her morning wrapper, had summoned him (and in all innocence he felt, too), to go with her to the cellar and help repair a broken part of the basement where the rats had come in, and that seeing her standing there with so very little on—well, they had both forgot themselves, and they were, for the first time, he swore, having . . .

"Having what!" Mr. Skegg had suddenly raised his voice in a fury as great as Aiken at his bullforce height.

"I was letting her have it, sir, when . . ."

Mr. Skegg offered to strike the horsetender, then thought better of it.

"I exculpate you, Aiken, for anything you did . . . Go on . . ."

"The cellar door opened, sir, and there stood Owen Haskins watching us . . ."

The entertainment of Aiken's narrative proved too much for the maggot, and absent-mindedly he drank some of the concoction he had prepared for the beaten youth.

"Then folding his arms," Aiken went on, "this boy who had looked up to me, this Owen, catching me in that helpless state where we are not masters of ourselves . . . Oh, Mr. Skegg!"

"Go on with your God-damned story!"

"I say," Aiken struggled on, his eyes filling with water, "he folded his arms like an angel sent by the Lord, except, sir, his mouth was foul, he spoke most foully . . ."

"Give his exact words, and quit your sniveling . . ."

"He said, *Why, Aiken, my lad, you're not equipped like a man, you've got the pizzle of a county-fair bull, and we'll have to put you on display. You've impaled Lady Bythewaite with your prize cock, and we'll have to fetch a surgeon to free her from your bullhide* . . . Or something like that . . ."

"And that is all he said?"

"Yes, by God, and don't tell me you wish he had poured out more!"

While Aiken paused, wiping his eyes, the old maggot mused. He had never been so pleased, nor so satisfied.

"I ran after Owen with the buggy whip," Aiken began again . . . "I caught up with him on the little hill near your mansion. I said to him, *Owen, you can whip me, and I want you to.* And he said, *I never harm a farm animal* . . . *Either you hide me, or I'll hide you, Owen*, I told him. *It's as simple as that. Whip me or I'll whip you till you drop in your tracks.* And Mr. Skegg, I had forgot he was mad. No, amend that, sir, he's the sane one, the only sane one. The rest of us are mad, and so he seems odd. I drove him crazy, when here he looks up to me more than . . ."

A look of almost royal insolent command from Skegg made the groom go on.

"Then Owen raised the whip I handed him, but I never knew

he would hide me to within an inch of my life . . . For I had to take it out of his hand at the last, though I damn near was unable to . . ."

"And where is this poor mad child, as you term him, now?" Mr. Skegg almost screeched from sheer excitement.

"I reckon he's run away," Aiken looked down on the floor. "I judge he's run off back to New York, worse luck!"

He helped the hired girl clean up after the traces of "massacre" about the house, even getting down, to her real consternation and resentment, on his hands and knees to "tidy up" with her, a procedure utterly unknown in this house or indeed in Prince's Crossing, and as he was in the midst of these menial labors, she saw, puzzled, a kind of surge of renewal sweep over the old man. There was no trace of his rheumatism to judge by his quick thorough movements, his heart, often so irregular in beat, now pumped steadily and rhythmically if his breathing and color were any indication, and he babbled to the girl about the old times when Indians had still lived about here and on occasion had visited his mother.

No, "fine stalwart" Aiken Cusworth had not been whipped in vain for several persons that cold uncertain spring morning.

"I hope, nonetheless, Aurelia, you will keep your mouth tightly closed over all this sad affair." He had risen almost with no difficulty, whispering his caution to her.

"Oh, Mr. Skegg," Aurelia whined, "you've gone and ruined your good trousers, sir!"

"Now, my dear," he edged up to his servant, oblivious she had spoken of ruined trousers, "we don't want young Aiken Cusworth to suffer from this any more than he has. Understand my meaning."

"But what has he suffered, Mr. Skegg?" Aurelia wondered. "Has he been throwed from a horse?"

Mr. Skegg laughed in many keys. Aurelia lifted her apron to her face, and wiped her brow with its hem, and wondered if he had begun to drink owing to his rheumatism.

"We have some wonderful men left in this nation after all, Aurelia!" he intoned. Drawing near the girl, arresting her attention so that she thought he was wishing her to hear some unusual sound coming from the house or the woods behind it, all he did finally was place his finger to his lips in adjuration of silence, and then from his pants pocket he took out a silver dollar, and put it in her palm, though she made every sign of not wanting it.

"Tell no one what has occurred here, Aurelia. Not a breath!"

And he gamboled off into his study, where for so many years he had planned and plotted, where he had made and destroyed fortunes, and ruined lives.

"I've got Lady Bythewaite, I've got Owen, I've got all of them!" He began speaking aloud to himself once the door was shut. "And blessed Aiken. Why, he's only now come alive, after I'd put him down as no more than a horse himself . . . He's no horse, no horse," he kept muttering.

But the thought of how Lady Bythewaite had "scalped" him kept coming back.

"She'll crawl here before me," he went on to himself while opening a big ledger, and touching the lines here and there written in different color inks, whilst still muttering, "Clarence will come back with his tail between his legs . . . And I'll put Aiken Cusworth in my will . . ."

He relived the keen pleasure of the morning. In a kind of delirium unknown hitherto to himself, the hours swam by while he went on thinking of how he had risen from entire weakness, imminent old age and death to a summit of control and jurisdiction again over all who surrounded him. He had suddenly by means of a horsewhipping on his own property become again, however briefly, the great maggot whose name was once whispered in Wall Street.

His peals of laughter reached finally the kitchen, where Aurelia and the cook exchanged looks of helpless wonder, shaking their heads at first, and closing their mouths tighter and tighter, but finally, since laughter is catching, even when its source is unknown, they too began to giggle and titter, perhaps at the thought that Mr. Skegg's secret, whatever it was, and whatever had happened with regard to poor Aiken Cusworth, would spill itself, and that all would be talking, in church and out, of the old maggot's latest wickedness, and more mud would be thrown at the gown of Lady Bythewaite, who once had said of all this: "The dung they have thrown at me, you see, has now dried, the fabric is intact, and brushed clean, the owner of the garment spotless . . ."

However defective Lady Bythewaite's memory may have been concerning these events of so long ago, of one thing she would always remain sure: she had always felt Owen Haskins was like Phaëthon, but since none of her acquaintances in Prince's Crossing were familiar with the sun-god's son, the name Phaëthon never stirred the faintest interest in her auditors—until the nephew heard her pronounce it.

The nephew had stood up on hearing it. The spools stopped. She was asked to repeat her statement, she did so: "He was another Phaëthon." And the spools, moving again, picked up the name, took it, and kept it.

But Owen had been most like Phaëthon, when he had run away from the vision of his mother in the embraces of Aiken Cusworth, who was his idol. She and Aiken thus became the agents of his running away, back to the splendor of his godly brother Clarence. It was this second flight to New York, she opined, from which all the ills of Owen and her life stemmed. Yes, it was a flight of destiny.

Lady Bythewaite's memory, never good, needed jogging especially now, for as this story, the only one which meant anything to her in her long life, receded in time, it often seemed to her that Owen Haskins had been more successful than Phaëthon, and had left Prince's Crossing every morning at daybreak, went to New York to see his splendid brother, and then returned at nightfall to be with her. Yet he must have gone away only twice, the first time by train—the second time—how?

He had gone, her failing memory tried to prompt her, he had gone this "fatal" last time, improbable as it might seem today, on horseback. Or perhaps—who knows?—the horse had died on the way, and Owen completed his journey on foot . . . However, Phaëthon had got there, and when he did, he was a much sorrier sight as he stood before his glorious actor brother than when that other bastard Phaëthon stood all but blinded before the glory of his father Apollo.

When Clarence Skegg had opened the door on his runaway brother, he had barely recognized him. Owen was covered with mud from head to foot, his forehead was cut and bleeding, and the clothes he had on his back, which were the ones Clarence had persuaded a wealthy patron of his to give the boy, were in ribbons.

Unlike Apollo, who had been pleased to welcome his bastard son to his abode of glory, Clarence could only say to his bastard brother: "Well, if it's really you, I suppose you'd best come in."

Then taking another long look at Owen, the actor had burst into tears of vexation and shame.

After gaining partial control over his displeasure, Clarence got out: "You dare to come to me in this condition, you dare shame me like this, Owen!"

There had followed their bitterest quarrel, during which words of such murderous vehemence passed between them that even Lady Bythewaite's imagination could hardly call them back from oblivion.

"You are no better than Aiken!" however, was the one refrain which came from the lips of the actor, and to his incomprehension, each time he mentioned *Aiken* strange hysterical cries came from the upbraided boy.

But he kept Owen for a while. Kept him because he was his own, and New York was not, and he had begun to feel even then, at his very beginning, the contingency of the sheer drop from the heights into the foundationless abyss of failure. And he needed money. Yes, money, money! He had turned down Mr. Skegg's bribe of a thousand dollars sent by this muddy Phaëthon on his first ride to the city, but now he needed much more than a thousand, and gazing at his brother, he wondered if Owen could not, after all, despite his just-concluded abuse of him, be persuaded to help him.

As Clarence spoke of his need for money, his affection for

Owen appeared to revive. He removed the boy's torn and be-mired clothing, and gave him another suit which fitted him quite well. He bathed his lacerated scalp and forehead in warm water and witch hazel.

But Owen could not stay! Phaëthon must go home again, and not scale the same heights as Apollo.

"I don't mean to send you back forever, as you put it, Owen, but only for a little while, don't you see? . . . Of course I will call you back, I'll summon you, demand your presence here! Don't you see that, childish boy? Did you ever know me to go back on a promise? But I am desperate for money now. My name is in lights, you point out, true, and I am a star, but look about you, at this tiny room, look at me . . . Only my erect posture and good looks separate me from the crawling scum you see in the Bowery. You must go back to Prince's Crossing at once, and see Lady Bythewaite comes to my aid!"

Clarence Skegg, or Maynard Ewing, was, as his runaway brother could not help noting, the most resplendent ever, narrow room or not. His new dressing gown of gleaming gold set off the shining midnight black of his recent masterfully designed coiffure, and his lounging robe and hair were in striking con-trast to his blue eyes, and the somewhat bluish red of his angry full impassioned mouth. His teeth were as white and menacing as Mr. Skegg's.

"I can never face Lady Bythewaite again after what she has done," the fugitive from Prince's Crossing now testified. He had already told Clarence three successive times the story of his hav-ing surprised Lady Bythewaite in Aiken's arms and each time he had given his account of the happening the actor had be-haved as if he were not taking it in.

"Oh, what do you mean by *what she has done*," Clarence finally blurted out indicating he had taken in the account of the "wrongdoing" quite fully. "One would think you were referring to the crime of murder . . ."

"Oh, isn't it worse, Clarence," the boy appealed in a whisper which wrung the older brother's heart in spite of himself. "And haven't I described the horrible thing to you in all its detail." Owen now sputtering advanced toward his brother as if to see some tangible reassurance from him that he at least was not wholly lost to him.

"But you are speaking only of a brief love affair, Owen, and with poor Aiken Cusworth . . . An episode . . ." And Clarence broke into guffaws, and then took his brother in his arms, and smoothed his hair. "You must grow up just a tiny bit, dear Owen . . . I thought your last visit here had taken some of the briars and thistles out of your unkempt head . . . Why should you begrudge Lady Bythewaite a little pleasure, at her age . . . I'm sure Aiken meant nothing to her . . ."

Owen Haskins disengaged himself from his brother's embrace, and moved, as far as was possible in the cruel narrow confines of the room, away from him.

"If you want to be with me forever, as you told me once," Clarence began again, studying Owen closely, calculatingly, making every word count in what was this important hope and plan of his, "if you want us to be together forever . . . go home and raise money for me."

"Oh, stop it, Clarence, for Christ's own sake, I can't bear any more pressure . . ."

Then putting his hands before his eyes like one who feels some excruciating pain, he cried, "I swear I will run mad . . ."

"Then leave me and don't help me and go back there and forget me, and be a good sane farmer which God marked you out to be, Owen."

A sudden spatter of tears came over Owen's face, as if they had been splashed there by some angry wave, and his hands fell to his sides.

"After what I've done, whipped poor Aiken, after what she's done, after what Aiken has done, I am to go back and say to Lady Bythewaite, *Clarence is in trouble, dear mother, you must lend him thousands of dollars, and he will be all right, and I will be happy, and I do forgive you for being a whore with your groom, and I forgive Aiken for mounting you before my eyes, and let me go down on my knees before all of you . . . Just give a small fortune to dear Clarence, whilst I am kneeling here in the mud . . ."*

Barely attending to this speech of whirling hysteria, Clarence's full attention kept centered on the recounting of the whipping of Aiken Cusworth. He had doubted somehow Lady Bythewaite had actually been intimate with Aiken—she was always caressing young men, after all!—but he never for a moment doubted that Owen had whipped the young horsetender. No, Lady Bythewaite's having surrendered completely to lovemaking he would not credit, but the whipping made him a true believer, and filled him with both a kind of nausea and a creeping dread of the slight nervous pale perpetrator of mayhem who stood bawling barely a foot from him at this moment, and whom he was determined once and for all to drive out from him forever. Collecting himself as best he could, he said:

"Owen, Owen, if I had your reservoir of feeling, well, call it I suppose passion, I would be the greatest actor in the world . . . Sit down, poor chap, compose yourself, please sit down, as I say, and don't wave your arms and roll your eyes anymore . . ."

"I can't go back there, dear Clarence," he implored, in abject petition.

"But you can't stay here either, Owen Haskins!"

The younger boy stared bewildered, dizzy at the transformed majesty of this personage once called Clarence Skegg, and his brother.

"I can barely keep myself here in this revolving inferno of an island . . . You must have guessed how I live, despite your mentality of an oaf . . . I live by hook and crook, by handouts, largely . . . The film people have cheated and lied to me . . . Nonetheless, my career will be a big one, you can depend on that, and as soon as I'm a real success, I'll send for you. But what you've got to do now is go back home, for my sake, for both our sakes, Owen. Get money from Lady Bythewaite, get more than thousands even, if you can . . . Tell her we both need it, don't you see . . . Yes, that's right, both of us need it . . ."

"But what do you want so much money for?"

"So much?"

"And how can I go back there, Clarence? . . . How can I bend my knee before her when she's so rotten . . ."

"Not rotten, Owen, human . . . She's had no love in twenty years . . ."

"You call that love, his sticking it in her like that, as you would poke into a . . ." He covered his eyes with his hands again.

"I can't have you here now, Owen, and that's all there is to it. You make the wrong impression on influential friends, for one thing. You're too raw, you puzzle these high people finally as to my own origins when I tell them you're my brother. And if you condemn Lady Bythewaite so vociferously for being a woman and whip Aiken for being a man, you will surely condemn and rawhide me one day when you find out who I really am, and how I live . . ."

"I would never condemn you, Clarence, no matter what you did." Owen spoke close to tears again.

Clarence bit his lip. But then, resolutely buttoning up his brother's coat, which he had just bestowed on him so that he would be a bit more presentable, he opened the door of the tiny room of "glory," and said, "I am not casting you out, Owen, mark this well, but I am telling you where your duty to me and yourself lies . . . It's in Prince's Crossing now, and when you've got the money from Lady Bythewaite you can come back and visit me . . ."

"*Visit* you, Clarence. I want to be with you . . . forever . . . I can't go back there! I don't belong there anymore!"

"You don't belong here either, double damn you!" Clarence hesitated for a moment, and then struck the boy a resounding blow across the mouth. "You've driven me to real fury, Owen Haskins. You're not, after all, my brother, in any case!"

"Who am I then, Clarence?" the boy called upon him from his cut lips.

"That's for you to decide, Owen . . . Meanwhile you know at least what is expected of you. And I speak for your own good also. Go back there where you came from and appeal for me, get help for me, or this is a real goodbye forever . . . Do you hear me? And don't snivel on your new clothes!"

He closed the door on Owen, and then held his back against the lock and muttered, "I don't hear his cries, and he is not my brother. I must be what I was intended to be. Nobody, nobody must stand in my way . . ."

Then turning round he yelled through the thick wood of the door, thicker and wider it did appear than all of the small cramped room which held him and his wardrobe, "Get gone, I tell you, you grieving bastard, or shall I come out there and beat you all the way home to the backwoods . . . I'm warning you, Owen, if I open the door and find you still here, you'll face the music, you'll . . ."

There was a deathly silence from beyond where his voice was rushing. He waited. A few weak sobs shook the actor now. At last he flung open the door. There was nobody in the gloomy hall outside.

No one saw anybody that summer in Prince's Crossing, the great houses were locked tight, blinds drawn against the heat, shutters secured, so that one would have thought their inhabitants were traveling, and meaning to be long away. Occasionally Aiken Cusworth stopped by Mr. Skegg's for instructions concerning some work to be done on a farm, a drainage problem, a mortgage overdue, but the operator of the bread-delivery van never went near Lady Bythewaite's, except for his duties in the pasture land with the horses.

Their summer would not have been so tranquil, their shutters and blinds not so firmly closed against mere heat had they known that Owen Haskins was not where they assumed he was, that is, with his brother Clarence.

In September, at last, for one whole morning, the voice of the new film star tried to communicate with the "central" of the local telephone line in order to reach Prince's Crossing. At last some shreds of his voice came through the primitive network. Lady Bythewaite, however, was not sure she had heard *his* golden voice aright. And he left no telephone number by which she could reach him, for according to his explanation, he was then calling her from some "fashionable" hotel, where he was only "visiting."

She walked all the way to Mr. Skegg's but found to her consternation and disgust—and surprise—that the door was tightly locked and bolted. She could not in her confusion remember where the bell was, but in the shrubbery she spied a brass dinner bell once used to summon the threshers for grub, and she picked this up, and raised the dogs for miles around.

At last the door opened, and Aurelia stood before her. Lady Bythewaite pushed past her without a word, advanced to take a seat in a crumbling luxurious silk-upholstered chair.

"Tell him to come at once," the visitor vociferated.

"He's in the . . ." Aurelia faltered.

"Go up and fetch him or I will . . ."

Then seeing the girl dared not move, Lady Bythewaite, throwing her head back like an auctioneer, called with lungs as resounding as the dinner bell.

Mr. Skegg came stumbling down the great staircase, his cheeks and chin covered with rich shaving lather which gave off the odor of lavender. His right hand trembling eloquently held an heirloom straight-razor. Somehow she no longer associated him with needing shaving, as if advancing age excused a man from this daily task, as nature excused a woman in later years from menstruating. But it offended her, his appearing lathered. Still, she had intruded upon his privacy, yet she could see that her daring had pleased him, and indeed had broken their stalemate.

"You can finish your shaving before that splendid mirror over there, and I'm sure Aurelia will fetch you a basin of hot water . . ."

This was all done, but the sound of scraping over old bones unsettled her nerves. She asked for coffee.

The hot drink was brought in an elaborate hand-painted oversized china cup with flowers so cunningly painted to life she regretted the coming death of florid summer.

"I know everything, Nora, for he's told me, you see, as you must have known he would." He patted his crimson cheeks with some strong-smelling abrasive.

"You mean my visit is uncalled for?" She gulped a swallow of coffee, which had been, rare for his house, freshly ground and brewed. "He just telephoned me long-distance . . ."

"Who did?" he cried, turning about. "You mean he has run off too?"

"Who in damnation are you talking about?" she retorted, staring at him with bilious impatience.

"Your onetime son, Clarence Skegg . . . who else!"

Refraining from patting his face after the ablutions he had

administered to it, he walked over to a little rack and picked up a *Stage and Screen* magazine and, opening it at the right page, tossed it to her.

Her worry about Owen, her shame at what had happened between her and Aiken were eclipsed momentarily by this "spread" with such prettified pictures and biography of Maynard Ewing as could indeed only issue from the success of being a great star in that epoch.

"So he's climbed the mountain," she whispered, and let the magazine drop.

"He won't be at the top of it long," Mr. Skegg scoffed, and he tightened the belt of his dressing gown viciously. He clapped his hands, and Aurelia came in with his coffee.

He began drinking, while looking down carefully at his high shoes, which in his haste he had not tied properly. "Well, then!" he scolded at his visitor impatiently.

"I have just learned from a long-distance telephone call from Clarence—are you listening to what I am saying, Mr. Skegg . . ."

He looked up at her from staring at his shoes, and the expression on her face made him look away immediately.

"My son has not been with Clarence in New York since last spring!"

Mr. Skegg's face remained blank.

"That's a good many months for a young boy to be nowhere," he said after a lengthy pause. "But you don't suppose I know where he's gone, do you Nora?" he half-defended himself, still avoiding a glance at her.

"I believe you would be the last to know where he has gone." If he would not look at her, she did look at him, and it gave her some comfort that his face had gone ashen despite all the attention he had given to it with his ablutions, and his mouth had drawn itself to one hard worried line.

"Clarence explained," she began again in her usual hard voice, "that he had thought Owen was here all the time . . . They had quarreled, he explained. They had indeed fought. They parted in anger."

"Owen has the temper of my father."

Mr. Skegg's sentence hung in the air like the report from a gun.

"That is surprising," Lady Bythewaite spoke just above a whisper, "in view of the fact you claim that Owen is not your son."

Mr. Skegg's complexion changed back from ashen to ruddy.

"If he had lain awake for a year thinking of how he could punish me, he has succeeded!" Lady Bythewaite summarized it all, getting up.

"Who?" Mr. Skegg cried.

Coming directly over to him, she took up his coffee cup and drank out of it a few swallows.

"Who but Owen of course, but since you wonder, I can add Clarence too, or Maynard Ewing." She shot this last name at him so that he might feel some of her pain.

Was he thinking of Aiken Cusworth and Lady Bythewaite in the account the horsetender had given him of Owen's "discovery" of them together, for his faraway look drew finally even Lady Bythewaite's attention.

"We must think what to do, Nora," Mr. Skegg muttered absently. "We must find him. We will find him . . ."

"No, no," she said. "It's too late. You sent him away once, but I sent him away for good. And as to finding him, or hunting him, 'twill be like looking for where a raindrop fell in the waters of the lake . . ."

Aiken Cusworth had run out of chewing tobacco, and he was a long way off from the store where he usually purchased it, but seeing a small cafe and gas station he drove his van to the rear of the latter, and jumped out. As he was paying for his package of Mail Pouch, his eyes roved to the interior of the adjoining cafe. At the rear was a long table at which a young man with a large floppy hat and an old Negro were seated, a few chairs apart. The hand that was about to put the plug of tobacco into his mouth stopped as short as if a bullet had arrested its movement, then with intense will he bit, chewed, and the muscles of his exposed throat moved spasmodically. He walked over to where the young man was seated, whilst the old Negro watched with riveted curiosity the two white men's encounter. With a movement as flowing as that of a bird which goes direct to its hidden nest, Aiken pulled off the hat of the youth, and as he did so the familiar brown shock of curls fell out, and two terrible, but hopeless, helpless eyes emerged blinking which told him he had uncovered Owen Haskins.

Aiken's tough heavy body, which had become tougher if not heavier since the springtime, lumbered into the unsteady chair of the table before him, his hands, which had held the tobacco plug, fell with a bang upon the hard wood of the table, the first brown trickle of the juice staining his expressive deep red lips, and soon reaching his chin.

"Shuffle off, why don't you?" Aiken turned to the old black man, who, staring malevolently at both Aiken and Owen, refused to budge. "Then *don't* shuffle," Aiken growled, scowling when the old man made no effort to move.

"You know she beguiled me," Aiken began at once, clipping off all the months of the calendar which had separated them, months which hung as a matter of fact in front of them now, and which somebody had forgotten to tear off since spring so that a large glossy picture of a swimming hole and beech trees looked down upon them wrapped now in heavy clothes against the frost and winds.

"I have never contrived or plotted against you, Owen . . ."

The younger man looked away, the blood left his face, for across Aiken's left cheek was a not pleasant somewhat large scar, which on the countenance, Owen felt, of a less manly person might have looked more ill than on him, and which he had put there with a whip.

"But it was wrong of you to stay hid, and worry us to distraction," the horsetender stumbled on, "even though you had the excuse of my shaming you . . ."

A look of such helpless torment now came over the face of Owen Haskins that Aiken's mouth opened in frank questioning of what such a deep expression meant.

"You'll stay then?" Aiken wondered.

"Where?" Owen gasped, like one who inquires of a fireman where he can jump from a collapsing conflagrated house.

"Why," Aiken said, biting off another piece of tobacco, spitting on the sawdust of the floor, rolling his eyes, "there be at least three doors open to you . . ."

Owen Haskins put on his winter hat again, and Aiken wondered how with such headgear he had indeed ever recognized him.

"Terrible big wind's rising up from the west," the old black man, who had stood up, addressed them in hushed alarm, even panic, and then indeed "shuffled off." "No time to tarry back there, gen'lemen," he called a last time to the seated two as the door slammed shut after him.

"You really hided me, Owen, with that whip," Aiken spoke with a short quick laugh and with a convulsive grasp took Owen's hand in his, and then almost dropped it, for it was as cold as stones in a brook.

"Aiken," Owen began, but his voice sounded swallowed deep within him or even gone out of him and through the floor.

"Speak your piece," Aiken encouraged him.

"I've long thought of this meeting . . . I expected you to kill me when we met at last, I do believe. I wanted you to kill me . . . But Clarence has made me see one thing clear. He never cared about me or anybody but himself. And when he drove me out, for he did drive me out, I intended to come straight back to you, Aiken, though I could not believe you would have me back, and while I hesitated where to turn, this bad thing overtook me there in the city . . ."

"But don't you see, Owen, if you talk of killing, I was the one who drove you away, and I am the one to grieve over it all, not you . . . And grieve I have . . ."

"You mean you have no hard feelings against me? . . . You don't want me gone from you too?"

"I . . . want you gone, Owen?" Puzzled, or perhaps overwhelmed, Aiken Cusworth took off his own hat. His hair had not been cut since that April day he had been attacked by Owen, and in addition to the stains from tobacco juice, the scar on his cheek, the color of earth was about his chin and ears, so that he looked like one who has sprung out from a ploughed field.

"I only know," the older man fumbled for what he wished to say, "I have missed you and I have regretted all I have done . . ." Having got this out, he pushed himself back in the chair and stared up at the high peeling fly-specked ceiling above them.

"I do not think of myself as a bad man," Aiken spoke again after a silence, still gazing at the ceiling.

"Nor do I," Owen muttered. "But things will not be quite the same between us, I don't suppose . . ."

"Oh, well, we'll see . . . But did you have to stay away so long, Owen, and break your mother's heart in the bargain?"

Words formed themselves in Owen's mouth and on his tongue, but they were rejected and like the sound of his voice seemingly descended to the floor, but at last he began again: "That is what I am coming to, Aiken . . . After Clarence drove me out, drove me out as if he had the real whip, I had this great trouble I have mentioned to you, and I can only tell this to you, for it has weighed on me so very much . . . Are you listening, and are you truly my friend?" He seized Aiken's hand tentatively, and Aiken, sensing his grief, held it. "I do not remember anything that happened from the time Clarence drove me out until you took off my hat here in the cafe. So help me God, that is true." His lips quivered, and shut off further speech.

Despite himself, Aiken withdrew his hand, and his face clouded.

"Clarence had rejected me," the boy went on, perhaps because of the silence with which his story had been received, and speaking in a faster tempo, "I was not Clarence's kind of man, after all, Aiken. But I didn't know where I was, don't know to this day where I have been all these past months . . . I swear, I swear it's so . . . Do you believe me, or if you don't believe me, do you forgive me . . ."

A kind of sick grin came over Cusworth's mouth.

"I mean I wandered about in the city there like you dream you are dead," Owen pursued. "I didn't know how to come back here, and I couldn't go back to him. He's grand now," he wailed. "You know he's a star . . ."

"Clarence, yes," Aiken agreed, but with a hesitant awkwardness he would have shown had someone mentioned seeing and meeting people living in the planets.

"Where could I go to . . . That was when I was lost, you see . . ." He mumbled on into silence.

"You fended for yourself all this time . . . *there?*" Aiken cogitated.

"There's a mean ornery wind coming up that looks awful bad," an elderly farmer cried, coming part way to where they sat. "Best for all of you to make for home . . ."

Aiken, dully turned inside himself, his eyes veiled, did not appear to hear the old farmer, or the rattling of the windows about him.

"He couldn't have turned you out just like that!" Aiken suddenly protested, and his hand cautiously touched Owen's fingers.

"Well, he did. Clarence did. He's not human . . . leastways in his feelings anymore!"

But it was Owen who stood up, for the wind, like a hundred thousand hands, was shaking the whole structure, which was like to fall about them.

Lady Bythewaite would not talk of the cyclone, would not put her lips into the whirring recording machine that waited to capture her breath and life. Either she had forgotten the cyclone, or found in it something too near herself to recognize, one great force refusing to acknowledge the prerogative of another.

"It was a bad storm." She would only go that far.

"But the annals say it was the worst cyclone in history," Eneas Harmond reminded her.

But she was mum, and so the whirring reels did not contain anything of the cyclone, but if Lady Bythewaite did not recall it, would not dredge it up from memory, the countryside still bore the mark of the fiend. There are whole forests there which lie pigmy-stunted and dead from the maniacal hands of the whirling wind.

It was the greatest cyclone the century had ever seen, so said the farmers, and it put Prince's Crossing on the map long enough to help finally remove it forever. It was, as they might have said, and I suppose they may have said it, the beginning of the end. What she did not know, which proves that great people often never find out what other people call them behind their backs, just as ordinary people never find out perhaps what other people think of them in their hearts, the cyclone was called Lady Bythewaite.

But while the great storm raged, to the consternation of the hired girl, Nora Bythewaite had thrown open the door to the lunatic winds, and gone out, whilst the maid cried, "Ma'am, you'll walk into your death!"

Some say she had taken too much opium that morning, but the general consensus was she had seen, as in some final vision,

Owen and Aiken Cusworth driving in the van, and toward these two persons Lady Bythewaite was hastening. His house being on a hill, Mr. Skegg too had watched the occupants of the van as he had watched some months past the horsewhipping. And again this time he had not been able to give his eyes credit, for he suddenly spied the three of them, Lady Bythewaite, Owen, and Aiken, who together with the horse stood in the very eye of the cyclone, while behind and in front of their strange "meeting" forests, farms, barns, houses went up into the air and were never glimpsed again, and the heavens looked like the ruptured bowels of great beasts. A kind of fearful white shaft of light came down upon the three persons he was observing. Mr. Skegg would have seen more but at that moment, hardly to his surprise, the roof of his own house moved up and out, three of his four walls went down, and there he stood, his field glasses in his hand, but suddenly there was a darkness about him so impenetrable he could not see his white shirt cuffs or his almost as white hand stretched before him.

Because Lady Bythewaite's house was the only one left standing, her sense of condescension dictated that she invite Mr. Skegg to "live with her" and her illegitimate recently returned son Owen Haskins until the old maggot could build or buy a new house for himself. Aiken Cusworth was to live in the barn, for his house in the woods was entirely destroyed, and the old folks who had shared it with him had been killed.

Perhaps she did not remember the cyclone because it had only accomplished what she had wished, had allowed her to take under her roof all her menfolks. She did not now even regret perhaps Clarence's absence. She thought of him, much as Aiken Cusworth had thought of him when Owen had described him for the horsetender in the nigger cafe, as having been transplanted to heaven, and there, receiving a new baptismal name, he shone down upon us here on earth.

Mr. Skegg had hesitated, they claimed, revolving in his mind Lady Bythewaite's invitation to live with her, unsure whether he should accept it, but at last, like a horse, at nightfall he had gone into a place that had shelter, and it was besides raining very heavily, and his head had been cut open by a flying beam.

But within Lady Bythewaite's thirty-five-room home, not a chair had moved from its place, not a windowpane was cracked, and the fire was blazing in the mammoth fireplace as in a picture book.

Passing by the barn one evening when he was at loose ends, Owen had heard a sound like that of a man sobbing to himself. He tiptoed into the barn, saw the red of the antique lantern, shining from an inner room, and went carelessly within. The sound coming from there was one of those which the ear knows as it does tides from the moon, cries known perhaps from before birth. The odor too emanating from nearby was both animal and flower-like, and though it was winter out, Owen smelled trees heavy with their blossoms. But the sounds of straw thrashing about struck some remote terror in him, as the breathing sounds and odors of flowers and beasts made his eyes heavy with some unremembered slumber. He walked on not knowing he was walking. A gleaming pitchfork barred his way to the little room whence the sounds came. He picked it up, looked at it not without a kind of sick admiration, then noiselessly put it in a corner, safe. The latch was open on the little room. He knew who he would find, but would he be alone? Where would he run to this time if that person was not alone? Tormented cries now came faintly, and again the stir of straw.

Opening the door, and then closing it behind him, Owen looked toward a corner of the room, and his jaw fell gently downwards.

Writhing with genuine pain, looking like one of the Titans hurled from heaven, with his belly defined in its muscles like a chart in an anatomy book, his fist holding his gross breaking bulge of sex, Aiken Cusworth let out a sudden spout, like the burst from a punctured wineskin, from his mouth and at the same moment sprayed a creamy jet from his tormented penis. At the same time his jaw seemingly dislocated continued to spout what looked like a full mouthful of blood, but which Owen looking at the bottle in the sufferer's other hand saw was only wine. After some more convulsive shakes of his entire huge frame, the horsetender raised himself on one elbow, and looked at Owen contemptuously and then down at his own wilting organ, giving the latter a nod of forgiving and entirely sympathetic absolution.

"Satisfied?" Aiken cried, and as the big man rose and came forward to him, Owen had the feeling he had indeed gone mad and was looking at Maynard Ewing perhaps in some new film role; however that may be, Aiken strode up to him and hesitating only a moment struck him a massive blow across the mouth, so that as if in imitation of his hero, Owen spat a perfect albeit smaller stream of blood which struck the older man in the face.

"You untouched good people!" Aiken roared. "Judge me, will you . . . Can't I be an animal when I need to without you judge me, Owen Haskins. And look who was behind your siring, won't you? Do you think you was sired by thinking. At least I ain't a *recognized* bastard, proud Owen Haskins!"

Suddenly seizing the boy, Aiken shook him until his teeth rattled, and then slapped him across the cheek.

Owen wheeled, looked out toward the room where the pitchfork stood as galvanized and vicious as Aiken's penis had loomed before him bedizened with the gouts of blood-like wine and semen. His hands stretched out toward the fork, and then everything turned black like the eye of the cyclone, and he fell down to the straw-covered floor. But he was not to know this time the mercy of unconsciousness.

Lying at Aiken's feet, he mumbled words like jangles from faint repeated abject confessions, begging, it appeared, in his incoherence, that he be set "straight" about "everything," about "life." Crouching over him, in due time, in all his naked unselfconscious grandness, in so different a mood and appearance from the quiet careful sympathetic Aiken of the nigger cafe, the older man now taunted the boy angrily for claiming not to remember all those lost months in New York as he might have shamed and taunted a common thief, and he hinted that he did not believe in his loss of memory, and warned him of the possibility of his own permanent displeasure with him.

And where before he had welcomed him home, and praised his character, now Aiken, as changed as the skies and countryside by the past storm, cursed him and, it did appear, cursed life itself.

"And supposin' Maynard Ewing does summon you back to his royal majesty," Aiken scoffed, after swallowing some more of the wine. "Well, will you go?" he wondered when there was no response from the supine form beside him, with the tightly closed eyes. "Of course you will . . . I know you better than you think . . ."

But the corrected Owen suddenly turned, opened his own eyes flashing with anger on the friend who had so suddenly turned against him, and the expression of menace caused Aiken to rise from beside the boy, put down his bottle, and begin ever so slowly to dress.

"Don't ever judge me again if you value your life," the older man finished in a voice as soft and collapsed as his penis which he guided now into his trousers, closing them over it. "Never call me—"

But at that moment Owen leaped to his feet, and speaking directly into the face of his persecutor said:

"Who told me to whip you? Who held the whip in my hand till my knuckles was raw, hey?" And rousing himself to greater tension, holding his fists up, he made an offer to strike the older man, who merely held those small fists together in a vise, and stared with worried attention at the sudden strange clouded aspect of the boy's eyes.

Then gazing with dimming vision into Aiken's eyes, and from the sudden rising memory of the smell of blood, flowers and blossoms of trees, Owen remembered that what had really made him strike the horsetender that past time with the buggy whip had been the sight of the still undried semen on his fly from where he had defiled his mother, and wrenching free from his grasp, the boy rushed out of the barn, and ran through the pasture land.

"I've lost him." Lady Bythewaite kept repeating these words as she choked down her morning cornbread and coffee, hoping perhaps that the more she said the short sentence the less she would feel the rage and loss. Her muttering was an accompaniment to the louder sounds of pages being turned, almost torn under her rapid fingers, for she was poring over the movie magazines, press clippings, and other paraphernalia of Clarence Skegg's glory, now metamorphosed into an all but unrecognizable Maynard Ewing. And she had begun it! On this one bedrock fact Mr. Skegg was right. She had turned the boy's head, turned it toward the stage at any rate when he had been little, and when she had been still—she caught now a glimpse of her fading self in a great mirror—well, a very striking woman, to say the least. They had rehearsed plays together by the hour in those days—she came back to this, for repetition never bored Lady Bythewaite as it did the present generation which could barely endure hearing a story even once—they had rehearsed and rehearsed, for Clarence liked repetition almost as much as she did, yes, perhaps more; she had taught him stage diction, cut away his drawling accent and homely expressions, while during all that time she had begun to lose her own stage accent, and now, she thought with grim humor, she spoke almost like any farm woman. Well, she was glad! She begrudged him his success, yes. All right. But she would get him back when success soured, as it always did. He would fail, fall, drop, he would come back to her, back to Prince's Crossing! She would have him again under this roof, though, this time, with the rest of her menfolk, for she had all of them now but him, and she would get him back if . . .

But there stood the wraith of Effie, the hired girl, waiting to say something.

"You quite startled me, Effie, coming in without a word." Nora Bythewaite put the rotogravure glories of Maynard Ewing down quickly on a huge blotting paper, and glared at her servant.

"Are you the bearer of some distressing tidings? Well, speak up, Effie, can't you see I'm in no humor to coax words out of anybody today?" And as she pronounced these words her glance fell upon one of the hitherto-unnoticed-by-her Sunday newspaper supplement photos of the great new star of the silver screen, and a flush suffused her face down to her firm breasts.

"I can't go on here, ma'am, on account of the carryings-on and the quarreling and the like . . ."

Whether it was this last glimpse of Maynard Ewing in prettified apotheosis or hearing some of her own unspoken fears blurted out, Lady Bythewaite felt her mind go blank.

"If you can't go on here," she guided herself now with the servant's own phraseology, "where do you propose to go, Effie?" She spoke softly, almost sweetly in her first bewilderment for she wished to gain time and also keep control over her own ungovernable temper, for her rage directed actually against Clarence was begging to be given its vent and turn against whoever might cross her shadow at that moment.

"I've been to see the preacher about it." Effie's words rose like a cloud in the room, and assumed a meaning as hard for Lady Bythewaite to comprehend as the exposed countenance of Clarence Skegg, turned star.

Effie began to quail at that moment under her mistress' silent and thundercloud brow.

"What preacher are you referring to, Effie, for I know nobody who is known as *preacher*."

"The preacher, ma'am, of my little church."

Effie had perhaps chosen the word *little* to avert Lady Bythewaite's wrath, but the wrath she saw had already been kindled and no one word could have added much more fuel to the heat she saw coming from those eyes and lips.

"Would you enlighten me as to what church you might be referring to?" Lady Bythewaite spoke now as a kind and reasonable judge who will hear the plea of a felon who seeks clemency. This kindness struck even greater terror into the mind of the "suppliant."

"He has advised me, ma'am, that I am in danger of perdition."

"But you have avoided my question, Effie, my child. As a member of what church does he so advise you . . ."

"Our church of the Pilgrim Brothers."

"Ah, your little church, yes." Lady Bythewaite stared into the eyes of her servant, who bowed her head.

"I do not know that church, Effie, and speaking now as your friend and as one who has advised you in the past, I do not believe you should know this church . . . For you belonged when you came to me to the True Church, Effie, you know, the only church with authority and divine sanction . . . Would you tell me again what church that was, which you once belonged to until you backslid and fell into error . . ."

" 'Twas the Established Church, Lady Bythewaite."

"Yes, it was indeed . . . But your craving for novelty, for the thrill of intemperate and rhetorical preaching and its dogma that all would be burned but your good pilgrims misled you somewhat, wouldn't you say?"

"Oh, Lady Bythewaite, I will not argue with you . . . I know the preacher is a godly young man, and would not mislead me . . ."

"That is just how he has misled you, for you have joined an organization not sanctioned by heaven, not guided by Christ . . . Effie, you are in danger of final judgment and eternal damnation even as we speak here . . ."

But the older woman had misjudged her own power of knocking all to the floor who disagreed with her, and instead of cowing her hired girl she stung her into unlicensed rage and indignity.

"I . . . sentenced to damnation . . . when you and these young men go about the devil's own business . . ."

Cut to the quick by this insolence, Nora Bythewaite waited, sat down, drank some more coffee, and then watched her servant, now convulsed with a kind of contagious anger. Walking quickly outside the great room and as quickly returning, the girl produced a laundry bag, and then suddenly raised it aloft and made a token of proffering it to her mistress.

"If you could see the undergarments of these young men alone
. . . But I don't need no proof!" she vociferated. "All knows
what goes on under this roof . . . And you are chief of the le-
gion, Lady Bythewaite!"

"And will your young preacher, with whom you are doubtless
in close intercourse, Effie, feed and clothe you?" Lady Bythewaite spoke softly, and then rising slowly but with an almost
priestly benediction took the laundry sack from out the servant's
hands, which had relaxed their hold as the girl began to weep
perhaps from sheer terror.

Seating herself in the principal chair of the room, Lady Bythewaite began going through the laundry bag with the righteous
weariness of one who has been wrongfully charged with falsi-
fying accounts.

"Who will give you a crust of bread when you have left my employ, Effie . . . Remember your old grandfather, and how it was
I gave to him out of my small bounty . . . And when before he
died, he begged me to look after you . . . And have I?"

As she said this, she pulled from the laundry bag certain pieces
of underclothing, but raising each one as if they were blessed
white fresh bread.

"Have I?" Lady Bythewaite repeated her question now, and
then waited until Effie had wept the desired number of tears.

"But evidently you were not grateful, though you kissed my
hand, but that kiss dated from the time you were a communicant
with the Established Church, Effie, and a good girl . . ."

Lady Bythewaite's fingers held—counting, one would assume,
or blessing, who knows?—the undergarments of both Owen Haskins and Aiken Cusworth. She looked at the garments carefully
but without surprise or undue attention, certainly without
squeamishness or dissatisfaction. Suddenly rising, she almost
pushed the garments into Effie's contorted face.

"No good girl," Lady Bythewaite began in the voice of a can-
non, "no girl who had, as you coarse farm people say, her cherry,
would understand the condition of these underdrawers. You
come here as a double hypocrite. To shame me and my men-

folk when you yourself are a lost soul, having given up the True Church, to follow apostasy and abandon your body in the arms of your young pastor . . .

"No good girl," she came as she said this directly up to the servant's face, "would know what is on these garments, which you pretend to judge as one unacquainted with sin . . . Look at them! Look at these garments! They are only the exuberance of health, the overflow of life!"

Seizing the girl by the nape of the neck, Lady Bythewaite rubbed the stained garments over the girl's face, rubbing hard and thorough, as if she would rub off the most ingrained and stubborn mask of grime from her face.

Crying out in terrified surprised anguish, the girl threw herself into Lady Bythewaite's own just abandoned principal chair.

"How dare you sit down in my presence, you impudent slut," the mistress said, but in a relaxed and calm voice, for victory was coming.

"Oh, ma'am, ma'am, ma'am," Effie babbled, her face unrecognizable, her small hands beating hopelessly against the sides of the heirloom chair.

"You have lived here and prospered and grown proud indeed," Lady Bythewaite proceeded. "Who buried your grandfather at her own expense, and put up a headstone for him in the Cemetery of the Established Church . . . You have desecrated his memory and his grave by romping off with your rioting pilgrim brothers and your fornicator of a pastor . . ."

"Oh, Lady Bythewaite, stop, please stop your torment!" was Effie's constant cry, and rising from the chair she kneeled before her.

"Have you been intimate with the young pastor?" Lady Bythewaite now spoke in a stage whisper, the kind she had taught Maynard Ewing so long ago.

"You may address me freely, my child," the mistress spoke pianissimo now, and helped Effie to rise, and gathered her into her arms, in much the same way she had gathered up the garments of Aiken Cusworth, stained with the exertions of perfect animal health. "You are with a true friend, stern perhaps, but forgiving . . . Have you been often intimate, I say, with the young pastor, Effie?"

"Oh, let's not go over it, or dwell on it, ma'am . . . My poor head is whirling . . ."

"Answer my question, my dear, for I must know the truth if I am to forgive, and help you. How many times have you given yourself to him, Effie, and where?" She pressed the girl's arm with extraordinary force as she said this. "The times, Effie!"

"Countless, countless!" came the words smothered in the cloth of the mistress' rich dress. "In the graveyard mostly, but anywhere there was grass, or shelter, ma'am . . . More than I can count!"

"There," Lady Bythewaite said. "Enough . . . Yet I am so sorry, after all, you want to leave my service," and as she said this she released her with the suddenness of a cord being cut. "I am sorry you feel you must go, for I know how without provisions you were for so very long in times past . . . But your young pastor will give you of his abundance, without a question of a doubt, my dear, and you won't miss us here in the big house . . ."

"No, ma'am, oh no . . . Listen to me. Listen. I must stay." She was babbling now, and Lady Bythewaite allowed her to embrace her again, though she drew back slightly feigning distaste. "I'll work on for you, ma'am. I'll take no wages, if you only will let me stay . . . I remember them bad days too well . . . And you've reminded me all of a swoop what I owe you, and how wrong I was to act the preacher here against you and your boys . . . Keep me, Lady Bythewaite, keep me for nothing by you . . . I will tell you all my wrongdoings . . ."

"We will see, Effie, we will see. Remain for the time being at any rate . . . Yes, you came here to condemn my own wickedness, and we have instead uncovered your own." She shook her head wearily.

"Oh, but ma'am, do let me stay on then . . ."

"I do not see why all cannot be forgiven you one day," Lady Bythewaite pondered the supplicant's plea. "In time of course you'll come back to the Established Church . . . We'll see then about your remaining on . . . And now, meanwhile, my dear," and as she spoke she kissed Effie on the forehead with lips that were to the girl cold as the lake in January, "now take these garments to the laundry and wash them out thoroughgoing, for we won't trust them to the regular laundress, will we, Effie, my child, you and I who know what life is, know also how to keep its secrets, my dear . . . Now wipe your face of tears, and go, and remember—I will carry your own heavy secret in my heart, and share it with no one . . ."

"Come in, Owen," Mr. Skegg's snoring words came from the cupola, where he now had his quarters in the aftermath of the cyclone.

Entering, Owen Haskins noted how cool and quiet and collected the room was, like the man, his alleged father, whilst wherever Lady Bythewaite moved and had her being there was the presence of fire and the sound of thunder.

"You remind me of the moon, Owen," Mr. Skegg went on, motioning the boy to seat himself near his roll-top desk, "pale and always wandering, and always, too, looking down upon mere earthly creatures. You are very unlike anybody I ever heard of."

"How tiresome," Owen said under his breath, but of course the old maggot heard it, and seemed to care not a jot about the ill-humor behind the remark, for he went on, "At your age, I was already in business and making a fortune . . . Yes, at the age of fifteen," he raised his voice on these last words in order perhaps to correct a look of disbelief on the boy's face. "Of course that was in the last century, the age of horsepower."

"I have not been myself, Mr. Skegg," Owen spoke up in the manner of one who states the reason for his having come to see the maggot, though, again, like the moon, he had had no plan in coming upon Mr. Skegg any more than he had intended to discover Aiken enjoying his own body sexually.

"You have indeed become quite a stranger to us, Owen," Mr. Skegg now began the scheduled interview proper. "You have been gone a long time for a young fellow, and this absence has never been explained. Your mother had given you up for dead. She had a mild stroke from it, and if you ask me, she has not recovered her faculties as yet. I doubt she ever does. She was prostrate for weeks."

"Who comforted her?" Owen spoke up with decisive sharpness.

Mr. Skegg was taken aback. His mouth opened with one word or phrase, discarded this silently, opened with another, and closed on it unspoken. "Well," he said at last, "we had the doctor of course. She was quite bad. He put her under a hypodermic for days."

"No one else was . . . attentive?" Owen spoke airily, a hooded look over his eyes like that of an owl surprised and made to fly into daylight.

"Your mother was deeply heartsick over your running off, as indeed in a lesser degree I—though I am not your father—was uneasy that you should have disappeared without a word to anybody . . ."

"I don't know that I disappeared so much as I was . . . driven away," Owen retorted with a kind of stumbling, but lofty, indignation.

"My own idea," Mr. Skegg began with a thought which appeared to comfort him, "is that you were making your own way in the world."

Owen considered this interpretation for several moments. "I am not bright like you, Mr. Skegg," he then began, "or strong, or courageous, or wealth-aspirant, or indeed anything. And in the bargain I believe I have lost my wits."

"Tommyrot! Why, you don't strike me as any madder than, shall we say, poor Aiken Cusworth!"

"Oh, damn Aiken Cusworth! I wish he was in hell! I wish he was a horse. At least I could ride him then and rub him down and think of him only as what he is, a beast."

"He's had no advantages, Owen, like you. And though he boasts of his ancestors going back to the Revolution, I don't think anybody in his family was ever married."

"You don't say so," Owen said, swallowing hard, and coloring, and closing his eyes briefly on this remark.

"I thought, however, you had been very much in love with

Aiken," Mr. Skegg spoke in the incautious manner now of the nineteenth century.

"In love with him! Good Christ, Mr. Skegg!" He spoke with eyes flashing.

"Your mother assured me he was a hero to you."

"Well, my mother, if indeed she is my mother, knows not a jot or a tittle, and has ignored me ever since I came back. She has not had fifteen words to say to me, Mr. Skegg."

"Your mother is not a well woman, Owen. She may go at any moment. So the doctor has told me. And this terrible farce which Clarence has dished up for all of us. We may have to emigrate to escape the scandal . . . You know his picture show is opening here next month. We are already the laughingstock of all the surrounding counties. He plays the role of a paid lover to some duchess in this film."

Mr. Skegg put on his glasses, and read from a handbill which was being passed about in the streets of the neighboring town of Stotfold, where the movie theater was located. "Maynard Ewing," he read, "plays the dashing inamorato of a titled woman; he is irresistible to all, he . . ."

"Clarence is certainly the direct cause of all that is wrong with me!" Owen pronounced, and stood up.

"You don't say so!" Mr. Skegg spoke in an offhand way so that Owen indeed wondered if the old maggot had heard his remark.

"I wish I knew what to advise," Mr. Skegg then pondered. He indistinctly shook his head several times. Then picking up a small bell such as lay near his chair, he rang. "Pray don't leave yet now, Owen, I have a favor to ask of you."

Owen did not sit down until the parlor maid came in. She had been weeping, or rubbing her eyes, and was indeed nearly incoherent.

"Would you bring in that newspaper advertisement I laid on the dining room table, Hulda. You can't miss it, for it's circled with red ink . . ."

The parlor maid inquired between suppressed sobs if the

young man would require anything while she was about the first errand.

Owen spoke up to say he would require nothing.

They waited in silence while Hulda was out searching for the desired advertisement, Mr. Skegg yawning from time to time, and Owen looking his sulkiest.

When she had brought the advertisement, Mr. Skegg went over it again and again.

"Owen," he began at last, handing him the advertisement, "as you see, this gives the local world notice Clarence is arriving in the village of Stotfold on the silver screen . . . I wonder if you would accompany me to the photoplay house in Stotfold to see his picture . . . I may try to wear some kind of partial disguise so that nobody will recognize me . . . I must go, you see, only in order to understand how far the boy may have compromised us . . ."

Owen was studying the photoplay advertisement in almost the same sort of bilious dread and aversion which Mr. Skegg gave evidence of.

"I believe Lady Bythewaite is planning to make a sort of outing of it for all of us, and you will be invited also . . ."

"You don't say so!" the old man responded in choleric disappointment. "She always gets her oar in first of course! . . . I had hoped you and I would be able to see him alone together . . . But if she has planned an outing, as you say . . . Oh, well . . ."

Owen had handed him back the advertisement. The cause of his being summoned for an interview in the cupola was not understood, but he went on brooding. The young man's strange abstraction at that moment caused Mr. Skegg to inquire: "And, Owen, you say you remember nothing of what happened from the time Clarence ordered you out of his flat until Aiken Cusworth discovered you in that nigger cafe?"

Owen blinked, the hooded expression swept over his orbs, but he responded rather rapidly to the query: "That is correct, sir. I really do not know how I lived or where after my fight with Clarence. Until I saw Aiken I remember nothing. Rather until Aiken took off my hat. I recognized him then and my head cleared."

"I regret you are having differences with Aiken. You should never have whipped him."

"Sir, you know he commanded me to do so. Ordered it on the pain of his hiding me to my marrow should I refuse . . ."

"I don't think you should talk against Aiken. He is very devoted to you, and I wish you would see more of him . . . Why do you snort like that? He worships the ground you walk on."

"I wasn't aware of that," Owen spoke very softly, somewhat mollified.

Then cupping his hands, as if he was holding a tiny megaphone, he called to Owen Haskins: "I am in exile here, in this hateful cupola. She has outstripped me in one farm deal after another. I'm nearly cleaned out, Owen. I'm not myself, either. Don't worry about your having lost six months, and of not remembering where or even who you were. These things happen to all brainy people, and you are brainy, Owen, though you may have no character. If I were your father, I would do for you. But I'm not. Your mother has not the best character in the county, but she is your mother. I want to recommend Aiken, however, to you again . . ."

"Ruin seize Aiken! You stop it, do you hear, stop it!" Owen screamed suddenly and held his ears with his hands. "Stop!"

"My dear young man, are you again unwell? . . ."

"I won't have Aiken shoved down my throat, do you hear? I am not unwell! I can't remember, that's all. And I think Aiken fucks the mare, too!" Owen added this without a pause between his thoughts, while rolling his eyes.

Mr. Skegg smiled deprecatingly and drank his milk with extremely loud and revolting sounds.

"You say, Owen, the mare *too*." He smiled broadly with white markings from the milk on his lips. "It's all of no importance, my lad," he went on in extreme good-humor, after he had belched a few times and caught his breath, and by the word *all* which he had pronounced Owen seemed to get from him that he meant just what he said, everything under the sun was of no real abiding importance.

"Your news that Lady Bythewaite is planning an outing for us all on the occasion of Clarence's first film showing in Stotfold rather spoils my plans for you and me to go see him together." Mr. Skegg now brought their meeting to a close with these words, and stood up. "I felt you and I were the ones to go together alone as I said before and say again now. It is a disappointment. She always manages to disappoint everybody . . . But I want to get to know you better, Owen, and I thought this would have been an occasion for better knowledge . . . However, there will come another time, no question of that . . ."

Stotfold is a "sleepy village" (in the jejune phraseology of an out-of-print guide to the Yankee State) which lies near but not too near the small lake which makes Prince's Crossing so idyllic a place in the eyes of its lifetime residents, but Stotfold is further enhanced by two winding rural rivers without names, which in summer are merely "creeks," according to the indigenes.

Stotfold had seldom, if indeed ever, seen Lady Bythewaite; indeed her public appearances were as rare as those of royalty or presidents; she occasionally appeared at communion at a nearby Established Church, where her frowning aspect gave the impression she was turning the wine to poison; her other visits were paid to a doctor, who had been an apothecary of note, and when the weather was fine, which was infrequent, Aiken Cusworth had been seen driving her for "outings" in her costly, shabby buggy.

Desperation, exacerbated desperation, drove her from her house in dank rotting November. Aiken drove. They went to Stotfold without stop or detour. All along the leaf-strewn road, whilst Aiken spat this time only pure saliva, for Nora Bythewaite forbade him to chew tobacco in her presence, she kept her eyes peeled for something, turning and tossing her head like one fearing ambush.

"What is this crotchet you have of spitting continuously?" she called out to Aiken, but he made no response, whipping the reins up and down. She held on to her big black umbrella, which she had owned since London.

Lady Bythewaite had come out for one purpose only: to verify "rumors," rumors as nettling to her as if her own name and photo had been reported placed on public view on the highway. For rumor had it that on display all about the roads and by-lanes of Stotfold and Prince's Crossing were giant billboards advertising the "coming" of Maynard Ewing in the "overpowering melo-drama" *The Eagle's Nest.*

She had to see the posters, the billboards, the "theater" itself where this public "immolation" of her former pupil was to take place. Several times she commanded Aiken to stop the carriage, while she got back her breath, if only temporarily. During their halts, she heard him uttering for her benefit, she was sure, his own most appalling hard-bitten indecencies of language. She was too ill to correct him, but when she reached home again, and got back her strength, she planned fitting punishment for him.

Without her realizing it, Aiken had drawn to another halt: they had stopped at a large billboard displaying a giant Maynard Ewing, half-undressed. He was fortunately unrecognizable of course.

"Drive on, for pity's sake, Aiken . . ."

They halted next at the crossroads beyond which stretched Stotfold, a more pretentious, if larger, Prince's Crossing, with a large green general store, a dollhouse-like bank, a huge rather beautiful silo, and (here she closed her eyes and felt she might die in the buggy) the Elysian Meadows motion picture theater.

"Go directly to the front of the theater," she called to Aiken, "and stop muttering, do you hear, open your mouth only when commanded to do so, or. . . ."

". . . or what?" he roared back at her.

She burst into tears. This unnerved him, and he nearly dropped the reins.

At the movie theater itself, Mr. Stephen Bottrell, the man-ager and owner, a young man who, so folk said, had been a stage actor in New York City some years before, rushed from the green purlieus of the lobby, incredulous, gaping at the sight of Lady Bythewaite.

He went up to the buggy, took her hand, and then gazed for a moment with confused revulsion at the animal insolence and rural abandon of Aiken Cusworth's huge frame. Nonetheless, Mr. Bottrell nodded coldly to the driver.

"He's been here and insulted me!" Mr. Bottrell began at once.

"Whom do you refer to?" Lady Bythewaite wondered, looking

about the wet streets, and holding her smelling bottle pressed heavy against her right nostril. She was, she felt, very ill, but her eye took in the monstrous photos of Maynard Ewing with some dwarfish female whom he held to his half-naked breast.

"I refer to Mr. Skegg," Mr. Bottrell spoke with the touch of a whine. "Who else!" It was clear, nonetheless, that the theater manager was beside himself with anger.

"Oh, Mr. Skegg. Is that all?" she deprecated any encounter Mr. Bottrell might have had with him. "Pay him no mind at all, dear sir . . ."

"He threatens to close my theater, is taking out a suit against me, he claims . . . He pushed me brutally . . ." He pointed to his sleeve which was bedraggled.

"When was he here?"

Stephen Bottrell thought a moment, unsure in his distress when the old maggot had made his appearance, although he had thought of nothing else since.

"No matter," Lady Bythewaite began to comfort the theater owner on seeing his growing agitation. "Suffice that Mr. Skegg was here. You must forget him now. That is the only remedy against such a man."

"Are you coming to the performance?" Mr. Bottrell had brightened a bit now.

"Oh, I'm much too ill, dear fellow."

"I can arrange, Madame, for a special matinee—just for you, where you would not be importuned by . . . anybody . . ."

Lady Bythewaite took his hand, implying she would consider this kind special attention, this unusual invitation, even though she planned to do nothing about it.

"How did he insult you, Mr. Bottrell, by the way," Lady Bythewaite wondered, after studying the ribs of her umbrella.

"It's too damned shameful to repeat," the theater owner began speaking ruefully and rapidly, almost in falsetto, and then in the midst of his complaining, he caught a look of lordly contempt, if not loathing, coming from clodhopper Aiken.

Looking directly at the horsetender, nonetheless, Mr. Bottrell said, "Mr. Skegg called me a sheeny . . ."

Lady Bythewaite now looked also at Aiken in the searching glance of one who held him responsible for Mr. Skegg's remark.

"When all the world knows I am Scottish back to the Battle of Culloden!" Mr. Bottrell appealed to everyone within earshot.

"Mr. Skegg has not looked in a dictionary for over fifty years," Lady Bythewaite explained the "remark" in this fashion. "Besides he is near bankruptcy, you understand, and could not sue a flea. He is also mentally incompetent. Quite. You got off easy with whatever name that was he called you. You should hear what epithets he brands me with . . ."

Here Aiken began beating angrily with the buggy whip against the cracked wood of the vehicle, and expressly to smart her, took out a huge plug of tobacco and offered to bite it.

"Aiken Cusworth!" she shouted, and Stephen Bottrell, a bit shortsighted, raised his head expectantly in the direction of the coachman. "I will not have it, Aiken . . . Categorically not!"

"When did you say the matinee would be held?" Lady Bythewaite inquired immediately of Mr. Bottrell, after her warning.

He named the hour and day.

"I will be here if I am alive." She took Stephen Bottrell's hand in hers. "But admit no one else to the theater during that performance, do you hear? And," she hesitated only a second, "may I bring the old maggot?"

Mr. Bottrell paused at hearing for the first time the epithet commonly bestowed on his enemy Mr. Skegg, but replied in forthright evenness of tone: "If you think it absolutely necessary, ma'am, then it's agreed, of course . . ." and the wheels, set in violent motion by the driver, came near to running over his feet.

"I do indeed think it necessary, Stephen Bottrell!" Lady Bythewaite's voice reached him from half a block away. "And I'll see that he never sues you or anybody else for that matter—you can rest assured on that score!"

She then fell back against the still luxuriant leather of her carriage, almost at peace, until looking up she saw Aiken take a great bite of chewing tobacco.

At ten o'clock in the morning of the day of the promised great matinee in Stotfold, Lady Bythewaite summoned sullen Aiken Cusworth. He was ushered into her bedroom where she complained of a migraine headache, and told him she was too unwell to attend the special performance Mr. Bottrell had arranged.

Aiken had gone not to the foot of her bed, where a livery stableman might be expected to wait upon his mistress, but went directly beside her pillow on which her black hair coiled like a trailing plant, her hand within nervous easy reach of a tiny bottle of medicine resting on the quilt.

"What are you looking at my eye for?" she cried at last under his persistent scrutiny. "Has it offended you, and will you pluck it out, impudent Aiken?"

"I don't believe you are ill, ma'am. I don't believe you have ever been ill."

He stopped and swallowed, his Adam's apple moving violently as if all the words of all the days he had lived were struggling to burst out at once.

She took his hand, but he rejected it.

"I know who you are at last, Lady Bythewaite."

She attempted to fix him with her lightning glance but she was repulsed and dazzled by eyes too like hers for her to blind them, so she had recourse to her tongue: "All the time I feared that it was Clarence who might corrupt Owen and render him unfit for life in the world, all the time I feared that starstruck boy's influence, it was you who had done your work . . . Why do you stain your handsome mouth and teeth with that damnable black juice?" she cried, and struck him a glancing blow over the mouth. "Go tell Bottrell I am dying, do you hear . . . Tell him I am already dead, if you like, but go!"

He rose, and walked with filthy feet over her white Navajo rugs.

"One moment, there . . . You have not been dismissed! . . . Now hear me . . . Do you love Owen enough to die for him?" She had sat up to cry out to the enormous hulk of his back and shoulders.

He stopped only long enough to say *Yes,* and left the room, his word causing her to fall back against the hand-embroidered pillowcases.

Then rising again: "Tell Bottrell we'll come tomorrow!" she shouted with great vigor for one on her deathbed.

Some few minutes after this "interview" between her groom and Lady Bythewaite, Owen discovered Aiken striking his fist through one of the wooden partitions of the barn. After knocking it through several times, Aiken drew his hand out running with blood, pieces of skin hanging down almost to his wrist.

Like a person who had been advised in advance of what was to happen, and who therefore could not be taken by surprise or squeamishness, Owen took the older man's injured hand in his, and held it with an expression of stunned and unbelieving expectation and gratitude, keeping hold of the hand like a gift. Aiken remained lost in thought, his eyes ever foreboding and of an expression which made most people look away from them, lost as they always were in some cavernous cogitation, the gift of his bleeding hand remaining in Owen's grasp, until suddenly coming to himself, Aiken rushed away to the pump and began washing his wounds with thorough vehemence.

"She's the cause of everything!" Aiken advised the boy. "I've had the scales removed—at last!" He touched his brow and eyes with his good hand.

"This is nothing," he went on, touching his injured hand severely, "compared to what she's done to me inside . . . Come here," he jerked his head to Owen, "come over to the strong sunlight," he commanded, taking the boy near where the barn door gaped open. "Look into my eyes, Owen . . ."

Owen had not balked at looking at the bleeding hand, indeed

the boy had thought in his terror for a moment that Aiken had torn his hand off in an accident, and he was prepared for the sake of his "hero" not to flinch if the hand were hanging by a thread, he would not gag, he would not faint, he would hold the severed hand, and go with his friend to the surgeon, but he had never been able to look into Aiken's eyes.

"Look or be damned, you fine bastard!" the liveryman snapped, and he pulled Owen roughly up before his eyes, and made him look to within a quarter of an inch of those black orbs. "Look your fill!"

And then he pushed Owen roughly so that he fell against a siding of the barn.

Then seeing Aiken come up to him so close that he felt the hairs in his nose move against the groom's breath, and whose teeth suddenly cleansed of tobacco juice shone white like an animal's, he heard Aiken whisper, "Did you observe?"

"I did, sir."

"*Sir?* Does one by-blow call another *sir?*"

"I've noted the cast in all our eyes a good many years," Owen spoke spellbound directly into the white teeth of his "assailant."

Aiken drew back almost in trepidation.

"You're a scurvy little liar as well as a shitten bastard!"

"But I didn't know it meant we were all—" Owen began, softly trying to appease the wrath coming up in the man before him.

"Tell me then what you do know!"

"I only know it completely now, Aiken, before your anger . . . Do you mean to kill me, because I hope you do. Life is not worth the candle in any case . . ."

But this only infuriated Aiken the more. Grabbing Owen by the scruff of the neck, he said, "Tell me what you know or I'll put that pitchfork through your guts and hear you thank me . . . But I forgot, I promised the whore I'd die for you . . ."

"Why, Aiken, I thought you knew when I did. I thought we knew the same things since we're of the same blood . . ." Then choking as if he would bring up a stone lodged deep within him, he got out . . . "Since we are brothers."

"How long have you known it?" Aiken wondered.

"I think from the beginning maybe . . ."

"And I knew only today," the horsetender mumbled.

As in the two previous times when Owen had discovered him at sexual culmination, all the strength in the big fellow now had gone, and he was the weak one, throwing himself now down on the straw, on his injured hand of which he was oblivious, his blood now, like his semen before, running freely over his clothes and over Owen's shoes.

"When I looked into the bitch's eyes today," he spoke to himself, "I saw she had the same cast in her left eye that you have, and I have, and even Clarence has . . . So that we're all of a pack . . . And you kept this knowledge from me," he turned with some mild show of savagery on Owen.

But the look coming from the younger boy made him pause. Not only did he see the strange bluish cast coming out in the light from Owen's eyes, he saw a kind of death-like dependence on that face, as once he had seen in the eyes of a favorite dog which was near drowning, and which he had saved.

"So you knew who I was before I knew who . . . you was," Aiken said, lowering his head.

As he always did when no more words would come to his relief, Aiken Cusworth took a chew of tobacco and was masticating solemnly, his black eyes shining in the comparative dark of the barn like strange bodies falling from a night sky, when Owen taking a position beside him said with a kind of mortal temerity, knowing how proud somehow Aiken was of his chewing, "Give me some of your chaw, why don't you."

Aiken looked forward at the boy from his sprawling length.

"You can take a chaw right from my mouth, Owen," he braved him, and he opened his lips which within looked as scintillating and malevolent as his eyes. "Dare you to take some from me . . ."

Then with monstrous condescension he lowered his mouth to Owen, who with only a momentary wait put his mouth to Aiken's, drew out a piece of the plug with trembling lips, and, staring at his "brother" with smarting eyes, and a mouth as terrible as his model's, began solemnly to chew the plug robbed from its owner.

"Damn me, if you don't chew good . . . But why should I be surprised?" he spoke moonily now to himself, "if it's in the blood, 'twill show . . . You chew that good now, Owen, for it's of the best . . ."

There was a guest room in that huge house by the lake which, since Lady Bythewaite was not fond of guests, was seldom if ever occupied. Nonetheless, like all the other rooms in the house, it was immaculately kept, though the blinds were immediately drawn after each house-cleaning, and in the center of the room resting on an heirloom carpet was a Circassian walnut king-size bed. Here one showery November afternoon, the day in fact of the proposed matinee in Stotfold, Aiken Cusworth in muddy boots appeared before its ivory portals (the room had double doors, with chains, and bolts and other paraphernalia), then unhesitating made his entrance, carrying on his back his few belongings. His heavy footsteps echoed through the house like an alarm of trumpets sounding through every room and beyond to the pasture and woods, so that Lady Bythewaite was awakened, and despite her "condition" hurried out of her sitting room and up the long staircase after him.

Inside the guest room Aiken had raised the blinds and was washing his face in water from a granite pitcher.

"You have gone out of your wits then," she addressed him, but in a voice of such indecision and weakness that her words were not backed up by the proper force to make them stick. "A livery-stable boy in my guest room!" She tried to bring her old authority and anger to this last statement.

Taking from a weathered cowhide valise a suit of clothes, which looked like they dated from the Civil War, and laying them on the counterpane of the bed, he began stripping in front of her. Then carelessly he began donning these antique-appearing clothes, which were of course those of a gentleman.

"I am warning you, either you will go back where you came from, or . . ."

"I have come back where I came from, Mother, and this room

suits me to a T. And you won't go for the sheriff, and you won't go for nobody. I belong here more than you do. If the sheriff is sent for, 'twon't be for Aiken Cusworth, but for you. I'll nigger for you no more. I'll live here as an heir. Yes, I'll drive your carriage for you, and tend your horses, you vile hellion, and keep you maybe from hanging yourself, I may, but this house is Owen's and mine. We know who we are now at last, and we'll live as we're meant to live . . ."

She rushed out, and approaching, in her wanderings in the long winding labyrinth of halls, Mr. Skegg's room, without bothering to knock, she entered the exiled domain of the maggot.

"We're all going to the matinee this afternoon to see your son," she called in her megaphone voice, though at that time Mr. Skegg was far from deaf. "And I won't take no for an answer from you!"

Mr. Skegg rose, not because he was indignant over her intrusion, or her invitation to see the principal shame of his life in public, but because he saw something in a way much more unhinging. The door of Aiken's room had been left open, and though Mr. Skegg was looking from some distance, and through winding corridors, he saw the new arrival as in a strange closeup stereoscope effect, for the horsetender stood before him as if at fingertip, imperious and got-up, with a gold watch-chain across his massive chest, wearing a scarlet cravat, gold cufflinks, and silver buttons, his lips curled like some princely Alexander.

"What in the name of reason is *he* doing here?" he cried, not in criticism or contempt, but in fear lest the cyclone had not only leveled his house but his wits.

"Aiken Cusworth will live here from now on, Mr. Skegg," Lady Bythewaite spoke in lofty finality.

"In that room?" the old man inquired with child-like confusion.

"What room would you assign to him then?" she spoke now almost coquettishly.

"Why, I never thought of Aiken as belonging here, that's all," he babbled, "leastways not in the guest room."

"Well, I have, my dear Skegg . . . I have thought of him here . . ."

As she was speaking Aiken strode out, his head in the air, nose pointed slightly upwards, without speaking a word, and went down the "everlasting" staircase with the assuredness and slight contempt for its many steps of one who had been climbing and descending there since he could toddle.

"I have long wanted someone responsible in the house, and he is that," she explained curtly, looking after his retreating figure. "I am not well. The cyclone has made all of us remember we are not permanent fixtures here. I will have him in the house, Mr. Skegg, and I will brook no argument whatsoever on that score." Here she began to sob so hard, she had to lean against the baluster.

"My dear Nora," Mr. Skegg began, but she held out a hand advising him to cease. "My dear," he went on despite her prohibition, "I will never understand you, not from day to day, but from minute to minute. A livery-stable boy, a horsetender in the guest room!"

Was there ever a group of people so solemnly assembled to see what they feared and loathed and disapproved of, as Lady Bythewaite and her retinue now about to go to Stotfold to see Clarence Skegg transformed for them as Maynard Ewing in a matinee performance. Why were they going? Did any of them know?

Nora Bythewaite looked in many ways more outrageous than the most scandalous poses of the "creatures" she pretended to despise in the movie magazines which she consigned to the dustbin, yet she was, on close examination, far from immodestly dressed, in a long flowing purple silk gown, with a gold chain, and little gold and diamond earrings, and white gloves with purple plume designs embroidered on them. But had an outsider happened by, he might not have known to what period of history Lady Bythewaite was to be assigned, save that it was most certainly a forgotten one. As she waited until she was sure everything was in order for the "procession" to begin, her black eyes shone as deep-set as those of Aiken's, whose glance she avoided and would avoid until a final day on which she would be required to look into them and then in vain.

Mr. Skegg, like Aiken, had donned a suit of clothes which would have been more recognizable in the ante-bellum period than the early years of the twentieth century. And Owen, to Nora Bythewaite's inexpressible ill-temper, was wearing one of the New York suits some carelessly lavish donor had bestowed on the boy during his visit to the metropolis. Yet Owen in a sense was, after all, dressed more inappropriately than the others, if that was possible.

"We must not keep Mr. Bottrell waiting at the theater!" Nora Bythewaite cried in a great iron voice, though it was actually she who was holding up the exodus. She then led the way down the long path from the mansion. But when all were finally seated in the larger of the two buggies which she had chosen for today's "outing," she discovered she had forgotten her "medicine" and with it her smelling bottle.

Owen raced back to the house to fetch them, and in his absence Nora Bythewaite said, "It's a pity, Aiken, you are so much broader in the chest than Owen, for otherwise you could wear one or more of the suits he has managed to carry back from New York . . ."

"Meaning you are ashamed of my appearance, ma'am?"

"Meaning nothing!" she flared up, so that Mr. Skegg, seated beside Aiken in the front seat, turned about to gaze at her from under the brim of his weathered felt hat.

Then they were off. The sun had come out, the gold fields and corn shocks looked beneficent, the crows rose in pairs as they approached, and a whirl of pink maple leaves ascended from the roadbed when the buggy wheels advanced toward Stotfold and the private matinee.

Mr. Stephen Bottrell stood in front of the tall green doors of his Elysian Meadows Theater, dressed in a tuxedo, his hair skinned back with Vaseline and water, ready to spring forward to greet them, or rather greet only Lady Bythewaite, for he could have little use for Mr. Skegg, as we already know, or for Owen, whom he regarded as a "permanent truant" from school and worldly affairs, and whose teachers were supposed to have called him "unteachable," and did one even need to mention the driver, Aiken Cusworth, far beneath the notice of a cosmopolitan like himself.

"It is most kind of you, Mr. Bottrell, to take all this special care," Lady Bythewaite had begun her speech of gratitude at being welcomed, but her words came more hesitant and less convincing than when she was in her own domain, and her attention strayed somewhere. "The only thing is I don't know that we shall be able to bear it," she spoke in a kind of aside, though her voice carried to the public square. "I warn you of our strong feelings on seeing poor Clarence, Mr. Bottrell, because I value you, and your courtesy and thoughtfulness are overwhelming. I know you will bear with us . . . We are of course all going in," she issued a kind of sharp command now, for Mr. Bottrell gave the appearance he was about to close the door on Aiken, and she had rushed to take the hand of the buggy driver in hers.

As she more or less pushed Aiken ahead of her into the lobby of the theater, she pressed something into Mr. Bottrell's hand, which he made a faint civil motion to decline, but Nora Bythe-waite had given it to him, and she certainly did not want it back.

Stephen Bottrell then led all of them to the "choice" seats in the theater, which had at one time been the site of the Established Church. The piano player, a woman of declining years, was seated before an upright, and directly ahead of her, looking at Nora, like the light from a storm, was the silver screen itself, on which soon Clarence would appear before her, magnified, prettified, changed, altered, gigantic and unrecognizable, to torture and unhinge her. She pressed something into her mouth from the little bottle.

Then at a signal from Mr. Bottrell, they were plunged into darkness. The silver screen rose like a forest illuminated by lightning and then froze into a square, staring dutifully but searchingly at Nora, and the untuned piano struck a chord. A strong odor of leather drifted out to her, and drafts from innumerable cracks and crannies attacked her neck and ears.

Then the jumping motes of hastening human figures began to afflict her retina. Faces, enormous, tall as buildings, atrocious mouths, teeth of an evenness and whiteness such as one never sees in nature, painted eyelids with eyelashes like those of fluttering insects, great dead even mounds of impeccably groomed hair, and then "titles" of idiotic brevity or inanity explaining what the grinning teeth and mouths had uttered. Immediately, so unlike any chapter in life, came caresses and love, simultaneous romance, painless dilemmas, and everywhere the whirring flitting motes of aimless movement, and the gang-bang on the eighty-eight keys of the upright piano in dwindling cascades of tunes from forgotten operas.

Then at last he came forward, Clarence Skegg came, yes, to

speak to her and to no other, the remaining faces and movement having vanished leaving only him and his peremptory beckoning to her. He stood before her, as high as her own mansion above her, his arms folded, staring with monstrous pupils into her eyes, the disfiguring makeup about his eyes accentuating the awful message he was conveying to her, telling her something she had never allowed herself to remember, let alone hear.

She had looked away, but the enormous face and eyes were everywhere, even when she covered her own face with her hands.

At last after what seemed hours of torment of gazing into Clarence's blinding countenance, she began to hear from far behind her a mild murmur of voices, from her menfolk. Only then did she realize that she had left them, that she was on her way walking toward the great silver square of the screen itself, up the steps to where preachers had once stood to admonish their farmer congregations concerning the Last Judgment, until she stood flush before the giant image of the boy she had reared and trained to dwarf her, to beat her now into the dust.

Her hands tore at the screen with a kind of rage as giant and towering as the enormous figure of Clarence before her, but he did not feel her blows, or hear her cries, he had got beyond her grasp or power. Her cries of impotent disappointment rose above the piano, which faltered into dissonant arpeggios, and then stopped.

It was Stephen Bottrell who restored order, threw on the lights, making the sky-high faces and the flickering motes which had beguiled their attention disappear again into a silver gray blank.

"Are you too distraught, dear lady, to have us continue with your matinee?" he spoke prayerfully, taking Nora Bythewaite in his arms, leading her back to her special appointed seat.

"We must continue. By all means," she assured him confidently. "I was overcome for a moment by the size of the faces, that is all . . . I do not know the motion picture."

She went on whispering apologies, explanations in Mr. Bottrell's ear as the theater manager still held her carefully, but she was looking away from him, in the direction of Aiken Cusworth, who, in turn, was looking, it seemed, at nothing.

"I do believe we will go ahead with the performance, dear patient kind Mr. Bottrell," she raised her voice now, and then her eye fell on Mr. Skegg. He was sound asleep.

Two unusual horsemen were now seen more and more frequently on the back roads leading to and from the villages and towns of the vicinity of Prince's Crossing. In the evening, farmers' wives would look up from their tasks as the hooves rushed past. The horsemen always came inevitably to a hemlock grove near the Civil War cemetery, and there the two stood in interminable confrontation. Later, people remembered these evening rides and linked them to the unbelievable events which were to follow. Both riders were expert, but the heavier and older of the two rode with an energy, a kind of sightless fury, so that one did not feel a man was seated in the saddle, but that the horse, possessed of no flesh-and-blood rider, flew with the secular winds from the beginning of time. The rainiest, snowiest nights, the grimmest weather, with roads sinking in mud, were of no bar or hindrance if the horsemen felt prompted to ride their beat or pursue their mission.

It was nearing December, and the wrathful sunset still lingered almost an hour after it had crimsoned the west.

"Look at you, Aiken, you're dripping with sweat even in this weather, and I am dry as a bone."

"Have you made up your mind—come to my decision?"

Aiken had ignored Owen's comment, and looked the boy searchingly in the eye. "Shan't we go?"

"I told you, Aiken, I was ready when you was ready . . ."

"You can stand the long trip west?"

Owen paused, his mouth and tongue moved several times, then his jaw closed tight, and finally he spoke: "I had a bad dream the other night, Aiken."

"Oh, a bad dream!" The older man spoke with rising spleen.

"I wish I had not had it," Owen cried, a rising wail of hysteria in his voice. "I wish I had not . . ."

"If we don't leave soon, we will never leave, Owen . . . You know that. You told me the other day you wanted to be free . . ."

"Our lives are not here, then, in Prince's Crossing?" Owen inquired almost piteously, and his horse whinnied and pounded with its front hoof the frozen earth.

"Our lives are out there, and together," Aiken pointed toward the west now the color of black gore.

Aiken was watching his brother with a studious attention tonight, but Owen kept turning away his face from this scrutiny and once or twice pressed his head against that of his horse.

A night bird somewhere accentuated the silence of the hemlock grove.

"Well, now what was your dream, Owen Haskins . . . Could it be so bad a one?"

When Owen did not reply, Aiken took the boy's chin gently between his thumb and index finger and pushed his head back ever so slightly.

"I dreamed you killed me."

Aiken's hand dropped. "Oh, Owen, you do cut me more than any other person I've ever known at times . . ."

"You've not known too many, Aiken, to cut you, though . . ."

"You do hurt me so." The older brother turned away and walked a few paces into the actual hemlock grove. "That you should even dream such a thing, when I'm the one who always wants to do for you. Owen, Owen . . ." He walked on into the grove, muttering.

"Well, damn you, I shouldn't have told you!" Owen shouted after him. "You asked me once that there should be no secrets between us . . . I've kept my part of the bargain . . ."

Turning about, coming out of the grove, Aiken was beginning to vociferate some large sentence punctuated by weary swearing and obscenity when they heard the wheels of a wagon. Racing past the hemlock grove, Mr. Skegg, alone, his white hair flying in the bitter wind of early winter, was holding the reins to an old farm cart in the back of which were loaded some few belongings. They heard his whip snap as he drove out of eyeshot.

"And where is that buzzard's mate off to on a night like this?" Aiken's wrath found a target for the moment in the old maggot and his flight.

"Old crazy Jehu braving the night!"

The horsetender stood a long time looking in the direction of the vanished old man, his white breath coming in and out with the same slow rhythm and wheeze as that of his horse.

He had been holding in his extended hands a creased and folded map of the far west, which of late he carried about with him everywhere he went, and which he had been about to go over with Owen, but suddenly he folded the map again for the hundredth or so time, and put it roughly away in his hip pocket, and spat on the frozen ground.

"We quarreled not at all, until he was leaving me with his goods and chattel. Then I forbade him to go, and he condemned me . . . on account of you, among other things." Lady Bythewaite found herself explaining Mr. Skegg's sudden departure to Aiken Cusworth the day after Aiken had seen the old maggot racing down the back road in his cart. "He could have stayed here forever. He knew that. But he wanted me to feel guilty, and stained. And so I do, I suppose."

She noted that Aiken had "condescended" again to be wearing now one of the suits of clothes which Owen had come home laden with after that first trip of his to New York. The seamstress too had let out the vest to give capacity to the dimensions of his chest, but otherwise the suit, she saw with real pique, fitted him all too well. Indeed, despite his huge frame, she sometimes on a dark stairwell mistook Aiken for Owen.

With cool careless demeanor Aiken sat down near Lady Bythewaite. His shoes were polished, and securely laced, and she felt she almost detected a scent of pomade of the attar of peonies coming from his crisp and ringed black hair. Indeed his youthful flourishing glory at that moment struck her dumb.

"So you quarreled over me being in the house." Aiken spoke gravely, like a counselor, rather than a usurper.

"Oh, we always quarrel, Mr. Skegg and I. It is our only form of intercourse."

Aiken's huge hands moved now with delicate fingers so that one thought he held a hat between them. She looked at those brown hands fixedly.

"This quarrel has quite unnerved me. He has tricked me, furthermore, again . . ."

Whatever their quarrel had been with respect to Aiken her attention had now gone back to her more daily, if not her master, preoccupation, and she became the Nora Bythewaite of sharp business practice and overwhelming ambition for the goods of the earth.

"I can't imagine anybody moving out at that time of night, and in such bitter weather . . ." Aiken spoke with suspicion and sly insinuation.

"Nor can I imagine any who would go horseback riding in gales and snowstorms and over freezing plains!" she retorted.

She stood up and shouted as if calling to the fugitive old man: "He has dug a hole for me while he was my guest, and I've fallen into it . . . Aiken, he's purchased Shapwick Manor!"

"Shapwick Manor," he echoed her in intensity of passion.

"What touches you so sorely there?" she wondered with a kind of uneasy apprehension softening her voice and abating the movements of her flailing arms.

"Shapwick Manor belonged to my great-grandfather," Aiken spoke in almost a falsetto, his fingers pulling roughly on the lapel of his fine borrowed suit-coat.

"You had a great-grandfather!" she scoffed with her old corrosive tone.

"So I was told by the old woman of Four Crossings, who read my hand . . ."

"So a gypsy gave you your family and your inheritance!"

A look of such pure assassination came over his face, she closed her mouth, looked away hurriedly toward the doors to see if they were locked.

"I mean, Aiken," she stumbled, "if it was your great-grandfather's, that was a long time ago . . ." Her manner tried to soothe him, and she indicated she would even like to drop the matter of Mr. Skegg.

"I knew my great-grandfather." And here Aiken rose and came up within a foot of where she stood. "He told me before he died how I'd been robbed of my inheritance, not once," and here he came so close to her that his spittle flew over her face which she dared not wipe dry, "not once but again and over again I was robbed . . ."

Lady Bythewaite could only stare in wonder, oblivious even to the danger she might be in from this unknown accuser, for she saw here greater eloquence than Maynard Ewing could give from the giant eye of the silver screen.

"We have all been robbed of our inheritance, one way or another," she said at last.

He had sat down, and the fingers again began to work on the imaginary hat brim.

"But Mr. Skegg has filled my mind with doubts and anguish on other matters," she began, and Aiken looked up then with a growing astonishment, for she spoke almost as a suppliant. "He knows now where to cut me down!" Then going much further, she hoarsely besought: "I want your trust. More, I want your mercy, Aiken."

His tongue came out in struggling indecision, almost caressing his nostrils. This gesture of his, more like the old Aiken, gave her some strength somehow to go on.

"Mr. Skegg tells me that you mean to rob me of Owen."

The blood drained from his face, but his eyes looked straight into hers, and she was the first to turn away her glance.

"Do you mean to rob me of him, Aiken?" she spoke in one of her "terrible" whispers which used to strike terror to his heart.

"I can never give up Owen, if that's what you mean," Aiken replied with a dry mouth. "Why should I give up what is mine, why should I relinquish blood when I have found it . . . in another . . ."

"When do you plan to take him from me, Aiken. For I must prepare myself, if not to stop you, at least to get ready to die."

"What do you mean by plan? I have no plans. No plans at all." His passion now roused the second time, the first having been the mention of Shapwick Manor, which he saw as rightfully his. "Is not Owen my brother?"

"How can you doubt it, since you love him so," she opined, no more like Lady Bythewaite when she said this than the piteous complaint of the mourning dove.

But she was soon herself again, with her iron voice: "Aiken,

I will give you anything you wish if you will leave us! Do you understand? I will get Shapwick Manor for you. I will ruin Mr. Skegg if necessary for you, do you hear. You want him ruined in any case, for he is your father. I will have Shapwick Manor in your name within six months if . . ."

"If . . . what . . . ?"

"I will restore your inheritance," she raced on, "I will give you a name, I will do anything, but you must leave Owen and me, and not be part of our lives . . ."

"Fair promises—lies. Yes, you lie!" he growled. "Shapwick Manor . . ."

She saw nonetheless the temptation working, and she let it work on his blood, then to her gnawing anguish and disappointment, if not surprise, she saw it fail, and fall, as she heard him say, "You can't rob me again with your bribes . . . Since even you admit it's him who is my brother, how could I give him up after I've found him, when I thought I had no blood relation. I find that both you and he are mine, and the day I find this out, you hellish she-wolf, you would turn me out again to rot in riches and property! Damn you to the hottest seat of hell! I'll stay here, because I belong here, and I'll have Shapwick Manor too, and I'll have everything! I'll have Owen. I have him. He's my slave if I will enslave him, though I don't have to in order to keep him . . ."

"You'd ruin him, then, Aiken?"

Touched to the quick, he rose and advanced toward her.

"Ruin the ruined, Lady Bythewaite?"

"Leave him, for God's sake . . . He can't live in any case." She lowered her voice.

"What's that you say?" He looked at the strange bluish cast in her eye moving as if of itself like some unheralded meteor in the sky.

"He's desperately ill," she said.

"You're a damned liar. If he is so, I'll bring him to health."

"And who then will be left for me?"

"Do I take him from you?"

"Yes, by breathing, you do! As long as you live I will not have him."

Aiken watched her. He had long known she was crazy, but he had not known she was so far gone in craziness. His own brain was reeling, and he touched his eyelids gently as one who wishes to stop the whirling of a top.

"One late afternoon, soon after his disastrous visit to his brother Clarence," she spoke in a faraway voice as if alone in some prison cell, "Owen lay sleeping on the couch in the front room. My grandmother's quilt covered him, or had covered him, but it had slipped to the floor. Then I saw you go near him. You crawled on hands and knees. You stood over him for what seemed to me hours. I could not move or breathe. I wanted to die . . ."

"What have I done wrong?" he thundered at her.

"It's what you've done better than me!" she shouted back at him. "Then," she went back in her monologue seemingly oblivious of his presence, of his intrusion, "you took the quilt so tenderly, and covered his legs. And then," but here he turned away from the wild look in her eyes, and the nervous tokens of execration in her lips, "you took his hand and held it with a tenderness no woman, no mother could know . . . I hated you then, I could have killed you and him both! Why cannot you be satisfied with roaming the countryside whoring and carousing as you used to do when you were really yourself, unclaimed by even a mother who had disowned you! Why do you have this strange tenderness and love for my son, why have you come back into my life to rob me of the little that is left me . . ."

"Because as even you have half-confessed, I am your son!"

"Yes, you believe it!"

"I know it . . . As touching Owen," he moaned, and if he had feared she sometimes rushed to the verge of insanity, looking at him she feared his mania now the more, so that she braced herself for whatever violence he might now rehearse in front of her, "he means more to me than life and always has. I know no explanation for it, anymore than cyclones and fire . . ."

"You worship one another," she cried in helpless terror. "And you, Aiken. You look but are not of the earth. I fear you to the marrow of my bones!"

In a dark corner of her great house, where no parlor maid or servant was allowed to enter, Lady Bythewaite stored certain keepsakes, mementos of her youth in London, of her "shame" at having had three illegitimate sons, at her long life of confusion, sorrow, and incurable illness. From a heavy bureau, custommade long ago, and whose drawers opened creaking like the door to tombs, she took out a dusty discolored small book into which there were certain dates, inscribed in gold letters, and under which she had written certain events of cataclysmic or epochal importance in her life:

1900

1902

1909

and under the year 1924, she had written

> They do not love one another like the sons of men but angels. Their love, which is not human, but of fire and wind, has blotted out my life. But I will not die now, though I have no purpose in life. If there were a God, he would intervene. I have seen beyond the veil.

She made ready to close the book. In order to have strength to reach her own bedchamber, she drank several drops from a tiny bottle, and waited until the powerful drug could begin to take effect, but today it did not work, and she was not in time to close the book before drops from her eyes as cold and blinding as snow blizzard and then as biting as acid fell upon the fresh ink of her entry blurring it but not effacing what her heart had dictated.

The never-ceasing sound of horses' hooves beat into her brain now at all hours—she heard them even when the horsemen themselves were sleeping, and the horses tied securely in the barn. Many nights, though, she lay sleepless while the horsemen raced and rushed about the countryside like phantoms, riding all the night, and more apt to ride on nights of foul weather, of sluicy rain and sleet, riding far beyond the hemlock grove or the Civil War cemetery, riding into some night of their own, some night of mingled blood and seed peculiarly obscurely theirs, beyond whose borders she and every woman was forbidden to pass as if by rings of blue fire.

Having lost, then, both Aiken and Owen, Nora Bythewaite, sleepless even when she helped herself liberally from the tiny bottle of opium which she saw was replenished by her apothecary friend near Fieldstone, her thoughts turned slowly grudgingly but inevitably toward Clarence, Clarence Skegg, her other, her first love, her "real" son perhaps whom Mr. Skegg had so early deprived her of. For Owen was lost to her forever she feared now, ever since he had discovered her in Aiken's embrace, yes, she felt he regarded her as too common for worship, and to punish her forever had given his love to Aiken.

And how well Owen rode! This angered her almost more than his slavish dependence on Aiken. How had he learned to ride as the wind rides, as the cyclone sweeps over the surprised earth. It was *his* horse's hooves more than those of his damned brother which beat within her temples. Indeed until she helped herself liberally from the little bottle, she heard nothing now but the hooves within her brain. Riding, riding, Owen-Aiken riding, those two fiends in the night on roads no farmer or traveler would so much as think of trusting his neck to. And Aiken, who had whored with every young girl in the neighborhood—how many bastards had *he* sired, she wondered—Aiken having found his "blood" and his "brother" seemed perfectly content to use all his overflowing animal vigor in these never-ceasing nocturnal breakneck races with death or destiny.

In her desperation, then, she turned to her last remaining son, hope, refuge. For the first time in many years, she was to write him a letter. Her fingers, lately unused to a pen, as Aiken's had been unused to tenderness until he had touched the ancient quilt to cover the feet of a "found" brother, trembled under the stiffness, under the passion, under the need.

My only darling she had begun, crossed that out to *My dearest Clarence*, blotted that, tore up the fine vellum page, chose another less expensive kind of paper, scrawled on that, tore it up likewise, went back to vellum, and wrote in great untamed letters of frantic appeal, *Clarence:*

> I am desperate for some word of you. Do you need aught, that I do not hear from you. I have seen your picture. Oh, Clarence, whatever may be your need, your anguish, know there is one here who will ever share with you, one to whom you can ever turn, who loves you beyond words,
>
> Your Mother.

In times past she would have summoned Aiken to take the letter to the post office, and now there was only herself to whom she could trust the message she had composed tonight. Sealing the letter, she went out to the barn, and looked at the mare, the patient animal Owen and Aiken now ignored and neglected. She kissed the "star" on the beast's long face, held it against her breast, kissed her eyes, one after the other. Then assembling the old buggy as best she could, she drove as wildly and recklessly as her night-riding sons, the rage in her mouth causing her spittle to fly through the air like the foam coming from the mouth of the mare driven by her to heedless and frenetic speed.

Clarence Skegg alias Maynard Ewing, alias many young men who haunted gambling clubs and whorehouses and private saloons, sat or sprawled over a marble-topped table in his hotel suite, a score of bills and summonses strewn over the dull Turkey carpet beneath his bare, rather ugly white feet, the nails of which were discolored and black from wearing tight shoes.

He had purchased a pistol that morning.

At the summit of his fame, he was also looking down on his

immediate ruin, eclipse, for he was soon to be, he felt, the laughingstock of the profession which he had scaled the top of like Jack and the Beanstalk, in one short delirious climb.

He had put the pistol in the drawer, postponing his suicide for a time when his hands shook less violently, and sorting through the new bills fallen due, fastening the cords of his crimson and gold dressing gown, he saw at the bottom of his pile of mail the imperious if slightly defective penmanship of Lady Bythewaite.

He pounced on this epistle, tore its delicate paper, from which emanated the old familiar scent of pressed rose leaves and lavender, and devoured almost with his teeth rather than his eyes her few lines.

"How did she know or divine or guess I was in these straits!" he cried.

The door opened from the room adjoining his, and a young woman, wearing one of his unmended pairs of pajamas, looked out upon him, lip rouge having moved from her mouth to her cheek and eyes so that she resembled a drunken Cupid.

"Did you say something, sweetheart?" the girl wondered, looking about unsteadily.

"Did I say I said something?" he sneered, not looking at her.

"You spoke, dear boy."

"I am not your dear boy. I am nobody's dear boy here . . . I am going home . . ."

"Home? You have a home? . . ."

He stared in her direction now with a loathing which made the overnight guest look away in sheer fright and confusion.

"I am leaving this spider house to go rot in the country . . . I prefer to rot among the grass and trees, Bessie, rather than be eaten piecemeal here . . ." He rose, tightening as he did so the cord to his dressing gown in such a firm way that the golden bobbing head of the cord came off and fell to the floor without its owner observing it. "Oh, how I loathe what they have made me look like, like no man ever looked . . ."

With a snarl which made Bessie move off from him, he

stamped and ground his heels into a collection of recent movie magazines which he had thrown to the floor in one of his tempests. Then he marched to the bureau and took the pistol out of the drawer.

"Oh, Maynard, you would not shoot me, would you?"

"You, Bessie, what would anybody shoot you for?"

"I thought you thought I had stolen your watch, since you couldn't find it last night. You said, dear, you thought I had stolen it . . ."

"I've pawned so many watches the past month," he mumbled, and reaching into another drawer of the bureau he fished out a cheap timepiece and handed it to her.

"You may have this to pawn, little lady. For yourself. I don't have much else to pawn, do I, sharp-eyes."

"But if you go back . . . home, Maynard, what will I do?"

"Oh quit calling me Maynard, I'm no Maynard . . . I'm a country shitass they've made up to look like an elderly woman's wet dream . . ."

As she protested against this statement putting her head against his chest, he went on, his nose in her hair, "You still have a body, Bessie, as you had before I met you, and you'll have one a few years yet to come before . . ."

"Before what, Clarence . . ."

"Well, before you feel like I do, seeing myself in those thirty-foot pictures wearing paint like an old harridan."

Suddenly with a force that recalled Aiken Cusworth he tore the dressing gown he was wearing in two, and stood before her like one suddenly struck by an assassin.

"But, dearest boy, you can't go back to a crossroads, after what you've done here!" Bessie appealed now to both Clarence and Maynard with what he saw was perhaps true sincerity.

"Oh, can't I? And why ever can't I, tell me. I can always do what I want, and you know it, Bessie."

She went up to him again, and tried to put his dressing gown into some semblance of repair and covering.

"That's your trouble, Clarence," she said, putting his gown to rights. "You can do anything you want, but . . ."

"What?"

"You don't want to do what you ought to do."

"I'll blow out my brains though, you see!"

She cried a bit at that.

"I will always be . . . what I was," Clarence said, striding up and down, little realizing perhaps that now he was an actor, if not of the grand Shakespearean kind, an authentic one he would never be before footlights or on the silver screen, "which is, in the end, I suppose, a dirt farmer, or better what I told my brother Owen before I drove him out . . .

"I said he would never have the horseshit off his boots, but it was myself I spoke of . . . And here is my death warrant!" he cried, shaking Lady Bythewaite's letter at her. "This is from a whore like you, Bessie, but she is too smart to leave her own whorehouse. She governs the world from her bed, without requiring one customer's money!"

"Clarence, this is not yourself speaking," Bessie struggled to protest, weeping and daubing at her face with one of his large handkerchiefs.

"Say that again! I was *never* myself. But I am less myself on that thirty foot, forty foot, how many foot screen, and I'll be damned if I go painted before those lights again and act the part of some bugger I never heard of or the world never saw and who never existed! . . ."

"But your career is just beginning," she pleaded, falling over her words. He saw her tears were not glycerin but real.

He sat down. He looked at the gun, the bills, Lady Bythewaite's scented page, and then at Bessie. He rumpled his brown ringed hair. He looked at his nails eaten to the quick by his teeth, so that one could hardly tell his fingers, chewed by wrath, from those of Aiken Cusworth's, broken and cracked from his exertions as a groom.

"If I stay I'll stay through hate, and to see them all buried!"

"Who is *them?*" Bessie wailed.

"The curs who have unmanned me!" he cried. "I want to bury them, bury them all . . . under the rock of this rotten island."

"They are plotting every minute of the day!" Lady Bythewaite called out in the empty rooms of Shapwick Manor to the old maggot. "They have a compact, a covenant, they have all but sealed in blood!"

Mr. Skegg finally made rejoinder: "There are two things wrong with your view of reality, or should I say you have destroyed your own natural mental faculties with two bad departures from normal conduct, first, your having been an actress at one time, albeit in London, and second, your relying on strong medicines which no doctor should ever have prescribed for you!"

"And am I to lie there suffering with no one so much as lifting a finger to help me?"

"You speak of compacts, covenants! Why, Aiken cannot be much more than twenty-four years old . . ."

"He is all of that!" she cried with such certainty, such precise knowledge that Mr. Skegg's eyes widened to more than a look of surprise, and his jaw slipped down as in those frequent periods when he dozed off in his big chair.

"And what is it, do tell, they are plotting about, to use your curious way of phrasing it?" Mr. Skegg now humored her, but she was too distraught to be aware of this condescension.

She went on much as she did when locked within her own study, alone: "Aiken must have Owen for himself and himself alone, and in order to make this wish of his come true, he means to beat you and me to our knees . . ."

"Aiken has already purchased the Dunthrop farms, you know."

Mr. Skegg had meant to surprise Lady Bythewaite with this announcement, which he had purposely not prepared her ears for, but he had not counted on the overwhelming effect his intelligence would have on her. She came directly over to his chair (there was as yet no other chair in the great room, for Shapwick Manor was still largely unfurnished) and, standing before him, studied his face as one studies the marks of bullets shot against one's door. He looked away, partly through fear, partly because he felt he did not recognize the face of the woman so searchingly studying him.

"It has begun then!" she managed to get out.

"Oh, you make everything melodrama, or mystery," Mr. Skegg ventured, though he spoke with less self-righteousness and conviction than he might have given to his words a few years back.

"And what on earth, for example, my dear woman, do you mean by saying Aiken must have Owen for himself, as if the boy were to be his chattel and slave . . ."

Mr. Skegg offered her his chair, he had offered it to her twice already, each time as again now, declined, and then he rose, unsteady, and the two stood together, like desperate persons who both wait their common punishment.

"Aiken is famished for blood relation . . . Yes, that is how I would put it." She stopped then and, looking at Mr. Skegg, was taken aback at his sudden dignity, even handsomeness, and his fixed authority: he had ceased to be an old man just then, and gazed at her as the great influential person he was once said to have been.

"Go on, Nora, and don't speak in riddles! You've left the stage."

"The truth never sounds like anything but rank craziness, and for all your years of living you've never found that out."

Then putting her hand on his shoulder, and bending ever so slightly toward him, she muttered: "He's found his blood relation in Owen, don't you see, and he can't get over the long thirst he's suffered these years without him, without having had him as his own . . . They're brothers! I thought you knew. They're brothers." She finished with a sound of rage and resentment and disapproval and bitter disappointment which were far beyond his power of understanding, and yet, very faintly, under the rush

of her words and the ardor of her presence, some understanding
came through to him.

"You have been very unfortunate, Nora," he said at last, and
he took her right hand softly in his.

"Yes, to say the very least, I have . . ."

Walking about the empty spacious room, dry-eyed and more
astonishing for being so, she tried to explain the inexplicable:
"I never knew Aiken was my son. Is that believable? Of course
it's not, but I swear it is true. Of course I am a liar before
God on many scores, but I say this is so! I never knew he was
my son until, one might say, without any stretching of the truth,
yesterday night . . . And he's gone demented on the subject of
blood. Do you understand that, Mr. Skegg? I do not, not well,
but that is what is wrong with him. He is demented on the score
of his blood . . ."

Mr. Skegg's heavily veined hands, with one great signet kind
of ring, beat against the back of the thick wood of his chair,
as if by his beating, these unclear matters, accusations, and whirlwind confusions might, if not be explained, find themselves paci-
fied and checked and dwindled and finally made to go away.

"Having found themselves in themselves," she went on, speaking in a voice so deep and distant and husky he cupped his hands
to hear, almost uncertain indeed if the voice was hers or if a
voice was there, "having learned of their need, through their
need of their own blood . . ." She stopped, for the words seemed
to be fed to her from some hidden source, from the waters of
the lake perhaps, "they are as inseparable now as if they were
one, Owen as spoiled as Aiken in this regard, they go riding
through the countryside like spirits . . . I believe they have shed
one another's blood to have each his blood intermingled, or their
undergarments are so often covered by stains . . ."

"Sit here now, my dear," Mr. Skegg managed to say, and
helped her into his place. "Now listen closely," he spoke with
a hollow throat. "You are to go home and rest . . . I will take
you in a moment. I have learned, dear heart, partly by knowing

you, not to think of human nature too closely. It is quite beyond us. I have kept to my figures, in which you have sometimes, I admit, by your very greater intuition, outstripped me. But it is best not to look within the pit . . . They will tire after a while of having found out so very late they are brothers, after the long years of their not knowing indeed who they were. They will return to the more ordinary concourse of daily life. As to their racing around the country, perhaps Aiken is looking for new farms and manors to purchase in order to outstrip us. Property is in his blood, too, you know, as well as his idolatrous worship of poor wretched mad Owen . . ."

Lady Bythewaite half-smiled, and then the tears which she had forbidden to gather and fought to restrain fell in sparse thick heavy drops, like gems, on her thin wasted hands.

Our Lady Bythewaite studied her new son with intricate ceaseless attention. As she had foreseen, he did not now race with his brother Owen every night, the unsleeping demands of his body made him return each eight days or so to a collection of ill-lit half-concealed buildings beyond Ferrensby and Ferriby, where he spent most of the night in a futile attempt to appease his onetime more appeasable flesh (so she thought) with ruined farm girls and discharged parlor maids. In times past, his schedules with his animal self had always given him a sense of buoyancy and renewed health, but of late, Aiken Cusworth, no matter how hard he rode by night on his collection of punished horses, or how many times he lay with one woman after another (his fame had traveled throughout the whole farming area as one whose capacity and flow were inexhaustible), a sour crabbed look grew over his features, his hands clutched at his buttons and hat, with the maniacal claw-like motions of Mr. Skegg at his worst, and the bluish cast in his black eyes shone with such brilliance that many persons taking a cursory look only at his distended iris decided he was blue-eyed and blond, instead of, as he once had styled himself, the color of a wolf's throat.

What double-stung him (as once angered at the lack of success he was having shoeing one of his own horses, he had picked up the hot tongs from the forge and branded himself across his own chest) was that after Owen had told him his "terrible dream" he dreamed almost nightly even when he had fallen asleep over some drunken farm girl's body that he saw his newly found brother lying massacred and still. And the last time he had gone beyond Ferrensby and Ferriby, the owner of the disorderly house had forbidden him entry on the grounds he was too savage and hurting to his girls, that their house was for the purpose, as all such houses should be, of pleasure and not some wounding contest with horsebreakers and wild animal trainers.

Then he took to riding alone, choosing for his night forays the most desolate barren stretches of the little islands beyond the lake. He would return at dawn, heard only by Lady Bythewaite, who had waited for him through the everlasting hours of night. He would go as always not to his own guest room first, but after he removed his boots she would hear him with the stealth of some small cat for so huge a fellow creep with inevitable step to the room where Owen had been sleeping for so many hours. She would hear Aiken remove the bedclothes from the boy, and she fancied she heard his heavy stertorous attention as he gazed down upon what was so precious to him, that he had found his hope and his lineage here asleep, and must be secure in his mind that it was secure before he could go to his own great bed and slumber some two hours or so until he would (just as he did before he had found his rightful heritage) perform the hard tasks of manual labor about the farm.

But all unknown to Lady Bythewaite, Aiken studied his sleeping brother not only to see that this body lived and breathed but that it was not covered with the marks of blood and disfigurement which his painful nightmares brought to him whether he slept by day or in the darkest midnight.

Then she would hear Aiken in his own bed move with the turmoil and unease of some wild animal tied with chains and chafed with fetters writhing and turning in torment from unseen, unknown captors.

Nora Bythewaite started from a deep kind of doze which had given her some few minutes of respite from her slumberless night to see standing in front of her a woman in black silk whom she feared to recognize. It might, for aught she knew in her anguished frame of mind, be some dreamed messenger of bad tidings.

"Nora," the woman in black said, and then she recognized her as the minister's wife.

She should have been angry, nobody had the right to enter her house unannounced, least of all some emissary from an institution which had done her no service, no good.

"I had a mother once, Isa. I would give the world to have her back today. When you stood there just now I thought you were she."

"I am sorry then if I startled you," Isa replied.

"Is the house on fire?" Lady Bythewaite wondered. She did not invite her guest to sit down.

"It wasn't burning as I entered," Isa answered, and she made no motion to seat herself, bidden or unbidden.

"What hour of the day is it, Isa?"

The visitor drew with gloved fingers from a deep side pocket of her heavy coat a small gold watch and blinked at its face. "Two minutes before the hour of two."

"And by the light coming through the shutters of course you mean afternoon." Lady Bythewaite squinted into the outdoors where between naked oak trees one glimpsed the gray chopped waters of the lake.

"I am a prisoner in my own house," Lady Bythewaite began. "Having taken in as a guest Aiken Cusworth, I find he and my other son," and she stopped here to see the effect of these words on the minister's wife, "I find," she went on, "that the two of them have signed a pact, to finally oust me . . . Do you know Aiken Cusworth?" she inquired but not so much in interrogation as command.

"My husband has died, Nora," the visitor now stated her business. "No, say nothing, I know your feelings about him. I have come to ask a favor of you . . ."

"A favor for you or the dead," Lady Bythewaite mused.

"A favor for both of us . . ."

"When did I take communion last, Isa?" Nora inquired. She motioned for the visitor to be seated.

"Oh, ages ago, I suppose, ages, and ages . . ."

"What favor do you wish?"

"The use of your two geldings for the funeral service . . ."

"Why only two, Isa?" Lady Bythewaite raised her voice. She picked up a huge dinner bell and whipped its black tongue about as if ceremony for some dire judgment were about to commence.

"Please, Nora, I want nothing in the way of refreshment . . ."

"You shall have spirits, Isa, or you won't get your favor. You need spirits as do I."

Effie stood before them. Had she been weeping, or was this sorrow her natural facial aspect now. At any rate, she was given the hard dry command and left, returning almost immediately with a huge bottle of something alcoholic.

"Look out at that landscape, and dare me not to give you some of this," Nora scolded.

Isa Heynings suppressed a great sob, while Lady Bythewaite sat staring at the minister's wife's courage. She had entered her home without invitation or knocking, and had come furthermore to ask a favor. At that moment Lady Bythewaite almost felt some sort of connectedness with this new widow, if no real sympathy.

"Am I greatly condemned?" Lady Bythewaite made sudden and unexpected inquiry, and pointed with her left hand in a vague general direction "out there," where, presumably, the rest of humanity dwelt.

"Oh, Nora," Isa said. She was sipping the strong drink nonetheless.

"You mean I am still condemned." Nora looked first to Isa Heynings and then to the world beyond the lake. Then she went on:

"I want you to have four horses, Isa. I will refuse you two.

I never heard of a respectable funeral service with only two . . . Four horses or none . . ."

Isa had finished her drink, her mouth puckered as if from wormwood.

Lady Bythewaite rose and began to replenish her glass. As she was pouring, a heavy step was heard on the bare floor leading into the reception room.

Aiken Cusworth stood on the threshold, not in his miry clothes as a groom but dressed in still another of Owen Haskins' fine New York suits.

Isa Heynings blinked at Aiken uncomprehendingly, then looked questioningly into her drink. Her face relaxed from the tension of her grief.

"This is Aiken," Lady Bythewaite spoke in her pealing organ voice. "My son."

Mrs. Heynings swallowed more of her drink. The word "son" in her shaken condition betokened some purely Christian appellation, she supposed, or perhaps one supposed she supposed.

"Would you care to drive the horses for Reverend Heynings' funeral, Aiken, for Reverend Heynings has departed this life . . ." She put her inquiry to him in tones of gay invitation as one might propose an outing.

Mrs. Heynings now wept bitterly, and then with a kind of angry resolution finished her drink. Lady Bythewaite, who was studying her, relaxed her own stern features and almost smiled.

Aiken, who had kept to the threshold during these moments, now entered the room and sat down in one of the wooden chairs with the small wormholes dotted here and there in its antique colonial surface.

Both Aiken and his mother slightly lowered their heads like persons bent on carefully recording the number and volume of Isa Heynings' sobs and the number of sips she gave to the strong brandy.

"I will drive for the Reverend's wife," Aiken spoke at last in a voice that rushed through the room and into the hall beyond. "Yes of course, you can count on me . . ."

No one had foreseen that Reverend Heynings' funeral was to be a notable example of infamy and disgrace in the annals of our crossroads. The breath of scandal had somewhat abated so far as Nora Bythewaite was concerned in recent years, and Prince's Crossing, if not sound asleep with regard to her past, was a bit drowsy on the subject.

But the funeral woke everybody up, if only for a time.

Had Nora planned this dishonor to our village?

She laughed as she recalled it even a half century or so later, though its queer resemblance to Mr. Skegg's recent burial finally, I believe, hushed her, but as she swore to her own innocence at perpetrating the deed into the spinning reels, her laughing finally froze into a brief sound of bottomless sorrow, then into quiet, as she considered it all.

A few days had then elapsed since Reverend Heynings' funeral, an event which was still fraught with greater shame owing to Aiken's part in it, as well as Lady Bythewaite's. But in the end all tongues accused her, and the growing awareness that he was her flesh-and-blood son only pointed the finger of guilt more strongly at her. As the indignation of the inhabitants mounted, she went to even greater lengths to keep her house locked and bolted, and admitted nobody. She had not only all the usual gates put up around her house forbidding carriages to enter, she dragged from the cellar other forgotten iron posts and bars, and had them sledgehammered into grim barricades. Then she sat in her great chair, both apprehensive and joyful.

But when one day she heard a pounding on her inner door with some heavy instrument, her surprised rage knew no bounds. Under the duress of the last few days, following the "scandal" of the funeral ceremony of the minister, she was apprehensive enough to take from a nearby closet her shotgun (which she still used occasionally to fire at the crows when they disturbed her rest in the afternoon).

Unbolting the door, she stuck the gun directly into the face of Mr. Skegg, who merely pushed the weapon aside and came in, his feet and greatcoat dripping with fresh snow.

She took her time, however, putting away the gun. It was clean, polished, and loaded. Nonetheless, it was clear that she was relieved to see him, for there had not been so great an outcry directed against her since she had refused to marry, a generation ago, and had been willing to be the mother of fatherless sons.

"I must sit down, if you will permit me," he began, "for I am sure the story you have to tell me will be a long one . . ."

"Do you think I care a straw about the odious minister's wife, or the rabble which stoned me?" she began at once, while putting the gun back in the closet. Turning about, she pointed to her forehead where a black-and-blue mark was healing by reason of her perfect cast-iron constitution.

"I too was insulted on my way here," Mr. Skegg informed her.

"I should not have been surprised had they overturned your car, for I understand that you have given up driving horses so that you may be more in tune with the age." She sighed, scolded him some more, and then sitting down, toyed with her mother's gold lavaliere which adorned her throat.

"There is after all, as is always the case with grave matters, very little to tell. Small things are what are complicated. Furthermore scandals always bore me to relate . . . Nonetheless . . ."

"This would never have happened, Nora, had you not taken Aiken Cusworth away from me," Mr. Skegg complained.

"You fool. I never take anybody from anybody. He came to me here for one and one reason only."

Mr. Skegg looked as blank as a dry cistern in August.

"I see you don't know which way the wind blows. Well, I understand even less of it, so there! These two inseparables want to be separated." She spoke now of Owen and Aiken. "They chafe and quarrel when they are near one another, but they howl when one leaves the other! Understand it how you will, for I make no pretense to understand it. I am blamed for everything and, unlike some people, I accept the blame. It was I who arranged for Aiken to drive the minister's remains to the cemetery, although the pious widow came here to beg my horses of me . . . But I never planned the outrage, and neither did Aiken . . . In fact, I don't think I ever planned anything in my life . . ."

"However that may be, Nora, this is a disgrace which has taken place, a disgrace these simple farmers will never forget or forgive!"

"Then I'll buy up their damned farms and drive them out from the county! I'll burn them to the ground with their own firebrands."

"And coming directly on the heels of Clarence's scandal," Mr. Skegg was beginning to muse, when Lady Bythewaite plunged directly on, telling him, telling *us:*

"Owen had been acting in a wild irresponsible way for some days, and contrary to Aiken's instructions had been riding without permission from anybody the most dangerous horse we have, indeed the one nobody has succeeded in breaking . . . This wild horse Owen rides repeatedly against Aiken's express command . . ."

Mr. Skegg waited. A comb from her hair slipped out and fell to the floor, and as she lowered her head to retrieve it, she complained of dizziness . . . Then anger or stubbornness having cleared her brain, she went on:

"As the funeral procession was getting under way, Aiken driving, we were all treated to the spectacle of Owen Haskins suddenly appearing from nowhere on this untamed mount . . . It was clear at once that the horse had become frightened. I don't know whether it was at the sight of the hearse, or the geldings' having been adorned with all kinds of funereal trappings, at any rate Owen's horse reared, and plunged, attempting to throw the rider . . . A farm boy came out and tried to subdue the animal . . . In vain . . . And what does our former groom Aiken do but instantly follow the runaway horse and rider at breakneck speed with hearse, casket, trappings, and all! The pursuit of the runaway horse with the hearse was soon ended, for a wheel came off, and as you must have heard, the casket and the dead minister fell out into a snow-filled ditch, the horses became unyoked . . . Aiken leaped on one horse, extricated it from the funeral procession, and raced after Owen . . . What followed, so far as my poor eyesight could see, was something out of a rodeo . . . At any rate, Aiken reached the runaway horse, the runaway boy, caught him from the ungovernable mount he was on, and brought him to safety on his own horse decorated with funeral pomp . . ."

Mr. Skegg's face showed as many violent and contradictory motions as the feats Lady Bythewaite was describing for him: surprise, shame, indignation, admiration, amusement, even suppressed laughter, and finally astonishment approaching terror.

"When they had fixed the wheel of the hearse," she went on, "and there was still no sign of Aiken returning, I maddened the entire party the most, I think (by now it was raining, a fine hurtful kind of rain, you know, and I or nobody else had so much as one parasol), by proposing to drive, since I recognized nobody about but old men, small boys, and tired women. I saw Isa's face both forbidding me to do so and commanding me at the same time to take the reins! Yes, I think this is what has angered them all and not Aiken's running off, for after all had he not gone to save the living and his own brother on a runaway horse? And so I drove the hearse to the funeral service, and later to the burial . . . There was a bare handful of people at the ceremony, Mr. Skegg. Therefore my presence should have been appreciated in view of the paucity of mourners. But all during the service that faded vixen Isa Heynings never left off staring at me with white fury; her anger at me had taken the place of the lack of grief she had for her reverend husband . . . And as I was leaving the cemetery, to take my own horses back with me, she took hold of my black silk coat, tearing it shamefully," and here Lady Bythewaite smiled broadly, revealing teeth as preternaturally white as those of Aiken Cusworth's, "and . . ."

Mr. Skegg waited, some sort of anger on his old drawn face, perhaps anger at such a long-drawn-out recital.

But Lady Bythewaite was having difficulty in controlling a laugh which resembled almost that of a barking animal.

"Isa Heynings said to me," she managed to continue, " 'God will judge you for this more than he did when you were the public whore of Prince's Crossing.' 'God grew tired of judging me years ago,' I replied to her, 'and has allowed me to be mistress of my own life . . . Do not desecrate your husband's obsequies with petty pique and jealousy, or with the envy that has gnawed at your old bones from the day you first set eyes on me . . .'

"It was then she spat in my face."

"And you—?"

"Yes, you heard right. I let her! Yes," Lady Bythewaite flushed triumphant, "it was an unhoped for piece of luck . . . It has also slowly worked in our favor . . . When our sons come back, if they ever do from their breakneck ride, Isa Heynings' having spat on me, I who supplied her with horses for her spouse's burial, my unappreciated generosity, spurned by this decayed vixen, will be all that they will recall! . . . And sleep again will overtake Prince's Crossing . . ."

As long as the two runaways did not return, were traipsing, adventuring she knew not where, she kept possession of herself, ruled the big house, saw the chores were performed, issued commands, and was herself, but when one early spring-like morning they came back, her anger and pride felled her. She lay in a darkened room. Dr. Applegate was summoned from fifty miles away, he administered a hypodermic, and gave her more medicine, and departed. Lying with pads of witch hazel on her eyes, she tossed and turned even with the opiates running in her veins, so that the bed had to be remade every few hours.

Finally, after twenty refusals, she admitted Aiken. She forbade him to raise one single blind, however, so that they communed in total blackness.

"A decent man would never have returned," she began.

"I am not decent."

"I was about to inquire where you get your sharp tongue." She raised herself up on one elbow. "That is hardly necessary now, though, wouldn't you say? . . . Well, Aiken, if you are not sorry you have disgraced yourself, let me be sorry for you. You will not refuse vouchsafing me with that, will you? Yes, I am sorry for you! I grovel on the ground where you should be groveling . . . I pity you . . ."

"I will not allow that," he raised his voice so that the spoon in her waterglass tinkled.

"You have no control over my mind as yet, or my soul, Aiken Cusworth. But that will come—is that not the meaning of your pithy *I will not allow that?* That is the real Aiken speaking."

"You speak of disgrace, lying there with your fancied illness."

"You don't believe then that they hate you now as much as they do me?"

"Why should I believe anything," Aiken responded. "I value

the living more than the dead. Anybody can drive a corpse to the cemetery. I have only one brother."

"You have *two* brothers. That is a luxury most people do not have. Even if they both are . . ."

But a movement from him stopped her short.

"I will tell you the truth because, Aiken, the terror you strike into me makes lying not worth the candle . . ."

"If *you* are going to tell the truth, let me move closer to where I'm to hear it," he said, and drew his chair up to her bed. "Shan't I raise the blinds also if you are about to speak it?"

She tried with shaking hand to reach for the little bottle. Aiken stood up, took the bottle out of her reach, and put it beside a plant of rich luxuriance.

"You can tell the truth without any help from this dope you poison yourself with."

But her mind wandered. His strength not only overwhelmed her from speaking, she felt her whole being dwindling, diminishing, drifting out to some tide in whose flow she knew she would never return.

"That you should prefer one person . . . to all others in the world. What kind of commitment is that?"

"You prefer that I give you my undiminished loyalty and love: that is why you are sick, and that is why you are always angry."

"You can never save Owen . . ."

"Yet I . . . will . . ." His features were distorted almost beyond recognition, the blood having rushed into his face until it was distinctly black before her own eyes even in the blackness of that room.

He seized her by the throat with both his hands, but then releasing her, he muttered, "No, you shall live, to witness more disgrace! You must see to the end what you have set into motion . . ."

"You must find some life beyond your attachment to him!" she spoke back to the darkness beside her, clasping her injured throat, speaking into the teeth of this menace which, not visible to her in any one place, seemed to swirl throughout the entire room like flame and smoke. "You are pursuing wind and air. I am warning you," and she touched again her throat where he had left his thumb marks in welts. "I want, I aim to save you . . ."

"You couldn't save a dog," he spoke with his back to her. "As to the wind, or cyclone, or hurricane—whatever force it is you call on, you speak as if I cared to live . . ."

"Don't live, then, Aiken, but don't die mad!"

He turned on her then so that she expected indeed he would lay hands on her in earnest. But the tempest was over for today. Going directly to the larger of the windows, he raised the blind. Outside the lake sparkled in the sun, and the trees were showing new red buds.

"And so this is where you are and have your being!" Mr. Skegg waved his arms about the great suite where the former Clarence Skegg now resided in New York. As was always his custom, Mr. Skegg never forewarned anybody he was coming, but simply, in the words of Clarence and Lady Bythewaite, "barged in," unannounced, unheralded, uninvited, unwanted. But not completely unwanted this time, for still crumpled in his vest pocket was the telegram which had brought him to New York, a terse message from Clarence reading "Come at once," and the old maggot had told Lady Bythewaite of neither this telegram nor his sudden departure for New York.

Facing ruin, Clarence was, Mr. Skegg presumed, nearing the end of one of those nine-day-wonder careers, drunk more times than sober, having lost much of his good looks, but worse than all these misfortunes, possessed of a soul weariness such as many feel only toward the end of life.

Yes, Clarence was glad even to see Mr. Skegg! He pressed his old father to his breast, but since Mr. Skegg had never embraced or kissed anybody in his life, man, woman, child, beast, the old maggot drew back in embarrassment and shame, but was pleased nonetheless, even though the brief pressure from his son left him with the distinct taste and smell of expensive eau-de-cologne and face powder.

Clearing his throat many times, Mr. Skegg gave Clarence a few particulars about life in Prince's Crossing.

Clarence sighed, cleared his own throat in a manner very like that of his father, and then said pensively, "And how is that terrible woman?"

Mr. Skegg was seated now, having paced, until he was comfortably tired, about the great room, seated almost protectively next his tiny valise (he had only two changes of clothing in his entire wardrobe, only one pair of cufflinks, only one pair of high shoes, only two stiff high collars, and he was said not to have worn underwear), and putting his index finger to his temple, as he had in his great Wall Street days, and somehow by his pausing, and his vacant look, he commanded Clarence's attention so that the young man realized he must have got some kind of his acting talent from the old maggot too, for he was, the son believed, a consummate hypocrite. At last the maggot said: "She is paying for all her mistakes through her son Aiken."

"Through her *son?*" Clarence raised his voice and approached his father. He moved toward a chair and more or less fell into it, though he was not drunk. He looked at his nails with a kind of stare of wide-eyed and complete disapprobation on contemplating these chewed and mistreated ornaments of his fingers.

"I said through her son," Mr. Skegg spoke in a very effective sotto voce.

Clarence stood up, he sat down, he stood again, he followed his father's example by pacing, and he returned to his chair and looked at the seat of it as if to inquire who had been sitting there a moment or so before.

"I'm afraid I'm completely in the dark as to what you are talking about," the actor spoke with a kind of wounded tone like one who had been both insulted and treated beneath his dignity by being forced to witness something in extremely bad taste.

"See here, can't I order you something in the way of refreshment after your long journey?" Clarence spoke brightening, almost cheerful, having hit on the idea that the fatigue of the long train journey had confused the old maggot's brain as to the parentage of Aiken, if indeed one could consider the horse-tender as having parentage of any kind.

"I would like a breakfast sent up of steak, potatoes, apple pie, and cheese, my dear boy."

"You shall have all of them presto!" Clarence rushed to the telephone with relief, and gave the order, and came back beam-

ing with the expectation that the matter of Aiken and parent-
hood would now be dropped.

But no sooner had the breakfast been served, and Mr. Skegg
had pounced on this fare with an appetite and dispatch which
Clarence envied, the pique of curiosity proved too much for
the actor.

He drew up a chair to within a few inches of Mr. Skegg,
though the sight of his masticating was not too aesthetic, especially for one with as weak a stomach as Clarence now had.
The old man kept his mouth open during his entire repast, and
he did not seem to chew anything thoroughly, especially the
beefsteak whose red juices threatened to stain his pale cravat
and high stiff collar, and so Clarence found himself helping his
father keep tidy and unspotted with generous swathing from a
thick linen napkin emblazoned with a monogram.

"My dear father," Clarence could no longer contain himself
from beginning, "you have said something . . . which deeply
upsets me, I'm afraid . . . Perhaps the fatigue of your
journey . . ."

"Fatigue, fiddlesticks. Slept all the way, Clarence. Easy reclining chair, helpful porters. A rest after the vaudeville of
Prince's Crossing . . ."

"Then what do you mean by saying Aiken is my brother! If
you are not overfatigued, how dare you say this!"

The old man waited a good minute before replying. "I didn't
exactly say he was your brother, Clarence." He stopped chewing.
He then lifted his fork and began on his pie, without having
quite finished all his steak.

"Well, you said he was Lady Bythewaite's son, didn't you?"
A short violent cough coming from Clarence caused the old
man to look narrowly at the actor.

Then laying his fork down rather peremptorily, even peevishly, Mr. Skegg gave a kind of last look at his beefsteak and
pushed it away.

"I confess it was news to me," Mr. Skegg spoke rather loftily,
"though I can hardly say I was surprised, to speak the truth . . .

Nora, your mother, in her youth was what we called an emancipated woman. I have no idea how many sons she may have . . . I do know that Aiken is one of them. That is I have convinced myself he is . . . But I wouldn't think of him as your brother. He has no legal claim to anything of yours . . ."

"But what about the claim of blood?" Clarence spoke so softly as to almost elude Mr. Skegg's hearing, but he heard him nonetheless.

"I wouldn't think about such a thing," Mr. Skegg cautioned his son. "It's too late in life to think about blood, as you call it. In the lives, that is, of either you or Aiken, it's too late . . . Why, Clarence, I do say, you are quite upset! Should never have mentioned it to you!"

"That great strapping lumbering . . ." the actor had begun muttering.

"No one should be ashamed of how Aiken looks," Mr. Skegg complained in a kind of offended manner, and then bringing back his plate to within convenient reach, he began chewing again on his beefsteak. "Aiken is quite personable, if not indeed handsome."

"I am in too great a difficulty here to care much about such a thing, I suppose . . . Just the same," Clarence spoke almost to himself, "we do have the same . . . Aiken and I . . ." Then, raising his voice much in the manner of the soon-to-be-eclipsed Maynard Ewing addressing his audience: "Are you Aiken Cusworth's father?"

Mr. Skegg put down his fork with the piece of beefsteak dangling from it, but he did not quit chewing. At a rumble of impatience from Clarence, however, he ventured:

"I am quite in the dark about it all, my dear Clarence."

"Now that we have opened one closet, if only to shut it, I may as well open another . . ."

Clarence stood over his father and folded his arms before going on: "My career both in the films and the stage, such as they were or are . . . they are all over . . ."

"But you've made quite a fortune, Clarence . . . I saw your

financial statements which your attorney was kind enough to send me . . ."

"Why don't you ever listen to what I say?" the young man stormed. "My career here is over! I am through!"

"And for what reason, pray?" Mr. Skegg assumed his magisterial role of cross-examiner . . . "Or, Clarence, am I not allowed to inquire, as I am not allowed to inquire of so many things."

"I'm afraid my explanation of my failure must be kept as vague as your explanation of who is the father of that young livery stableman Aiken Cusworth . . . Imagine my being his brother!" he modulated his voice as if in prayer. "I don't know which overwhelms me the more, that I'm ruined here, before I've properly begun, or that nobody back home knows who sired whom or when . . . Somehow I don't care, don't have the strength to care . . ."

"Oh, Clarence, there's nothing wrong with you that we can't fix up back home! And I have Shapwick Manor for you . . ."

Clarence was weeping hard now, and with each tear there was less and less of Maynard Ewing, until finally dry-eyed, he looked very much like he had when he had been expelled from West Point, and had come home to his father to take his punishment, but Mr. Skegg then as now had been too puzzled and confused to do anything but pat the boy on his knee and offer to leave the room.

"It will all come out in the wash, my boy!" Mr. Skegg's voice came over to a dazed Clarence Skegg. Indeed he was too stunned to want to get drunk. He was going home to Prince's Crossing, in a day, a month, a year at the most, and he had a new brother he had seen but never recognized, and all the while he hated New York with a passion his Scottish ancestors had reserved for the Devil or the Pope.

"And so when will he be home then!" Lady Bythewaite's up-braiding voice startled the old maggot from his dozing. He sat bolt upright. He thought he was still in New York with Clarence, instead of here in Shapwick Manor, with the sound of the one voice (hers) which would pursue him he was sure beyond the grave.

Rubbing his eyes he explained: "I would have sworn I was still in New York, for Clarence's voice was as audible to me as yours is now . . ."

"I don't know from your tale if Clarence is dying or indeed dead or successful or in eclipse, or all these things in succession. And I don't know whether I wish him to stay and be successful, or fail and return, but I get no more out of you than if you were talking in your sleep," she was going on with her monologue.

"What have your wishes got to do with Clarence's staying or returning. Why don't you think of him! You speak as though he owed you his return or his staying, whichever is the one your mania of the moment dictates . . . After all, Clarence has been gone for *years!*"

"Years?" Lady Bythewaite spoke with genuine astonishment. "How many years?"

Mr. Skegg knew that in this one area she could not calculate correctly, was indeed lost. Her concept of time had always been dim, but now she had lost track of the actual season, month, day. Before Aiken claimed his inheritance and had acted with some kind of daily responsibility it was the horsetender who reminded her always of the time and season, but now, and here Mr. Skegg sighed deeply, Aiken was as nebulous and unreachable as Lady Bythewaite or moonstruck Owen.

"Have ten years gone by?" Lady Bythewaite, imperious, shook him by the shoulder.

Mr. Skegg shook his head wearily.

"Ten years from when?" Mr. Skegg finally spoke in an attempt to capture her attention, which had not only now but for some time been wandering away from her first son, Clarence Skegg, an attention entirely absorbed by Aiken Cusworth and his ascendancy over herself and Owen.

And now that he had mentioned "time" he found she did not listen. Whenever he began to describe Clarence's life in New York, his suffering from fame (he omitted mentioning the signs of dissolute life which were to the old maggot the most prominent aspects of Clarence's New York sojourn), the boy's utter disinterest and dislike for his "profession," and his ambiguous homesickness, Lady Bythewaite only looked puzzled, or tired, or vague, or annoyed.

"Well, why didn't he give you a direct answer as to when he is returning to Prince's Crossing?" Nora Bythewaite, coming out of her reverie on time, suddenly demanded.

"My poor distraught dear, have you heard nothing I have said?" he spoke with a real indication of concern.

"If you value your life, Mr. Skegg, never show to my face that you pity me." She spoke this sentence having lowered her body and face from her standing position so that she could look directly into his large unclouded eyes. "When I ask for answers to my questions, which you are of course incapable of giving, I do not require your last-century patronizing of me . . . What I need is for someone to come here and chain that fiend Aiken!"

He had not been quite prepared for her last sentence. She had come, he had arranged for her to come, to discuss only one topic, Clarence Skegg's failure in New York and his inevitable return, as a result of the old maggot's visit to the metropolis.

Having mentioned Aiken, she picked up a huge vase which was sitting near them, and Mr. Skegg closed his eyes expecting her to throw it through the window, but finally opening his eyes he saw she had only picked up the vase to deposit it in a more ornamental location.

"You should fill this beautiful article with flowers," she spoke softly now, wiping her eyes. "At least you could put some bulrushes or bittersweet in it . . .

"Now, my dear Skegg," she raised her voice as she paced about the room, quite a different person now, at any rate more like the world's idea of Lady Bythewaite, "describe again his New York life to me! I was much too overwrought at your first telling, and you were much too sleepy while you were telling it to me . . . Never tell anything when you are sleepy. You said some very peculiar things in your doze . . ."

"But, Nora, there's so little to tell . . . And now I'm back, I don't really believe I have been there, to tell the truth . . . Why, his life is more dreary and boring than ours, despite his living in a large suite. He does nothing but pose in front of a camera, and come home to this suite to complain, and weep, and . . ."

"I knew there would be an *and.*"

"I told you at the height of your inattention that he's drinking too much," Mr. Skegg spoke throatily.

"Ah, if drink were all that is wrong with Clarence Skegg!" (Mr. Skegg could not contain a movement of surprise when she said this.)

"And," she began, steadying herself by holding on to one of his stoutest chairs, "did you not tell him how I am a prisoner in my own house, how a certain former horsetender has gained ascendancy over me, so that I cannot do a thing without consulting a former stable boy . . ."

"The emergence of Aiken has quite crushed him." Mr. Skegg's directness here astounded her.

"He understands my plight?" She threw back her arms as if at last some kind of respite were to be given her for her lonely anguish and separation from her former self.

"He understands now that Aiken is your son."

"You told him?" She sat down in a straightback chair before a huge deal table. "And did he believe you?" She spoke this last sentence only after a struggle with herself.

"It was not so much that he thought of your case, Nora, as

he tried to digest the fact that Aiken whom we always thought of as a kind of blacksmith and groom . . ."

"Which he is!"

". . . was his brother. The idea Aiken was his own flesh and blood he could not digest."

"I see . . . There was no room in his heart for concern over me, or my plight . . ."

"Clarence is too beside himself to think of anybody else," the old maggot raised his voice now. "I shouldn't be at all surprised if he . . . shot himself."

But Nora Bythewaite, who did not know if Clarence had been gone one year or ten, was pacing the floor again, and it was doubtful if she had heard what Mr. Skegg had said, or if she had heard it, it would come back to her like regurgitated food in the dead of night, for often she did not hear what people said to her at the time of their speaking, but hours later their voices came to her as clear as chimes, and she then wished to make answer to them. This would happen now with Mr. Skegg's statement about Clarence's going to shoot himself.

"He keeps this close watch on Owen because Owen was lost to himself for over six months, and he counted every hour and minute of that absence!" She would have gone on with her monologue coming out now irrelevant, non-sequitur, like talk from a chamber at midnight, had not Mr. Skegg in great impatience cried, "Who is this *he* you are speaking of?"

"Who is this *he*?" she gave a start, for he had indeed brought her back from her own kind of absence. "Who is always *he* but that tobacco-stained devil, the one who upset a hearse and overturned a dead man in his coffin to go in pursuit of his runaway new-found brother! Aiken is who! Aiken! And Owen is his slave, and he keeps him his slave because the boy cannot remember! All he would have him remember indeed is that he is his flesh-and-blood brother. Oh, I have heard their catechism together. They stay up half the night whispering together when the wind forbids sleep. They are worse than lovers! Yes, it would be better for all if Aiken enjoyed the boy's body than keep this mastery over his blood and soul . . ."

Mr. Skegg had stood up. He was deathly pale.

"I am glad," she spoke through a calm smile, "that something I have said has reached for once more than your ears, Mr. Skegg."

"You have said a great deal," the old man mumbled, and he looked out the window where trees, bushes, and flowers were beginning to burgeon. The sun too was out but clouded.

But Nora Bythewaite, who had not finished, in her quietest tone was speaking on:

"Because Aiken had known him from birth, from beyond birth, and forasmuch as he followed me about when I was pregnant as if he knew he would claim the soul of the child I carried in me . . ."

"Nora, for pity's sake!"

". . . forasmuch as he knew this son would be his, let us say, he was ever jealous of any who showed the least attention to the boy. Having had nothing, no confessed parentage, no mother or father, no inheritance, except for that of his own great strength and the soil he worked in, horses, the grass, he waited for the birth of this son as his own. Owen was to be his heritage, the meaning of his life . . . And so, perhaps there is not so great wonder he tortures the boy and himself over the missing six months, the missing New York months!"

She pronounced the name of the great city as if it contained in her mouth and in her brain the vilest taste and meaning of anything under the revolving sun.

"The six months Owen Haskins was away," she answered his questioning eyes. "You insult me because *I* do not remember. Do you remember not your own sins, Mr. Skegg . . . Who sent my son away? . . . Who lost him those six months? Where was this boy all that time, a mere child? . . . That is what has driven Aiken insane, for have no doubt in your mind, he rages, if not outwardly, inwardly more than any of your common cyclones which rove the earth but for a few minutes . . . Each night the two of them, nestled together like twins in the womb, go over everything together! They are not just twin brothers as they whisper and confer—they are one flesh . . . And he will wrench out from Owen this knowledge, don't you see. He will find out . . . or kill him . . ."

"If I were to bring Clarence back, do you think he could set the family straight, do you think all might be reconciled . . . ?" The old maggot was appealing to her, though she gave no indication she was being reached by it. Without her being aware of words or embrace, he had placed his arm about her shoulders, he was walking with her about the room as though she were his aged mother and not the woman whom he had loved and given sons to.

"How can the drowning save the drowned!" She thus dismissed Clarence's return. She shook off his embrace.

"I don't want any help," she spoke to the floor. "They say even God cannot undo his own mistakes. I pray only for strength to endure the great thing that is to come. I practice strength day and night. There they are, even now, in my great house talking. They know the awful thing is coming also. They have very little time, forasmuch as . . ."

"Forasmuch as what?" He took her by the shoulder, shaking her, then raising his hand he was in the attitude of one about to strike her, when releasing her, he said only, "No, I will only be an ear, not a hand . . . You may come here, Nora, anytime you wish, but I will never do more again than listen . . ."

She had long thought of God as her adversary, her personal enemy, as One who constantly thought of how to outwit and debase and humiliate her.

But now she found she prostrated herself often at the side of her bed, calling upon some Power, she knew not what, a Power that heard mothers perhaps, calling upon him or perhaps on *her* to save her and Owen.

"Let the mother and the son go out of this bondage. Amen . . ."

But even as she helped herself up to her feet and looked out upon the troubled lake in the rough springtime air, she felt her plea would not be granted. Nothing had ever been granted to her, all she had ever got she had taken by main force. For she had met with a strength greater than her own. She had no key, no map, no insight into the whirling confusion that was Aiken Cusworth's soul. Even now when she went to speak with him, she felt a breath come from his body which swept into her own, and blew out from her inmost being all thoughts, all light, all the fluttering breath of words. Perhaps Aiken had come straight from God, perhaps he had no mortal father after all but she had become pregnant with him by some unknown whirling force, and he was her punishment and her judgment. For time after time she had studied his face, and once when he had been worn out to the point of sickness by his manual exertions, and had thrown himself down nearly naked on his bed, falling into snoring unconsciousness, she had stepped to the threshold of his room though shaking with terror and studied this unknown though familiar person, hoping by gazing at his face and form to understand her enemy and guess at his origin. But all that lay there was the body of a young Titan with some of her features in the nose and mouth, and had the terrible eyes opened, her own eyes would have gazed back at her, but blacker than hers, and in the end not of human expression, nor even of animal or serpent . . .

Then as she closed the door on her son who had come to claim his inheritance, a thought came to her so chilling, as if by mischance she had fallen from her room into the icy waters of the lake, that she did not wish to escape Aiken and his enslavement of Owen, else she and Owen would long since have been gone! . . . But with reflection, with a sip of strong whiskey poured into her coffee, she saw that this reflection was not one which would stand up to reason . . . For no matter where she and Owen fled—and they were such poor fleers!—that indefatigable horseman would follow after them.

And so after all her own earthly wanderings and trials, she

had met a force, if not greater than her own, her equal, she had met with one who would not let her go . . . would not let her be! And she could explain it to nobody, least of all herself. For look, the doors of her house were open at least to her, she was the mistress of this mansion, and true, a stable boy and horsetender had moved into the guest room, but this was explainable to all and sundry as her fear of robbers and cutthroats. Life went on smoothly, orderly, her acknowledged son Owen was more sober and industrious than he had ever been to her knowledge, they sat down to evening supper like a well-ordered happy family . . . So was the whirlwind only in her mind? No, she knew better. Aiken knew better. Owen likewise. They accused her of having lost track of time, though her house was full of ticking clocks—she dared not count the number of the timepieces—but there was no time in her heart, she had only sons whose hearts as long as they beat kept time for her.

Spring is coming even to this bleak part of the world.

Owen was sitting in the front parlor which looked out on the lake when he heard his mother address this remark to one of the many attorneys who now came traipsing in and out of the house on some momentous land deal. The words were said loudly enough to reach him, and, he felt, spoken purposely so that he might know she had words for everyone but him. Aiken too had disappeared unaccountably, though before he went, he had just as unaccountably given Owen a thick packet containing money and had asked him to keep it in a safe place for him. He put it away, after a thoughtful wait, in the family Bible.

"For you are the only one I dare trust." Aiken's words kept coming back to Owen now.

We will have to sell all the property east of Chipstable.

The words from his mother broke his absorption somewhat in the packet Aiken had entrusted him. He heard her unfolding the map of all the farm districts she was discussing and the sound was almost identical to that of when he touched the thick packet of money coming from the hands of Aiken.

Of course I will live to regret it, but I am in need of money at once, and if those farmers have to be dispossessed so much the worse for them. Sell all the land beyond Grovely Wood and to the north of Chadwick.

Owen stood up and placed his back to the direction in which her whirling words were coming. He had not opened the packet of money, but now the auctioneer volume of her voice, the note of desperation, the need for immediate cash made him take down the huge family Bible and remove the entrusted packet from its thick pages, on one of which he saw the date of his confirmation. He held the envelope in outstretched hands.

Suddenly he tore open the envelope, and even as it sprang

open he wondered why he had done so. Was it his mother's hysterical need for "ready cash" which had made him look within something put in his own safekeeping, or was it the desire to touch something which belonged so deeply to Aiken. At any rate, there they came bulging out, a huge roll of U.S. bills, whose number and denomination astonished, even appalled him. And all of the bills were like Aiken himself, stained with the marks of earth and sweat.

The deep concentration within him consonant with touching something which was Aiken's and which Aiken had earned and entrusted to him, together with his sudden homesickness for his brother, made him unaware that Lady Bythewaite had finished her business transactions for the spring quarter and had entered the parlor unnoticed by him, and was indeed now standing directly over her one acknowledged son.

"I have never known a young man before on whom people were always bestowing gifts," she began, "and gifts which if they make the donor proud seem to distress the recipient so deeply."

With a handkerchief redolent of sweet lavender she brushed the tears from his cheek.

She seated herself on the mahogany footstool at his feet, and took his hand in hers.

She felt reconciliatory, kind, protective until all upon a sudden as his heavy breathing broke open his outer jacket, she saw across his vest the gold watch chain which also belonged to Aiken.

Rather than snatch the chain from his vest, instead, in her anger she tore from his trembling fingers the packet containing the bestowed money, and though he gave her a gasp of shocked disapproval, she had caught him too unprepared, too guilty to fight her at once.

She was counting the money before his pained observance, and with each thousand-dollar bill noted by her, a choke of grief rose from Owen's distorted throat.

A cry of derisive laughter came as she looked at the last thousand-dollar bill.

"And how did he earn this money?" She turned her fury on Owen. "And what, pray tell, are you doing with it?"

His eyes had dried almost shut, and she studied with a little uneasiness the angry curves of his mouth.

"Do not push me, Mother."

"Do you realize that you were holding a fortune here in this shabby envelope?"

"I am only his safekeeper of it. I had not looked within."

"Then why had you unsealed the envelope!"

He dared not tell her he only wanted to touch the bills that Aiken had touched, that he had no connection now with life except where he could touch where Aiken touched.

"I want you to go to New York and fetch your brother Clarence home . . ."

"You told me once that that was the last thing on earth you would ever permit me again . . ."

"You are older now," she spoke with a ferocious energy, and then looked up at the wheezing moribund grandfather clock. "You are nearly . . . eighteen years old, aren't you?"

"And let that painted drunk clown revile and mock me again!" Owen raised his voice which, changing now, came out suddenly in the deep baritone of Aiken Cusworth.

"A lot you know about mocking and reviling!" Lady Bythewaite spoke dryly, and began to move away from him. His few words had spoiled her argument, and she stood now by the window to look at the waters of the lake, and to gain time.

"You'll go if I tell you you must go!" she finally managed to say.

"I will do no such thing . . . You have no power over me anymore." He stared at the opened packet which she still held in her hands. "I've found you out, and I will not obey you ever again."

"As this livery stableman's star rises, ours is setting evidently," she whispered, and she slapped the packet of Aiken Cusworth's fortune down on the family Bible but held it still in her hand, and indeed soon took it up again and clasped it tight.

"Your brother Clarence, I need not repeat, is ruined . . . I've sent him enough money to open a bank with . . . He's not only a drunkard but a gambler. He was about to be arrested two months ago . . ."

Her head swam dizzily, she went over to the great wooden colonial settee, and sat there, letting her head fall between her knees so that she might not faint.

"He has blackmailed me for a year." She reviewed her own folly also: "That's why you heard me a few minutes ago giving commands to sell my land . . . And while my land and money go to New York, your stableman brother is getting rich!" She looked again, almost murderously, gazing at the packet of money.

Then speaking as if in prayer and alone, she began: "I dare not send Clarence any more money directly . . . I need some trusted messenger to go to New York, and accompany him to where this last payment is to be met, someone to see that it goes where it is meant to go, and not let it fall into the bottomless place where all the rest of our fortune has gone . . ."

"And how would I know how to do that, may I ask you, since when I went to New York the last time . . ."

She had again forgotten until this moment the unaccounted "six months" in the life of Owen Haskins which was one of the principal torments of Aiken Cusworth.

"You are my only hope, Owen," she proceeded, ready perhaps to risk another "six months" loss. "I can't send Mr. Skegg . . . He would never give Clarence such a sum of money in the first place. He would let him go to jail . . . Or he would meddle, with his Calvinist uprightness, and indeed send him straight to prison . . ."

"It's gone as far as that?" Owen wondered, and he stood up. But she saw no willingness or love there, only memory of something which had happened to him in New York, of being in arrears to Aiken Cusworth for six months of lost memory and time. Owen knew, and she knew, that money meant nothing to Aiken, furthermore, and that this packet of a fortune could be thrown into the flames tonight in the grate, and he would never turn a hair, but Aiken expected and would find out where the six months had gone in the life of his brother, whose keeper he was now and forever, and New York would not be permitted, and nothing originating from Lady Bythewaite would again be permitted.

Aiken Cusworth had come indeed late into the world, she saw, to judge them, to dispossess them, and in the end his word would be law.

"Owen, you no longer love me. I have known that for some time of course." Lady Bythewaite spoke in the whisper which used to make shivers go through his body. "He has tampered with your most delicate inner workings." Her eyes sought out the great clock ticking in the hallway. "You are in imminent danger, let me warn you . . ."

But she saw only an impassive face now watching her, hard and determined, which indeed might never shed tears again for her.

Taking the packet of money which she had held all during this colloquy, she threw it in his face and rushed from the room.

Lady Bythewaite began to go "everywhere" then with Stephen Bottrell. When they were not taking long rides in her buggy, they met in a candy-kitchen ice-cream parlor as their convenient place of rendezvous (set a mile or so from the Elysian Meadows movie theater) which had hidden booths in the rear, a favorite spot not so much with lovers as persons engaged in land deals. Here in secret safety Stephen Bottrell would pour out his heart to her for hours, during which he always managed to ask for an introduction to the great Maynard Ewing, would revert to his own incurable homesickness, and then would listen with incredulous half-attention while Lady Bythewaite inventoried her own troubles—that she had lost all her money, that she was about to be put, with her belongings, into the road by her, yes why not say it! by her son Aiken, who had managed to buy up all her old past-due mortgages, and that Stephen's own idol, Maynard Ewing, far from being a success, was in debt, penniless, that she had sent him a fortune which he had squandered, and that Owen, her favorite of all, had turned on his mother, and had some strange ailment which threatened his life.

A bit stifled by this unexpected saga of woes from a woman, from a "house" which he supposed above anything as common as money troubles, Stephen though struggling with partial disillusionment finally got out: "But it has not spoiled your beauty!" He spoke in a rushed panting voice, like one who has to pull this statement out from his pockets, which were always bulging with receipts and checks and loose dollar bills.

"Which of my features do you find most fetching?" Lady Bythewaite retorted almost immediately, for she felt his flattery might be intended to confuse her, and that in her confusion he would make another advance in his conquest of her.

But Stephen Bottrell was as quick-witted if not as brilliant as Lady B. He replied: "Your beauty is an overall effect, and to be appraised must be studied as a whole."

"It is a great shame we did not meet twenty-five years ago," she reflected, and picking up her ice cream spoon, licked it clean of the chocolate syrup. Indeed this syrup tasted so good, she ordered another dish of ice cream from the soda jerker who had been transfixed, from the front of the store, staring at her.

"You could easily pass for thirty, and you know it," Stephen managed to get out, though blushing furiously at his own mendacity.

"And where on earth, dear Stephen, would I be able to pass?" she wondered, for his flattery, outrageous and downright as it was, had been the only happy thing she had heard for many a revolving year.

The soda jerker had also brought Lady Bythewaite, unheard of in this place, a fresh cloth napkin, a huge tumbler of water, and he was busily polishing a solid silver spoon, which when he handed it to her she examined briefly and then looked into the boy's eyes with careful aim.

Stephen Bottrell had now regained his own equanimity and was determined to go on with his flirtation, no matter how many times he slipped, and Lady Bythewaite chewing her ice cream was waiting for his next speech.

"What I wish to do is invite you to a private showing of Maynard Ewing's newest film."

She put down her spoon and soiled the fresh linen napkin.

"Wait, wait . . . There would be no one in the theater but ourselves, that is, your own company and I, and of course the operator."

"Is it true, my dear Stephen, that these films often catch fire, and burn the audience and the operator to cinders?"

"Oh, only out of rank carelessness."

"But even barring the occurrence of a fire, do you think I would be able to endure Clarence's new film . . . I mean considering what the past ones were like . . ."

"You would not have to endure anything, Nora . . ." His eye rested on a large brooch on her bosom.

She had not corrected his using her first name because she saw how frightened he had been when he took the risk of saying it.

"Why don't *you* go into the movies," she wondered, looking into his face, but she saw at once the reason, had seen it from the first. Stephen Bottrell, granted he was star-struck, still had a look of such fierce, if ordinary intelligence and will, he could never for a single moment have persuaded anybody to believe he was anything but what he was, a sharper. In order even to portray the nonentities which Maynard Ewing was required to bring forth into flickering life, one had to be both addled and inspired, and Stephen Bottrell was entirely clear-headed.

"I have told you a good many things today in this place which should have been left unspoken, I'm afraid," Nora Bythewaite reflected.

"I would count myself the most fortunate man in all the world if I could be your friend, Lady Bythewaite." He underscored her "title" with hard, almost passionate emphasis and reverence.

"I must tell you a thing, then, Stephen Bottrell . . . I'm sure it will not surprise a young man of your experience, and worldliness, but it ought, I opine, yes, it should be said . . . I have never known friendship . . ."

"Not for anybody?" he cried, surprised in spite of himself.

"For absolutely nobody."

Then all at once she could not finish her second dish of ice cream, and she pushed it over toward him so that it touched his spatula-shaped fingers with the somewhat unclean nails.

His spoon fell almost mechanically into the ice cream she had barely touched, and he brought some to his mouth, and his lips opened and took it in.

"I have often wondered," she went on, "what people meant by friendship . . . As I go down the 'shady side of life,' as my mother called it, and the only thing that seems definite is the grave, I think more and more of the grandiose words and ideas people use in this flickering brief existence . . ."

"What words, Lady Bythewaite?" he wondered, and his nervousness and disappointment appeared to have given him an appetite, for he was quickly finishing her second dish of ice cream for her.

"Why, all the paraphernalia, you know, we come into the world hearing from the beginning, God and justice and splendor and of course friendship, and love . . ."

Her face suddenly looked as if it had been slapped by a strong palm. He feared indeed she was about to weep, her irises were so inflamed, her pupils so bulging.

"I only know that everything is beyond me, and those words, one of which you have mentioned, only make life more difficult, more *un*-understandable . . . If I said that they were plotting against me, however, you would tell people I was mad . . ."

He put his hand on her sleeve.

"I would believe anything you say, and I would do anything you commanded me."

"Perhaps I could put it another way," she spoke with a foggy abstraction which indicated perhaps she had not heard his last statement. He waited for her to continue like one who has waited all his life for the words that were to issue from her mouth.

"Aiken and Owen," she confided to him, after another struggle when her tongue and lips refused to obey what her heart prompted them to pronounce, "my sons want me out of the way . . . I am no longer needful to them . . . They rule, or rather the blacker of the two rules."

Coming out of her meditation, she took his hand in hers, and gave it an unwonted pressure, strong as a man's, her rings pressing into the pliant flesh of his hand.

"Of course I will come to your private showing! And of course I will write you a letter of introduction to Maynard Ewing . . . He shall see you! Or I will know the reason why. Unless of course he has shot himself." Then not having prepared him at all for her lips, she kissed him on the mouth. "He threatens to kill himself every other Friday," she finished with lungs of brass, and Stephen Bottrell fell back a little from her, and brought his right hand to his heart.

"Do you know what?" Stephen began, reeling a little toward her, and now she did look at him with studied coquetry as she waited for his sentence. "You are the most wonderful woman I have ever known. Perhaps in your heart you despise me, but I love you."

He covered her mouth with two fierce kisses.

Lady Bythewaite's mansion had even more mirrors than clocks, each mirror like each clock an heirloom and therefore nearly priceless, and if she could not always see to remember time, the clocks whispered to her it was passing, and the mirrors showed her not only her own approaching old age, but allowed with their expansive reflection her eye to rove into the purlieus of the kitchen, the buttery, and the hired girls' rooms without so much as stirring from her post.

Her lips still fresh from Stephen Bottrell's kisses, lips which had spoken not a word since she promised she would attend a "private showing" of Maynard Ewing's newest film on the morrow, Lady Bythewaite, removing her hatpin from her great flowered velvet hat, had entered the house with the impression she was alone. Stephen's kisses and a certain strange calm in the landscape without had relaxed her features; the gloom of the parlor showed no gray in her black hair, few wrinkles in her throat or forehead, and she was about to say she was indeed not too old for this new love, half her age, for where someone dreams of love, he will take, she knew, almost any sweetheart, when looking into the reflection of one huge pier glass mirror to another she caught sight of something which at first she thought was arising from an overdose of her medicine. She pricked herself with her hatpin, her hat came off, and with it her long hair partly came down. She held on to the little end-table in front of the great mirror in whose depths two figures seemed as large and menacing as those flashed upon the silver screen of the photoplay house. She closed her eyes, and waited, then, slowly opening them, saw an old woman looking at the reflected image of two young men in the kitchen.

She saw, then, Owen Haskins, seated in an improvised barber's chair, his child cheeks lathered with obscene gouts of thick stiff white soap, and directly behind him, his sleeves rolled up beyond his biceps, his great hands holding a straight-razor, his great starting black eyes showing for the first time in her memory merriment and pride, Aiken, turned barber, giving her youngest son his first shave.

Their cries of fun and joy struck her as heartless and unfeeling as if they now frolicked about her open casket.

She kept her eyes closed, the blood from where she had pricked herself with the hatpin running upon the little peach end-table, and into the palm of her hand, which lay on the wood as lifeless as if it had been severed.

Why, she tried to study herself, why should this scene so overwhelm her, why did its innocence and intense pleasure so far as the two participants were concerned shrivel her inner organs, dry up the spittle in her mouth, and make her knees buckle. She moved to the armchair, from which she could still see this scene reflected in one resplendent mirror after another.

She fancied she heard the razor move through the thick white gouts of lather. She must not move, or speak, or breathe, or the razor would slip. But it was not this contingency which threatened to overwhelm her . . . Then her hand which had been searching so long found the little bottle, and she took this time more than the prescribed dosage. She did up her hair, occasionally having to look upon the floor for a misplaced hairpin. *How tar-black my hair is,* she kept repeating to herself.

Then she found herself on the threshold of the kitchen. The merriment ceased. The old sour crabbed look returned to Aiken's face, and he began rolling down his shirt sleeves to cover the brawn of his forearms. Owen stared up at her with eyes of real terror.

"His first shave!" she exclaimed in tones as false and unfeeling as Maynard Ewing might have envied in the new melodrama now playing continuously at movie theaters, *His Secret Fortune*.

"You're not angry?" a voice which seemed to come from every corner and roof of the house reached her. She sat down in order not to fall.

"Angry!" Lady Bythewaite answered the voice, and she had the distinct impression she was back in London, and some old titled gentleman had brought her a bouquet of American beauty roses.

Then there was Aiken kneeling before her, his hair all in curls from the effort of his exertions as barber.

"His cheeks had got more than downy, ma'am, he was getting beyond the corn silk to the unkempt and shaggy, why, it was . . ."

Owen, too, had risen from the barber's chair, and approached his mother with the lather still not wiped free, and found himself kneeling by Aiken's side.

"Did I criticize you boys," she spoke at last, scrutinizing their look of appalled expectation, and then they waited in the silence which followed her first words, a kind of slow-coming bewilderment both at her strange unnatural voice and at the deep pallor on her almost unrecognizable face. "Did I give one word of reproach," she got out in choking exertion to swallow the real words which struggled within her to be said, and which must not ever be said.

"Lady Bythewaite," Aiken began, rising considerably confused as to how he had found himself on his knees.

"Silence, no more words," she commanded. "This indeed I do believe," she began then in a moment, her eyes filling with water, "this is the scene I have beheld in dreams, my dreams, you know, and which I knew would one day happen."

Her two sons looked down on the worn hook-rug of the floor, as if in prayer along with her words.

"Why, Aiken, if he needed shaving, you of all would know," she talked on in her more common daily intonation, and she laid her cool hands on Aiken's weather-beaten scarred and open face, but shrank back suddenly in dismay as she saw that some of the blood from her pricked finger had come off on his face.

"I would never have done it, ma'am, had I thought . . ."

Was it Aiken's words of regret or his real awe at her disturbed features which restored her for a moment to some kind of equanimity?

"I do believe, Aiken, that whatever you do is right," she spoke directly to him. "I mean, we have a guiding star, don't we . . . Now go on with your shaving," she commanded, already passing out of the room as she spoke.

She went into the tiniest chamber of her house, where the newly installed telephone rested in its specially built cupboard like a black skeleton beckoning. She took hold of it roughly, raised the receiver, talked awkwardly if angrily to the "central," commanded her that the voice of Mr. Bottrell be brought into her domain, from the Elysian Theater, and by some miracle got this voice at once, and said into the unfamiliar horn of the apparatus:

"My dearest Stephen, this is again your friend Lady Bythewaite . . . I have thought over your kind invitation of this afternoon . . . I accept it . . . But I should like to see you this very night, that is correct, at the theater . . . Pray see that nobody else is admitted at that time. Yes, yes, show the new film, but the main thing is that we are together and alone. No piano player, the silence will be perfect . . . Oh, well, the projection operator, if he is absolutely needed . . . We two, then, Stephen . . ."

She kept her eyes averted from the mirrors then, but she heard still the scraping over flesh and bones from the razor, but there was now no merriment or laughter or joy from the two young men. His first shave was nearing completion in sober silence.

When they heard Lady Bythewaite drive away, the restraint and also the feeling of shame she had conferred on them was gone, and Aiken broke into such a torrent of foul language and cursing that Owen stood rapt in admiration and deep attention. The forbidden words and their images coming out of Aiken's mouth brought the color back to the boy's face and lips, so that he appeared to be taking a refreshing bath in a tingling stream. And since it was established now that she was also Aiken's own mother, many of the things which the horsetender now said and which would have been interdicted by Owen a few months earlier were permitted and in a silent way applauded.

Inspecting his "charge" carefully, Aiken began closing up some of the wounds conferred upon him by the straight-razor by means of a curious treatment of his own, saliva applied more or less by his fist, and a bloody stick of styptic. Then with a final eyeing of the boy, with a melancholy pride as if he had created him from his own strange musings, if not from his very spittle, he said softly:

"You'll do, Owen."

Immediately wheeling away from the boy, walking up and down the kitchen, struggling with something he would say, lowering his head again as if he could not, would not say it, and then finally blurting out:

"Once you asked me about that little house in the woods far out beyond Cawkwell."

Owen's Adam's apple moved convulsively under the thin covering of Aiken's spittle and styptic.

"Shall I take you?" Aiken said, but he had averted his glance from the questioned one.

"You can take me anywhere, Aiken, I suppose."

"Oh, *you!*" Aiken cried with a hurried joy, and turned about and faced him. "I can, huh?" He broke into some of the merriment he had lost after their mother's entrance.

"You won't hold it against me later though?" Aiken wondered. "Or tell the old dame?"

"Oh, Aiken, don't you know me better than that by now?" Owen chided, feeling his "new" cheeks.

"And by the way, where *is* she on a night like this, do you suppose!"

Looking out he studied the torrential spring rain staining the windows with whip-like marks. "She's killing that fine mare with her damned racing around . . ."

Giving a last inspection to the results of his tonsorial art, the horsetender cried, "By God, we'll go then!"

It was difficult to reach the "little house in the woods" even by daylight, for even at that time the village of Cawkwell had ceased to exist except for a farmhouse here and there, and the tiny inlets from the big lake, quaint little clumps of forest, and huge boulders which had arrived here from before time itself, made the route thither a painstaking quest.

And Aiken's criticism of his mother's reckless driving did not prevent his own managing the horse and buggy tonight in the most reckless manner, a result of which was they were landed in a ditch more than once, and came again and again close to careening.

Then having reached where Cawkwell had once stood, they paused before a weather-beaten oak door, with the red glint of light coming from the inner recesses of the house.

His fist raised to beat against this door, Aiken hesitated, nearly turned back. He put his hand on Owen's shoulder. Then with a spurt of fury, anger, he chided: "No, you must get completely out of her hands!"

He pushed open the door.

A very young woman with long skeins of corn-colored hair was seated at a brightly varnished table playing solitaire. A glass of dark wine stood within easy reach of her hand adorned with one great glittering false gem. A look of poorly controlled distrust spread over her full mouth and well-defined chin.

"I've brought you somebody who may be more to your lady-like taste tonight, Lucy . . ."

She smiled in spite of herself, and took a sip of wine.

"And what if I say I won't, Mr. God Almighty?" Lucy retorted, studying a card she had just laid down.

"Then I'll have to order you, for we've little time, and I've no inclination to be civil about it. You're here for it, you owe me favors, and you'll do it."

"Now look here," Lucy threw the whole pack of cards down, "you're in my house, for your information . . ."

But like the trainer of some prized athlete, Aiken was already helping Owen off with his clothes.

"I won't have refusal from the likes of you, Lucy, and you'll not speak of your house here, for 'tis more mine than yours. In any case I'll have none of your lip." He turned his full attention to removing all the rest of Owen's clothes except for a slip of underwear, which he allowed, somewhat contemptuously, to remain.

"In all this world," Lucy addressed Owen, "there doesn't walk a man under the revolving sun who has such black deviltry or pride in his heart . . ."

She had strode up to her persecutor as she said this and struck at him with her fists, but he caught her arms, and held them up, and kissed her solemnly on the mouth several times, and she subsided very much as Lady Bythewaite did when she had touched her mouth to her little bottle.

"Then do you sit in this room," Lucy said, when he had released her arms, "while your pupil and I go yonder." Having said this, she put her arms about Owen, and drew him with her into the adjoining room.

Alone, time ticked by, each minute like an hour, and then by and by Aiken found a half-hidden bottle of her homemade wine, opened it by breaking the neck of the bottle, and having extricated little pieces of glass, tasted cautiously its bitter flavor, grimaced, spat it out, and then spent some time examining his water-soaked boots. He looked into the face of a great-grandfather clock, as ancient as any of those in Lady Bythewaite's mansion, and with a countenance as superior as and even more contemptuous than those of the great house.

Finally in a gelid rage after an hour or so of unaccustomed passivity, he went to the closed door, and beat upon it. When there was no answer, no sound even from within, he called like some worried sentinel in the night: "What are you doing in there, raising a God-damned family?"

Then he flung open the door.

Lucy was already dressing, and Owen, reclining on a high chair, his eyes glassy, his mouth a weal of red marks, was looking apprehensively at the approaching horsetender, who went directly up to the boy and, like an impatient and overworked surgeon, took rough hold of his penis, pulling its foreskin roughly, until from its beginning-to-wilt head came pale thick drops depositing themselves freely on Aiken's palm and fingers.

"And high time too!" the elder brother exclaimed, grinning, wiping his hand dry on his trousers, and then giving Lucy some dark incomprehensible look, pulled out a billfold of ancient creased cowhide, took out some bills, and attempted to hand them lackadaisically to the girl, who, having refused them twice, at last seized them and flung them into his face, and then rushed from the room.

But Aiken's attention had turned now back to the boy, dreamily.

"It's good . . ." he had begun to speak, but some immoderate hoarseness moved up as if from his own groin into his larynx, cutting his voice forthwith.

He pulled Owen almost angrily to him, and held him against his chest, and then to the boy's real if vague terror, gave out three short gruff sounds whether of grief or joy—who knows? —but which resembled very much those of Aiken's fist knocking through the sidings of the barn. He held the boy's head tight against him in a kind of silent thanks until he was quiet again from whatever turmoil he was undergoing.

Then in great clatter and commotion the two left the house, like robbers who never intended to return again.

Stephen Bottrell would never forget how Nora had looked when she entered the Elysian Meadows Theater that evening. The rain, her own tears, her turbulent feelings arising from what she had seen in the mirrors of her house, and later what she had witnessed, without reflection from glass, in the kitchen, had made her (he thought) a beautiful if Gorgon-like vision. And they must have both forgotten her age and where they were, for they embraced with the fresh hunger of new lovers who had been unjustly parted for days rather than a few hours.

Speaking in phrases not unlike the "titles" which helped bear the burden of narrative on the silver screen, Stephen began whispering: "What has gone wrong for my darling while she has been gone from my arms?"

Disentangling herself from his embrace, Nora spoke suddenly very much like the brilliant real-estate financier she was rather than the woman of his dreams:

"He has outstripped me again . . . His cleverness knows no bounds. I know the next move will be my own eviction from my own house."

The thought that his Nora might suddenly become impoverished, homeless, chilled Stephen Bottrell's present ardor.

After clearing his throat, and arranging the crushed carnation in his buttonhole, he proceeded: "Please tell me exactly what has gone amiss, Nora . . . And is *he* you speak of Mr. Skegg?"

A look of grave disappointment swept over her countenance.

"There is only one person who knows where to plunge the knife, Stephen, and then to twist it with the craft and deliberation of the greatest of all criminals . . . I used to think Clarence was cruel . . . But I have met . . . my equal . . ." She had struggled for the word, and *equal* did not please her, but she could not bring herself to say either *master* or *captor*.

"What has *he* done, then, so to overwhelm you?" the photoplay manager inquired, offended, and more than a bit hurt at her interdiction of his words.

She took his hand and held it to her breast.

"Doubtless knowing I was about to return, having waited for the propitious hour, having long rehearsed it in his mind, as I come into the house exhausted, I look into the mirror, to see Owen in a barber chair, years before the boy is ready . . ."

Here cries of impotent rage prevented Nora from continuing,

but his caresses against her breast, the sweet soft breath coming from his mouth against her cheek, encouraged her to get out: "There, tied down by a great white cloth by that devil, covered with thick white froth and foam, *he* was scraping those smooth untouched cheeks and lips with a razor that looked as immense as an executioner's axe!

"And you ask me who *he* was who brought this to pass!" she pulled herself from his arms. "There is only one man with breath in him who could have thought up this kind of punishment for me."

Stephen Bottrell broke into unrestrained laughter at that moment, a laughter of a kind she had not heard since, as an actress in London, she had played in farces, and yet, she stared, open-mouthed at him, for this was his own genuine and characteristic laugh.

"You dare to mock my anguish!" she uttered her cry of warning after a full minute in which she drank in his derision, and then slapped him with forthright deliberation across his rather homely mouth. Unlike Aiken he quailed under her blow, and held his hand to the place struck. But noting that her anger was the real article, that he had misjudged her, that she acted only one role, her own, and that if he wished to prosper he must swallow both his anger and the small amount of blood she had brought to his lips, he was soon back in form, holding her to him, asking her forgiveness, agreeing that she had been right to be so upset, that shaving a boy who as yet had no beard was not the "right thing," and that Aiken was indeed out to destroy them all.

"Well, my dear Stephen, shall we save any further acting for the picture show you have promised me?" she finally spoke in her old confident assured manner, and kissed him on the cheek.

Then they both laughed, and then Lady Bythewaite daubed her eyes with a brocade handkerchief, and said:

"Let us go into your theater . . . I think the horror of seeing Maynard Ewing in a new photoplay may cure me of one grief by giving me yet another . . ."

Overjoyed that she was "game" after their quarrel, Stephen led her inside, but this time he had had the unusual foresight to bring in two overstuffed chairs and a divan of sorts, some pretty Scotch lap robes, and a small table on which rested bottles of "refreshment."

"You have not overlooked a thing, have you?" Nora Bythewaite commented, glancing about from the bare floor to the high vaulting ceiling.

She began to sit down in the overstuffed chair, but then pleading giddiness, she reclined in the generous amplitude of the divan.

"It will be rather a pity without music," Stephen ventured, but she kissed his mouth closed.

By the time Stephen Bottrell had given his command to the operator and the lights had gone out, and the great giant faces were swimming across the screen in front of them, Lady Bythewaite's rage, maternal defeat, presage of coming old age, rancor, bitterness, and true sorrow had been partially replaced by a hunger both for revenge and pleasure, neither of which had ever, she felt, been even faintly satisfied in her long, hard, disappointing life. In the factitious midnight of the photoplay theater, Stephen Bottrell's lips were almost as inviting as the crushed eloquence of the beet-red mouth of Aiken Cusworth.

"I have been unhappy long enough," she told her somewhat unready companion. "I need all and everything you can give me . . ."

When he hesitated, saying, "I must tell you something so that you won't perhaps be too greatly disappointed . . ."

"I already know, my darling," she smoothed the soft cheeks which certainly had not known many more shaves than Owen Haskins. "You have, like all those before you, not had much experience . . ."

"I have had none." He spoke in a choking voice and his head fell across her bosom.

But Lady Bythewaite had known this too, but she also knew there was very little time, as if she had brought all the clocks from her mansion along with her, and all her mirrors too, so this was not the occasion to be proper or dilatory or careful or decent or in deference to any of the other clutter and paraphernalia of the fool's world about her, and then she immediately brought out the throbbing hulk of his flesh from his trousers while cries issued forth like that of an animal which caught, but not injured, is expressing its deep troubled awareness of entrapment.

Lying back at last in his aroused embrace, in the midst of this tumultuous unhoped-for pleasure, she could look then with cool and cautious, relaxed and indifferent eyes at the giant faces which raced across the screen, for as life had betrayed and cheated her, she could cheat and betray it for a few minutes in this dark dank photoplay house where housewives and retired farmers and young men and their girls came to dream, and where at least the pressure of his hard young flesh gave her the fleeting sensation of being herself alive at last, and she smothered his groans and whimperings, his occasional prescience of pain as she commanded him to begin the act over again, and at his renewed exertions which he dared not disobey she swallowed the flow of his saliva and sweat by seeming to cover his entire swimming face with her mouth.

But Stephen's fresh untiring embraces could not efface the vision of Owen's being shaved by the hard earth-stained hands of the horsetender. The ceremony haunted her like an open grave. And Stephen's having laughed at her grief over the shaving of her favorite and only acknowledged son rankled in her bosom long after the pleasure of his lovemaking had been dissipated. And all the time she had lain in the photoplay manager's arms, instructing him in his first act of love, she had thought she was unaware of the giant face of Maynard Ewing on the silver screen or of the giant faces of his numberless passing sweethearts: all the faces indeed had flown past like forests and hills at the window of an express train. But now in the solitude of her room, Maynard Ewing's face came back to her in pitiless detail, almost threatening to efface from her memory the direful vision of Owen Haskins' head slightly bowed, breathing through half-opened lips, his eyes, smarting from the strong soap of the lather, his flesh contracting from the scraping of the straight-razor, his chestnut hair more curly than ever from the exertion he gave to please his barber-brother, and over all his countenance a look of surrender and abject submission to the hand that swept with the open blade.

And the photoplay manager had dared laugh at her anguish! So, it was only a young boy having a shave, being lathered and scraped by his older brother! No more than that! . . . She saw again the gulf that separated any man's vision from her own—even so compliant a specimen as Stephen Bottrell had the veil drawn tight over his eyes, and would never understand her. She was furious now that she had surrendered to him, for the pleasure, now that it was past, seemed small, and his incompetence, the wretched dank darkness of the photoplay theater, the blinding rush of the images on the screen, all lingered on with her, so that she felt she would never walk in sunlight again. She despised herself, and at the same time, even now when her distaste was at its height, she was glad she had done it. She would do it again. It was all that relieved both her tedium and her anguish. She would find more young fools, if necessary, especially should Stephen prove in the future indifferent and inattentive to her needs.

Coming out of her room, and scurrying down the hall, she ran directly into Owen himself. He appeared to be walking in his sleep, and she had to struggle with her own wish not to gaze into his face, which appeared greatly altered even in the imperfect illumination of the hall. Despite her feeling of embarrassment, and helped by his seeming bewilderment as to where he was going, she took his face in her hand, and looked at this face as if she saw the sun shorn of its beams by dismal clouds.

"Am I such a stranger to you, Owen Haskins?" she murmured, resting her hand upon his shoulder. "Has someone else completely supplanted me? You have room in your heart only for him?"

She was a bit taken aback at her own speech, certainly unplanned, but she had not been prepared for a startling change passing somewhere over his face.

"Owen, Owen, what is wrong with your eyes!"

He put his hand up as a kind of shield as if the effect of some sustained injury to him was now known.

She took him in her arms and held him against her breast much in the manner with which Aiken had held him to himself after he had dried his body from the dripping semen of his sex.

At her mention of something being amiss with his eyes, the boy suddenly let out a cry of real pain, and calm now, as she always was when something grave threatened, she helped him into her own bedroom, and held him until he could lie down on a horsehair sofa, while her own eyes looked over various bottles of medicine.

Sitting down beside him, she watched him with hungry perplexity, avoiding the ominous clouding of his pupils. He had then put one hand again over his eyes, but she gently removed this protection and looked into his eyes. What she saw struck her into frozen silence.

Then Owen felt the heavy solid silver spoon with the red medicine against his teeth.

"No, no," he said, "I don't need it, Mother."

"Can you see . . . aught, Owen?" she whispered, holding the spoon still to his clenched teeth.

"Only the smallest ray of light," he responded.

"When did this occur?" she wondered.

"Only just now."

"You must take this medicine, and your eyesight will clear . . ."

When he refused again, angry, she put the spoon in her own mouth, and swallowed it, for it was after all only cherry cordial.

"It will pass, dearest Owen," she comforted him. She waited

beside him until his regular breathing told her that he had fallen into sound slumber.

Before all the traces of winter had gone, summer came with flies, birds, countless flowers and green heavy trees, the air was filled with light and sound, and then the afternoons, which had been cold and blinding, became golden and somnolent.

But Mr. Skegg had no time for the beauties of the season. He stood in a long shaft of sunshine today holding before him a huge sheaf of papers in his trembling hand, papers which, though white, looked to him black as a river of tar. He stood silent before the man who had served him the papers, and on his lips rose words of regret coming from deep within, regret concerning his decision some twenty-four years ago to recognize Clarence legally and take him away from Nora. And though he had been threatening to disinherit Clarence almost from the day he had "recognized" and adopted him, he had had no intention ever to do so. He had no intention of doing so now when the "legal" man from several towns away had handed him the mass of documents which he now held incredulous before him. No, Mr. Skegg would not desert someone who had got himself over his head into the most complicated and appalling financial difficulties he had ever come across in all his years in business.

A Mr. Emscote had brought all these papers and made him a gift of them. Mr. Emscote was even older than Mr. Skegg, was always dressed in inky black, and wore a necktie which resembled a pair of discarded shoelaces; on one hand he wore a real diamond ring, which sparkled in a kind of accusatory manner. Mr. Emscote only appeared, like the undertaker, when total ruin had already overtaken a man and his family.

"And you have the gall to stand there and tell me you went first to Lady Bythewaite rather than me about this grave matter?" Mr. Skegg began at last, gazing down at the bulging sheaf of legal papers which the process-server had bequeathed to him.

"I stopped at her house, sir, I did indeed," Mr. Emscote answered back, not as loftily, however, as he might have wished.

"And why, may I ask, did you stop there when it is I who am the father of the ruined Clarence Skegg and who am alone responsible?"

Mr. Emscote considered this question lengthily in silence, too lengthily and too silently for Mr. Skegg, who proceeded:

"Did you not know furthermore that Lady Bythewaite is too ill to receive visitors?"

Mr. Emscote seemed puzzled by the notion that illness, any illness could exonerate one from being informed of his or her financial ruin.

"It was my understanding, Mr. Skegg," he recommenced, after a pursing of his lips meaning he would not now take up the peripheral question of illness, "and my weighed judgment that only Lady Bythewaite would be able to meet the responsibility and obligation which the papers in your possession challenge one to shoulder without further ado!"

"I see!" Mr. Skegg vociferated, stung at this bold reference to his financial disgrace. "And how, do tell me, did Lady Bythewaite receive this very great knowledge on your part concerning her responsibility and obligation?"

"Lady Bythewaite, Mr. Skegg, like you, may face a lawsuit in the very near future, for she forcibly drove me out of her house." The old attorney spoke with roused irascible dignity and also certainty of coming legal redress.

"You wouldn't refer to assault and battery, by chance," Mr. Skegg could barely restrain a sneer.

"I do refer to assault and battery, sir, for your information."

"Then may I ask you to leave my house immediately, Mr. Emscote, before I commit the same breach of the peace on your person as did Lady Bythewaite!"

How long Mr. Skegg stood with the papers in his hand, he did not know. He had been unaware of the precise moment of the departure of the process-server, as a matter of fact. He had been carried back in memory to his Wall Street days, to the black Monday when he had been "destroyed," and had been a few days later forced to come home to Prince's Crossing and begin his fortunes all over again as little better than a dirt farmer. That bleak day, some thirty years ago, when he had acknowledged himself ruined, he had found himself wandering about Broad Street in the financial district of the metropolis, in a state of incoherence, without his hat, which to Mr. Skegg then and even now was almost as great an impropriety as appearing in public without one's trousers.

But today as on that day so long ago he had finally come "to," and searching out his hat, put it on, and looking about now and seeing no sign of Mr. Emscote, he shook his fist in the direction of the departing old shyster, and walked out onto the main highway.

Mr. Skegg walked all the way to Nora Bythewaite's house, although his brand-new car, which Mr. Emscote must have studied or rather inventoried as something not long to be in the maggot's possession, was waiting to convey him there. To his added consternation, if anything could add to it, once arrived, he found all the gates and other impediments which made Lady Bythewaite's property resemble a military fortress opened and unbarred, and her front door gaping open, allowing an army of flies free to enter.

Mr. Skegg stood respectfully on the threshold, hardly daring to advance a further step, thinking indeed that Mr. Emscote's visit had proved decisive and that she had killed herself from chagrin after reading the papers which the shyster had submitted for her perusal.

At last, Mr. Skegg cried in the favored manner of the inhabitants of Prince's Crossing, "Whoo-hoo!" and waited to learn if she had done anything rash.

Death had not arrived, and Gorgon-grim she faced him, but it was clear she did not see him, either because of her own imperfect eyesight or because of her present deep preoccupation.

"My dear Nora," he began, but she raised her arms in so peremptory a manner that the words were cut short in his throat.

Going directly up to her, and taking her hands in his, he corrected her mistaken impression: "No, I am not old Emscote come back to plague you . . ."

"Then you've seen, you've been with that molting old carrion! You know the extent of your ruin!" She spoke with some of her old invincibility. "Cannot you still smell him?" she inquired, sniffing the air. "There is no stench like that of a feasting vulture . . . We are fumigating at any moment, so be brief with your business, Mr. Skegg."

She motioned for him to sit down, while she gave the impression she might go on standing forever.

"You have come here doubtless, Mr. Skegg, to upbraid me, to join your voice to the chorus of disapproval which is rising against me," she began to his own considerable astonishment. Having said this, she waved a small envelope in the air as if she held a weapon recently employed by her assailant against her.

"Upbraid *you*, Nora, I? when if anybody is to be put to shame it is me."

She turned her full gaze upon him, wondering.

"Certainly Mr. Emscote has told you both Clarence and I are ruined."

"Ah, and so you are," she acknowledged this. "There is no doubt on that score . . . But you speak as if you had not counted on one friend who will help you."

The old man looked wearily away from her face of lightning.

"That friend stands here, Mr. Skegg, but calumniated." And having ceased to wave the letter about in the air, she thrust it into his unwilling hands.

"Read it."

Perplexed how any letter could take precedence over the crash of fortune whose messenger Mr. Emscote had been, Mr. Skegg adjusted his spectacles and began poring over the epistle, but soon concluded his reading with the cry "Why, it's only anonymous!"

"But do you believe what is written there?" she countered.

Mr. Skegg began to be almost relieved at this sudden change

in the order of business, though the letter, while somewhat trivial to him in the face of his own and Clarence's ruin, was of course scurrilous.

"But, Nora, everyone knows you are not a . . . common whore," he quoted with some hesitation from the letter under study. "And you could not be the *lover* of young Stephen Bottrell!" He shook the page of the epistle briefly as if perhaps some further elucidation might fall out from it.

"I am, you mean, neither a whore nor Mr. Bottrell's lover, Mr. Skegg, because I am too old to be anything but the bride either of death or of that ancient buzzard Mr. Emscote, the public prosecutor!"

Instead of replying, Mr. Skegg folded the anonymous letter and handed it back to its owner.

"Mr. Emscote, nonetheless, will not forget the interview which he had with me this morning. He will remember it on his deathbed, he will dream of it in his grave!"

Walking up and down the room, in her original manner of trying to remember her next lines, and swallowing hard several times, she went on: "As to *your* ruin," she addressed him now with supreme contempt and condescending pity, and then going rapidly up to where he sat she took from him all the accusing papers which Mr. Emscote had conferred on him, "as to your ruin and Clarence's, hear one thing! I am prepared to sell all I have to buy up his debts and yours. I can live with the name of whore and seducer of my own sons, but I cannot live a bankrupt . . ."

"But there is no need to ruin you . . ."

"No one is going to ruin Nora Bythewaite!" she shouted into his unprepared face, her saliva, like that of Aiken Cusworth's in anger, spraying him generously, and her anger defying him to wipe his face dry of it while she gazed at him.

"I have told Emscote I will buy up all these (she struck the legal papers), but I have also told him that he will not be permitted ever to enter this house again, for I will shoot him as a housebreaker should he do so . . . And I'll have the writer of this letter brought to the bar of judgment!" she went on, tearing the letter now into a myriad of little pieces. "Death is too good for the writer of this!"

Then, as always was the case with her, the tempest had passed, and she sat down in her armchair, and began reading through the many documents which chronicled the fall of Clarence and the old maggot. However, even her recent bravery and effrontery was riddled a bit by this close perusal, her jaw dropped slightly, and as she paused over this documented record of folly, her mind would go back to the face of Maynard Ewing as it had flitted for her across the silver screen, and her mind recalled the explanatory "titles" as clearly as if she was back in the Elysian Meadows Theater holding the hand of Stephen Bottrell:

> If we should part, it will only be because fate is stronger than even our love.

Her eye returned from the remembered "titles" of the great screen to the damning documents before her. She read on, but the denomination of the figures, the extent of Clarence's indebtedness, the black and white record of such daring follies stunned her brain, her eyes smarted from the accumulation of all she had seen, and her attention kept creeping back to shadowy Maynard Ewing and the "titles," as if now and now alone and for the first time she was a witness to one of his films:

> I loved you first before all other women, and my love for you will be my last.

"Nora!" Mr. Skegg sought her attention. "I do fear this has unhinged you more than it has me . . ."

But her closed eyes could only see more great words on the screen:

> It was you who sent me away, cruelest of the cruel, when I would have remained with you forever.

All the recorded accumulation of Clarence Skegg's foolishness had fallen from her lap to the floor, and Mr. Skegg was at her feet, gathering the papers together, when, whether because of her confused state, or out of remembrance of old vanished tenderness and the common bond of their exiled son, she took his white head in her fluttering hands, eyes open now, and held it fervently.

Just as in the silent movies when something all too often went wrong with the film, and the lights had to come on in unforeseen intermission and the spectators awoke full of sleep, so the great-nephew's reels often broke during that long recital, and then, rolled back, began to repeat the whole story over again, and I (Eneas Harmond) would jump up then from the slumber of listening, a slumber as deep as if I rested under all the waters of the lake, and then rising to the water's surface, blinked into the morning sun.

But even in these intermissions in which the eye opened suddenly and as suddenly the giant faces and the "titles" vanished, one saw and heard (so it appears to me) the "silence" of the story louder and brighter than a thousand suns exploding before the eye.

"What shall we do, my dear?" he whispered against her cheek. "We can't let him go to prison . . ."

"But so much money, dear Nora. More than a fortune!"

"I will sell more or all of my farms."

Then extricating herself from him as she would have from some impure embrace, as Lucy had used to pull her body from the brutal "mount" of the horsetender Aiken, and become now again cold Lady Bythewaite, she rose, she thundered:

"This grief you have shared with me is as nothing to what I suffer now under my own roof!"

He raised his eyes in astonished sympathy.

"I am not mistress in my own house! I am a prisoner to him! He has no pity for me, he loves only Owen, whom he has taken away from me forever. Why mention the author of my own ruin, you know his name, as you know Lucifer's . . . This is my pain . . ."

"Oh, Nora," Mr. Skegg was again the postulant, "I wish you would not speak in these riddles, or of things that make no sense, when these very real palpable dangers press home so . . ."

"Oh, Almighty God," she cried, leaning against the peach wood of her desk, scattering sheets of figures everywhere, "am I never to know one calm moment, one respite from rolling time . . ."

She thought then of nothing but Clarence's ruin, and her anguish could find respite only in her eternal pacing of the floor, and doing up her long black hair in one style after another, ceaselessly taking in and out her ivory hairpins, absent-mindedly bringing one of them to her lips. Her authority, diminished by grief, caused the two brothers Owen and Aiken to run even more wildly about the bounds of her enormous estate. Once looking out the dormer window she caught sight of Aiken stark naked as he went about his endless tasks in the sun. But she was actually only to "see" this vision of her own dethronement with any retention of its meaning when she was riding on the Big Four train to New York a few days thereafter.

For she was pacing in so disconcerted a manner now because she knew she was going to New York. There was no one else to send, for one thing, all her messengers had achieved nothing, and she knew, too, her own mission would be to no avail. It was too late to salvage Clarence, but she might, she thought, prevent him doing any greater mischief. She would tie his hands. She would bring him home tied.

But how could she leave her "kingdom" where no one contradicted her, where she had no rivals, and where even her own mirrors most of the time softened the truth, at least reflected no other mistress than her. She had not been to New York in over twenty years! She had nothing decent to wear, she did not even know what women wore! She who had once been, at least for a short time, of a style all her own. Clarence would be ashamed of her. He might not even recognize her. But then recalling Mr. Skegg's grim picture of his ruin, would it matter? If Clarence was as ruined as the documents showed, he would not notice or care that his mother was démodé. And then the peril of leaving her house and property in the possession of safekeeping with Aiken Cusworth! No, she could not go. And yet she could not stay.

The heat of summer had begun, and her sons did not go to bed now until the worst of the heat had gone out of the old house. They sat in the kitchen playing endless games of dominoes. The sound of the oblong pieces being moved made her uneasy; she felt people were playing with human bones, and the tiny pieces banged down on the table had a fateful depressing sound to her ears.

One evening, angered by the incessant shuffling of the ivory oblongs in their game, she had rushed to the kitchen to interdict another move of the dominoes, but having arrived on the threshold noiselessly, unobserved, she stopped short in her tracks. A look of such perfect contentment, peace, even fulfillment was on the faces of both the young men that she had not the heart to shatter this fraternal bliss. She retreated to her own black mood, her doomed lonesome pacing, but depressed even more by the thought that their happiness, the perfection of their communion would not last, but like perfection itself, like all things from the hand of mysterious creation, would soon change, be no more, be forgotten in dwindling time. She was not even jealous any more. She felt for them, despite herself, a sense of satisfaction, even fulfillment.

The next day Aiken noted she was packing. Astonished, he stood at the open door of her room, in the respectful, bowed manner which had been characteristic of him when he had been only her livery stableman.

"Yes, Aiken," she called from within, "I am going away for a spell . . . I am not running off, and I will be back, though I wonder if you would not be happier if I never returned . . . I am going to see Clarence Skegg." Here she stopped, overcome by many conflicting sensations, so that she felt as if a great cloud had settled in her lungs.

"I have noticed something that troubles me, Lady Bythewaite." Aiken addressed her with the calm formality of older days.

She looked up and studied him sharply. Whether it had been his winter of hard riding, his new clothes, or what, Aiken had turned to pure sinew, whereas before he had had a certain touch of stoutness coming from perfect health.

"I believe he has something seriously wrong with his eyes," Aiken spoke almost inaudibly.

"Whose eyes?" She flung these words out while inspecting a flowered cotton dress, and shaking her head over its unpromising character.

"Whose eyes but Owen's," Aiken responded somewhat tartly.

She let the dress slip from her fingers and studied him more closely.

"They seem to cloud over, and then for a minute or so he cannot see . . ."

"It's your rough horseplay, Aiken. You wear the boy out . . ." But the horsetender could see that something troubled her too in the information he had conveyed to her.

"I know that I will be leaving Owen in good hands," Lady Bythewaite indicated she would not pursue the subject of Owen's vision further. And now rare for her, she took Aiken's hands in hers, without pressure, but without coldness.

"Why are you going, Lady Bythewaite?" Aiken spoke almost boisterously, certainly loudly, rousing her from reverie.

"There's nobody left to be sent to him but me. Clarence has gone through two fortunes. He's bankrupt, penniless, in great debt, perhaps faces jail. His career as an actor seems over. So I am told. He hardly knows his own face when he sees it in a mirror. Do you have my reason for going now? And besides who else can stand to go . . ."

"Shan't I stand it?" Aiken protested, half-raising his hand in a strange entreating gesture.

She stared at him. "I've already told you there's only one person left who can do it. You're facing her. You mean, Aiken, you don't think I'm up to it?" She laughed her special hollow kind of laugh. "Well, I'm *not* up to it. I don't know that I've ever been up to anything. Perhaps nobody is up to whatever is handed him to perform in this world. That could be. I will look pretty awful in New York, having lost touch with everything for so long. But he's too far gone to care, I daresay, how out of date I look or am. He may even be glad to see a familiar face, or it may be too late for him to know a familiar face."

Then having folded with growing repugnance some last articles for her valise, she walked up close to Aiken and said:

"Owen has always had some trouble with his eyes since he was a baby. Don't let it afflict you."

She made this statement with a kind of angry tone of defense and humiliation.

She had expected the world to smirk at her, deride her, find her clothes and her face cast-offs and period pieces. But everyone before whom she appeared, from the Pullman porters and conductors, on to the taximen and the manager of the modest hotel at which she registered, gave her more than an ordinary recognition and reception. Was it her manner which arrested their attention, the remains of her once stunning personal endowments, her imperiousness, or perhaps her contempt of the world, more thoroughgoing than that of a saint. Whatever it was, whatever she had, Lady Bythewaite's appearance in New York at least was a success. She found of course nothing to her taste. The buildings were too ridiculously tall, the physiognomy of its inhabitants too dark and low of forehead, its speech the accumulated detritus of languageless immigrants, its haste, appetite for money, and delirious pleasureless lust for novelty and noise immediately disgusted and wearied her. She was ready to return home after an hour within the metropolis' confines.

But first, after her all-day-and-night journey, she must rest, be calm, be stronger than she had ever been before in order to meet the one person who had outstripped her both in glory and in ignominy. She wondered whether she could forgive him for either accomplishment. She would try, but she felt she was not a generous woman, and her love for no human being had ever been truly tested. She also knew that as she stood at the threshold of old age, she was to be tested beyond the endurance of perhaps even her own indisputable strength. Of course, she muttered, every breath we draw is a test, a kind of contest and torment, including the last we draw when the soul at last—well, she would not now think of *at last*.

The more the time drew near for her meeting with Clarence Skegg, the less prepared she was. Her eyes, always the weakest point in her constitution, bothered her more and more. She remembered with trepidation too now Aiken's warning about Owen's affliction, but her own present malaise drove even his suffering from her mind. Whether she closed her eyes or opened them she saw now only the motes from the silver screen darting everywhere, the giant face, the giant "titles" with their imbecilic sentimentality and melodrama, which to her continued surprised disgust somehow moved her, the vulgarity of the emotions touching her, as certain loathsome smells invite the nostrils to continue whiffing:

> Before there was time,
> we loved.

She held her hand over her eyes, still seeing his giant eyes, mouth, billowing hair.

The silver screen, she mused, was, however, less monstrous than the island of Manhattan with its inhuman towers and the ape-like cacophonous speech of its deracinated inhabitants, and here everyone everywhere who appeared before the reeling eye was selling or sold, or discarded, eaten to husks by the steel and concrete of the machine that was the island's only soul or substance.

> Are there no flowers
> bare winter brings?

Then finally, despite her many hours of self-prohibition, she took her tiny bottle and from it extracted its smallest dosage, and then the motes and the idiot "titles" of love stopped, the giant faces swam into nothingness.

She was ready for Clarence Skegg, for Maynard Ewing was, if they had apprised her right, and unless that molted vulture Mr. Emscote was only a phantom messenger of ill-tidings, Maynard Ewing of the silver screen had been vanquished and was gone forever.

She waited a day more, when if not eager to see Clarence she felt at least resigned to her task, and then, haunted by the knowledge she might also have to become a detective in order to find him, she set out.

When she appeared at the gold-turreted hotel at which Clarence had had his quarters, and from which he had composed such terrifying letters and telegrams to the father who had disinherited him, her unheralded appearance created more than a mild sensation. The manager, coming out from a saffron room filled with anemones, took her immediately by the hand, mistaking her, she saw at once, for some celebrity in her own right.

Lady Bythewaite's attention was fixed, however, not on the inquiring white face and dyed sideburns of the manager, who implored her how he might serve her, but on his soft womanish wrinkled hands, which she felt should be covered with white gloves to hide their unpleasantness.

Convinced as he was he had with him some prestigious, undeniably great woman of the past, of whom he was unfortunately in black ignorance, the hotel manager raised her calloused hand to his lips, and then led her in subdued triumph into his sumptuous receiving room. Tea was served, and a string of unsteady compliments was thrown lavishly, if carelessly, by him in her enthroned direction, and then, in growing confusion, if not panic, the manager asked her sotto voce with whom he had the honor of conversing.

"Lady Bythewaite" came her stentorian reply, given without affectation but in genuine forgetfulness after all that this appellation which passed for common coin or at most a fanciful nickname in Prince's Crossing was here in the metropolis open to misconstruction.

At the sound of her "title," the manager blanched and quailed, and his mouth became too dry for speech, for it had been a lengthy age since aristocracy had occupied his great damask chair.

Presently, however, he came to himself, and said: "And why,

Lady Bythewaite, did you not announce yourself far in advance of your coming, my very distinguished visitor?"

"Because, sir, I do not come here on my own account but on that of my son Maynard Ewing, the star of the silent screen . . ."

The manager stood up. He looked about him like a man who has been whirled through the air and then violently and unceremoniously dropped into a room unfamiliar, if not unfriendly, to him.

"*Your* son, Madame?" the perplexed manager echoed this statement, blinking violently.

"You could not have mentioned a name which would have given me a greater sense of pride had it been spoken even a short time ago, say a week, dear Madame," he began with a kind of mechanical fluency and a certain regaining of his composure. "But for today, let me confess it, the name gives me personal sorrow, if only because Maynard has left us so unceremoniously . . ."

"And of course in debt!"

He waited with a certain lengthy condescension as if this last remark had been unheard.

"Allow me to introduce myself," the manager spoke now in a sad humming voice so that he brought back to mind the manner of Mr. Emscote in his role of official vulture, bestowing upon her his papers. "I am, Madame, Mr. Lobthorpe."

Lady Bythewaite did not take his extended hand, indeed she did not even see it.

"Your glorious son," Mr. Lobthorpe nonetheless went on, "needless to repeat, is no longer with us . . . I hope I do not pain you if I say that you cannot be ignorant of his recent eclipse, if not his fall . . ."

"I have not come here, Mr. Lobthorpe, to speak of his eclipse or his fall, but of his whereabouts . . ."

"Precisely, quite so," Mr. Lobthorpe bowed to her correction. "But allow me to say only this . . . Maynard Ewing, whatever the world may say today, will rise again! No question of it! He will again be over us in all the illumination of his past glory."

Lady Bythewaite stared at Mr. Lobthorpe with a deepening scowl.

"You do not have the information, then, sir, which I have come seeking," and she indicated that she would now leave his reception room in consequence of the bankruptcy of his knowledge by half-turning from him.

"Don't spurn one who would do all for you if he could!" On this speech pronounced by the hotel manager, Lady Bythewaite wheeled round, for his words sounded like something spoken to her in her night of dreams.

"I did all in my power, dear Lady Bythewaite, to save him, for he was far superior to any and all who ever resided in this gilded world . . . But he left in anger, and with no wish to be saved . . ."

He took her hands now, and kissed them profusely.

Then quickly walking with his old pomposity into the lobby, Mr. Lobthorpe clapped peremptorily, summoned employees, young and old, strange large-bosomed women with the war paint common then to the New York feminine face, and strange men of indeterminate age with haunted eyes and long eyelashes, house detectives who resembled seriously ill bulldogs, and even a threadbare paretic old man who summoned taxis for the grand and the wealthy. But despite Mr. Lobthorpe's relentless questioning of them, none knew, none remembered where Maynard Ewing (whose name, she saw with sad half pride, stirred something in their ruined characters), where that great giant face had disappeared to. He was gone, on that all agreed—certainly he was not here.

And so, with a few "possible" addresses and other information handed to her by a rueful Mr. Lobthorpe, she began her search through a city which she despised more with each glimpse she got of its imperial wealth rooted in filth and rats and decay, going from one end of the island to the next, stopping first at more or less medium-priced hotels and lodging houses, then shabby ones, then wretched ones, and finally, on a tip from one of her later chauffeurs who knew the name of Maynard

Ewing, in lower Broadway, she came to a place whose door looked like the discarded filaments of innumerable cobwebs. Her heart—was it?—more likely her bowels—told her where she was, for this was certainly the place. But she would take no medicine, for she felt stronger than if she had swallowed her whole bottle of opiate, strong as she had felt the day the cyclone struck, when everyone had looked to her for strength.

She nearly turned back, nonetheless, when she faced the creature at the register of the "hotel." He was, however, more frightened by her than she was of him, for drunk and asleep, he had opened his eyes to look into a countenance of such fierceness, anger, disapprobation, and judgment that he felt out of all the years of his own life brought to ruin he was about to hear for the last time the old cry *The prisoner may approach the bench.*

"It's room number twenty-three, Madame," the registrar managed to inform her, after a lengthy wait, during which she had repeated her question many times, since, as was to be expected, her son had not given his correct name, but the man at the desk had known almost from the moment she had appeared who it was she was seeking.

As she started up the creaking, careening staircase, she heard the man from the desk say, "Regulations forbid ladies to go upstairs."

She turned her head slowly and fixed him as if with her hatpin.

"I am Lady Bythewaite."

When he still hesitated, putting his hand on the banister almost against her dress, she opened her purse and, with a movement of acute loathing, gave him a bill.

"Whatever you do," she warned him as he withdrew from her, "do not come upstairs. Is that clear?"

It was pitch dark inside his room, hardly wider than her own arm stretched out to the form on the tiny cot.

"I want nothing." His voice, recognizable but so changed, pronounced these words.

She raised the shred of a yellowed blind, but she did not look down on the cot from which the voice came.

"Is there a chair to sit down on, Clarence?" she wondered listlessly.

"No. Use the floor."

She sat down on the cot beside him, but her eyes were closed.

"Clarence," she said at last, but when she opened her eyes, for all her years of training in a harsh school, and for all her fortitude and backbone, she let out a great short gasp as she saw him, "I've come to take you home . . ."

One could smell the blossoms of plum trees, and the mixed, ever intermingling perfume of countless other blooms, wild flowers, silent nodding trees in foliage, and everywhere the eye rested, long waving grasses.

Occasionally Aiken would lift his nose, sniffing, from his task of repairing an old cart he planned to use that day, like a man who fears all this verdure and mingled delicious attar might unnerve him for work. At his side, in mute obedience and admiration, sat Owen with the peculiar glaucous expression in his eyes.

"Since the lady of the castle has deserted us we'll go for as long drives as horse and cart will take us," Aiken spoke almost in singsong.

From time to time he would give Owen a piercing look with his own unclouded brilliant black eyes, those eyes Owen feared always to look into, but sometimes now Aiken would insist, as a kind surgeon might, and he would look into the boy's eyes fixedly, but would then counterfeit his feelings and thoughts and look away, or bark at Owen's *What is it, Aiken?* a ferocious command for silence.

"We'll enjoy the countryside, and we'll throw our cares to the wind," Aiken exclaimed as he finished the last of the repairs on the old cart. "No cross, no crown!" he quipped, borrowing one of the stock expressions from church meeting.

But unlike their wild country rides of last winter, when the roads were all but impassable, and the icy winds and sleet made sensible travelers stay inside, while they had raced like the very elements, Aiken was now in the mood to drive at a slow ambling pace, as if the soft perfume from the plum trees had softened his incomprehensible savagery and made it slumber.

Indeed, today he took so long to say "Gee-hup," the reins

lying slack in his brown hands, that Owen blinked up at him, wondering, if nonetheless content, and then at last the boy heard the command to the horse, a command which seemed to come tunneling up from under the cart, from within the dark earth.

The quiet ambling of the horse and cart sometimes made Owen fall fast asleep, and the driver, with both impatience and gratification, would pull his head over toward him to prevent a fall, and Owen would lean then on his shoulder, and the two would ride on like this for miles in a kind of drowsy, dozing incoherence so that they looked indeed more like sleepers at midnight than riders under the scalding sun of high noon, and farmers who knew Aiken for his rough manners, vile temper, and pugnacious even bloodthirsty ways, stared in patent unbelief at so brutal and uncivil a man plodding along with loose reins and nodding head, resembling one who had come at last into some peace and understanding with himself not exactly promised in this life.

But as the sun westered and passed from sight, something of his old irritability and anger would return, he would shake the boy roughly and jerk him into attention, and they would drive on at a more rapid rate, stopping occasionally under some huge oak tree, not yet in full leaf, to drink some cider and munch thick, rather dry pieces of bread and roughly cut pieces of beef.

Then as the shadows lengthened into dark, they would ride on, through back roads and sections of woodland peopled now with the cries of unseen birds and stealthy small beasts.

One night, far, or so it seemed, from their home, Owen was awakened from his secure place against his brother's shoulder by great angry cries, his nestling position was abruptly denied him, his head fell against the cart, he heard from a short distance Aiken's impassioned imprecations, and it was he who heard this time the word, rotten, vile, but unknown to him except in its blinding blasphemy, a word like, yes, *whippoorwill*.

Looking up and over, he saw Aiken protesting against what a knot of young men had evidently taunted him with, that word, but between slumber and half-waking, he could not credit his eyes with what he saw. The men stood on the porch of a tavern which had once been a farmhouse, from within which pale kerosene lamps burned sickly flickering. Aiken's impassioned tones again arose through the night, the crickets stopped their chirping, and some lone night bird gave out its throaty note in the far edge of a woods.

Then the sound of knuckles beating bone, the fists flying, the cries of pain and astonishment.

Aiken was surrounded by the knot of men, and then Owen saw with more than his pride dare dictate the knot diminish and dissipate as Aiken struck down one after another of his insulters, until one burly man remained, and next with great slowness Aiken knocked him against the pillar of the old frame house, which like a bunch of matches gave way and split in two. Then he glimpsed Aiken pommeling yet again that man. He rubbed his eyes hard, they blurred, he saw nothing for a minute, then he saw a thousand suns explode, and then darkness, and then Aiken sitting beside him again, his hands, his knuckles flowing with the blood he could not see, but nearly taste, and deeply smell.

"You'll have to drive, Owen, for I've considerably damaged my hands on those lowdown fuckers."

When Owen did not respond, he shook him roughly.

"Damn you, I said you was to drive, you contemptible little whelp. Are you blind!" He struck him across his face, then gasped, and drew back, for the blood from his contest with the men stained the boy's face as completely as if he had been painted with a red brush.

"God-damn it all to hell," the older man cried, taking the reins, and then, busted knuckles or not, drove off like a wild comet into the thick of the night.

"Looking like she had stepped out of a bandbox!" Clarence Skegg had smiled from out the face which his mother had found unrecognizable, and which had made her eyes, strive as she would to prevent them, stream with corroding tears, silent, but which he saw. Indeed she had thought at first, and the idea kept coming to her, that she had crept into a total stranger's room, for did not look like either Clarence Skegg or Maynard Ewing, or indeed anybody whom she had ever even known, but his voice, that she knew, and the voice that now spoke to her was Clarence Skegg's, the country twang in it, the slurred syllables, the homely accentuation, a far cry from dramatic school.

She tried to look at his face but could only take it in with short hurried oblique glimpses, and each sight of his ruined features brought up from within her such violent motions the chair on which she sat (which she had fetched from a room nearby) creaked and appeared to give.

"You should have come when I was in my glory, sweetheart," he said, struggling feebly to rise on one elbow.

She barely nodded.

"You never change, Nora Bythewaite," he whispered, for his voice, even when he could summon it forth, seemed now to be gone, and even this whisper came from a very far distance. "It must be the open air and sky which makes you so good-looking." His mouth, pressed downward, was speaking into the filthy mattress he lay on. "Or perhaps it is the sun . . ."

"I want you to come home with me, Clarence," Nora Bythewaite began after an endless wait, and she fingered the clasp on her great purse. "Now."

"Never, never, Nora Bythewaite." He stopped because of the cough which came as if clear from the boards beneath them, then got out: "I don't even want my body shipped back to that collection of mud puddles." His exertions to speak made his wasted face even more unrecognizable, if possible, and she looked at him intently, for what in all that chalky whiteness could she call her own son? "Go back there, Nora, dead or alive, and have them laugh at my rise and fall, as they crow from their dunghills whenever anything noteworthy passes . . ."

"No one need see you but myself, Clarence . . . And if you wish we will sell all our lands and property, and go far off, never return, never so much as look back . . ."

"Never return," he considered this phrase, and something of his old dramatic flair came through feebly.

"You cannot stay here in any case, Clarence . . ."

"Oh, I don't know. It's not so very terrible when the light's out," he opined.

There was another silence, during which she closed, then opened, then closed again the clasp on her purse, evoking sounds like those from a ruined clock.

"I'll never go back, Nora . . . I'd be happier with a rat, with a spider's nest than to go back there . . . And how, by the way, is that sailing corpse, Mr. Skegg?" He sat bolt upright now and roared with some sort of unpremeditated rage.

She laughed at his remark in spite of herself.

"You would never need see him, Clarence."

"*Clarence*," he mused. "I once hated that name, but it sounds sort of good now, don't it? I suppose it's me, after all, if I have a me. Nora . . . You know," and he turned fully toward her at last, blinking, "you were my all-in-all, you know that . . . The realest thing about Mr. Skegg was his watch chain, and his high shoes, and maybe his stiff collar. What was under all those appurtenances, I often wondered. You, on the other hand, Nora, are all mistakes and fever and blood, and so I hold you dear, but you can't help me any more than he did . . . No, I belong with the rat that lives in the wall, and the trap-door spider over yonder . . . Go back to that crossing? You know that cannot be . . . Our love is done, Nora. My life is done. I long so for

rest, final rest from myself . . . Don't call me back to life . . .
Go home, go home!"

He drew the sheet over his face and turned his eyes under
it in the direction of the wall.

How many years had he been gone? It seemed an eternity
and yet it may have been only yesterday. Time was not one of
her strong points. And how long did she stay in that "house"
with him which was one stop before the crematorium? She could
not say any better than she could tell her own age, or when
Clarence Skegg had left home. But she came to the black awful
house daily, brought him unwanted sustenance, which he refused or partaking usually ejected, she waited with him all
through the night, scandalizing those who were beneath or beyond scandal and calumny, mystified the world, and went out
at last beaten and alone.

"Go away," he had said to her at last. "I never want to see
your face again in this life or the next, do you hear? You marked
me with the thing that is eating me up, so spare your theatrical
sighs and tears . . . Oh, you are acting every minute of your
life! This is a great scene, made-to-order for you, your eternal
madonna role . . . But go back to your own stage and leave me
to rot in mine, Nora Bythewaite. You're rich and beautiful and
have everything, but you shall not have your eldest son. Never
again. Sit here till this claptrap island itself drifts out to ocean,
I'll never be yours again . . ."

After the free-for-all, and driving home with the greatest difficulty, for his hands seemed badly damaged by his fistfight, assisted from time to time by Owen, who, despite the boy's failing eyesight, seized the reins when they were about to fall from the driver's numbed fingers, Aiken Cusworth could barely drag himself to the great kitchen, and there on a small davenport provided for the exhaustion of cooks and pantry maids he threw himself down with a finality and surrender which made his evening companion tremble and shudder.

Kneeling beside the davenport, the boy began taking off Aiken's heavy boots, and this done he walked unsteadily into the next room, which appeared, as he tried to look about, a shimmering dazzling array of the indistinguishable objects, but at last he found what he sought, the Scotch lap robe, and stumbled back into the kitchen and threw it over the fighter's limbs. Then he listened to the heavy arhythmic breathing, punctuated by snorts, and with peering difficulty he studied Aiken's battered fists, and probed the bones under the flesh. There was nothing broken. His hero would live, he guessed. A great sigh of relief came up from the boy when he heard, after a bit, steady snoring from the horsetender. Owen lay his own head on the davenport and blinked his eyes. How long he lay there he did not know, for he felt so at peace, until he heard a voice so much deeper than he remembered Aiken's being in daylight, a voice which indeed sounded as if it came from some black sunken hopeless kingdom:

"Where was you all those six months?"

Was the speaker tossing in sleep? was he addressing him? Yes, he was indeed, for he felt the injured hand take up his head, and he felt Aiken's breath against his face. Aiken was looking into his failing eyeballs.

"You never told me, Owen, and it has given me many a bad night, when I've laid up there wondering, for I blame myself . . ." He violently let go of the boy's head and fell wearily back on the gutted davenport. "You must one day remember, and you must come to me then when you do . . . I am the one you must come to, remember . . ."

After what seemed hours, Owen heard his brother's voice again:

"Six months in the life of a boy, a young man like you—not accounted for! Why does nobody ask for a reckoning for such a blank!"

He lifted himself up now painfully, and again began staring at Owen, who kept his head down, like a postulant who expects final rejection.

"You don't withhold this information to make me feel guilty, Owen, do you?" Aiken spoke almost with a pathetic querulous note, which recalled Lady Bythewaite when she had imbibed too many drops from her medicine bottle.

Owen raised his head at last, and there was anger in his voice when he said, "I've given you everything I have, I will give you my life if you demand it, but I can't give you what I can't fish up. Where is it, how would I know!" He peered hard toward his interlocutor to see that black face begging him for knowledge in the gloom of the kitchen.

"What I have to give you I will give, but don't ask for more!" he shouted at last so that Aiken himself was astonished into silence.

"And," the boy began, babbling, incoherent, "what *word* was that they shouted to you tonight that made you rush toward those men like some wild swollen river at floodtime! What terrible word was that which should make you foam at the mouth? Answer me that, you who fish for things that are beyond anyone's reach!"

"I don't know what word you are talking about, save that they yelled some insult at me." Aiken spoke in muted neutral tones, and turned his face away now from his questioner.

"But what was the *word* that should make you so boiling mad, for look at you," the boy went on with vehemence, and picked up his brother's damaged fist, "all for what?"

"They yelled, I say, some insult," Aiken spoke gravely but absent-mindedly, and it was clear he could not or would not recall what word they had shouted. "They're a mean low-down lot, and have been spoiling for my fists," he finished with more decisive satisfaction. "I'm only sorry I didn't kill two of them . . . But my not remembering some crud of insult ain't the equivalent of your losing six months! I tell you, it unnerves me, Owen, it is a thing that will not let me be . . . Why does *she* not worry about it? And will it come again?" He spoke almost whispering and reached for the boy's head, but he eluded his persecutor, and then beginning to speak in some mumbling inaudible speech perhaps to himself, Aiken stood up, but reeled and fell against a great cupboard so that all the dishes within rattled like a flock of birds a hunter has shot at.

"I must be told as soon as you know," he spoke again to Owen.

"You'll have a long cold wait then."

"So. I'm the man to stand long cold waits . . . But I'll have it, and you know I'll have it . . . For it was me that drove you off, that's why, and I've the right to know . . . I'm the one who will look after you when all are gone, don't forget . . ." And now he searched in the dark for Owen, and found him at last, and held him in almost the same pressure he had held the man who had insulted him tonight, a bit at arm's length just before he punished that insulter with his fists, and holding Owen then just as far from him, and then bringing him close to his chest, he said, "You are my all-in-all, Owen, don't ask me why, for I don't know why any more than you can't remember the lost six months. I feel more tender for you than for any woman. Why is that? But you shall not cheat me of those months!"

"Aiken," a voice spoke as elusive as the voices of the whippoorwills, "you are scaring me with your mad talk, and pray stop, won't you . . ."

He heard Aiken throw himself back down on the ruined davenport.

"Everything I have ever learned come out of tearing it from its source," Aiken spoke after a while. "I am in the dark about everything, and when I light one light, another goes out, leaving me like I was before . . ."

Aiken Cusworth was seated in lordly splendor at the fifteen-foot-long dining table, a silver coffee service at his bandaged left hand, a steaming pile of griddle cakes before him, his white teeth dutifully chewing a slice of ham, when looking up he saw the angry outraged face of Mr. Skegg who had come in unbidden. Aiken did not rise, did not stop chewing, and at last with the most mocking and deliberate fastidiousness wiped his full red lips carefully with the thick damask napkin, and stared at Mr. Skegg until the old gentleman lowered his eyes.

"You have made yourself most comfortably at home, Aiken." The old man had slipped into a chair now, and was making an effort to be careful of what he said.

"I *am* at home." Aiken helped himself to another serving of griddle cakes. "I am where I belong. Others may not know where they are. I do."

"I see." Mr. Skegg could not restrain a snort of ire. "And where, if it would not tax your hospitality to tell me, is the lady of the house?"

Aiken furrowed his brow, and looked about the room as if searching for the cat.

"Lady Bythewaite! Where is she, and where has she been!" The old maggot beat upon the floor with his walking stick, which he rarely if ever carried with him.

"The last we heard of her," Aiken spoke with full mouth, dark syrup trickling down his carefully shaved chin, his tongue quickly following the trail of syrup and bringing it back into his vigorously chewing mouth, "the very last news we got of her was she had located . . . Maynard Ewing . . ."

This mention of the pseudonym *and* the son caused Mr. Skegg to rise from his seat precipitately and then begin pacing about the room.

"Why in the name of God does she not keep me informed!" Mr. Skegg looked out in the direction of the lake.

But Aiken seemed so deeply absorbed in the animal-like enjoyment of his food, the water beginning to come to his eyes at the pleasure of his chewing, his head bowed silently as if in praise of such rich victuals, he did not appear any more to be conscious of Mr. Skegg's speech or presence.

"A thousand things need to be looked after, a thousand things need to be tended to . . . She has picked a fine time to decamp if you ask me!"

"And so, in your irritable, cantankerous old way, you think to scold and blame me for all of it because there is nobody else about!" Aiken proclaimed. "You come into my house unbidden, unannounced, and in your unmannerly bear-like way interrupt my breakfast, as if I was the cause of Lady Bythewaite's never having married you . . . I won't have it, by Christ, and I won't have you in this house if you've come to order me about and blame me!" Aiken suddenly threw his napkin in the direction of a struck-dumb Mr. Skegg.

"You dare to speak to me in this fashion!" But when the old maggot had delivered himself of these words he merely sat down again as if his knees had buckled from a gunshot.

"You have taken away my appetite!" Aiken storming rose from the table and went to sit in one of the larger chairs, the largest, to his displeasure, being occupied by Skegg.

"You are no more what you were than ice is fire," the old man mumbled, shaking his head, and occasionally looking out in the direction of the lake as if he half-expected to see Lady Bythewaite arriving any moment on some vessel coming across its waters.

"All these years before I knew I was her son," Aiken was going on, "I have niggered for the both of you, for all and everybody, and been paid in halfpennies . . . Look at me!" he had risen and shouted into the face of Mr. Skegg.

"What is wrong with your fist?" the old maggot wondered.

"My fist," the horsetender grimaced, looking down at his bandage, "my fist is angry that I did not kill the sonofabitch who roused my wrath!"

"That is precisely the reason I am here, and when you calm down, I will talk to you."

"When I calm down, Mr. Skegg, the Day of Judgment is near . . ."

"The sheriff has been to see me about you, Aiken . . . Indeed he has!"

"And what has that down-at-the-heels shitlicker had to say to you . . . ?"

"Aiken, Aiken this will never do!"

The younger man paced up and down the room, and again as on that day when he had come horsewhipped into his house, Mr. Skegg felt more admiration than anger for such a demonstration of passion and indignation.

"We have had a most serious talk." Mr. Skegg had begun now to speak in his old realtor's sensible manner. "The sheriff will take no action at this time . . ."

"Aha," Aiken replied, glaring now too in the direction of the lake.

"But if you go on the way you are going on, Aiken, let me warn you: you will be put under a peace bond—or worse!"

Whether it was the slightly ridiculous gesture with which Mr. Skegg made his warning—a shaking of his finger at Aiken as one would at a five-year-old—or the impotence of any threatening in general, Aiken burst into one of his laughs which made all who heard it uneasy, for it resembled some tormented cry of a shame and confusion which could no longer be borne.

"With all your good qualities, my dear fellow, you have nonetheless been always one of the worst boys in this part of the country, at least after the sun goes down, and you know it . . . But we would not part with you for all that . . ."

"You will not part with me because everybody knows who I am, and the sheriff, though he's an asshole and a crook to boot, knows this, and even I at last know it, and there'll be no peace bond, Mr. Skegg, unless, moreover, you're put under bond too,

so let's not talk of tales out of school . . . Peace bond, my foot!
I'll kill any man who calls me names, and don't you forget it
either . . ."

Such a strange musing sadness had come over the old maggot
however that even Aiken Cusworth's tempest of hate was somehow abated a bit. Mr. Skegg looked very old, though he had
always looked quite old, perhaps counting and numbers make
one old, but now he looked bereft and lonesome and staring direct into the blank that faces all who have long forgotten and
lost youth and love.

"I see." The old maggot got up, and began heading for the
door.

"Come back," Aiken shouted at his retreating figure, for he did
not like his victory now he had it. "Mr. Skegg, come back." He
had lowered his voice.

The old man turned and looked sharply at Aiken.

"Have you decided to give me a fisticuff too before you dismiss me, or will you boot me out the door?"

"I would like to invite you to a bite to eat before you go
out, Mr. Skegg, for you look quite down and feeble, if you don't
mind my saying so, and the wind promises rain . . ."

The old man struggled with different emotions, different
phrases, but as in his former financier days, he was never too
much a fool to admit defeat, and, besides, the coffee and grub
Lady Bythewaite served were superior to what he now had in
his own house.

"I could stand with a bite of something, I judge, Aiken . . ."

Mr. Skegg had barely sat down and tucked a clean napkin
under his chin, agreeably nodding over Aiken's order to the cook
to put on another batch of cakes, when a great grinding of buggy
wheels was heard at the back of the house, and a familiar voice
calling in the tones of a certain chosen model "Gee-hup" reached
the breakfast table.

"What on the face of the earth—" Mr. Skegg began.

"Damn him, double damn him!" Aiken began his string of imprecations, throwing his napkin ring on the table with a resounding echo to his own voice.

"It's Owen of course," he offered an explanation to the wondering Mr. Skegg, "and he's no more fit to drive than a child-in-arms . . ."

"But, begging your pardon," Mr. Skegg protested, "Owen is a fine horseman, and it was you taught him to be."

"*Was,* Mr. Skegg, sir, *was!*" Aiken countered, and his chest rose in violent motions, causing his watch chain to tinkle against the buttons of his vest. "His eyes, Mr. Skegg, are all but bereft of their light."

Frightened and shamed by one giant of a brother, Owen Haskins, half-blind but trusting to the patient intelligence of his mare and their common trust for one another, was racing to see the other giant brother, in his last day on the screen in the outdoor spectacle *Beyond the Canyon.*

Several times on the road to Stotfold and the Elysian Meadows Theater, nonetheless, Owen's vision became so clouded that he could barely, in his apprehensive state, hold the reins, and the mare finally came to a halt under some cottonwood trees. Owen sat there, chewing his ire, and then closing his eyes for a few moments, he opened them and could see the road tolerably well again.

"To Stotfold, Meg," he called to the mare, "for I'm 'reft of my eyes today, girl."

The mare started up, even quickening her pace, and they went on then without stopping, passing few if any other vehicles, and about one o'clock in the afternoon, Owen's dilapidated buggy drew up before the hitching post by the Elysian Meadows Theater. But after securing the vehicle, another great cloud of darkness descended on him, so that he stood fixed to the spot, incapable of seeing a thing, then waiting, holding on to the flanks of the horse, gradually the spell passed, but this time the figures of men and buildings had become amorphous, of strange purplish color, and the earth and its world was floating—floating away from him. A short sob of terror came from his throat.

He hobbled away and presently stood in front of the theater entrance, which was as shabby and worn as his own buggy.

"Why, Master Owen!" He heard a familiar voice coming from some indistinguishable, invisible location nearby. "What a nice surprise." It was of course Stephen Bottrell, the photoplay manager, but his voice seemed to come from the sky. "Come in, Owen, there's almost nobody here today, and you shan't pay, you shall go in free . . . Why, Owen, I didn't know you cared about the art of the motion picture . . ." Here Mr. Bottrell's laugh came from all kinds of directions, from space itself perhaps. "But, Owen, what on earth is wrong with your eyes . . ."

"It's an old complaint of our family," the boy responded, smiling, while turning his dying pupils in almost every direction except that from which the manager's trained baritone was coming. "It will pass, Mr. Bottrell," the boy said after a long silence, during which he puzzled as to where his questioner now stood.

Far from certain that the young man was suffering only from a "complaint," Stephen Bottrell helped Owen into the inner recesses of his theater, and seated him as he would have some ancient invalid.

"I'll sit here with you, Owen," Stephen spoke with tremulous concern, and he took Owen's hand, which the boy permitted him to hold.

"Shan't I call your folks?" the manager wondered after they had sat like this for some time.

Owen shook his head. He was staring in the direction of the silent screen. By reason of the piano playing, and the stir of people's feet, he was aware that a performance had now begun, and towering beyond him and Stephen Bottrell and the rest of the audience was Maynard Ewing, who was looking at him also with sightless eyes.

"I can't let you remain here like this without your family knowing about it, Owen," Stephen Bottrell finally insisted.

"Oh, Aiken will be so furious with me, there'll be no containing him!" Owen turned obliquely toward where Stephen's voice was proceeding.

"Furious be damned . . . Even a brute like him will recognize what plight you're in," Stephen supposed. Patting the boy's hand, as if fearful he would somehow now disappear, the movie house operator went into the next room, where there was a telephone. But it was difficult to get through, and he found himself talking to empty air, so that presently he went back and sat down with Owen, while he waited for "central" to connect him with Lady Bythewaite's inaccessible mansion.

"And now there is he again for you, your brother," Stephen whispered, languidly pointing to the screen.

"Oh. And what is he doing?" Owen wondered.

Stephen Bottrell hesitated, coughed. "Well," he began, "he is seated in this great room with flowers all about him, and several ladies sit with him, you understand, with jewels and broad-brimmed hats . . ."

The telephone rang, and Stephen gladly excused himself. He swallowed hard when he heard the glacial ireful voice of Aiken Cusworth on the other end of the wire.

"Young Owen is here at the theater, sir," Stephen spoke in a voice which he himself had trouble recognizing as his own. "He is in most pitiable shape, and I do believe he is *blind* . . . He can't see his own hand stretched out before him . . ."

After hanging up, Stephen Bottrell stood stiffly, holding the receiver still some few inches from his face in astonishment, disbelief, wonder at what he had heard proceeding from the mouth of Aiken Cusworth, for he had certainly not heard words: what had he heard? He did not know, and a sort of nameless dread swept over him as unsettling as his perturbation over wretched Owen's condition. He had heard coming from the horsetender, he now tried to recollect, sounds such as came from afflicted birds and animals when the hunters had wounded them . . . But he stopped, and drew away from his own thoughts, and went back and took his place beside Owen.

Owen was eager to hear described for him the faces and dramatic action coming from the actors on the silver screen, and so in a halting but methodical manner, Stephen Bottrell did his best to convey all that his own eyes saw, and his tongue could manage to report. He not only read the "titles," which now when they were spoken out loud were even to him a bit "thick," but he interpreted from out of his own actor's training and experience the staggering emotions which the characters in the photoplay were undergoing.

"I do so fear for Aiken," Owen said peremptorily in the midst of one of Stephen's lengthy commentaries.

"Fear for him, Owen?" Stephen turned clear about to study his charge.

"He won't be patient with this new trouble, Mr. Bottrell . . ."

Stephen Bottrell sat back and began reading rapidly the "titles" on the screen.

One matinee ended, and the housewives and retired farmers filed out, and another matinee began with even fewer spectators to fill the seats, but there was no sign of Aiken Cusworth. From outside one heard with tolerable distinctness the beginning of a thundershower, the spattering drops audible above the harsh waltz number coming from the upright piano.

Then at last the heavy step, and stertorous sound like that of a horse, and Stephen rose and withdrew as Aiken stood for a moment before the seated form of Owen. He kneeled before the boy, perhaps the better to inspect the extent of damage which his eyes had sustained. Then Mr. Bottrell thought he saw the older brother had waved his hand in front of the afflicted boy.

"Owen, Owen," at last came the tumultuous voice, "how could you do this to me?" Aiken had begun like the thunder outside, and Mr. Bottrell, in his ignorance, thought he heard only anger, or a passion of disapproval and blame in those tones.

"You have no right, Owen, no right," the maniacal voice went on, "no right not to . . . see . . . see . . . me . . ." Some other mumbled, incoherent words flowed from his lips then.

Was he drunk or mad? Stephen Bottrell drew back at the

apostrophe just delivered, yet was unable to leave the company of the speaker of these words, words as strange and indeed unrelated to any life he knew as the "titles" of the silver screen he had been reading for Owen's benefit.

"Where is my face, Owen?" the voice went on again, appealing to the seated boy. "Touch my face . . ."

Owen, who now resembled some figure carved in rock, nonetheless raised his hand, and with direct movement touched Aiken on the brow.

At this moment, to Mr. Bottrell's great relief, Mr. Skegg entered, with a great umbrella such as farmers employ in county fairs, and Stephen exchanged some words with him, but his attention was still almost entirely riveted to Aiken's incoherent apostrophes, and then to his even greater astonishment he saw Aiken take Owen's extended hand and bring it to his lips, and then, as the "great lummox" rose suddenly, he raised both his arms perhaps at Mr. Skegg, and then fell directly forward toward them, his head banging against the floor. The audience stirred peevishly at these punctuations and outbursts, these interruptions of their pleasure at the photoplay.

But whatever had occurred, and Mr. Bottrell was never sure from that day forward, it was clear both to Mr. Skegg and himself that the person needing immediate relief was a man who had never known a moment's illness or even been afflicted by so much as a cold or fever in all his life. Aiken Cusworth was hoisted up from the floor, unconscious, and half-carried, half-dragged into the "private" room off the lobby, whiskey fetched and forced past his white clenched teeth and set jaw, and Mr. Skegg slapped him none too gently and quite thoroughly into a kind of attention, but the eyes staring at them, on opening, with an expression of horror and unbelief, eyes which appeared even blinder than those of Owen Haskins', and looked indeed in their redness and lack of focus as if a hand had attempted to gouge them from their sockets.

Aiken repeated, with great strings of saliva falling from his mouth, the same incomprehensible dictum: *"Why did he choose to do this to me?"* and then shaking his head and rolling his own seeming-sightless eyes, much in the manner of Lady Bythewaite when she discovered the world had no use for her.

And so, bent ancient Mr. Skegg and thin nimble Stephen Bottrell helped Aiken into the back of the buggy, with as much care and caution as if he had been run over by a fast train, and then went back to lead a much more calm and collected and indeed "seeing" Owen to sit in the back seat by the side of his collapsed brother, who immediately took Owen's hand as if his own death were moments away.

"Shan't I drive for you, Mr. Skegg?" Stephen gazed at the old maggot, as the latter took the buggy whip in one hand and the reins in the other.

"Not on your life," the old man replied, smiling. "Much obliged, though, for your offer." Again over his white chalky face had come a wave of high pink circulation so that he looked considerably spryer and more youthful than when he had entered the theater. "It's no trick at all for me to drive them home, Mr. Bottrell . . ."

"I'll accompany you nonetheless," Stephen offered again.

The old man studied the photoplay manager lengthily.

"You've got your own hands full," he negated the offer, and looked at the theater with his old eye of disapproval, "with your own business and all, Mr. Bottrell. But I'm most grateful to you for what you have done, and I won't forget it . . . in the days to come . . ."

Then craning his neck to the seat behind, he cried in his trumpet-voice: "Aiken, are you among the land of the living, boy?"

"Here, here, Mr. Skegg," a response to this question came as if from some cave beyond the depth of exploration.

"Then we're off!" the old man cried, and shook the reins, and the wheels creaked and moved through the wet town streets.

A knot of curiosity-seekers had gathered round Stephen Bottrell, and all their eyes followed the buggy out of sight.

To her grateful astonishment as she stepped off the sleeping compartment of her pullman, Lady Bythewaite spied weaving baggy-trousered haggard Mr. Skegg waiting for her at the junction on a gravel road behind which breast-high sweet corn was moving languidly in the breeze.

Mr. Skegg moved back a bit also in astonishment at the sight of her. She looked not unlike that first glimpse he had had of her when as a young woman she had just arrived in Prince's Crossing, and when her eyes had still possessed confidence and benign expectancy, now clouded over by a vague musing and querulous expression, and with a mouth ever braced, in a thin line, to receive more tokens of disapproval from what she called always, as if it contained all the buffeting enmity of destiny, "the world."

"Little did I think to see you or any of my menfolk here," Lady B. extended her hand, and then, rare for her, at the strange look of measured supplication on his weather-beaten face, she kissed him on one of his furrowed cheeks.

"May I beg of you the favor to take you to Shapwick Manor first, for the very briefest of talks . . . I have had a little collation prepared for the fatigue of your journey, and you may even lie down a little . . ."

"What is amiss, Mr. Skegg!" She took his hand in hers.

"Nora, you will be doing all of us a service if you will, for this once, obey me, and obey me in silence. I beg you, I command you, and so say no more . . ."

And without more ado, he put her luggage in his slightly used Studebaker, which had no top, and they drove off in the direction of Shapwick Manor, Lady B. having somewhat the flattering impression she was being forcibly driven off to be married against her will.

Unlike herself, she made no more protests, indeed she had made none, for her grueling experience with Clarence had robbed her of any will to fight for the moment, and had also slightly numbed her to the awareness that Mr. Skegg had more bad tidings in store for her.

Sitting under a glimmering chandelier in Shapwick Manor, she tasted a bite of cheese, sipped some homemade wine, and drank cup after cup of strong black coffee, stirring a tiny solid silver spoon with a heraldic design against the thin edges of his hand-painted china.

From the centerpiece of the table came the pungent odor of nasturtiums, with their hopeful bright faces and lily-pad leaves, so winning that at last she reached out and took one and held it to her nostrils.

"We have had very bad news, Nora," he began at last. "But the thing is perhaps not forever irreparable . . ."

"It's night-riding Aiken, I suppose," she began, though she felt of course it was not he at all, but she was stronger by mentioning his name first.

"It's both Aiken and Owen," Mr. Skegg corrected her.

"Oh, how well that is said! Never the one without the other." She opened her purse and took out an immoderately scented handkerchief and wiped her eyes. "Owen and Aiken, Aiken and Owen, yes . . . Before we begin on them, I may tell you that I first saw Clarence in the most abject circumstances, and had frankly given up all hope . . . I will not tell you now or in any future conversation where I found him, or what it was like. I do not believe it yet. I do not believe I was there . . . But as I stayed on, he came out of his ashes like phoenix, how, do not ask me, for he has disowned me in a more real sense than you ever disowned him. I believe his hatred and contempt for me and my wasted pity made him rise out of his deathbed and walk . . . He is now, I believe, at work on a new film, living in moderate poverty, beginning all over again."

Lady Bythewaite spoke on and on, describing Maynard Ewing's rise and his fall, hoping she supposed that by talking so fast, and explaining so much so quickly, the dark glowering brow of Mr. Skegg would clear, and he would tell her that her two Prince's Crossing sons had bad colds and were confined to their rooms for a few days.

"And now I am ready, Mr. Skegg." Nora Bythewaite had managed to speak at last, and she sat back with eyes averted.

"He has gone blind, Nora, and we have had the doctor of course and there does not seem to be any hope he will ever see again."

To his considerable puzzlement, Nora Bythewaite merely nodded at this and puckered up her lips as was her wont when he had in times past advised her concerning thorny business transactions, mortgages, and foreclosures.

"But there is more," he went on, turning his head out toward the pasture ground. "More, and worse . . . Nora, I do not believe Aiken is any longer, shall we say, compos mentis . . . Perhaps this sorrow will pass, but he has behaved . . ."

It was this last intelligence which did its work, for a soft but far-carrying moan such as he had never heard come from her or any other human throat swept across the room and out like a living winged thing to the horses standing in sweet pasture, who whinnied then and shook their heads.

"I cannot credit what you have said, and I will not!" She spoke with the strong defiance which comes from hearing another voice the secret counsel of one's own heart.

"You shall judge for yourself, Nora, when you meet him."

"Meet *them*, you mean," she countered, dry-eyed, her face as chalky white as his, her eyes mere slits from which red darting illuminations came and went.

"How blind is Owen Haskins?" she demanded at last.

His fingers moved over the edge of the hand-blown glass, bringing from it a kind of sickly chime.

"Blind as the grave."

She nodded. She had become again impassive, cold, almost collected.

"And what proof have you of Aiken's being mad?" She suddenly was accusing him.

"You must be the judge of that for yourself, Nora . . . I will say no more . . . I did feel it my bounden duty to warn, to prepare you. I could not let you go to that house and see them as they are!"

She had seen them finally. It seemed a long time, looming up from her own disturbed memory, since Clarence Skegg had branded her with his hatred, and ordered her out of his hovel, or flophouse. That rose up before her now, New York rose up before her, as she looked back, as a mere "outing," finding Clarence in infamy, prepared to die, and then, as in a photoplay, she mused, reading the "titles" on the screen, this same Clarence had "got up and walked," and gone about his business . . . But it would come back, she opined, everything came back, nothing in life left us once it had appeared and made its motion to us, all, all, in the chain, or from the ashes, whichever, returned, and then made its claims on us.

There they sat, then, some days having passed since Mr. Skegg had tried to warn her, after which she had crept into her own mansion with the stealth and lack of familiarity in her groping and stumbling through its many halls and rooms as some housebreaker at midnight.

She had not found them bleeding, with their scalps hanging down over their foreheads, their hands severed, their eyeballs disorbited, but she had found the quiet and the stillness almost worse. The hurt and damage and doom were hidden under silence and softness, and mocked by the soft summer day, and the blooming sunflowers nodding their great top-heavy faces behind which Aiken and Owen now sat, shuffling the dominoes. She looked only at their hands. The hands perhaps are the last to die, and are the most human of all our appurtenances, she thought. Everything else about the two young men seemed dead at that moment but their dealing hands.

So, as she best remembered, she had sat as invisible to them as the winds, and watched them play, or perhaps she did not look at them. They paid little mind indeed to her, and appeared forgetful that she had ever left or returned to them.

"Playing dominoes under the sunflowers," she whispered. "Did anyone ever see the like?"

Owen of course had shut her out from the light long ago, she mused, and Aiken had never really allowed her to stand clear and revealed in his line of vision, or rather she had failed to allow him to do so . . . And poor as her own eyesight was, she had begun to crochet these days, in order to distract her mind from the incessant banging down of the "bones" of the dominoes on the hard marble surface.

Though Owen Haskins saw nothing, did not see her, and used his hands only to play with the dominoes, or to touch when in confusion the sinewy arm of Aiken to guide him, the boy walked about the house alone with the assuredness and skill and with his old perfect posture perhaps gained from his horsemanship or from his hero model, as if nothing at all had gone amiss with him. Once to her thrilling terror he had stopped in front of her chair, and his sightless pupils leveled themselves at her. Unlike many blind persons, his eyes seemed clear and searching still. She put down her sewing, stopped breathing. Was she sure, were they sure indeed, he saw nothing. Or was this all some hoax to torment her and bring her finally to her knees prior to their putting her out on the street and closing the great "castle" against all the world, and living together like exiled potentates, the hero and his pupil in heroism.

One night when Owen sat alone in the confines of the sun porch, blinking toward the declining rays of light, Aiken unaccountably came over to Lady Bythewaite and sat down on a small hard-oak footstool beside her. She had the feeling that, blind as his bastard brother, he had not even seen her, did not know where he was, and had indeed never known where or who he was.

"Aiken, you must marry!" Her own voice speaking astounded

her, for she had not known she thought this until she had spoken it. He moved his head in a slow arbitrary manner such as deaf people do when they hear a sound which arrests or warns them of something suspicious, if not dangerous.

"You long for a son! Hence this devotion to him. It is your deep longing for a son, which all men have, which is the source of your . . . sorrow, I think . . ."

"What sorrow, Lady Bythewaite. I know only joy."

She came close to pricking herself with her needle, she swallowed hard, and she flushed knowing that he had heard her throat struggling with her old turbulence, if not with her lies.

"You would be a perfect father, Aiken." She put down the needle and thimble, and then looking at the thimble for a moment, for it had been her mother's and seemed solid gold, she went on, "There are very few fathers who would so patiently teach their sons to be men."

She looked into his eyes now to see if his madness, if that was what it was, if Mr. Skegg had known what it was, showed in these windows of his soul. But she saw only Owen in his eyes, there was Owen in the face and body of a rustic Hercules.

"Not too long ago," she proceeded, putting on her thimble again, and his mouth opened in his old fashion, like that of a handsome dog, the saliva coming out onto his hands stained as if he had shelled black walnuts, "in fact only recently I saw Lucy Weymouth, who spoke so warmly about . . ."

"Where did you see her? Naked on a pool table?"

Lady Bythewaite drew back from these words of rage but did not look up. She did not go on.

"You liar." Aiken spoke in tones of incurable rage.

She put her hand on his, nonetheless, and said, "Lucy loves you . . . She would marry you . . ."

"You would breed me so that you could have more bastards to harness and serve you," he whispered, and he picked up the sleeve of her worn but outrageously costly dress. "I, a father . . . You would take my son if I had one, and I would never see him again. Breed me to whores, will you! They've had out of me all they'll get. All have had out of me all they will get. I am my own master now, Lady Bythewaite, my own man." He got up, and in his old fashion threw back his arms, stretching as if no care or sorrow had ever been felt within his frame or his heart.

"You will think over what I have said, nevertheless, Aiken, about your having a son, for a son you should have."

He bent down looking at her narrowly, his lips working convulsively, his tongue exiting from and entering into his mouth, with mute eloquence, the spittle falling on her faded fine garments.

"You . . . cursed . . . bearer of false witness!" Stammering, he barely managed to get it out. "You . . . nurse of pain and shame!"

"Be careful, Aiken Cusworth!" she began in her former ruling manner, and for a moment he obeyed her, and then letting out a curse word which reached Owen as he sat like some remote somnolent judge, the blind boy stirred and agitated his fingers, and a low cry very much like that of the night birds in the woods came to their distracted ears.

A few days later, Lucy Weymouth arrived with her few belongings, which included two empty bird cages, and a county-fair kind of colored umbrella, and was installed in a small, unused maid's room down the endless hall which led by many windings to all the sleeping chambers. Nora Bythewaite's severe reception of the girl gave little indication that the great lady had all but got down on her knees to persuade her to come. As she was talking to Lucy in one of the innumerable unused rooms of the mansion, the girl looked up with an expression of tenderness, dread, and unbelief. Owen stood at the threshold of the room from where their secret whisperings issued, his eyes like wreathing and flickering motes in setting sunbeams, and his mouth smiling as if he heard dance music.

"I will be with you directly, Owen," Lady Bythewaite spoke with sharp confused irritation.

"Whatever for, Mother?" he replied, his extinguished eyes looking in the direction of the newcomer, and he stalked out, walking and moving with an assurance indeed very little inferior to what he had had before he had been stricken.

Lady Bythewaite gave Lucy a last severe silent warning, and followed after her son.

The mother and her one "recognized" son had not been alone together since he had gone blind. She would not trust herself hitherto to such a lacerating confrontation. But she saw at once that their being alone together at last had come too late. She saw all the marks and signs of unappeasable anger on Owen's face, and as permanent blindness settled over him, he looked more and more like Aiken, and she felt shut out forever from his love.

"What have you brought that whore to this house for?" Owen began then after a long struggle to say something, during which his tongue had moved in the same animal ferocity so common to Aiken.

"I beg your pardon." Lady Bythewaite spoke in the offhand weary tones of elocution common to an actress reading from a script which fails to impress her.

"Beg nothing of me, Mother, nothing. But does Aiken know Lucy is here?"

They heard all the great collection of clocks then wheezing and ticking and marking the passage of the seconds and minutes of time.

"It is not good for a man of Aiken's energy and endowments . . . to be unmarried." Her voice barely came audible over the sound of the clocks.

A laugh of such demonic but pathetic wretchedness came from Owen that it made the mother lower her own eyes to her tightly clasped hands.

"You must have noticed," she went on doggedly, "how, though Aiken is happy with you during the sunshine hours," and here immediately she began to stumble as if again reading from what someone had shoved at her in the shape of a poorly lettered script full of blots, mistakes, and corrections, whose elementary meaning escaped her, "when darkness comes, though he loves you more than any other human being—he is your slave, Owen! —when night has fallen, he must be in the company of those who can give him relief!"

"Relief?" Owen cried, the same chilling laugh coming out, filling the corridors with sound, "Relief for Aiken! Do you think his fire can be put out, Mother, by darkness. You do surprise me, since you were, if one can believe your testimony, once in the world, though what the world has to do with Aiken, I know not . . . Relief!" He touched on this word again . . . "Everything in nature may have relief, Mother, but not Aiken! Fire can be put out, the cyclone grudges itself out, and disappears, and the sea quiets down, but Aiken, relief! You are either a fool or a hypocrite . . . Make that whore taste the door before he comes back, I warn you . . ."

"I do believe it is you who bring out these black things in his nature!" She stopped, in pursuit of her handkerchief. "I see I do not know you after all, Owen . . . You two young men bring

out all the dark things in one another's souls, I do believe . . .
No, no," she held the handkerchief to her bone-dry cheeks, "I
was right to bring Lucy here, it is one of the things that I have
done which is right . . ."

"Suit yourself then, Mother, since you are the only one you
ever wish to suit in any case. I do not care how many whores
you bring to him in any case, for he can never be appeased if all
the gaping gaps in all the women who ever tempted men from
Eve down were offered to his inflammation . . ."

"Owen, where do you get this speech, so unlike you . . . What
have you been studying, what terrible books had you been poring over before the time of your sad accident . . ."

"Hearts!" he shouted at her, and then from his dead eyes small
rivulets of blood began to trickle as if tears were too poor a
thing for him to shed.

"Owen, Owen," she whispered, starting up, and drew him to
her, "when you know that it is only you I ever loved, and live
only for your good . . ."

His head and body rested against her but without nerves or
sinews, seemingly, or the coursing of blood within him save for
the trickling drops of red from his eyes, and he neither gave
nor resisted love.

"All shall be ordered and designed for you and you alone
. . . If the whore must be sent away," she fell easily into his
phraseology, for was it not an old play they were in, or perhaps
photoplay, "we will send her away . . . Did you think I meant
to take Aiken away from you by bringing her to this house?
That was never my thought . . . I fear his terrible energy! See
how it has brought you to sorrow, Owen . . ."

But she stared now down at her charge. There seemed no
breath or motion in his loved form. Almost falling against him,
she listened bending over his chest, and taking in her hand his
wrist, and from his chest to his wrist recording if she could any
beat or motion. Yes, strong as the current of the lake, it beat,
or like all the heirloom clocks, the rhythm and motion were
there, marking time.

Owen did not need his eyes to know when Aiken entered the house, his brother's step told him all, and had Owen been deaf, his nostrils would have forewarned him it was Aiken by reason of his forest smell, half flower-like, half animal, and had his nostrils come to be useless as his eyes, his blood coursing in his veins would have told him, and in death, which he thought was never far, his soul would know Aiken in that final night.

Aiken's heavy step came to a halt near the table at which Lucy and Owen were now playing dominoes, and the heavy breathing changing almost to gasps warned of the tempest, but Owen's hand closed over Lucy's, which held a single domino, protectively.

"With the rose blood on his cheeks, he looks a proper man indeed," Aiken's voice came out at last, in menacing tones, and he took Owen's thick head of hair in his hand and pulled his head back with no gentleness and stared into the blank eyes.

"And so they have brought Cuntgrope Lane into my house," he spoke directly to Lucy. "Yes, I've an ill-blooded nature, so what! Who would not be put out of countenance . . ."

Owen could hear him sit down heavily on the stool near the dominoes.

"I have been a-dancing, and am drunk," he said after some more cogitating. "But drink don't take with me, and maybe never has . . . How did you get in?" he raised his voice now to Lucy, but he had forgotten she was used to his "ill-blooded nature" and she ignored him, still holding Owen's hand in hers.

"When I gave him to you that night, Lucy," Aiken began, after the lengthy pause during which both she and Owen could hear his breath come and go like an expiring runner, "I didn't give him to you for keeps . . . Who admitted you here? But you don't need to answer. You were sent for of course . . ."

"She was sent for, for you," Owen declared, stung to anger.

With a kind of godly melancholy, Aiken responded: "Oh, so, for me . . . She never gave me respite that I know of, did you, Lucy . . ."

"Until the lady orders me to go, I'll stay," Lucy spoke out, "and Owen and I will play, if you won't," and having said this with considerable defiance, she freed herself from Owen's hand, and dealt the dominoes anew on the marble-topped table.

"We'll see if you can bring the sun to shine again here," Aiken scoffed, and jumping up went into the next room, but returned immediately, and sat down again, studying the two as they played, Owen feeling the black marks on the "bones" with his clever long fingers.

But drink, which Aiken said did not "take" with him, began somehow to have its effect, and after a bit he threw himself down near the feet of Owen, indeed rested his head on one of Owen's boots, and made out to snore.

"And where is the lady of the house?" Aiken muttered after a long silence during which they had thought he was sleeping.

"Lady Bythewaite asked me to tell any callers that she was not in parlor condition to see anybody tonight," Lucy spoke with calm collected sureness both of her place and her future here.

"My ears tingle," Aiken responded. "That means one of us will take a journey . . ."

Owen had stopped playing and passed his fingers across his eyes. Lucy pretended not to notice. Then a small cry of surprise or discomfort escaped Owen's lips because Aiken had put a steel clamp about his ankle, as if he fought with an enemy.

"So," Aiken began to babble, "so a burning word falls from my peevish lips, am I supposed to stand what I have had to stand and be ice and wood, Owen . . . Answer me that, you who are so perfect . . ."

"When was I perfect?" Owen wondered, pushing the dominoes toward Lucy for reshuffling. "You bring me news, Aiken

Cusworth," and he said these words to Lucy's consternation in the absolute voice and cadence of the horsetender himself.

"You are her only son," Aiken said, pulling the boy's leg so that suddenly he fell from the table and sprawled beside his brother's prone form, his sightless eyes struggling to see in what plight and accidental position Aiken had pulled him to.

"Deny what I say, that of all the bastards you are the one welcomed with open arms into her abode and grace . . ."

Aiken shook him like a retriever with a prey too delicious for saving even for the hunter.

"Don't deny what I say, Owen, or I'll close your wind-pipe . . ."

When no sound came in response, Aiken picked him up with one hand as one would a small parcel and plumped him down hard in his chair so that many of the pieces of dominoes fell off from the table.

"I'm going then," Aiken intoned lazily, stretching himself, "and will leave you two lovebirds together for the night . . ."

Wheeling about, thinking perhaps he was making for the door, but instead with the plummeting motion of a diver going into water from a great height, he plunged instead into the massive glass of an old china closet, and then, stuck between its broken teeth, was held there as if garroted.

As aware of what had happened as if he had seen it, but unable to help, Owen began to make strange sounds in the back of his throat which alarmed Lucy almost more than the grave accident, stirring in her some thrilling nameless fear. But like Lady Bythewaite, Lucy Weymouth was accustomed to accidents and the spilling of blood, and very little could happen which would prevent her from going about her business. Yet it was with some real difficulty and time that she extricated Aiken from the jagged, broken face of the heirloom china closet. Almost as strong as a man, despite her genuine grace and good looks, and finally with Owen's coolheaded help, they freed the drunk man at last, and deposited him on a davenport of sorts, less elegant than most of the furniture of the room. From above them, they heard Lady Bythewaite's querulous cough, and Lucy tiptoed into the hall and closed one door after another in order to deaden any further sound from reaching the upstairs.

Having closed the last door, turning about, her eyes fell on the brothers then as if she were seeing them for the first time, and a momentary sensation came to her that something too had gone wrong with her eyes, for looking at Aiken and the blind boy she had the distinct impression she saw only one "brother" there instead of the two who were of course sitting together in close proximity.

"Do you hate me so passionately, Lucy, that you look at me the way you do?" Aiken's voice reached her.

Coming to herself, Lucy went over to the speaker, and looked down at him carefully.

"You are badly cut up, Aiken," she spoke at last in angry professional tones. "I will have to bathe your cuts and even, who knows? perhaps sew you up."

Then shifting her glance to Owen she saw with great puzzlement the look he sometimes had of seraphic contentment, for soon the door of the house would be closed for the night, and he would be secure tonight at least against Aiken's running wild alone through the sleeping landscape.

Aiken would not believe that Lady Bythewaite had brought Lucy to the house to appease his own unappeasable nature any more than he would believe, in the end, that there was any human being on earth who loved him. He had not slept all that night after his accident, but sat in his erect military posture by the ruined china closet, as if guarding now where a thief had entered.

It was five o'clock in the morning, the hour the mistress of the house usually appeared, and if not really "up," she at least made her rounds at that hour, sipped some of her own brewed coffee, and in Aiken's words "planned the strategy and the campaigns of battle" for the day.

She was as surprised as she could possibly be at the sight of the horsetender sitting like a sentinel, the ruined china closet, to say nothing of his "massacred" appearance. She said nothing, however, for the moment.

While going through Aiken and Owen's clothes the night before, signaling which piece of their apparel, trousers, vests, or coats could stand mending, a diminutive notebook had slipped out from the horsetender's trousers. Her trembling fingers could not resist the temptation to open the book. Once opened, there spread before her Aiken's untutored handwriting, not so much resembling that of a child or a savage, but looking more as if a tree flailing in the wind had put down its arms and twigs and written a message on the naked white paper. But what followed even she was not prepared for. If the entries were true, if the stratagems listed had come to bear fruit, Aiken was a rich man. All the time he had passed for a bread delivery boy, a "handy" man, a groom, and tender of horses, he had been making money, buying up one small farm after another, or some few acres, and then selling, and buying again, and now, look at him!

And like some youthful outlaw or professional gladiator, he sat there now, desperate and forlorn before her cold scrutiny, and then without warning, like vomit from his mouth, came out the long list of her crimes, and his acerbic accusation:

"You brought her here to set him against me, to bring division, to win him away from me so that I would have nobody, as I did before!"

"You could have all the world, Aiken Cusworth, if you would not knock everybody's teeth down his throat who tries to be your friend!" Still these words from her did not come with her old confidence or force.

"You brought her here to take him away from me!"

"How anybody could take him away from you," she spoke with real torment, "when he would eat the dirt you have trodden on! When he never cared or looked up to anybody but you! I am not his mother, though I have confessed it on my knees to him. He spurns me. I am not his kind of dirt. But wherever you tread he kisses that footprint!"

Throwing down the small worn book of ciphers and figures of his aggrandizement into his lap, she shouted: "You have deceived all of us!"

"If so, I have been taught by the fount and origin of deceit itself!"

"Yes, you are eloquent, if unlettered, Aiken . . . Thanks to your early church upbringing, I suppose. You know how with a small phrase or word to wound and turn the knife in the wound. You are always bleeding," she spoke now almost inaudibly, surveying him as if for once and all time. "Hardly a day goes by you do not bleed from your own rashness and ungovernable temper. But I am cut to ribbons inside of me. What is wrong with this old body of mine!" she now raised her voice, "that it does not burst and free me from this torment of you boys! Have I not suffered enough?"

"No, you have not, Lady Bythewaite. You lie like that whore upstairs. And your tough old sides will hold until you have been cut to much finer than ribbons. Pity you! Pity the wind and the ocean and the hurricane!"

"I brought Lucy for you, not for him . . . Bring that great strapping girl for a blind boy!"

"Well, he's enjoyed her body long ago," Aiken lashed at her with bitter triumph. "Long, long—" but Lady Bythewaite's ringed hand struck him across the mouth.

Spitting out at her, though his lips moved sluggishly by reason of her blow: "Being blind, he'll only be more appetizing to her, and less able to escape her blandishments . . ."

"Then go, Aiken, get out of my house!" Lady Bythewaite commanded now. "You shall not rest under this roof another night."

He rose with his look of final triumph, and waited for her to tremble more violently.

"And when and if I go," he began then, "and I am going, you will crawl all the way to wherever I am to bring me back. Provided you find me . . . For he won't live without me. We breathe through the same pair of lungs, and he has no eyes, no eyes now! No eyes but mine, Lady Bythewaite."

As he pronounced these words, she attacked him with all the violence even she had kept partially under control through the years.

When Owen came down for breakfast he discovered his mother seated near the confusion and scatter of the broken cups and glasses and plates as if it had been she who had hurled herself through the fine glass of the china closet.

There was no sign for him of Aiken, no indication in the air, no movement in the room to betoken his presence, and besides, Owen had heard him drive away on his horse fully an hour ago, with a violent speed of one who will not stop until he has reached the shore of the ocean.

At the nadir of her misery, who should appear, decked out in the latest fashion, looking younger than anyone under her roof, without a care in the world, radiating health and infinite satisfaction to be alive but Clarence Skegg himself.

In his glory again, restored to grandeur, he had done all he could to try to forewarn her of his coming for the great gala and celebration which had been prepared for him by the mayor of Stotfold, for he was to be honored as the most celebrated of all the hometown boys of the entire region, the only young man who had gone away and made a name for himself in lights.

To prepare her for his return, for his country apotheosis, he had stood by the phone for days trying to get through to Prince's Crossing, but either the wires were "down," or the connection could not be made, or the phone was not answered. He had tried telegrams, but there was no real telegraph service near Lady Bythewaite, a fact which had perhaps slipped his mind, and so his messages were returned to him stamped NOT DELIVERABLE. He guessed that his letters to her had long been left lying unopened or unread on her great mahogany desk, gathering in piles, for he sensed that when Lady Bythewaite saw the handwriting and the postmark *New York* her courage failed her, and in all his letters to her he had never been able to bring himself to make one reference to Owen's blindness.

But some telephones were working even in Prince's Crossing, and Clarence had finally reached Mr. Skegg, but the old maggot had thought it best to say nothing to Lady Bythewaite concerning the meteor's return, and had gravely warned Clarence not to expect his mother to share in his homecoming celebration owing to Owen's terrible mischance.

And so, since that black cloud-laden afternoon when she had walked the long set of steps to his room in a flophouse, and had, after he dismissed her, returned, and forcibly, with the aid of two men, removed him to a better lodging, he had come up green and growing, like the countryside after a cyclone, and was more than flourishing. He had made three films since their meeting in despair. He brought her gifts, a coat which must have cost a fortune, and might have looked a bit costly on the shoulders of present-day royalty, and then from out an ornate jewel-encrusted sack, some gems, rings, and bracelets.

"Nothing is too good for you, dear heart," Clarence said again and again.

But she soon saw that his gaiety, his happiness, his success were a little too exalted. He was too grand. He was feverish in splendor as he had been in wretchedness. But she would not think of that now. No, she was mistaken, perhaps, since he had arisen, and her doubts must stem from the great suffering which Owen and Aiken had inflicted on her, and which she began now to tell him of, in a torrent he was unable to check, though he attempted to check it, again and again.

"Let's not take time for sorrow now, dear Mother," he had said. "I am much too happy. I'm here, you know, for the celebration which Mr. Bottrell has arranged for me . . . I believe you two have been introduced, so he wrote . . ." Clarence Skegg stopped a moment. "If I am not mistaken, indeed, you have become friends . . ."

But Lady Bythewaite was too distracted to understand that Clarence was fishing for information, so he went on, "Stephen has organized a really grand celebration for the 'local boy' . . ." He stopped on this hackneyed phrase, wishing perhaps he had not said it, or that he was not this boy in question. "Yes, it's all a bit countrified, but they believe back in New York it may help a little . . . I'm willing at any rate to submit . . ."

She had forgotten about it all, she apologized—the celebration that is, in her worry over Owen, and she poured forth her regrets, and begged his understanding.

But Clarence Skegg did not want to hear about Owen, and tried to change the subject, but she pressed him.

"If he can't see me, darling," Clarence stood up and walked to the window looking out critically at the waters of the lake, "I mean, since he is blind, don't you think he would appreciate it perhaps if I didn't go in to see him, at least just now . . . It would be painful for him, I've no doubt . . ."

Lady Bythewaite was speechless at this, and Clarence then, turning back to her, noting her mood, tried to amend his statement a bit: "Of course I mean to see him, I shall see him. But I don't quite know how to act in the presence of a blind person."

"He's not *a* blind person, Clarence, but your own flesh and blood . . ."

The actor bit his lip, and looked into the next room jampacked with heirloom furniture.

"Lady Bythewaite," he began firmly, "I'd rather not, but if you feel it would make him and you happy, I will see him."

"But what about your own feelings? Shouldn't they dictate that you wish to see your own brother, no matter what painful and terrible destiny has overtaken him?"

Angered, Clarence began walking about the room. He now saw everything as it had always been, only this time it looked much smaller, though it was not small, he was aware, the lake was not small, it was immense, the pasture out there with the horses, the great meadows stretching beyond with their countless flowers and grasses and the sweet air, no, none of it was small, but it looked small, too small for him, too still, indeed contemptible.

"Of course I shall not insist, Clarence," Lady Bythewaite's voice barely reached him in his reverie. "I know you have many appointments and obligations. You are after all what none of us is or ever will be, famous . . . But it has been a crushing hard siege for your mother, believe you me . . ."

"Oh, of course I'll see him," Clarence cried, angrily removing his "traveling coat." "Where did you say he keeps to himself?"

Lady Bythewaite hesitated.

"He's as a matter of fact in the kitchen," she spoke after a struggle with herself, and barely keeping any composure.

"Is that where you keep him now he is in this . . . condition?"

"Clarence! . . . He prefers the kitchen because it has the most light." She touched the great cameo brooch on her breast with shaking fingers. "It's not just an ordinary kitchen, you know," she spoke now with some of her old anger and tartness, but under this anger was a dark and terrible sorrow which gave him pause.

"Then let's go and see the poor chap!" Clarence cried heartily, and put his arm about Lady Bythewaite, but even as he did so the telephone rang, and Effie came hurrying in to inform him he was wanted.

While the celebrity was away talking, Owen entered the room, apprised by the stentorian voice in the front room that there was a visitor.

"Sit over here, Owen, why don't you, for Clarence has come to see you." Lady Bythewaite spoke in cold harsh wounded tones, but her eyes belied her harshness, for they were full of tears. "Let me straighten your tie and shirt, why don't you . . . Oh, my stars, you've gotten almost as slovenly as dreadful Aiken."

She took a comb from her deep pocket and tidied up his hair, and then standing off gave him a look of mingled admiration and cureless pain.

"You look splendid for him, Owen," she whispered.

"Doesn't he!" boomed Clarence Skegg entering with so light a step he had not been heard.

"Owen, Owen! It's so wonderful to see you, after all this time . . . You've grown into a young man! Hasn't he, Lady Bythe-waite," he turned to her like one with new-found joy.

"It has been some time, that is certain, Clarence," she spoke with a dry throat.

"They want me at the local theater," he went on, his volubility on a par now with a certain glacial control, and his new-found New York accent filling the rooms with this unaccustomed cadence. "And so I must be off! I don't know when I'll be back for a longer visit, but of course that will be easy to arrange, now that I am in the vicinity again at last." He laughed here a bit edgily. "Are you both coming for the celebration?"

Lady Bythewaite looked confused.

"I know you don't like public celebrations, my dear, so don't feel you or indeed Owen need come . . . I realize you must have additional duties now also," he finished rather lamely.

And so he had gone, like some wonderfully colored peregrine bird which by mistake had flown into their unprepared room, had displayed its exotic incarnation briefly, and then vanished.

"He'll be back to see just you," Lady Bythewaite said studying Owen's face with careful worry. "In his profession, you see, he has no time . . ."

"Oh don't gloss it over, Mother," Owen responded to this remark in the firm male tones of Aiken Cusworth. "He couldn't bear it, that's all . . ."

"What is *it*, Owen dearest," she wondered, and immediately wished she had bitten her tongue off.

"What do you think it is!" he retorted with savage bitterness.

"Owen, you have never looked more handsome for a homecoming," she told him, then regretted this statement also, for a look of inexpressible torment crossed the boy's face.

"Listen, Owen, I will fetch him back for you . . . I mean Aiken of course . . . I promised I would . . . I sent him away, but I will fetch him back . . . But you shall keep Lucy too, for she's so kind and considerate of you. I have seen your dear face in her company soften and glow . . ."

"I doubt I need anybody now, Mother."

She waited until she could breathe a bit more easily, then went on: "I know Clarence's manner was very abrupt," and she remembered her own mistakes, tormented by a conflux of wild indecision, confusion, foreboding, ever-present sickness. "Success goes to some people's heads, you know, even petty success like his . . ."

"Is that how you read it?" Owen spoke in an expressionless voice, but he looked at her as if his eyes had never been robbed of light.

At that moment Lucy came into the room, and took her accustomed seat near Owen.

Lady Bythewaite had never liked women in general, and any woman in particular, but she had grown to care for Lucy. Lucy had brought something into the house, if not into her life, she would never even have thought of searching for. Yes, without the girl's presence, she might have run mad. And though a woman is not enough, Lady Bythewaite had often meditated, for someone like Owen who worships a hero, Lucy did more than very well for him indeed.

"Allow no more visitors today, Lucy," Lady Bythewaite said, going out the back door, and then wended her way over the expanse of the great meadow.

All the small villages close by and even at some distance from Prince's Crossing had turned out to honor Maynard Ewing's return. The folk had forgotten perhaps he was really Clarence Skegg, and since his parents did not come to claim him, a kind of general impression was created by the committee in charge of the gala event that the little communities themselves were his progenitor. Both Mr. Skegg and Lady Bythewaite were in seclusion during the "triumph" and homecoming, and to tell the truth, Maynard Ewing was more than relieved they did not appear with him as he drove in one rose-bedecked open carriage after another, surrounded always by young girls in shocking pink and carrying great waxen bouquets of gladiolas. Yes, people had forgotten he was Clarence Skegg, son of the old maggot, expelled from West Point, and of dubious other escapades, in their deep emotion and dogged determination to honor the thirty-foot face which had appeared to them on the silver screen of their photoplay houses, the intense flickering embodiment of youth and glory and riches, come briefly to earth before he would be snatched up again away from them into the great crucible of dreams and shadow, only to return to earth again at some distant time in an as yet untitled great melodrama of flickering motes and "titles."

Maynard Ewing's only present comforter, guide, and consolation in all the uproar of his apotheosis was his old friend Stephen Bottrell, who, in the absence of the boy's family, was never more than an arm's length away from him, whether the star appeared in flower-decked carriages, bandstands covered with bunting, or before the pulpit of some church to which he had been invited to speak briefly while doting ladies of the missionary society and preachers' wives from this town and that looked on.

But like the cut flowers with which he was constantly presented, Maynard Ewing was wilting badly under the summer skies. Owen's dreadful fate (Clarence Skegg had never been able to bear the sight of sickness, old age, or death in any of its manifestations) had an accumulating debilitating influence on the actor, and all he could think was that he never wished to see the boy again. He would see Lady Bythewaite again of course, *had* to see her, for he had some pressing business matters to discuss, but he could not look at that martyred face of poor Owen. And then, though Maynard Ewing was now sober, had not so much as touched a drop in many many months, every so often a phenomenon took place which recalled to him his worst days, his humiliation at having sunk so low the day Lady Bythewaite had appeared out of nowhere: for from out of the crowd, just when his own sense of his importance and glory had reached its acme, it would seem to him, no, not just seem, he did see a face which he should have remembered, but which he was sure he had never known, a face as recognizable as what he saw when he looked in the mirror, and yet, he had to admit, of a greater handsomeness and stronger features, a face like that of some rugged archangel who looked toward him with judgment, with controlled but vigorous scorn, and with some hint of direful prophecy. Again and again as the brass bands played, and he was dragged up one street and down another, he thought he caught sight of this apparition of a young man's face, but the moment he would call Stephen Bottrell's attention to it, the face vanished, and Maynard Ewing could only rub his eyes as if he too feared he was losing his vision.

Then one day, after a wearying series of receptions, appearances at lodges and ball parks, autographing and handclasping, on his way to see his father, he had perceived leaving Mr. Skegg's back driveway that same young man, that same face, driving off fast as Jehu in a damaged buggy, with a horse that rushed as if it were devoured by flames. "That's him!" he exclaimed to a startled Stephen Bottrell, and he ran up the front steps of the old maggot's house, rushed into his father's presence like that schoolboy of some years past, and before the astonished mouth of the old man cried: "Who left here just now as if he had set the house afire!"

Mr. Skegg rose, greeted Mr. Bottrell with a glacial nod, and then indicated to Clarence Skegg, or Maynard Ewing, that if he wished to discuss private matters Mr. Bottrell might wait in the next room for a few moments.

Alone together, Clarence repeated his question with a splenetic vehemence.

"The man who left here in such a hurry, Father! Cannot you understand English anymore!"

Mr. Skegg gazed at his son with insolent pity. "The man who left here in such a hurry, Clarence, will soon buy and sell both me and Lady Bythewaite, for your information . . . Do not be surprised if on your next visit to your birthplace you see her and me begging in the streets . . ."

"But who is he? I see him, I fancy, everywhere I go . . ."

"That's odd," Mr. Skegg considered his observation. "For he keeps pretty much out of sight since he has even less use for the world than any of us, I daresay . . ."

"But, Father, who in blazing hell is he . . ."

Mr. Skegg looked both offended and disgusted. He threw down a pencil with which he had been checking some figures and calculations.

"Do you never stop acting, Clarence? Must you always, like Lady Bythewaite, turn everything into a scene of some sort! Who is who, you fool?"

"That thunderbolt that just left here in his threadbare contraption of a buggy."

"That's your brother Aiken Cusworth, in reply to your question, and you'd better have some respect for him and what he may be."

Clarence sat down, wiped away the perspiration and with it the slight cover of theater makeup he had put on for his various receptions.

"You told me that once before, that Aiken Cusworth was my brother. I didn't believe it then, and I don't now . . . He was, ever since I can remember, some sort of fellow who worked with his hands, and was always around horses, and a blackguard to boot . . ."

"Well, whatever he was then, you're related by blood . . . And if you don't want to believe it, why should you, Clarence . . . You've always preferred pipe dreams to life, and it's too late, I judge, to change you now . . . Certainly I'm too old to care about setting people right about what's a fact and what's not a fact, and I'm now indeed so old that I don't always see anymore the difference between a fact, and what a man chooses to believe is one . . ."

Clarence turned away with contemptuous brow from his father's statement, and then champing his jaw as if it held an iron curb, he cried:

"Well, I will seek out this fellow and talk with him, whatever you may think."

"I would not do that if I may offer you a word of advice."

"You would not see him," Clarence quoted from his father's statement, but there was no hint of sarcasm as he spoke, and he looked lost in thought, resembling, even his father must have noted, one of those photoplay scenes in which he was so adept, and speaking quietly and very much like one of the "titles" flashed on the silver screen: "Aiken Cusworth has changed, Mr. Skegg, so that I for one would not have known him from Adam. He looks like someone who commands not just men but hosts and armies . . ."

Mr. Skegg's fingers moved about in search of one of his pencils, and his lips formed themselves into their characteristic tight single line. "I don't follow your comparison, I'm afraid," Mr. Skegg said with such emphasis, if not irony, that Clarence looked over at his father.

"You mean, sir, you see him now just as when he was some little blacksmith or stable boy . . ."

Mr. Skegg grinned. "Oh, well, Clarence, he has dolled himself up a bit since then, especially now that he's buying up all the farms and pasture land Lady Bythewaite and I have had to let slip from our fingers." He looked accusing at his son. "But Aiken's face and . . . his hulk appear the same to me, whatever the clothes he has on his back, or the deeds and mortgages he holds in his hand . . ."

"But where did he get his clothes, may I ask?" Clarence went on in the mooning wondering manner which always stimulated Mr. Skegg's bile, "Why, the suit he had on today looked as if he had called down four tailors to pour him into it . . ."

"Should you meet with him, Clarence, which will be your greatest mistake, mark my words, you may inquire then who picks out his wardrobe for him . . . But until then—" and here Mr. Skegg indicated he must be left alone now with the pile of papers and figures which awaited his attention, and his fingers at last closed over the particular pencil he had been searching for during their colloquy.

But though "dismissed" by Mr. Skegg, the actor stayed on for some minutes later, in a deep fit of abstraction, so that one would have thought he was listening to the sounds of the pencil as it rode over the ruled pages of the ancient ledger on the desk of the old maggot.

Clarence Skegg's homecoming triumph was further put in the shade shortly after his dampening talk with Mr. Skegg by the very person who had arranged the whole gala affair in the first place.

Pressing Stephen Bottrell for more information about all the "affairs" which had been taking place in Prince's Crossing, Clarence learned in more detail what Mr. Skegg had only hinted at, that Aiken of late had become so clever in real estate both Mr. Skegg and Lady Bythewaite's "vast holdings" were threatened, were indeed jeopardized.

Clarence sat on gloomily, after this disclosure, in Stephen's front parlor, and then suddenly asked boldly for whiskey.

"You promised me you would never touch it again, and would certainly not imbibe while you were home," Stephen reminded him of their "understanding."

"All right, all right," the actor snapped. "But let me tell you something, or rather fill in your ignorance. You mentioned a moment ago that Lady Bythewaite and Mr. Skegg were in danger of losing their property to Aiken . . . A more exact statement, Stephen, would be that they lost their property through my debts. He has merely bought up, I suppose, what they lost to keep it in the family, on the bastard side it is true, but still, the family." He let out a laugh of such unpleasant stridency that Stephen jumped in his seat.

"How about my drink now, Stephen, don't I deserve it?"

The photoplay manager shook his head gravely. The information concerning Clarence's debts and the possible ruin of Lady Bythewaite and Mr. Skegg troubled him.

"Then if you won't give me a drink, Stephen, at least go with me to the court house, and let's see how rich Aiken Cusworth is!"

Clarence spoke with an ominous crafty kind of supplication, and a new facet to the actor's character appeared before Stephen Bottrell's confused observation.

"If you promise me you won't drink, Clarence," the young man began after struggling to find some order in his thoughts, "I'll go indeed with you to the court house, or anywhere else."

He stood up and went over to where the actor held his head in his hands. "But why torment yourself, Clarence!" He touched his friend gently.

"How could Aiken be rich or Owen blind!" Clarence was weeping now. "Why did I come back! You should never have made me do it, Stephen. I was happier, if such a person as I can speak of happiness, when I was in the gutter than coming back here and seeing what it is I came out of . . ."

"Well, thanks for your appreciation of my efforts!" Stephen retaliated, and drew away, and going over to a little end-table, took up his summer hat. "Well, shall we go to the recorder's office then and see how rich your brother is?"

Clarence winced at the word *brother*. He hesitated a long time, then rising, going up to a pier looking-glass, he straightened his tie, put some saliva on a handkerchief and wiped off some traces of dust, moistened his lips again, and dried the few tears which still clung to his long black lashes.

Having arrived in the court house, the division of records, and after receiving several effusive welcomes from the clerks there, Clarence Skegg, with a rather consummate efficiency for an actor, began going through the record files of late real estate transactions, while Stephen Bottrell sat waiting on an uncomfortable spindly chair, mopping his brow against the accumulated summer heat emanating from this pre-Civil War structure.

He never took his eyes, however, off Clarence Skegg, and if the actor regretted having come home, Stephen regretted his having fetched him a hundred times more.

Out of respect for the distinguished visitor and hometown boy, a set of rusty old fans were set going, and these grinding wheezing contraptions put Stephen's nerves even more on edge, so that at last he was about to jump up and excuse himself on the grounds he had pressing business elsewhere when he caught sight of a look of such overwhelming astonishment on that face of Clarence Skegg that he was glad he had endured the discomfort of the wait in the court house.

Clarence motioned for Stephen to come over to the files and take a look. And looking his fill, Stephen felt that his own face, had anybody observed it now as he stared into the mass of deeds, mortgages, and other related papers which Clarence moved before his eyes, yes his face would have been as much a study for any observer as Clarence's had been for him.

"Isn't that enough to satisfy your curiosity for one visit, Clarence," Stephen whispered, and put his arm on his friend's shoulder. "Don't look anymore . . ."

"I could come back tomorrow perhaps," Clarence thought now out loud, his eyes raised to the moldering Civil War flags in the corridor, rigid as if they were made of caked sand.

"Or," he came out of his reverie, and looked into Stephen's eyes with a sightless and yet vehement expression, "I could go in person to the lion's den . . ."

"Well, you won't be that big an Almighty-God-damned fool, will you?" Stephen raised his voice, and closed the file of the papers they had both been examining.

"In our family," Clarence mumbled, and there was no trace of dramatic inflection now, "we always do the wrong thing, Stephen."

Stephen Bottrell led Clarence Skegg away, in a deep study, almost by the hand, to a small confectioner's store where there was a player piano going full force to drown out whatever they might say, and a booth in the back where he hoped Clarence would not attract the notice of any passing admirers. Stephen ordered two cups of the local coffee, over which Clarence made faces, complaining not very convincingly that it was too gritty. Nonetheless he drank one cup and ordered another, while all the time they sat in the booth an augmenting crowd of curiosity seekers politely and silently stared in the direction of the celebrity. Stephen studied his friend. Clarence appeared genuinely unaware of, or completely disinterested in, the knot of admirers peering at him, and though the actor continued to look as though he were a thousand miles away, the photoplay manager wondered if perhaps for the first time in many years, perhaps for the first time in his life, he was home at last, for all his thoughts, painful, and all his feelings, exacerbated, were directed in blinding concentration on Prince's Crossing, which was claiming him whether he claimed it or not, and his main thought rested especially on Aiken Cusworth.

After moving his lips silently, and then awkwardly beginning to whisper something to himself, but without any touch of histrionics, and no longer recalling a photoplay actor so much as he did a man about to defend his life in a court room crowded with lifetime enemies, Clarence at last blurted out:

"Where does he live, Stephen?"

"Where does who live?"

"You know God-damned well who . . ."

"Don't keel over, then, when I tell you," Stephen snapped in growing shortness of temper, and there was now such a look of stony disapproval and fierce censure in his eyes and on his brow that Clarence's mouth opened with a dawning apprehension of some future bad disclosure.

"But for Christ's sake, don't go," Stephen raised his voice in an appeal. "Clarence," he begged in lower but even more insistent earnestness, and took his friend's hand in his, "go back to New York at once—this minute!"

"That bastard upstart, crossroads robber," Clarence mumbled, pulling his hand away from Stephen's pressure.

"No, no," the photoplay manager cried in disagreement, and wondered at finding himself in the role of defending the horse-tender, whom he feared and hated. "Aiken did it all up and above board!"

"And owns all this part of the country!" Clarence stood up and overturned his cup of coffee. "All right, if you won't tell me where the nameless scum lives, I'll find out from the next fellow I meet up the street . . ."

"All right, then," Stephen made retort, his fingers painstakingly and slowly tearing up the tiny napkin he had just seen Clarence wipe his mouth with. "Aiken lives, if you can think of him living anywhere, at the Acres . . ."

Despite his years of training in the theater and before his own looking-glass, Clarence was so astounded at the pronouncement and mention of this name, that he sat down into the booth again, and passed his hand over his brow like a man who has heard a final blasphemy.

"Would you please repeat what you just said again, Stephen," the actor mumbled, his eyes half-closed.

"I don't need to repeat it. You heard it right the first time."

The Acres, Clarence now reminded the young manager and reminded himself, in a long and often inaudible, if not incoherent, speech, free, however, of posturing, and too dry even for snobbery, the Acres had once been the grand show place of this entire part of the country, and though in great disrepair, was still the touchstone of grandeur vanished, and of imperial, if disappeared splendor. He was about to say more, but at the last, perhaps remembering that Stephen Bottrell was after all only an outsider, he kept it to himself.

There was a long queer silence, and then Clarence, looking up as if appealing for Stephen to assure him that they were at least still among the living, and in their right minds, merely said again, "Acres, imagine that," and repeated the name of the estate over and over.

"Why don't you leave, Clarence. The celebration is all but over, and you've done more than they ever expected you to do . . . You're bushed . . ."

"There's a banquet for me tonight," he announced with his old peevishness. "No matter . . . I want you to go over this all with me again, for you know everything," and he turned relentlessly back to the subject of Acres.

"God Almighty, what you and your family subject me to!" Stephen now went off on his own impetuous divagation and private anger. "I had to watch your young brother go blind, and see your other brother go crazy over it! Now I have to tell you he owns the Acres, and see you, why, I do not know, foam at the mouth over that!"

"But Aiken can't *own* them, Stephen," Clarence went on, oblivious to his friend's complaint and sense of being exploited. "I didn't see any mention of Acres in that drawer of his robberies at the recorder's office . . ."

"Well, Clarence, tell me since when is ownership robbery . . . Aiken owns the Acres. Everybody in Prince's Crossing knows it."

"A livery-stable boy, crumbling with horse shit, smelling like a steaming dray horse, who never bathed for ten years . . ."

Clarence stood up now again, his teeth gleaming, his eyes not quite in focus.

"If you go there, my friend, you're a bigger fool than even Mr. Skegg takes you for," Stephen said with complete effrontery and daring, though as he spoke he turned his face toward the wall, and his eyes, in angry inflammation, filled with hot tears.

"Oh if only being a fool, Stephen, was all that was wrong with me," and he took his friend's hand and wrung it.

Stephen Bottrell, who was after all "from the outside," so far as the world of Prince's Crossing was concerned, had not understood, could not understand why the mention of the estate known as Acres had touched his friend so deeply, and it was on this that Clarence now meditated in black concentration. When Clarence was a small boy, he and Lady Bythewaite had been guests at the estate many times. Its then rightful owner had been a woman of much greater qualities than any other person Clarence had ever met—Mrs. Macconall, who had taken a great fancy to the boy, and had personally shown him and his "lady mother," as she called Nora, through the endless numbers of rooms, salons, corridors, banquet halls, and then up to a parapet such as a castle would be proud of, to where the water of the indigo-blue lake lapped in disquieting sound.

"I want you to think of this as your home, Master Clarence," Mrs. Macconall had said on his first visit, and on one of his last visits, she had taken the boy's hand, and spoken in serious mournful tones: "This great place will be yours one day, Clarence, I am sure of it." This statement, unforgettable as a prophecy is, remained forever locked and unexpunged in his memory.

And often when either at the pinnacle of his "fame" in New York, or in the depths of his degradation, he had thought that if he had Acres, as promised him, and some spending money, he would ask nothing more of life.

The final banquet in honor of the hometown boy was in full swing at the Knights of Pythias Hall, and Clarence, immersed in a kind of trance, or deep stupor, had nonetheless the presence of mind to pass up all the libations and toasts, and drinks, but was otherwise oblivious to all the details of the festival, hardly knew next to whom he sat (it was the mayor on one side, the Congregational minister on the other), or what he had sipped (turtle soup), or pretended to eat (porterhouse steak, cheese soufflé, and drowned-in-homemade-dandelion-wine apple dumplings). He came "to" during the lengthy divagating belly-rumbling after-dinner speech and eulogy by the mayor:

> "From our own roots and background, where he had his beginnings, he has reached to the highest ramparts of our national life. With no knowledge of the world and only a rudimentary introduction to the craft of the theater, but imbued by nature and his own genius, our young man has scaled the tallest ladder in the history of world entertainment. The face we took for granted as our own and our native son's, as familiar to us as our skies and ploughed fields, has, in a single vaulting leap of energy and enterprise, become the face known and dreamed of throughout this entire peopled world, and without exaggeration, adored by all who look upon it . . ."

Rising from the table at this point, carrying his monogrammed linen napkin in his hand, without excusing himself, Clarence had rushed through the hall and outside, and then without quite knowing what he was doing, though he was cold sober, he had proceeded through a back road—the only road there was which led to Acres. He would not—he now remembered Stephen's warning—for he was afraid, the only time he had experienced this kind of fear—he would not go in. He could not go in! He could not see all that he found grand and noble and of any dignity or meaning in the black hands of a bastard livery stableman.

He stood a long time before the shrouded bulk of the great house. A mist common to that part of the country had come up from the now silent lake, and was proceeding aimlessly over the stretch of greensward directly facing him, as if shepherded by invisible hands. The mammoth gate was closed, but in a section of the hedge he spied an opening large enough for him to pass through.

He proceeded up the long gravel path then overgrown with wild flowers and thistles, passed under the spruce trees, and walked round a few motionless willows. But he had been wrong about there being no light, for as he stood now within a few rods of the main entrance, he saw from the deep recesses of the mansion itself a small but strong, if intermittently flickering light coming either from an illumination of candles or a gas lamp, certainly not electricity.

He turned to go, but then a deep anger overtook him so that had he been within reach of a glass of whiskey he would have taken it and drunk it down at one gulp. And so instead he would drink down, swallow his good resolutions made to Stephen, he would enter the mansion, he would speak his piece!

He strode up the crumbling stone steps, and stared at the elaborate frosted glass of the palatial doors. Without knocking or ringing any bell, which he presumed like everything else was out of use, he entered the hall itself, then stopped, for he could hear his heart thundering within his chest. Some tiny current of sound was audible inside, but this sound, whatever it was, only accentuated the deathly stillness of the great abandoned estate, where even the trees were invisible and silent in the moving mist from the lake.

He opened only one door, beyond which there was revealed the one person he had made all this trouble to see, unbidden and uninvited. But for a moment he had thought he had made a mistake for he did not recognize the man seated at a huge lengthy table such as a board of inquiry might choose for its deliberations. No, a stranger sat there, one who did not resemble a groom or muscular gladiator, but a pale, in the light of the guttering tall candle, thoughtful face absorbed in reading perhaps a roster of the dead, for the eyes were lowered, moving over the pages of some great tome. The face looked up, unsurprised, but not entirely impassive, for the beautifully formed mouth appeared to be ejaculating *No*.

"Has the banquet in your honor let out so early?" Aiken Cusworth inquired at last, moving his eyes from the ledger to a huge clock and barely including Clarence Skegg in that rapid glance.

"It has indeed let out," Clarence replied like one hypnotized.

"There is only one chair here," Aiken raised his voice, and rose. "You are welcome to it."

"Who are you to welcome me to so much as a stick in this mansion which does not belong to you by right, which you have cheated and lied to gain access to!" He had recovered his sense of outrage and anger after his first start on seeing the horsetender in possession, but he had not got his voice, which came out a ragged whisper.

Aiken folded his arms, and as he did so he no longer resembled the ascetic pallid judge of others' misfortunes and errors as when he had been seated but some county-fair wrestler or battered pugilist.

"You are welcome nonetheless to my house, and to anything I have, Clarence."

Unprepared for this response, Clarence fell into the proffered single chair, so that the effect was now that Aiken stood behind the actor like a faithful retainer awaiting his orders.

"If you have left a banquet in your sole honor to visit me in my house, then you are welcome indeed." Aiken's voice came in even measures from behind Clarence's bowed head.

"Wait till my brain quits spinning, and I will have an answer for your vaulting insolence," Clarence whispered. "Let me recover myself . . . The banquet you harp on be damned, and your hospitality and you assigned to the hottest seat in hell, you unleashed cur!"

With cat-like quickness, Aiken picked up the candelabrum which held only the one oversized candle, and set it on a smaller rosewood table directly facing Clarence, and began to study the face of the actor, his own arms now loosely hanging by his sides.

"What have you to say in your own defense?" Clarence thundered at him. "That you have tricked and deceived and beggared all who ever helped you, that you have bought and sold your own kith and kin, and disinherited by your thefts those who rescued you from the mire you were born in . . ."

"I disinherit *you!*" Aiken's voice now found its own volume, and came rushing from his own expanding lungs so that the sound issuing therefrom filled the room, and rushed out of doors as if to rouse all who had ever had ears, living and dead. "Speak of the disinherited, will we! You dare taint my honor so!"

"Yes, you grimy bastard, we will speak of it!" Clarence's eyes flashed at the man standing over him, and his tongue came and went from his open mouth in writhing menace. "We shall speak of it, and we shall settle once and for all your pretensions and your theft!" He sprang to his feet.

"I have no pretensions, Clarence, and you know in your heart I do not." Aiken spoke coolly into the distorted mouth and eyes facing him, but as he spoke he made a monstrous sound as if with his pronounced words he had swallowed some great draught of brine.

"This house, mansion, in whose premises you are so angry to see me installed as its rightful master," the horsetender went on after a struggle to regain his breath.

Here a cry of rage from the actor made Aiken hesitate, but he proceeded:

"Yes, Clarence, I am its master, search the records, you'll see . . . This house, mansion, and all others I have purchased are mine not due to a bastard's having disinherited you, but because your mother and father had to sell all their farms and estates to pay your debts . . . They are both ruined . . . I bought up all they had had to sell, and the Acres in the bargain so that all this property so long in their hands would not fall to strangers . . ."

"Why, you are the greatest stranger that was ever born in a ditch!" Clarence was trembling from head to foot, and he moved about dizzily, like a man who holds speech with a phantom, which taunts him from the safety of invisibility. "You were never born, in any case, you filthy tramp . . . Or if any woman was your mother, she was a horse!"

"She was your mother, and you know it," Aiken said. "You have always known it. You knew it from the first day you set eyes on me."

"Say that again, and I will kill you," Clarence now advanced toward his tormentor.

Aiken again looked at the intruder with calm clear eyes, and Clarence, despite his clenched fists and snarling lips, merely turned away.

Then beginning to babble again, Clarence said: "You would have me believe that an unlettered brute such as yourself has done all this reaping of fortune on your own . . . Who is *your* master? Who sets you on? From whom do you receive your orders?"

"I must warn you, Clarence, though I bear our father and mother great respect, and despite all my own many shortcomings, I say, I warn you, you are standing on my rightfully gained property, and I will not hear myself abused, by you, or by no man . . . I am not a brute, but you are not a man. I despise you, rather I pity you. But you are my brother, and I will not harm a hair of your head . . ."

"If you ever again claim blood relationship with me, I warn you, Aiken Cusworth, you shall pay a final penalty for it . . ."

"Well, there is no penalty I fear anybody can exact from me, I suppose, by now, save—" and suddenly as if a secret spring had been touched, he stopped, turned away, musing.

"Save Owen Haskins, I suppose!" Clarence cried, having during Aiken's strange abstraction come up within an inch of his face, and hissing these words into that unprepared mouth so that Clarence's rash words appeared indeed to issue from Aiken's own lips.

"Yes, your secret is known! Your appropriating of Owen, after you had ruined him, so that you could hold an upper hand over Lady Bythewaite and Mr. Skegg, and indeed all of us, and then through lessons with the devil himself, you have learned to cheat and steal."

But a kind of glow of such unearthly aspect began to diffuse itself over Aiken's features that the actor stopped for a moment in wonder. Then his mania, rising again, carried him on:

"I will ruin you if it's with the last breath I draw . . . You shall not have Acres, you shall not pose as my brother, you shall not appropriate Owen, whom you have made blind . . ."

As if asleep, for his eyes were closed, Aiken began moving his hands and fingers slowly toward the chair, and then firmly seizing it by its arms, he raised it over Clarence's head, and his eyes came wide open.

"Hit me, kill me, why don't you, for you have only your strength and cunning from whatever pair of animals were your parents . . ."

As if too unsure of his purpose or indeed where he was or who it was pouring out these words of torment, Aiken suddenly put down the chair, sighed, and stood as bereft of motion as Owen Haskins was of light.

Picking up the solitary chair the master of Acres had put down, Clarence raised it to a dizzy height and brought it down again and again upon the upright body of Aiken Cusworth, but no matter how many times he struck his brother with it, splintering the wood, and driving those remaining splinters until they were like giant toothpicks, nothing moved this upright figure, so that at last, seeing it was as if he struck a simulacrum of a man made of iron or indeed perhaps only of mist, the actor left off his blows. Only the torn clothing and streaming rivulets of blood gave notice he had struck a man.

Then beginning to leave the room, but searching unsurely for the way out, for he felt both drunk and insane, Clarence stopped at last on reaching the threshold and looked back at the upright thing which had dared to call himself his brother, and said:

"I am not through with you yet . . . I will have justice from you, and I will have Acres, and you shall not turn us out of the house and home without you pay with your own blood . . ."

After a long wait, in which Aiken was not sure if Clarence was still in the room or was yet going down the long flights of stairs leading to the front yard, he walked, dazzled and spent, with the stiffness of a man encased in armor to the head of the stairs, shouting into the night:

"I never bereft him of his sight, Clarence! Never, never touched him or his eyes! I am innocent of that, innocent . . ."

"No, no, my dear Bottrell, I cannot credit your tale!" Mr. Skegg was speaking loftily to the photoplay house manager. "You always remind me somehow of Lady Bythewaite in your fondness for hyperbole, and though I thank you for your coming here at this hour of the night, and for your seeming concern for my family, the scene which you purport to have occurred would be more convincing on the screen of your picture show house!"

Stephen Bottrell had roused the old maggot at two o'clock in the morning, and though Mr. Skegg, if one were to believe him, hardly ever closed his eyes in bed at night (which may have explained why he was so often asleep during the daytime hours in his big chair), he was, Stephen thought, just short of an inhabitant of the cemetery, impossible to wake.

Mr. Bottrell's own temper, however, was getting frayed, but rather than flare up he gazed with somewhat less than appreciative eyes at the old man's sleeping apparel, which was a darned cotton nightshirt, a most unbecoming nightcap, and some gray mittens owing to his suffering from chilblains, but it was the nightcap which most engaged Stephen's attention and drew from him the most amazement, for since he was city-bred, it was the first nightcap he had ever been privileged to see, and his persistent staring at this article of apparel finally put Mr. Skegg out of countenance, and then roused the spleen which he now poured out against the movie theater owner.

Mr. Skegg now reviewed the fight between Aiken and Clarence, as reported by Mr. Bottrell in the dim morning hours. He retold it as a false communiqué, and indeed snorted. He walked up and down the floor, and denied it again, quoting pieces of a paraphrase of his own retelling. Then turning with great accusation to the bearer of the news he said:

"I cannot credit it at all, dear Bottrell, that a big strapping fellow like Aiken Cusworth would allow his . . . brother . . . that is, Clarence, to attack him with . . . you say a chair?"

Mr. Skegg, however, now appeared to be ready to believe that a fight might, however, have occurred.

"I have more news, besides, than what I have told you, Mr. Skegg, but if you do not choose to credit anything I say, we will drop the whole thing, and I will go home . . ."

"No, indeed, you shall not leave . . . I will not dismiss you, sir . . ." Then with an attempt at mollification, the old man whispered: "We will ring for sustenance first . . ."

And lifting up a great bell such as must have been once used to summon threshers to a noon banquet, the old man moved the iron clapper of the bell which spread its alarm to the most distant landscape rousing many dogs immediately to bark.

"Now we will be cautious and calm, Bottrell," he said, and to Stephen's even greater exasperation, he took out from his nightshirt a notebook and a small two-inch pencil. "We will write down the facts, sir, and of course the complaints—the entire picture!"

Hearing nothing but silence, Mr. Skegg then looked up impatiently at Stephen, like a police officer about to interrogate a suspect. "Well?" the old man cried in the face of this augmenting silence.

But at that moment, a middle-aged woman, fully dressed, and wearing pince-nez, entered the room with a tray, a large pitcher of something, glasses, and napkins, giving Stephen the impression that this red-faced weather-beaten worthy person sat and waited throughout the night hours precisely for the earsplitting bell to ring, and wonder of wonders, he saw that whatever the pitcher contained it was steaming hot. To his disappointment it turned out to be milk, which he loathed, and now rejected.

"Would spirits tempt you?" Mr. Skegg inquired with gelid neutrality. "I keep spirits purely as medicine."

Stephen nodded, and the woman servant withdrew, returning in a very short space with a bottle of sour mash, and a large cut-glass tumbler, which Stephen stroked appreciatively, rather to

Mr. Skegg's disapproval, for he distrusted the worship of furniture and glassware.

"Now, my dear fellow, whom did you say you accuse?" Mr. Skegg had begun the inquest again, after barely sipping a bit of the hot milk. "And what is the storm you say is about to lower?"

Stephen drank heavily from the glass, and tried to hide a great starting tear in his eye which arose from the strength of the spirits. But Mr. Skegg mistook his tears for weeping and weeping in men he found even more detestable than their liking antique tumblers, and he tapped therefore with his pencil fussily against his tiny notebook.

"Mr. Bottrell, we don't have forever! Would you please come to the point."

"He has purchased a gun!"

Mr. Skegg wrote this down, but then, raising his inflamed eyes, cried, "Who?"

"Who, Mr. Skegg, but the assailant!" he responded, falling into the police station atmosphere evoked by the old maggot's manner. "Your son, Clarence Skegg, has purchased a gun to kill his brother with, kill Aiken Cusworth with!"

"Kill whom?" Mr. Skegg's face became more chalky than usual.

"He told me," Stephen swallowed hurriedly some more of the sour mash, which was not merely the strongest he had ever put to his lips but the most corrosive, "he assured me, Mr. Skegg, that he would kill Aiken Cusworth before the sun rose tomorrow, which is, sir, today . . ."

"More melodrama," the old man cried wearily, and put the tiny stub of pencil behind his left ear. "I seem to be surrounded by persons who think they are in photoplays," he went on complaining and appeared about to confide this statement to his little notebook. He removed his nightcap then, and his mound of white hair suddenly rose perceptibly like a great pile of meringue which is ready for the oven.

"I don't know how you can expect me to be calm and collected when I have had to see what I have seen tonight. I actually felt sorry for Aiken Cusworth, for he has been brutally beaten . . ."

"You mean to sit there and tell me again that Aiken would permit a fellow like Clarence, of so much less physical prowess, to beat him, as you claim, to a pulp . . . and never raise a hand to defend himself in return?"

"That is exactly what happened, Mr. Skegg . . . I don't know what had passed between the two of course, except for some wandering account Clarence dribbled out to me, but shortly after whatever did occur Clarence purchased a gun. He also began to drink. And he also disappeared . . . Then I had to make up my mind. That was when I went to see Aiken Cusworth, though I'd rather have gone to hell instead, but I went, and for the first time in my acquaintance with him, he treated me politely. He listened to everything I told him at least, but, Mr. Skegg, he did not seem to hear me, or care even that a man is searching him out to kill him . . . My warning, my concern for him was all to no good. I might as well have warned the treetops . . ."

Mr. Skegg was about to say again he would forbid melodrama coming into the conversation, and his lips indeed formed to say something along this line, but finally a sort of involuntary hardening of his entire countenance, coming over him like the forming of the ice in the lake at the beginning of winter, made him mute. He put away his small notebook, though he permitted the dwarf pencil to remain lodged behind his ear, and he painstakingly put back on his nightcap, for he felt cold, and very old, and very scared, and a bit nauseous.

"If you don't mind, would you pass me the bottle of the sour mash," he requested of Stephen Bottrell. He poured a small quantity of this elixir, no more than a tablespoon, and drank, with even more of a grimace than that displayed a short time ago by the photoplay manager.

"I don't like to call the sheriff," Mr. Skegg confided, "but I think I may have to . . . But perhaps we should wait till morning . . . Or perhaps we should not . . . Oh, if I were only twenty years younger, Mr. Bottrell, I would put a stop to this nonsense myself, and *now* . . . It is all Lady Bythewaite's fault! She has ruined all our lives. I hope she will feel satisfied and fulfilled and even proud when she sees us all in our caskets and knows then that she has achieved what her purpose in life has been . . ."

At this very comprehensive explanation of all their difficulties, Stephen Bottrell in his embarrassment and general confusion poured the old maggot another tablespoon of mash without receiving permission or a go-ahead sign to do so, and though Mr. Skegg frowned at first at this audacity, he drank nonetheless from the freshening of his drink, and with an imperious sign from his knitted brow commanded Stephen to pour himself more likewise.

At about four o'clock in the morning, with a heavy driving rain falling, the servants at Lady Bythewaite's mansion looked out the great blurred splashed window with as much astonishment as they could summon up in view of the fact that astonishment was, so to speak, their steady bill of fare in their present employment, and saw Nora Bythewaite herself driving her buggy out from the yard, and—all the servants agreed among themselves—she was very poorly dressed for such inclement weather, and indeed looked as if she were in her night clothes, while sitting beside her, but wrapped up a bit more sensibly against the bad weather, was Owen Haskins. And following Lady Bythewaite's carriage was another, in which sat ancient vigorous Mr. Skegg bolt upright.

The servants had been awakened by shouts and curses, and had with some difficulty, and then only after having opened a score of great doors, heard Nora Bythewaite protesting against some sort of desolate dark mission which the old maggot was evidently forcing upon her at "this ungodly hour."

"You would have me drive out in this hurricane rain, to *him*," Lady Bythewaite's voice now reached all the ears of the servants easily, "to one who hates me to the death, who has attempted my life, in order to save his life from the alleged threats of a stage-struck fool . . . And hear this . . . He told me, and who is he, but Aiken," here she seemed to have shouted owing to Mr. Skegg's slight deafness, "*he* told me that the day would come when I would have to crawl on my hands and knees to him, beg his mercy, ask in effect that I allow him to put his heel on my grateful face, and then twist it there until he was weary . . ."

Mr. Skegg's hoarse crow's voice then rose even over hers, saying again and again as in a chorus, expressionless and catarrhal: "But to avert calamity, Nora, only to avert calamity! . . . Have I ever come at such an hour in all our career together! You know I at least am no playactor!"

"Nor have I ever known you to come with liquor on your breath!" she cried. "You are drunk as a lord. No wonder the heavens are falling upon us with all the rain and thunder. Mr. Skegg of Prince's Crossing is drunk, and out driving at four o'clock in the morning in a cyclone and combined hurricane. And Lady Bythewaite is about to get down on her hands and knees and beg Aiken Cusworth, her former livery stableman, to resume his position as head of her household, and order her to eat bread and water in the broiling attic . . ."

And after a few more crashes, vividly brought to servants' ears, and many thuds, whether these were brought about by accident or in rage, came a stunning sound of breaking glass, then the silence which usually follows such crashes in domestic arguments, and then more doors closing, footsteps, and then a young man's voice, and Nora Bythewaite's exclamation: "At least perhaps now Owen will partake of food, for he has eaten not a mouthful since his idol departed . . . Do you hear me, Owen?" —her voice rose in crescendo—"we are going to Acres, where your mother will humble herself to your hero!"

And having pronounced these words halfway between crazed laughter and complaining sobs, Nora Bythewaite and her son drove off in one carriage, and Mr. Skegg alone in another into the pouring rain, and the great house, behind them, settled down into a kind of wheezing half-silence, over which the summer thunderstorm sounded almost like a benediction.

Would they arrive too late? the old maggot wondered, shaking the reins and the whip, or was this all some more than vivid nightmare he was having, or was he as crazy as his loved ones, and as crazy as Mr. Stephen Bottrell who had set them all on this night-riding expedition. At any rate, he would have pneumonia tomorrow, for looking down he saw he was sopping wet, yes, he would get his death of cold, no matter who planned to murder whom over property and lineage.

This strange crepuscular procession was coming to avert, or perhaps witness murder, but none of the three had been quite expecting what awaited them. One expects one terrible thing only to be handed by grim mischance a surprise. They began to be forewarned, however, as they drove closer to their destination by the sight of tall billowing towers of black smoke, an occasional glimpse of orange and red banners of flames, and an indefinite roaring sound calculated to make the heart sink. As they approached closer to Acres, Owen Haskins lifted his head and moved it in the direction of the great estate, for the glare from the conflagration gave him the momentary and peculiar sensation he had regained his vision.

"Great God Almighty!"

This barked outcry was emanating from the throat of the old maggot, who had alighted from his buggy and was standing in the road shouting and waving his arms. He was unlike himself, there was nothing in his cries or motions to remind one of a financier, a calculator, or a man who condemned melodrama. Nora Bythewaite, who had stopped her horse, sat in rapt attention and unbelief, and gaped at Mr. Skegg, who was gesticulating still, though more feebly.

Approaching her, the old man moaned hoarsely:

"The greatest show place yet standing in the nation is going up in flames, my dear!" He spoke now like a preacher, when he despised preachers along with actors, indeed he spoke both like a preacher and actor, and cries of unbelief and extreme pain followed from his throat, for if Acres was no more, Mr. Skegg felt that he had nothing anymore to set his foot against and call solid ground.

Standing now by their dripping black buggies, the three travelers kept their safe distance from the buckling half-consumed palatial structure which belched and vomited, roared and whined, and then finally gave out a kind of sigh like some mammoth in the invincible bonds of death.

But Nora Bythewaite and Owen Haskins did not share exactly Mr. Skegg's outraged pain and bereavement over the witnessed demise of a great estate, though Nora at least had as much or more knowledge of what was going up in fire and roasting conflagration than the old maggot, and what old ways and customs were sinking into rosy and gray ashes.

What held both Nora and Owen in rapt attention, in concentrated and frozen silence was a kind of thoughtless almost brute wonder that if within the collapsing walls and incinerated heirlooms of Acres there might not sit or lie charred and unrecognizable Aiken Cusworth, whom alone they had come in pursuit of. Hardly daring to breathe, let alone voice their fears, mother and son merely stood, one or the other occasionally, in sheer desperation to do something, touching the great iron fence gingerly, for it had long begun to partake of the heat and fury of the fire.

Then from a clump of small young maple trees a dark hulk of a man, dragging one leg, slowly began advancing toward them. He appeared a stranger, and there passed through all their minds the wonder that this was some old retainer who had refused to leave the mansion for all these years, but had lived on like a raven or bat in the highest recesses of some pile of masonry. The figure seemed both as charred and red as the collapsing walls of the estate, as he advanced toward the three travelers.

"Oh, Aiken!" Nora Bythewaite spoke at last, "nothing could cheer my eyes more than to see you at this moment!"

Whether she slipped as she said this, or deliberately genuflected before him, at any rate she fell upon his naked feet, and as she did so, he caught her hand and tried to bring her up, but she refused to rise.

"Thank Clarence Skegg for all of this!" Aiken cried out to

them now in the manner of some speaker on the town band-stand, but with a chilly insouciant contempt, far short of real anger. "Don't contradict me with a sign or word, Mr. Skegg . . . He has done his worst, and thank him for it . . . I know him, and his works!"

Mr. Skegg could only bow his head, and look down into the rainy earth, for killing Aiken Cusworth would have been one thing, and doubtless a terrible crime, but to actually set fire to Acres, to have wiped out all that he had felt was the country and the nation, took away speech, and dropping his cane the old man fell into Aiken's arms.

But the old financier, held up by his former groom, had only stumbled, and was both conscious and determined, and begged all to allow him to remain until a house of such immemorial significance to him should be unmoving still ashes.

Nora Bythewaite, pulling Aiken away from Mr. Skegg's embrace, led the former owner of Acres away with her, and in the vigor and resolution of her grasp warned him he must never doubt again that his place was with her, if not above her.

Aiken stopped for a moment in his proceeding toward the buggy, and a look of bewildered unlooked-for respite came over his face, for studying Nora Bythewaite's eyes he saw that for her, having found him again, the death of Acres meant hardly more than a box of kitchen matches gone up in smoke.

In the midst of these great disturbances and griefs, Owen's eyesight cleared slightly so that he could partially distinguish objects a bit better, and could make his way about the house with more assurance, but even this discovery did not lighten Nora Bythewaite's heart, though she brightened a bit as she promised to take him to a great specialist as soon as there was a breathing spell.

It was Aiken Cusworth about whom she wished to talk, and she knew she had a rapt auditor ever in Owen.

"You must have noticed at first, Owen, how he was calm and collected"—she referred to the complete loss of Aiken's property Acres, the stench of the burning from which still lingered in the air—"but as in certain grave diseases or wounds from gunshot, the pain and suffering come often much later, and the sufferer then knows very little respite."

Lady Bythewaite then commanded Owen to go and sit with Aiken much as if the former groom was the one who had lost his eyesight and was in need of company, and she spoke of an appointment she had with Farmer Cuthbert, and hurried off.

Owen passed into the next room where the horsetender was sitting in a rough wooden armchair, staring out into the expanse of a lemon-colored sky, and an eternally gray lake. His hands moved delicately like leaves rising from winter beds from the east wind, but otherwise he gave no notice of the blind boy's presence but sat on, as described recently by Nora Bythewaite, "having lost his purport, his tenor, and his self." He did, however, stretch out his hand to help Owen sit down on a footstool which was placed by Aiken's great chair.

The two ruined brothers sat on then in total silence except the sound that came from their rather heavy breathing. From the distance one heard the front door open, and Farmer Cuth-bert's heavy voice greet their mother.

Nora Bythewaite had explained it all to Owen, though she did not need to explain anything about Aiken to him, but she had hinted at and then finally discoursed on the subject of Aiken's pride, which was that once he had owned Acres, all his past would be blotted out, and if Owen had looked up to him from the very beginning as some sort of primitive athlete and hero, how much more would he, and the whole community to boot, look up to him when he was the sole proprietor of the once greatest show place, the prize piece of real estate, if not in terms of actual dollars-and-cents value, in imaginative glory and renown. And this dream and pride was all ashes! That is why, Lady Bythewaite said, he sits like some dying dethroned king, or defeated general.

"You need not sit with me, Owen," Aiken began after this long bitter silence during which they had both been thinking the same thoughts. "You must have more important things to do than sit with the horsetender . . ."

When Owen tried to protest, the older brother roared out at last: "I am back where I was, don't you understand? A grimy bastard brute, living in the stable . . ."

"You're living with your family, Aiken," Owen spoke as if an iron band were about his windpipe.

"Living? or taken in by them?" he scoffed. "Yes, great families do take in broken-down grooms from the stable, I have heard tell . . ."

Owen lowered his head, and covered his sightless eyes with his fingers, and wondered at Aiken's voice, which though it spoke bitter words had no longer any real tension or vibrancy in it as of old, but resembled that of Mr. Skegg. Indeed Aiken re-sembled the old maggot more and more in the days after the holocaust, for he seemed content merely to sit in this chair, look-ing at nothing, barely moving his sinewy brown hands with the bulging but sculpturesque blue veins. Even the smell of him, as it was constantly borne over to Owen's nostrils, was more now of reined leather and ledgers than it had been of open country and animals and grass.

They now heard Nora Bythewaite's voice raised suddenly, talking to Farmer Cuthbert, but there was something new in her manner of speaking which struck both the young men instantly: she was addressing the farmer in a tone of partial respect, a respect which must have its origin in the fact she was ruined, if not as dramatically as Aiken, almost as thoroughly. The phrase *a thousand acres of rotting hay are there and nothing is being done, Farmer Cuthbert* drifted over to their ears, and Owen stirred uncomfortably, but Aiken sat immovable under her voice, for he suddenly appeared deafer now than Owen was blind, and again a phrase reached their ears: *The oats are pretty good everywhere.*

Lady Bythewaite's voice now came as clear as if it had been by Owen's side.

The blind boy took Aiken's hand for a moment, in dread perhaps at the stentorian voice enumerating bankruptcy, but the older man indifferently withdrew it.

A mingled cascade of speech now came into the room, an altercation, a dispute, a summation between the farmer and the former mistress of lands and houses:

I nowhere saw a bad field of barley, what do you mean then we should not have planted?

But that is purely corn country, I am talking of barley, Farmer Cuthbert. And the work is still all done by horses there, not machines!

That is all dry land and gravel and stones . . . I'll not think of planting there.

In the midst of these and other apostrophes to crops and lands and herds and mortgages and buying and selling and deeds and losses and banks and beggary and the suggested presence of death, one voice losing itself into the speech of the next voice, so that in the end one could barely distinguish where one speaker began and another finished. Aiken Cusworth suddenly rose from his chair and extended his arms so that one felt he could easily reach the twenty-five-foot ceiling above, then his eyes rolled, as if he did not quite know why he had risen or in whose room he was, and having got up did not know where to move his body.

No, no, it's all pasture land. You are purposely not attending to me, Lady Bythewaite . . . You might as well talk of planting it with canary seed!

But the riser from the chair was bending over the blind boy, and also in the paroxysm of orotund speech:

"If you came here to sit with me and pity me," the speech had begun, with fully restored vigor, even venom, "I say, take warning, Owen Haskins, look sharp . . . I have no pity on anybody, and should I note the least sign of it in you, pity I mean, I will tear it out of your heart, do you hear . . . I have earned no man's pity, understand? Do you?" He waited, or Owen, in his darkness, thought he waited, but heard only now

But the corn crop is always sown at the time of barley in the throttled voice of Farmer Cuthbert.

"You mean nothing to me, Owen!" Aiken's great voice drowned out that of farmer and mistress, and the boy felt his brother's fury turned against him by reason of some present movement of air. "You owe me nothing! I owe you nothing! And I will not have your sad and pitiful looks, do you hear? I will not have sadness and softness! I will tear it out from your guts, if you show it, hear?"

Then there was a kind of movement from Aiken's boots as if he had trodden so hard upon the floor it had given way, the back door a little while later crashed like dry boards demolished to smithereens, and then one heard his savage rage riding off in the old cart wagon.

As if his eardrums had been punctured along with the light of his eyes, Owen caught now only disconnected phrases coming from his mother and Farmer Cuthbert:

This is all grass land.

What about the turnip crops then?

The cattle will starve on that crop!

Five or six hundred acres then. Alfalfa there? No more pasture land, you say. The corn is not breast high over there, mind you.

All right then, Farmer Cuthbert. My hands are tied, you understand. No matter what the crop, sell. Sell.

A week passed, then two, and soon a month had carried them to midsummer, but Aiken Cusworth did not return to Nora Bythewaite's house, or send word to her or to Owen where he had gone. He had, one felt, gone up in smoke along with Acres.

Nora watched Owen suffer. Without his eyes, he had been more attached to Aiken than ever. At the same time, she now felt almost greater respect for Aiken's own suffering, whatever its exact nature was, for she knew it was without bottom and sank into the unknown depths of earth itself.

One cloudless still afternoon, driving in her buggy back from a brief visit to Stotfold, she passed Stephen Bottrell on the road, walking bareheaded under the frying sun. She pulled her vehicle to an abrupt stop, and then hallooed him. As he approached, she called out a peremptory invitation to accompany her back to the house.

Stephen Bottrell hesitated, casting his eyes on the ground where pink and white meadowsweet bordered the dirt road on which he stood.

"Come not for my sake entirely, Stephen, but to cheer up that poor blind boy whom his brother—no, amend that to *brothers*—have deserted . . ."

The photoplay manager smiled vaguely, and hopped in the buggy.

Arrived at the great house, she had hitched the horse without his help. Indeed he still sat in the buggy for some time deeply musing.

"I was surprised nonetheless by the marriage," Stephen Bottrell remarked in a somewhat scared very loud voice as he followed Lady Bythewaite up the interminable driveway which led to her mansion. She was only a few steps ahead of him, though he had shouted as if she were a mile in advance. Lady Bythewaite stopped abruptly on the irregular wandering path overgrown with wild clover. He had halted likewise, but she did not turn about to face him for a long time, and there they both remained halted, like frozen figures overtaken by some disaster of nature, his one foot bent slightly and then raised so that it appeared from a distance about to touch her shimmering violet skirt. Then she wheeled about and faced him.

"Who do you say has married, Stephen?" She spoke in awful accusatory tones. He stepped back a pace.

"But I supposed you knew *who*, Nora!"

"You supposed too soon then!"

He came directly up to her and looked into her eyes. Then he slowly extricated from his breast pocket a cutting from a newspaper, and handed it to her. She looked him now steadily in the eyes for an interminable length of time before looking at the cutting, which in any case she could not read without spectacles.

"We will peruse this in the summer house," she said finally, and they walked on toward a little latticed enclosure which stood under a mammoth elm tree.

"I said I was surprised by the marriage," Stephen Bottrell repeated his statement under the impression perhaps she had not heard him speak the first time. "You could have knocked me over with a feather when I read the account in the paper."

He helped her sit down, in stiff ceremony, and she took off her big floppy white hat, with the daisy on it. Her lips moved in a forced strange grimace of a smile, her lips resembling something stuck on her face and struggling to escape and fall from her.

"You did use the word *marriage*, Stephen," she began her inquiry, as composed now as she would ever be.

Very deliberately, gently, his eyes never looking at her again after he had seen her lips move so violently, he took back the cutting from the newspaper from her shaking fingers, and held it under his gloomy scrutiny.

"Pray do read it, for I've come away as usual without my reading glasses . . . But wait one moment, dear boy, before you begin. Let me catch my breath. You know we are on an incline here . . ."

He did not wait as long as she perhaps would have wished, but such a wait Stephen knew would have been till Doomsday.

Later she realized she had only heard the first sentence of the newspaper account, but perhaps there had been only one sentence about the marriage in the Stotfold paper, only a few black little characters of print which conveyed such damage:

> *Mr. Aiken Cusworth has taken to wife*

She later tried to remember if the quaint country newspaper style put it that way or only

> *Mr. Aiken Cusworth was married in a simple ceremony today*

or did she hear merely

> *The bride and groom, Aiken Cusworth and Lucy Weymouth*

She found suddenly that she had torn the cutting from his languid fingers, tearing it into fine bits, and then unaccountably having put some of the cutting toward her open mouth, as if too blind to see her death warrant, she might taste it, her saliva falling on the paper and down on her spotless dress. She heard Stephen's great exclamation of concern.

"I will see that marriage dissolved if I have to kill one or both of them!" Her voice swept past disconsolate Stephen to reach the big house, from within which a door opened almost immediately within its endless expanse.

"Nora! That I should be the messenger of news that hurts you so much!" He bowed his head.

"Aiken has done this to spite Owen and me . . . He cannot love Lucy Weymouth. He cannot love any woman. He can only love Owen and me. Now I will tell you the truth, for he has betrayed my trust. He burned Acres himself. Do you hear what I am saying? He burned it."

"Oh, Nora, think what you say, and please lower your voice. One can hear you for miles."

"He burned Acres to spite Owen and me, and to spite himself . . . He has confessed it to me with his own lips . . . He will come here again one day of course, but on that day my door will be closed against him forever . . . Meantime there must be a punishment to fit the crime . . ."

She had stood up. Then looking down at the photoplay manager, she saw to her inexpressible anger that he had tears in his eyes. Bending over him, she shook him vigorously as she would a schoolboy or more exactly as she would have shaken out a priceless small rug from the upper story window when some careless houseguest had deposited mud on it.

"I cannot bear to see you in such a state of . . . lack of control." She rattled off an explanation of her displeasure.

They both were silent now, for they had become aware Owen Haskins was standing at the open door of the little summer house.

"I do believe your eyesight has improved just this past week alone, Owen," Nora Bythewaite spoke in collected cold tones. "Yes, considerably." She advanced toward her son, and helped him be seated near Stephen. "I am grateful for that."

"Why are you screaming?" Owen turned, however, in the direction of Stephen.

"I have," Nora Bythewaite spoke with contemptuous indifference, "I'm afraid, torn up what I was screaming about, for it has cut me to the quick . . ."

"Have you lost all your remaining farms in a fire?" Owen inquired, but there was such cynical contempt and loathing in his voice that Nora was as cut off from her next speech as if an iron clamp had been placed on her tongue.

"The news is much worse than burned farms, though it is perhaps connected with burning," she responded after a silence, and she sat down, and touched the brim of her hat. "But Owen and I have known only bad news from the beginning. We are old soldiers where it is concerned."

"Well, then if we are so familiar with it, let me hear it, Mother."

"Your brother Aiken has seen fit to get married," she responded with a swiftness which was crueler than his asperity had been, and she saw the mark which her statement had made across his face, like a scattering of gunshot.

"And what is more," Nora Bythewaite went on like an iron bell ringing, "it was he who burned Acres to the ground. As revenge. Yes, he burned it himself. There was no poor Clarence to blame, for all these weeks in the silence of the real culprit we have taken it for granted that it was the work of Clarence Skegg, but he was already on the train, far from here, when the torch was put to Acres."

Owen's eyes seemed to have regained all their luminosity, fire, and that fearful vision which had lurked within his pupils long before he had been blinded. Lady Bythewaite regretted now she had not spoken more slowly, and yet, no, she regretted nothing.

"But Acres was mine, Lady Bythewaite," Owen had begun to speak like one testifying now for the prosecution. "Aiken had long promised it to me from the time I was a small boy."

"Do you know what it is you are saying?" Nora spoke, unconcealed astonishment on her face. "*Promised* you? This is news to me! Promised you Acres?"

"From the beginning, yes, he had promised me the great house," Owen returned to this with implacable insistence, and with overwhelmed concern and unbelief at her "news."

"Aiken has wanted to get back at us, Owen, I fear. He never, I do believe now, never loved us. He has wanted his revenge on us somehow . . ."

But Owen had risen and gone out of the little summer house, and was striding down toward the carriage house.

A few minutes more and they saw him ride out on his horse,

and then take the direction of the back road, out into the lonely unfrequented dust and weed-choked lanes and turnings.

Only some minutes later, plunged as she was in thought, did she realize that a *blind* person had gone out riding, and it was too late then to send after him.

"Do you see that?" Nora Bythewaite murmured, mostly to herself, and shook her head. "Yet, Stephen, he is as safe on that horse, I suppose, as he is walking over these treacherous acres of ground . . . Safer . . ."

The words, however, froze in her throat as she saw Stephen Bottrell take something from the pocket of a light macintosh he had carried on his arm against thundershowers.

"Don't be alarmed, dearest Nora," he spoke, placing the package on the table on which pieces of the newspaper cutting were still fluttering.

"Oh, I wish you had not brought it, Stephen. I do wish you had not."

"This gun," he said, pointing to the box which held the firearm, "Clarence purchased after he and Aiken had had the altercation together . . ."

"Aiken had no altercation with him! Clarence had an altercation with him, which was sought out, chosen . . . You must learn how it is, Stephen. Aiken is the one who has been most wronged. You can blame me. Why not blame me! Every day, in every neighboring county, at every hour, by all men's voices, I alone am invoked, accused, impeached, rebuked, heaped with reproaches. Blame me! I expect it . . . But I wish you had kept the gun . . . No, it is safer here, for no one will know it's here, and I'll tell no one. But never condemn poor Aiken again. Of all my sons, it is he who has had the worst bargain, though they have all had a bad bargain, Stephen . . ."

"You blame yourself too much. I would like to praise you."

"Spare your speech. Do you think praise, even if it came from God, would lift up my heart. Do you think anything will?" She put her hand over her brow.

"I am glad at any rate, Nora, that you are aware it was not Clarence who set fire to Acres."

"But he did," Lady Bythewaite countered in her old stubborn perverse strain, without uncovering her eyes.

"I beg your pardon . . . Clarence was well on the way to New York, as you yourself said, when the fire occurred. . . ."

"Oh, you young fool," she said at last, and put her hand down on the table with the shreds of newspaper cuttings. "Clarence put the torch to that house or palace, to call it by its rightful name, much more than poor unclaimed Aiken. He put the torch to Aiken! Of course the actual setting of fire was not Clarence's. He didn't need to do that. He knew Aiken would do it after he had cut him down, shamed it, made him crawl."

She stopped on that last word. Then after moving her lips many times, and unable to find any words which would frame her thought, she touched the fluttering pieces of newsprint, and then at last got out: "And to complete his degradation he has married that whore. But it will not last, Stephen!" She rose. "Aiken will be ours again!" She walked out into the garden, and stood there. She appeared unmindful after a while that her guest and messenger, the photoplay manager, was still seated in the summer house. But then looking toward him, she began again: "Aiken will come back, mark my words, and this time he will be only ours, no one else's, for he is and always was only mine, don't you see?"

She stared fixedly now at the photoplay manager, but he was gazing at the gun with the glassy dazzled look of one who has handed away something he would give all the world to have back in his safe possession.

There was a kind of ever-present fragrance issuing from everywhere, and from nowhere, which warned Aiken Cusworth even before the disastrous night visits began that "someone" was coming. Great things which change the foundations of the earth occur within the space of a second or two. The coming of the horse's hooves whose rider was blind, whose coming had been presaged by the smell of nasturtiums did not break his wedding sleep next to Lucy. Aiken had not slept since he had been married. And though he had explored Lucy's body with his own in every variant of motion and tempest in much earlier times, in a past that now seemed antedeluvian, in their present wedded relationship he lay next to her as limp and unresponsive as if he were neither a man nor imbued with coursing blood or responsive flesh. Lucy wept, and while weeping feared his brutal cuff, but his brutality was gone also. While she wept silently in the presence of the horse's hooves, Aiken shivered, but when she tried to cover him with the comforter he responded enough to throw it off. Only his breathing, heavy, almost ocean-like, recalled the old Aiken, and then all at once they both saw the horse which had come directly up to their window, its heavy breathing equaling in sound and rhythm that of Aiken.

Jumping up at last, Aiken stood at the broad expanse of the window of Lucy's cottage. She could see his mouth and jaw moving, but nothing presently came out.

Then: "Give me some rest, why don't you, Owen! You hear?"

The horse whinnied, for it recognized the speaker.

The rider, almost shrouded from their perception, by a kind of mist or fog which had come up, moved off with his mount now from the window and stood under a spruce tree.

Aiken passed his hand over his hair and brow as if a sticky

strong filament of something had come off on him from the mist circulating in the air outside.

"Rest!" he shouted with expressionless volume into the night. "Rest."

Then putting on his shirt, he walked to the door, and stumbled out into the shadows, not, however, going directly up to the horse and rider.

Lucy had risen likewise and watched from the window, wondering if she was open-eyed and seeing what she saw.

"Aiken, Aiken!" she called out at last, for she doubted her own grasp of reason, as she saw the two men merely staring at one another, one looking out of sightless eyes, which seemed nonetheless to pierce the night as well or better than the thunderbolt glance coming in return from the awakened bridegroom.

Then without warning she heard the horse and rider race off, though no command of any kind had been given for departure.

She returned to her bed, and waited what seemed eternity, then somewhere in time, though she knew it had been only a few minutes in all that the rider had come and gone, she felt Aiken's weight on the bed beside her, and immediately after the pressure of his body on the gutted mattress she heard his cry which resembled an invocation for the rafters above them to fall. She tried to think where she had heard such a sound before, never indeed, she was sure, from a human throat, but where? she wondered with mute terror had she heard it in her brief troubled existence. The sound was so dreadful it dried her tears, gave her the strength to rise and go into the next room. She sat down in her grandmother's rocking chair, but she did not rock or move.

Her tears had dried clean into her throat with a dryness as if they had been touched with an incautious hand holding sandpaper, but deep inside from where perhaps those inhuman shouts from her "husband" were puncturing the night, she felt fathomless sorrow stirring mute and immovable. She felt she would never weep again, would never speak again, and nature had deprived her of the kind of breathing which gave him lying in there in her bed some half relief.

Each night thereafter the horseman returned, waited, drew

the couple from sleep, communicated something to the "husband" in blind silence, and then vanished.

During the period of the "visits" Lucy felt that Aiken waited for her to interdict his accompanying the rider, for what other reason did the horseman appear than to take Aiken away from her?

As in long sieges of fever, Lucy could not recall how many nights then passed in these senseless inexplicable deeply painful visits from "slumber" itself.

Then at last she had seen Aiken go out, like one who abandons himself to duty or death, and get on the horse with the rider. She had screamed at last then, but with the kind of relief which one might feel had an assassin each night held the naked razor to one's throat, and then had withdrawn, not slashing the flesh, and when on one final night he had invaded the flesh itself and let the blood spill from the prepared vein, there was that relief which she now experienced: the worst had happened. She even wept a little after all, but her main purport was to get all her belongings together, and not stay one moment longer than necessary, for if he returned from his ride with the horseman or never came back at all, she still felt herself in some strange danger, not so much from what any hand might touch her with, but from some menace within herself which the night and its sounds would draw out from her and upon her if she remained.

Before leaving this cottage and him forever, she was arrested by the sight of the bed itself, for it had a look so changed and different from what she had remembered.

There was of course the indentation from the weight of his body, for he had always weighed on her like iron, but this imprint was different. About the pillow and around its edges was a kind of foam, and intermixed with this and indeed spread all the way down over which the imprint of his body still remained there was more than one bloodstain, which came, she supposed, from his old habit of pushing his nails against himself in his fathomless rages, or, who knows? she thought wearily, perhaps in his rabid sleep he turned his own teeth on himself.

Stephen Bottrell wandered about the streets of Stotfold as confused and distraught as if he too belonged to the house and destiny of Mr. Skegg. Like bad dreams borrowed wholesale from the photoplays he exhibited, like visions half-remembered from fever, he walked on past the main part of town and his own theater to the little lanes and byways which at length approached the then silent and mysterious countryside. He stopped caught up in its quiet and verdure. But his eye at last fell in the distance on one isolated shack of a cafe where one could procure illegal liquor, contraband tobacco, and where other secret and seldom-spoken-of things transpired.

In almost no time at all he stood before the screen door of the establishment, thick with black flies, his fingers not quite resting on the broken knob.

The heavy hand of a man motioned to him from the dark recesses of the cafe. Stephen opened the door and went in. The strong sunlight outside had made his eyes temporarily incapable of seeing the person who was beckoning to him.

The figure which had waved to him now watched him impassively. It was Aiken Cusworth dressed in a traveling suit, thick cravat of indeterminate color, watch chain, barbered cheeks and hair, and he was, if miracles are not to cease, drinking a cup of tea.

"Sit down, why don't you, Mr. Bottrell, that is unless you are ashamed to be seen with me," Aiken began. "You have no need to fear me. You have never had any reason to hate me, or distrust me . . ."

Stephen stood for a few moments longer, then absentmindedly seated himself before a man whose physical presence alone had always given him a feeling of annihilation. In his acute discomfort he looked up and away at a huge piece of flypaper weaving in the breeze coming from an open back door, which, screenless, let in one buzzing insect after another.

"I would like to ask you a thing before I go, for as you see, Mr. Bottrell," and he looked down at his own formal attire with surprised curiosity, "I am leaving . . ."

"Where are you going to?" Stephen wondered with naïve curiosity, still not looking at his interlocutor.

Aiken Cusworth picked up a large map which he had kept by his side. By reason of its many creases, worn edges, folded quality, and thumb marks, it was plain he had pored over it for more than a few days, or months, or who knows? years.

"I am going here, sir," he pointed to a dot far west on the map, which in the dim light bore the name of Canyon something or other.

"That is certainly far enough," Stephen opined, barely looking at the map stretched before him. Even as he said these few words, suddenly feeling faint, he then did an unaccountable thing for him. Without waiting for Aiken's permission, he took his cup of tea, and raised it to his lips.

"Excuse me, Mr. Cusworth," he apologized abjectly as soon as he had swallowed a mouthful to the consternated albeit pleased owner of the tea. "I felt that queasy . . ."

"Then do drink all of it, why don't you?" Aiken studied his guest with somewhat appalled curiosity, yet with a kindled sort of kindness in his words also. "The heat is very pronounced indeed," he went on thoughtfully, and he touched the map with an index finger in a questioning and skeptical manner.

"But what advice did you give me, Mr. Bottrell?" Aiken began in much the manner of a Lady Bythewaite or Mr. Skegg who had summoned someone for consultation beforehand, and watching Stephen drink more of the tea, and then seeing he had finished his cup, he took the teapot, which had not been visible earlier for it was hidden behind some artificial roses in a huge vase, and poured him another cup.

"Should I see them, do you judge, sir," the horsetender was going on, "see them, I mean, before I go, that is what I would

like to inquire of you . . . Oh, by the way," and here he rattled
the map in a reproachful way, as if it had contradicted him, "I
have left my wife, I should explain, or rather, she has left me.
She has gone . . . east . . . There is no reason now to stay."

"No reason to stay!" Stephen's surprise coupled with shock
and anger broke the quiet now of their "interview." "What on
earth do you mean by such a statement, Mr. Cusworth! When
two people depend on you for, well, for everything there is to
depend on anybody for . . . Lady Bythewaite and Owen Haskins." He muttered these two names almost in prayer.

Aiken mused a long time.

"I can bear no more," the horsetender said after tugging on
one of his vest buttons.

"But what will that Canyon give you, for God's sake." Stephen
did not lower his voice, and touched the map held between them
with one gingerly outstretched finger. "You are from *here*, Mr.
Cusworth, almost more than anybody there is, and what is that
out *there* do you know for all your poring over that map? What
does it have, cliffs and deep hollows, where there is perhaps even
no water." He looked at his empty teacup.

"I've been over your argument in my own mind of course,"
Aiken spoke impassively. Then looking into the photoplay manager's face searchingly he inquired: "Do you hate me so very
much, Mr. Bottrell, that you look at me the way you do, or are
you feeling sick from the heat?"

"I don't know whether I hate you or not . . . I am . . . awed
by you."

"Awed?"

"Awed! It was what I said . . . But why do all of you of the
house of Mr. Skegg afflict me! I have no more to give any of
you! I've told you all I know . . . And I knew so little to begin
with . . . You have all taken me over, when there was so little
to take . . ."

The photoplay manager had begun to rise, but whether because of his faintness or no real desire to leave an Aiken Cusworth who was by some miracle gentle and conciliatory albeit

fearsome, he fell back into his seat and put his face down on the wood of the table scrawled by penknives with initials and unintelligible words from occupants and passersby lost in time's passage.

"It would not be right nonetheless for me to stay either," Aiken had begun again, with his old custom of letting his tongue come out of his mouth as if it would pick up information and advice from the air about him. "All my hopes, and all my wealth certainly, went up in the smoke of Acres. I cannot live that down here or there . . ."

"My advice to you then, Mr. Cusworth, is that you depart at once, that is if you are bent on leaving, as you seem to be, and never see another soul here, and never communicate with another soul, and be gone for ever, and all time!"

"So final!" he gave out with a cry of admiration at so complete a "reading" of his situation.

"But listen. My real advice is that you stay where you belong . . ." He moved the teacup about on its saucer. "I can leave. I do not belong anywhere except perhaps in the baked concrete of New York City, the real canyons for the buried-alive." He laughed as he said this, and then poured himself more tea, and gulped it down. He took off his hat and fanned himself, and then eyeing Aiken narrowly he fanned the horsetender ceremoniously so that Aiken opened his eyes wide as if someone at last had bestowed on him an unexpected balm of kindness and recognition.

"Stay, no matter what it may cost you, Aiken Cusworth." Stephen banged the battered teacup down, and rose with deliberate alacrity.

"You're unwell, sir." Aiken put out his arm to steady his visitor.

"It's my usual state of health. Were my nerves to become calm and steady, I doubt not I should perish immediately, Mr. Cusworth . . ."

Aiken stared at him over this pronouncement, then nodded perhaps because he liked the explanation.

"Stay and be damned, Aiken Cusworth," the theater manager

went on, waving his hat again for a moment through the heavy air, "or go to your Canyon and sink into its hollow and be nothing to no one ever again . . ."

Aiken heard the screen door slam, and he was alone again with the map and the black flies.

The fall rains had begun though it was barely September by the calendar, but the weather and the season were unpredictable in Prince's Crossing. They were fine little rains, but cold, and the leaves on the trees appeared shrunken and even withered under the constant ceaseless dripping from the skies, the cold wet preparing them for the sleep of winter, or their restless passage through the winds of autumn on the wings of which who knows how far they would fly.

The great house of Lady Bythewaite stood before Aiken in the dwindling light of evening. There were few if any lights in the mansion. She now believed herself ruined and poor. She half-waited for summonses which would evict her, or a bailiff who would bear her off to the county poorhouse. So, she would economize on light, on heat, and on air, if she could. For everything was running out. She would garner all things unto herself at last, and then say, *There is no more! All's exhausted and spent.*

He would follow strange Stephen's advice, and not go in, indeed he had made a mistake already by standing here like some housebreaker before her forbidden domicile, into which he had so many times been summoned, then ordered out, drawn into again, taken to the inner sanctuary, his body virtually stripped and studied, enjoyed, whipped, and exiled and expelled, a ceaseless seesaw of pain and confusion, sick yearning, and, as now, helpless frozen inability to let it all go, sever himself, sink into the far-off promise of the unpronounceable names on a begrimed map.

Under a great elm whose leaves occasionally fell onto his shoulders, he took his seat on a chair borrowed from her summer house. Here the rain was only a sound such as the ear might hear in the deepest slumber.

He lost track of the hours, but it was between midnight and

morning, he supposed, when he woke stiff and chilled, his hands icy with raindrops falling from the elm leaves, and saw her light in the room which had always been hers alone. She was looking down on him surely. He gathered up his things to go, but the arc of her hand moving downward and toward him arrested him yet again. She was commanding him to come forward, but he would not do this.

It was now raining hard long bitter sheets as she came down the stone steps which led to the meandering grass-choked path which had as its own terminus the elm tree. She had no hat or umbrella, her face had no expression of greeting, memory, desire, or indeed semblance of life, nor even the death-like aspect of a mask. Her face resembled the reflection of one looking into deep water.

"If you go without giving Owen goodbye, you will kill him, Aiken . . . Mind you I do not question your wish to go. I say nothing about that. But you can give him your hand, if not your blessing."

"I will not come in."

"You will not, or you dare not."

"Explain it any way you care to."

"I'm sorry, Aiken, but you will come in."

With a strength which many a strong man might have envied, Lady Bythewaite, placing her hands with might and main on her long unacknowledged son, brought him up from the chair on which he had sat through the principal hours of night to his feet, and struck him then a blow that would have felled almost anybody but this same unacknowledged son.

"You shall march into that house and bid goodbye to one who worships the ground you walk on, or I will drag you by the hair of the head. I will not have him forsaken without a leave-taking, you damnable coward!"

He stood before her, breathing again like one of his spent horses, his eyes rolling about in their sockets, also like those of a horse that has been ridden beyond endurance, his face so wet from the long night's downpour it too looked as if it floated in the rising waters of the lake.

He picked up a gray dilapidated valise, the one which he had brought when he had moved into the guest room and claimed his birthright, and then followed her weaving and slow but straight into the house. She could hear him behind her yawning convulsively, and this sound annoyed her the more. He would always be an animal! she thought to herself.

Aiken sat in his usual military posture in the front parlor, cogitating, his thoughts, as they had been perhaps from his birth, a thousand, ten thousand miles from where his sorry circumstances always rooted him.

"Oh, look at you, Almighty God, look at yourself!" Lady Bythewaite's voice reached him, and he felt then the pressure of the expensive glass tumbler against his mouth. "Drink this, for you are sopping wet . . . You cannot go from here in those wet clothes . . ."

He drank thirstily of the strong bourbon, and sucked in his breath.

"All your life is here, Aiken, and you are needed so!" She had half-kneeled as she said this, to replenish his drink from the bottle.

"I want to go where there are impenetrable canyons and hollows, Lady Bythewaite," he mumbled, his mouth against the glass.

"I should think the ones here would do for anybody, but I suppose in your case they will not. Of course that is so." She sat down heavily beside him.

"If you wish me to see Owen, best to summon him, Lady Bythewaite, for I must be going."

But Owen was already standing in the room near them, and it was Aiken now who blinked as if he was the one with both imperfect vision and bad hearing.

"I am trying to get up my strength to leave, Owen, as I've said to Lady Bythewaite," he spoke at last in his usual great resounding male voice.

"He has been sitting this livelong night in the rain, Owen," Lady Bythewaite spoke with great unease, and her eyes kept looking about the room as if in search of something of paramount importance which she had mislaid, and her memory went back in sick flight to the last time she had seen Stephen Bottrell, and what he had entrusted her with on that final meeting.

"If you have lost your courage, Aiken, you can't think that Lady Bythewaite and I would be able to give it back to you, do you, even though you've waited all night in the rain."

As Owen delivered this short speech in a kind of rhapsody, the very weight of the words seemed to force him to sit down on the edge of an overstuffed chair, and he put his hand cautiously to one of the side pockets of his jacket.

"Owen, what kind of a homecoming are you giving your brother," Lady Bythewaite spoke in an expressionless numbed voice, and her eyes fixed themselves on Owen's jacket pocket.

"What is it, Mother?" Owen cried, watching her nervously, his voice soaring in swooning hysteria.

"You had best say goodbye to Aiken now," she began, "and let him and me have a talk . . . For he will be back one day, I am sure, Owen . . . He will not find his canyons, however grand they may be, as much to his heart's desire as wretched Prince's Crossing."

Looking from Aiken to Lady Bythewaite, and back again to Aiken from his ruined eyes, Owen had risen slowly from the edge of his chair, when perhaps he saw or heard at any rate his own heavens crash, for Aiken Cusworth, his idol and hero, was weeping, yes, the tears of his brother fell like those of any photoplay actor.

"How do you dare!" Owen cried. "Aiken, Aiken, this is more unworthy of you than your leaving!"

Aiken watched the boy from eyes now red as Lady Bythewaite's.

"I will die if I stay, Owen," he responded in choked unrecognizable almost falsetto tones. "You know it is true. I can bear no more burden!"

"You lie," Owen said in quiet fury, and he went quickly and closed the door to the room. "Face me," he said, wheeling about in the direction of Aiken's voice. "Face me and tell me you are a liar."

Even more to Owen's anger now, he was aware of Aiken rising from his chair and approaching the younger boy, and in an attempt to take hold of his hand, he stumbled, and fell at Owen's feet, and then seeming to like this supplicant position which he had never assumed before any other human being, he kept it.

"Release me, Owen, for Christ's sake, do! I want, I long to be free also."

Lady Bythewaite, having risen also from her chair, could only stand, arms hanging by her yellow dress, her eyes seeking the meaning of the closed door, and watching the bulge in Owen's jacket pocket and wondering about the other "mislaid" article which she had sought for throughout the house earlier, and indeed for days past.

"Why should I release you, Aiken." Owen's words were all that one could hear now, or take in. "Never, never. You may leave, you may run to the ocean and back, but I will not release you . . . I owe you my blindness. My blind eyes will not release you."

"That is not true, Owen!" Lady Bythewaite cried, more like herself for a moment.

"No, no, Owen is right," Aiken cried. "I don't know how it is so, but he is always right."

"I will never release you, Aiken. Never in life or death. You bound me to you from the beginning. When nobody else claimed me, you claimed me particularly. I have no other life but you, no eyes or lungs or soul but you."

"Then, Owen, your love is too great a burden even for my shoulders," Aiken spoke like a man in prayer, and rose to his feet. He dried his eyes on his fist, and looked at Lady Bythewaite with an expression which she, not being able to bear, turned her back on.

"You had no mercy on Acres, which you burned to deprive me of," Owen now cried in a wild outburst of fury.

But Aiken was already on his way out, and had begun to try to open the stubbornly closed door.

"Don't try to open that door, Aiken. I warn you!" Owen called out. "It has been bolted in any case!"

Turning around again, Lady Bythewaite then saw it in Owen's hand, Clarence's gun, which she had so foolishly accepted from the photoplay manager.

Aiken gazed into the barrel of the weapon leveled at him, and a look of satisfied appeased longing came over his sorrow.

Owen shot once, and the bullet touched Aiken's shoulder, staining his coat almost immediately as if the blood came shot from the gun. Aiken removed his coat, and pulled open the buttons of his vest, whilst Owen waited.

Pointing with his finger to his breast, Aiken said, "The target is here, Owen."

Owen fired again, but this shot too was wide of its mark and struck Aiken somewhere on the upper part of his throat, and this blow seemed to please the horsetender the most, for a smile of satisfaction broke over his brown face, erasing all the trace of former grief.

Then Lady Bythewaite, with a sound such as one might hear when lightning hits a row of maple trees, seized the gun from Owen's hand which fought her efforts to possess it like some untamed parcel of winds, and the gun went off into Owen's face, seeming to explode his head, and then a final bullet cut sideways at her own breast, which was immediately scarlet.

Later, so much later, she had tried to remember it all.

The gun which she had held in an effort to spare them both, this gun in her struggling hands, turned, flashed against his precious forehead and scalp, tore out his brains and eyes, which present jewels fell to the ingrain carpet before her.

As she stood there, she saw Aiken kneeling beside his brother stark upon his back with socketless eyes, and heard him say, "Oh, Mother, you have killed my only one . . ."

Then to her own swooning horror in which her ears suddenly went dead, for she could barely ever hear again, she saw Aiken pick up the eyes which had been Owen's in their bleeding rings of flesh and cartilage and hold them to his mouth, while a kind of silent terrible groan she knew came from his entrails but seemed to come out of the earth, as he lifted the eyes more closely to his mouth.

"Aiken, Aiken, have some pity on your mother!" she whispered, but he was far beyond hearing her, as he placed the eyes of his *only one* in his mouth and closed his lips on them.

Lady Bythewaite woke one day, and looked down at her arms and hands. They were bound, not too tightly, against the counterpane. She turned her head briefly, and stared over the great expanse which led to the lake. The maple and oak trees were bare, snow was gently coming down upon the brown prepared soil, the vaulting heavens above were like the color of dead bark. Something was wrong in her head, and it was all numb, and she would have liked to touch her ears, for they must be stuffed with cotton, and she heard everything as if sound itself was velvet.

"Aiken! Aiken!" she called, and heard her own voice as far away as the slate-colored lake.

Mr. Skegg opened the door, came warily in, pulled up a chair. She smiled with lips that appeared fastened to the bones of her cheek by tough threads, and she looked down at the thongs which held her wasted hands and arms.

"If you will promise me you will not harm yourself again, I'll untie your hands, Nora," Mr. Skegg spoke with a great unburdening of both hope and despair.

"Mr. Skegg, why did you not tell me it was winter?"

"It's an early winter, Nora. We had almost no autumn, you see."

He was loosening her thongs, and she held her fingers once free up to the light, and rubbed her wrists.

"These are no more my hands than they are those of the old woman who used to row on the lake. Remember her? . . . Mr. Skegg, I *am* an old woman! Behold these terrible hands!"

"Nora, you have been fearfully ill, but you are much better, I do believe . . . Thank fortune!"

"Fortune," she murmured, the difficult smile breaking again

and turning her whole worn face into deep wrinkles. "Have I dreamed, then, the whole story, Mr. Skegg?"

A woman unknown to her in rustling white skirts entered the room with a tray on which sat a glass of something steaming hot, which Nora Bythewaite refused to touch, but when Mr. Skegg held the glass to her parched lips, she managed to sip from its mysterious contents.

"Have her wait outside!" Lady Bythewaite now spoke for the first time, since the dread last August day, like her old self, and Mr. Skegg smiled in spite of himself at this faint echo of old vanished imperious ways, and she caught his smile and returned it.

"What is this potion you have administered to me," she wondered, "for it coats the mouth and tongue like whitewash!"

She lay back on her pillow after saying this, admiring ever so feebly the snowflakes, but her mere admiration of their frail forms vanishing into air as they fell tired her.

"You must rest now, Nora, and I'll not put back those tiresome thongs if you will promise me you won't . . ."

"Mr. Skegg, I am too weak even to gather one of those snow-flakes, let alone harm myself . . ."

"But don't leave, for God's sake!" she cried, and attempted to rise from the pillow again. "Now that I have seen you again, please do not go. Don't leave me again to my dreams, Mr. Skegg."

"We will talk when you are stronger, Nora, and only then."

"We will talk now," she spoke with scanty breath, closing her eyes, and the drink, whatever it was, had given her something, for a pervasive coolness was coming over her hot brow and burning eyes, but with this respite from fever and pain, memory stirred, a greater pain.

"Where are my boys, Mr. Skegg?" she said at length, not looking at him.

"Nora, Nora, all this can wait, *must* wait, for you need all your strength . . . Do you know, dear heart, how long you have lain here without being yourself?"

"Where are they?" she spoke raising herself up, but he saw

there was no mania in her eyes or voice now, as in the months just past, but only a hunger to know.

Hesitant, trying to remember nurse and doctor's orders, trying indeed to remember what was unrememberable, he said, after a struggle to speak almost as great as hers:

"One of your boys still lives . . ."

She touched his outstretched hand, not wanting yet to hear which one, until her heart beat less violently, not daring likewise to tell herself which one lived, and which belonged to the shadows in which she had lain for so many weeks.

Mr. Skegg had bowed his head, and held his hand over his eyes, and as she looked at this hand, and his eyebrows, for a second she thought the window had suddenly come open and the snow come inside, for he was white as the flakes, he had grown all white whilst she had lain here in her thongs.

"Aiken lives," Mr. Skegg said at last, and did not look in her direction.

"Aiken," Nora repeated in the manner of a deaf mute who at last has learned to say one word, and perhaps will never learn to utter another.

"And is Aiken . . . well," she wondered after an interminable wait.

"Nora, be warned, you must not tax yourself more . . . Aiken is alive. I don't know if he will be well again, but he is alive . . ."

"And the other boy?" Nora pleaded as if to the lowering sky.

Mr. Skegg failed to reply.

Then to his own deep troubled sorrow, he saw her take the thongs and tie her own arms and fall back against the pillow.

"One only lives," she said after a time, speaking through her muffled grief, "but he is not well."

He sat with her through the long day, though it was a short one here, for dusk now came at three o'clock in the afternoon, and night fell with complete authority at five.

The lake stirred under a northeast wind, and its slate color turned raven black, but she did not hear the lake's motions, would never hear that far again.

By spring she came downstairs, and in a week or so thereafter, she was walking about the grounds, and resting in some chair weathered by countless winters, while her eyes never strayed far from the water of the lake.

She had decided to get strong not in order to live but in order to see *him*, see Aiken Cusworth.

"When you are strong enough," Mr. Skegg repeated to her endlessly each night as she was trying to drift off to sleep, "when you are perfectly recovered, we shall journey there."

"There." She marked the word and made it her own.

"How strong do you require me to be?" she said one early evening as he sat with her by the lamp. He thought over her question with great thoroughness and calm, for everything was to him business of course, but she could see a difference nonetheless in him too, for all, everything but the lake had changed. And of course Mr. Skegg had moved in months ago, was "ensconced" all over again, would never, she hoped and prayed, leave her again, and so she was quiet and patient as she waited for a response to her question.

"You must be stronger than you were ever strong before," Mr. Skegg replied at last.

A slight cry escaped her lips at that moment, which she immediately stifled as if she had closed her own mouth with a backward blow of a whip. Near the hand-carved legs of the ottoman lay an oblong something. It was a yellowing domino. Ignorant of its meaning for her, Mr. Skegg had picked it up, thinking it was something she desired, and handed it to her dutifully and gently. Though she feared the domino as much as if he had handed her the gun itself, she took it in order to convince him she was as strong as he required and that she could take the journey *there*.

"I am recovered, you see, Mr. Skegg. I will be even better." She closed her fist over the oblong piece of yellow ivory. "I will rule again one day, Mr. Skegg, though only among the dead . . ."

"We have buried Owen at the edge of the rose garden." Mr. Skegg spoke with the suddenness of a bird descending almost vertically and without warning, for he had not known for many weeks how to tell her of the grave, and her willfulness now also vexed him, and at the same time if she meant to go to the lunatic asylum to claim her son Aiken, she must be tested, and so he told her.

Her hand relaxed on the domino, and she handed it to Mr. Skegg.

"Tonight we must take a short drive," she said at length. "I have missed the sound of the horses' hooves. They soothe one so, Mr. Skegg. Tonight we must take one short trip in the carriage."

"Nora, the horses have been sold . . ."

He saw with a touch of relief her old imperiousness come back, or a shred of it, her hands half-raised to bestow again caution, admonition, punishment.

"With no one to tend them," he stumbled on, "you understand, and their being neglected so . . . And my dear, you know yourself how long you have driven in buggies and carts long after your poorest neighbor went about in autos and Ford trucks . . ."

"What have you done with the mare?" Lady Bythewaite wondered, but her words resembled more the humming of some few notes of song, and he did not respond, and she did not press him.

"No horses," she muttered after a while. "No tender." But there was something in the way she said this which encouraged him, for it had a harder note, a more confident summation of sorrow and obstacle, more like the old Nora who had said *Sell all the grazing land, turn the other acres into feed corn. Plant all the rest with alfalfa!*

"I will be strong enough next week," she told Mr. Skegg and he believed her.

It was a cold, almost bitter March day, but there was some sun, though fitful, and there were a few indifferent snowshowers from time to time which one barely noticed. Mr. Skegg drove his Studebaker, and they had found a young farmer to accompany them for what reason she did not inquire, or even wonder at. Lady Bythewaite had, however, looked him over before they got into the car, and had decided he was perhaps better than having nobody, and his name pleased her for some reason, for she repeated it several times: Eneas Harmond, until it had got fixed in her memory, and he had assured her he could lift his own weight over his head, and more.

But once arrived in the vicinity of the great sprawling gray-brick institution with bars and armed watchtower, desolate surrounding fields where nothing grew, and spike fences stretching in all directions, topped with barbed wire, she hesitated. She fumbled in her purse for something, but that something was no longer there. This somehow pleased her, and indeed gave her hope.

"No one need accompany me inside," she announced in level cold tones, for both Eneas Harmond and Mr. Skegg had got out of the car first. "I want nobody else to come within!" she repeated her command. "Thank you," she spoke to a puzzled Eneas.

"Nora, my dear," Mr. Skegg began, advancing toward her, and taking off his hat, and holding it to his chest, "you are making a terrible mistake of judgment here." He spoke with some firmness but also in a piteous way she had never heard from him before. She smiled her refusal and turned to go up the long walk. The steady way she went up that long boundless stretch of paving stone to the frowning entrance cheered him in some indefinable way. She did look somewhat like her old self, though her gait was that of someone who, if not old, was laden with troubles, but her hair, her hair was still jet black!

Gates now closed behind her. At first the official in charge refused her permission to go to the room in question, on the grounds that her coming had not been proclaimed in advance. Then Lady Bythewaite, her patience exhausted, announced her identity, she scolded, threatened, finally she raised her voice and commanded. Officials came scurrying down the hall in the wake of the commotion and disturbance, other persons were summoned, and finally a doctor, though Lady Bythewaite by her scrutiny of him did not yield him any deference of recognition or authority, stepped forward to hear her business and her complaint.

Removing pince-nez from red inflamed flesh about his eyes, he spoke as from a pulpit: "It is most inadvisable for you to go to his room, Madame . . ." He thought for a long while, adjusting his words and knowledge for this occasion: "I will not minimize the danger, or his violence . . . He is . . ."

But at a glance from her, he shrugged his shoulders, and bade her follow him. Past more limitless halls they went, and winding corridors and turnings and twistings, and huge doors, being unbolted, they went through those, and heard the doors closed and locked behind them, while other heavy iron-appearing doors opened, and likewise locked themselves behind them, while the sickening odors of sweat and vomit and carbolic acid and stale urine afflicted the nostrils, and then at long last *that* door sprang into view. It looked like an enormous eye. It was his room.

The doctor unlocked and opened the door, and she rushed in.

Though Aiken was secured in a strait jacket, and his face badly bruised, one eye slightly blackened, and his naked legs tied with some repulsive-looking cord, the expression in his eyes and about his mouth had a kind of benignity which gave her at that moment the strength not to totter, as she had in times gone by, and fall at his feet.

"Aiken, are you at all glad to see me?"

His eyes watched her mouth as if from that red pair of lips was to be pronounced at last something he had so long eagerly awaited, and a slight movement in the deep lines of his face seemed to indicate an expression of assent.

"Remove this thing that is around and about his arms and chest, would you please!"

"It is against all regulations, Madame . . . I cannot vouch for . . ."

Turning away from the doctor, who went on speaking, Lady Bythewaite herself began tugging at the complicated jacket which pinioned him, and then the doctor, having finished his speech, gave in and, while warning her again, undid the last fastenings which had held his patient for so many months.

Aiken's head fell down slightly, giving one the impression this release had caused him to feel an unaccountable drowsiness.

Standing over her son, not daring to draw one breath, it appeared to her that a great beam of both light and heat came from his liberated form, his bowed countenance.

"Pray stand up, Aiken," Lady Bythewaite commanded. He rose almost immediately and then again studied her lips.

"Oh, Aiken, are you willing and ready to come home with me? Will you let me do for you for as long as you desire?"

His head lowered slowly in a kind of eloquent, terrible bow of assent.

"He is ready now to come home with me!" She spoke in rapt thrilling tones to the doctor.

Then the voluble little man of medicine gave his long speech, his condemnation of the layman and the meddler, but to his textbook fulminations neither she nor Aiken paid any heed, gazing into one another's eyes and lips from time to time, while now from the same doctor came names of his terrible disease, given, it seemed, in several languages, warnings, prognostications of his dangerous character and deep-seated violence, while a nurse, summoned by somebody, in the midst of his oration, brought Aiken's clothes and shoes, and hat.

"How thin you have grown, Aiken, oh how spare you are under these wretched institutional rags!" And while the nurse helped him off with these clothes, to put on his own garments again, Lady Bythewaite turning to the now silent doctor, cried:

"How dare you clothe a son of mine like a convict!"

Folding his arms, after having removed his pince-nez, the doctor again began his lengthy discourse: "You have broken every rule and regulation this distinguished institution was founded on . . . You have set at naught both science and medical care . . . You . . ."

But the doctor's words were coming from behind Lady Bythewaite and Aiken, who were now walking down the endless corridors away from "prison," and then at last out into the air and toward the open fields.

But at the sudden vista of space, air, birds wheeling in flight above him, the movement of trees, he collapsed on the ground, but the young farmer and Mr. Skegg were there beside him, and suddenly Aiken did speak. "Eneas Harmond!" he cried, astonished, pleased, and took the young man's hand, and was helped up.

Lady Bythewaite, triumphant, almost herself again, sat with the sick boy in the back of the car, as they drove off, and her anger having found a target in the doctor and his institution, and anger, as always being a whetstone put across her tongue, allowed her to pour out now, as in old times, her vituperation and condemnation of the world of men and their institutions, of bars and chains, of churches and officials and governments, and this whirlwind of words fell on astonished but pleased ears, and finally the face of an Aiken Cusworth, unrecognizable to any but to her, turned and looked into her eyes, as if beyond the memory of this existence he had caught some glimmering of another time and place when all had been one, in harmony and perfection and assured peace.

Lady Bythewaite's ineffable joy at having her son with her again was much too perfect for Mr. Skegg to spoil by reason of his own deep sorrow, a sorrow which only Lady Bythewaite and Aiken's need for him had kept him from revealing to her. So, providence sometimes retains a useless unobservant and not very loving old man for some final purpose, he once wrote down on the margin of his ledger, beside the quotations of the prices of corn and turnips.

He even longed for the company of Stephen Bottrell!

Stephen Bottrell, that windswept butterfly, had long since gone back to his own canyons in New York, but he wrote to the old financier regularly, and these letters (since Skegg never or seldom received personal letters from anybody), the old maggot read over and over again, like certain persons who master Latin late in life, and triumphantly read some short poem by Horace again and again, marveling they have been able to comprehend so much as a word. But Stephen's letters from the metropolis were few and far between, after all. One such letter, creased and torn by constant rereading, slipped shortly after Aiken's homecoming from the old man's ledger, and lay unobserved by him in the far corner of his sitting room, for now that Aiken had returned, not so much a prodigal as from the dead, the old maggot spent a great deal of his time at the young man's side, often to the incredible astonishment of the servants who had never known him to be able to stand the pressure of human flesh, who now saw him take Aiken's hand and hold it, and sometimes rub the horsetender's arm where the circulation seemed to have failed perhaps owing to his having been in the binding corset of a strait jacket.

But Lady Bythewaite knew there was something else. Some secret lurked in the air, and had changed Mr. Skegg. This new relationship between the old man and an oh-so-unresponsive yet tolerant Aiken Cusworth betokened some past event which her long illness had made her ignorant of. Yes, both Aiken and Mr. Skegg knew something which was kept from her, and their eyes exchanged this knowledge with one another constantly.

Then there was Eneas Harmond. He had, in a time of rare events, found favor in Aiken's eyes, for they had known one another since boyhood, and Lady Bythewaite, first with invitation, then when the youth displayed reluctance, with open bribes, and when these failed, with threats and vituperation, gained his agreement at last to remain as Aiken's companion and constant surveyor. But Eneas refused the sums of money Nora Bythewaite tried to shower him with, for the longer he remained in the great house, the more he realized perhaps that after all he was needed more here even than on his father's livestock farm. At any rate, slowly accustomed to the ways of the mansion, he fell, as some said, under its spell, and he promised *her* he would slowly bring back the horses, and tend them, and that she should not be without her buggy and carriage.

Lady Bythewaite had of course sometimes tossing in her sleep thought of the morose doctor's warnings about Aiken Cusworth, but what kept her awake and pondering more than any real risk from his "violence" was the calm with which Mr. Skegg sat in front of an Aiken who was supposed to be dangerous. From the beginning, Mr. Skegg had shown no fear of being alone with him, no worry about the future, no belief evidently in medical prognosis. This sublime frame of mind on the part of the old financier puzzled her. But then, her thoughts went back in time, when had Mr. Skegg ever been really afraid of anything? Had he ever actually experienced quaking dread, drowned as he was in phlegm, age, and inevitable surrender to failure.

But they all knew something she did not know.

For one thing, to explain Mr. Skegg's "calm" with Aiken, it had slipped out one day in conversation that the old maggot and other "callers" had gone to visit Aiken daily in the asylum. And then at this disclosure, looking narrowly at Mr. Skegg's face she had seen the devastating change which had settled over his features, one might say almost the change present in his aura. For he had of course been old before, he had always been old, but he had not been snow-white, as he was ever since the day she had opened her eyes that bitter winter afternoon when she had begun to come back to her own realm and time. What, then, had turned him to a ghost of hoarfrost? what had dug even deeper ditches in his already hopelessly wrinkled face, as if hot lead had steadily fallen there on the flesh instead of just tears. Yes, like all whom she had known, like all the others, he had lied to her, and had hid his sorrow.

Since Aiken required very little care or attention from her (though one day he had smiled tentatively at her like a child who gradually becomes aware that some frequent passerby in front of his window means him no harm), she had toiled about the house ceaselessly inspecting it for dust or need of repair, watering the plants and closing the windows more tightly, straightening a rug, picking up a piece of lint fallen from someone's clothing. One day she had gone on a special errand upstairs to check on the parlor maid and see that all in Mr. Skegg's chambers was in shipshape condition. She found, as usual, traces of dust where there should be not even so much as a speck, a breathmark on the window, carelessly cleaned, a chair out of place, but her anger rose up in her full force when she saw a clearly noticeable something which lay impudently under a chair and which she mistook for wastepaper. She hurried over to its offending presence and stooped to pick it up. She saw, however, it was not wastepaper, saw handwriting, a flamboyant stamp, pink sealing wax, the postal cancellation *New York, N.Y.* Quickly, guiltily putting the letter in her pocket she hurried to her own room, fumbled in the drawer for her spectacles, could not find them, and then moving to a strong light by the window devoured the letter from Master Stephen Bottrell.

Her first astonishment, reading, was not what he said, for that was little, but that the boy was illiterate. Scarcely a word, even the simplest or most elementary, came from his pen without some peculiar misspelling. His sentences began and ended nowhere. Even neglected Aiken had done better than this! But then both her eye and her blood seemed to congeal at the postscript (the earlier part of the letter was an effusive and slightly hysterical "thanks" for Mr. Skegg's economic help to him, which at another time in her life would have struck her as so phenomenal as to have required days of contemplation and study to fathom), a postscript which said simply:

> *Since dear Clarence's death, I have hardly gone to the theater once.*

She had heard that those who have lost legs or arms often feel some pain or discomfort still arising from the missing appendage. But she had not read or heard that the heart being savagely stabbed again and again is finally indifferent to the knife. Yet in her case, she felt almost this was so, or rather she felt she was at last dead too, and perhaps awaited Clarence's coming to visit her ghost in this great house with its resounding endless doors and corridors. She marveled at her own strength and calm, but she knew it was pure deception. Her mind, her mouth, stuffed with horror, would take in this new death in time, would focus it on some great screen, the eye would absorb the image, and would bring it into the bosom and tell the heart, and the heart, peaceful up till now, having grown fond of quiet and of rest, of oblivion and of dark, would begin to throb again, and the nerves lulled to slumber by time and many medicines would respond to the savage heart's alarm, and all sinews, fibers, and senses would combine in unison with the thousand manifold pains of unappeasable grief.

The tailor had arrived the day she found the "lost" letter from Stephen Bottrell, and she was wanted therefore in the great front room where Aiken was now established, almost always surrounded by Mr. Skegg, Eneas Harmond, and, at Lady Bythewaite's own firm insistence, by Lucy Weymouth, who, however, would stay only an hour or so at the most, then depart.

And so there he sat in his great chair, the horsetender, seeing all, moving his head and arms occasionally, gracefully, it is true, but as far removed from them as the invisible stars above the lake in broad daylight.

But the change in Mr. Skegg was, if possible, even greater than that in Aiken, for Aiken had always been regal even when covered with grime and mud, he was incapable of not carrying his head high, and now in his complete ruin he gave the impression he held the scepter and wore the diadem. But Mr. Skegg! Her eyes now moved toward him with poorly controlled amazement. Mr. Skegg had come from a distant, cold abstruse financier to a devoted servant, almost nurse of his former groom and handy man, and his only pleasure in life was to take his place in as close proximity as possible to Aiken. Yes, of the two, the change was indeed greater in the case of Mr. Skegg, for Aiken, she mused bitterly, had always been beyond them. And even the letter from Stephen Bottrell which had just come into her hands failed to explain Mr. Skegg's metamorphosis.

Lady Bythewaite watched the tailor, and the fitting, and in spite of herself smiled. In times past, the old maggot would have been most irritated, indeed outraged, by the summoning of a tailor (and this one was a disdainful snob from New York) for any member of his household, and in distant days would have been horrified by the very thought of an Aiken Cusworth being measured and fitted by an expert in cloth and linings, cuffs, and sleeve lengths, buttons and pleats, all hand-sewn. But it was Mr. Skegg now and not Lady Bythewaite who was fussing and measuring along with the tailor, it was he who inspected the samples, pinched the wool, worried over color and style.

And so she half-understood, taught by the letter. He had no more sons but this one, whom he had denied all his life!

After the fitting, during which Aiken Cusworth had cooperated with every command, turning his body this way and that, raising a foot, lifting an arm, but always, so it seemed to her, with his eyes fixed on the invisible stars above the lake or in its waters and never on them, and with certainly no interest in or knowledge of the rich fabric being selected and bought for him, displayed and put in his hand for his judgment, and at last only the three of them were left alone in the great room, Nora, Mr. Skegg, Aiken.

After lighting the lamp, she had taken Stephen's letter from the recesses of her long silk dress, and handed it to the old maggot.

It lay for a long time on his lap.

"You have run your eyes over this of course," he said finally.

"I have certainly read the postscript," she snapped at him. He looked at her aghast. She spoke in as overbearing, contemptuous, and even heartless manner as the "Lady" of old. One would not have known from her voice, the way her head and shoulders rose in such statuesque assurance and frigid poise that she had read more than a description of some earth tremor in the Himalayas.

At the height of Mr. Skegg's astonishment, Eneas came into the room, and Aiken, immediately rising, accompanied him to the adjoining room, where there was a large gleaming table, at which the two sitting down, Eneas began to deal from a pack of cards.

"We should retire to a part of the house where we will not be overheard," Nora began.

Mr. Skegg in his new-found role as father, if not husband, however, demurred: "There are no more secrets now, Lady

Bythewaite. I wonder, however, at your calm," he added, furrowing his brow.

She studied that old face, a shipwreck countenance of everdeepening wrinkles which ran in all directions like a collection of tangled spider webs which had a weight nonetheless to bring down the wall on which they had been spun.

"Does Aiken know this," she finally asked, and tapped the letter from Bottrell.

Mr. Skegg looked toward his "son" as if to say, *Does he know anything?* Then he nodded vigorously in affirmation.

Lady Bythewaite studied the two men playing cards, the two farmers. Both indeed played like sleepwalkers. She wondered indeed if the game was real, or whether they were merely throwing down cards like small children to have something to do, nobody having instructed them it was a game, unaware that numbers and plays had to be counted and remembered, but suddenly she caught a flash of intelligence in Aiken's eye, and he put down a card with a triumphant snort.

"Aiken was a witness to Clarence's end."

This sentence cut short her small happiness.

Nora rose and began walking toward the window. Her "pose" had gone, her shoulders sagged, and her breast caved in, and though she tried to remain erect, she could not, and came back, and sat in the small chair beside him.

"If you are to tell what happened, Aiken will hear," she pointed out.

"Aiken hears and sees now only what he wishes to . . . I have not studied him for nothing all this weary fall and winter. Besides, he is most intent on his card playing. He is a fine player by the way."

Looking down at the childish handwriting of Stephen Bottrell, Mr. Skegg remarked: "Your curiosity has always been greater than your common sense."

"You seem to feel, at any rate, that I am strong enough to hear what you have to tell me," she spoke in her dryest tone.

"I am not sure I am strong enough to tell it, though."

Mr. Skegg had smoothed out many of the creases and folds, and torn edges of Stephen's letter, and then reaching for a folder which lay on the table beside him, he put the letter inside the folder, secured it with a paper clip, and closed the letter within.

"At first Aiken was not mad after Owen's death, but he was near death from the wounds which had come from that struggle. He lay between life and death as people say, but actually he lay only within death, if you ask me, though he breathed. He had no will, no pulse to live . . . Clarence of course had learned of this accident in our lives, and returned from New York against my wishes. He complained to me of remorse! Oh, he complained of everything. Yet he was hopelessly changed. His career was over. He was also indeed ruined, I saw. There was no Clarence left, no Maynard Ewing. He had only this remorse. I believe that his remorse was real, perhaps the only real thing he had owned. But it was all he had, and it devoured him."

Nora's mouth opened wide owing to Mr. Skegg's calm. She herself was not calm, although he mistook her motionless hands and face for tranquillity. She was frozen, but Mr. Skegg was calm.

"Clarence wished above all else to be forgiven by Aiken. He harped only on this, prayed and cried only over this. He said he had wronged Aiken. He called him his brother. He wished to claim Aiken, yes, I believe that is what he said, claim him for his own—his brother. I tried to discourage him."

Lady Bythewaite's eye had roved toward the card players again. But neither of the two horsetenders, for that is what they were and what she now almost desperately wanted them to be, neither paid any more attention to what was being told her than had Mr. Skegg been speaking to her of barley and oats.

"But Clarence was more like you than any of our other sons!" Mr. Skegg suddenly exclaimed, and then looked in the direction in which she was looking, but he gazed now at the young men with the impersonal scrutiny which he had given when required to attend a motion picture show.

"Clarence insisted he would make everything right between

him and Aiken, do you understand? Against the wishes of the
doctor and contrary to the rules of the hospital, against all common sense, he began paying calls on Aiken, whose life we felt
was perhaps not to be spared us . . . I have very little information, Nora, as to what passed between them. You must remember
Aiken was almost never conscious in those days . . . But Clarence told me he went there time and again not to ask for forgiveness (for he felt that was out of the question), not to ask Aiken
to let him make up for what he had done, for his part in the
loss of Acres, the death of Owen, the loss of his good reputation
. . . All he asked was to admit he was Clarence's brother . . .
But he could not get beyond the wall of sleep into which Aiken
was plunged . . . Then the final thing itself occurred . . .

"Clarence on his last visit, after repeating his request for the
final time, cut his throat with an old-fashioned straight-razor in
front of Aiken, cut it with a vehemence and rage which all but
severed his head from his body. The wounded boy lay there a
long time without attendance. I am not sure how long, two
hours? three? When he was discovered, Aiken had come full
awake, and was holding dead Clarence's hand. I say he was
awake, but the world claims him crazy."

Having finished, Mr. Skegg looked again in the direction of
the card players, but his gaze now had a strange expression, difficult to fathom let alone describe.

"Nora, what is it?" Mr. Skegg inquired at last, and now a great
wave of fear and foreboding swept over him.

"Don't be alarmed about me, Mr. Skegg." She spoke in quiet
if distorted tones, and he sighed with relief. Rising, he bent over
her, cautiously watching her, while at the same time a kind of
shadow moved over the two of them, and looking behind him,
Mr. Skegg saw Aiken Cusworth had also risen and was standing
by them, an inquiring look on his face over which the color came
and went.

"You have finished your card game early today, Aiken," Mr.
Skegg remarked matter-of-factly.

Kneeling, and as if his kneeling were his response, Aiken

waited for whatever more words Mr. Skegg might care to bestow on him, but Mr. Skegg, to Nora's incredulous eyes, touched the crown of the young man's head with his hand, and his hand remained there for a lengthy time so that she felt at last all things had been acknowledged in front of Aiken and that Mr. Skegg had said in loud words that he was his only son, recognized and confessed before men, his scion and heir.

There seemed very little time remaining, so ran Lady Bythewaite's thoughts. She felt that indeed the hours, minutes, seconds were become visible at last and, like ropes of sand or blades of grass, were falling ceaselessly, being coursed and counted through her open spare fingers.

Clarence and Owen were far away, were her sons in some far-off previous eon, and there was only Aiken. And though he never spoke to her, never showed he heard anything she said, never touched her when she touched him, appeared unaware of her embraces and comforting words, there were occasions when he turned his eyes toward hers, and it was then that he spoke with a glance and this glance indicated to her that time was indeed running out, time which in her old ruling days she had somehow thought would not end, but like air and water would prove inexhaustible.

So that the day Eneas Harmond brought the new horses into the pasture, behind the great barns, and came into the front room, taking off his hat, which was dripping with his sweat, this together with the smell of leather and harness brought both Lady Bythewaite and Aiken to a readiness and alert attention they had not had for a time out of reckoning.

"They are all arrived, ma'am, and you may come out and see if they are up to your expectations."

Aiken heard that, and rose, but she was not jealous he heard Eneas and not her, she was only grateful he had heard something, and led by Eneas they walked through the back hallways out into the strong sunlight and cold air, beyond the barns, weather-beaten, if not crumbling, to the pale green pasture, and saw the eight horses. But at that moment, Aiken pushed ahead, left them far behind, and moved into the circle which the new horses had formed. The animals almost immediately drew near him, surrounding him, making him the center, like spokes radiating about the hub of a wheel. All the horses raising and lowering their heads, putting their mouths against him, recognized him, ceaselessly touching their heads and mouths now to his hands, as he caressed them, and spoke low words to them, now as he lay his head from time to time against them. Both to Eneas Harmond and Nora Bythewaite, it seemed he would never return from the horses, and when at last she called to him to return, the horses whinnied and shook their manes in the manner of creatures showing displeasure and contradiction at the sound of her command.

At last, at a motion from Lady Bythewaite, she and Eneas moved away from the pasture land and began going back to the house, though Nora looked back from time to time, uneasily, if hopefully, with a kind of rush of glad sorrow.

"Perhaps later in the day you and Aiken might go riding together," she spoke to Eneas.

The slight hesitation on his mouth displeased her, but then with a real effusion he replied: "I think it would be a fine outing for him, ma'am."

"You will be most careful, Eneas," she spoke now almost below a whisper, and touched his arm.

"You can count on me, ma'am . . . I won't go back on you or him."

"Then," and she began to forget dwindling time for a moment, "perhaps one day we can go riding together, all of us, in the buggy, for next to his horseback rides, he did enjoy the carriage outings I do think the most . . ."

She looked up from this reverie to see Eneas studying her face with thoughtful care and kind attention.

And so, despite her failing hearing, which had come to her on the terrible day the gunshot had pierced her breast and deafened her, she began to imagine at least the sound of horses' hooves, as looking out her dormer window, she got glimpses of Eneas and Aiken riding about, sometimes going so far as the edge of the lake, which looked almost purple now beneath a lemon sky. And though Aiken rode as he had always ridden with effortless ease and perhaps with even more grace than before, one need only look a moment to see something profoundly wanting. What was it? she wondered. And then the rush of terror again and recognition . . . for Aiken rode now like a blind man! Yes, that was what she had seen. A great, incomparable equestrian, but blind!

The farmers and retired folk who dwelled near the lake had a fresh phenomenon with which to occupy their attention and puzzle their comprehension, for by day and by night now one saw Lady Bythewaite's old buggy, somewhat refurbished, drawn by a vigorous young gelding, pass endlessly about the environs of Prince's Crossing and the unquiet waters of the lake. In the front seat, with Eneas Harmond driving, sat rigid Lady Bythewaite, and in the back, sitting all by himself with erect stateliness, almost grandeur, but with eyes fixed on nothing, was of course Aiken Cusworth. Back and forth the buggy went, round little forests and lonely desert places, tracts of land unowned by any known person, over which hawks circled ceaselessly, to the very brown shores of the lake, in endless unwearied journeying. At night, under a gibbous moon, one often caught sight of the old buggy going at a slow amble, the reins slack in the young driver's hands—was he too dozing?

"You are not unhappy, Eneas, away from your own horses and farm?" Lady Bythewaite would inquire again and again fearing that it was the lavish sums of money which she forced into his hard brown hands which was keeping him with her, with *them.*

Eneas, holding the reins a bit more tightly, turned to her, and she saw that this horseman had *blue* eyes, which somewhat astonished her, as if all horsemen were supposed to be dark-eyed, and then he replied:

"I do it, and I stay, Lady Bythewaite, because I want to honor him."

His reply struck her as if with a thunderbolt. It was, his statement, more than she could have hoped for, it was the finest thing which anybody had ever said of Aiken. But her thanks, so unlike the old Nora, could only be poured out now in tears, which, she supposed, Eneas honored too, for her crying did not embarrass him as it did Mr. Skegg, or anger him as it had—and the pain of even the thought of his name rose again—as it had angered Owen.

"Eneas Harmond," she said when their ride was finished that night, "I must warn you. You do not have very long to honor him, but it is my hope you will stay on even when your task with him is done."

Eneas nodded almost violently, a white globule of saliva rose to his fiercely red fresh lips. Yes, she mused, he had understood all that she said, all that was necessary to be understood.

"I think I can persuade my Dad to stay on with you . . ." Eneas spoke after wiping his mouth gently. He had stopped on a word which his mouth had formed but not pronounced, the word, she knew, was *afterwards*.

One night when there was full moonlight, Eneas Harmond awoke in a cramped position in his cot which was situated immediately beside Aiken's bed, and for a moment was not able to get his bearings, forgetful while he slumbered that he was not in his father's house, but lived with strangers. Looking over toward the bed which was Aiken's, he saw at once that his charge was absent. Starting up, he rushed to the window. In his direct line of vision he saw at once Aiken in the pasture outside, and approaching him was a horse which did not belong to the farm here, and was unknown to him. It was saddle-less, and with something about the way it moved and shook its mane that made it resemble a wild horse. The horse approached Aiken, and he reached out as if to touch it, but the beast hesitated to come closer to him once it had come within a few inches of his outstretched hands. It was then that Eneas, leaping out over the high back porch, raced to his "threatened" charge.

Hearing Eneas' running feet, Aiken turned to him, and with a kind of exhausted flailing motion of his arms threw them about Eneas' shoulders, his back to the strange horse, leaving Eneas' eyes riveted to the wild animal's form.

Was it the nearly full moon with its almost sickening light turning the green grass whitish blue, was it his own bad dreams, his disoriented position in this great house and once great farm, his own fear perhaps of Aiken who now held on to him in gentle but firm embrace, perhaps asking him to shelter him against this vision of the horse. And then to Eneas' own shocked horror he saw, or thought he saw, that the horse had a *rider*, but of such insubstantial form that had Aiken not been holding him so tightly to him he would have surely rubbed his eyes. Then the horse, and if it had a rider, yes, horse and rider vanished, but oh so easily like the clouds being wafted about the full moon.

"Will they come again?" Aiken whispered, his mouth pressed against Eneas' terrified ear. They held one another there in the shifting light from the moon like two anguished children shelterless in a desolate wilderness.

"Take heart." Eneas heard his own voice comforting his companion, but holding that companion with too much stringency and force to be the comforter. "The mist from the lake, Aiken, is so deceiving, and the cold has got to your very marrow, for see how you are shivering . . . We will light the fire in the stove, and have some hot whiskey."

"Yes, if you say so," Aiken replied, but held his face safely against that of Eneas, and not looking out in the direction of whatever it was the two had seen.

It was only after the third night in which the horse and its seeming rider had "visited" them that Eneas spoke to Lady Bythewaite.

Nora was seated with her face looking in the direction of the lake and the expanse of pasture land, and within easy view of where this incredible thing was being reported by her new horse-tender. She was sewing diligently on a great white linen tablecloth, which, having been in her possession so many years, she was not content to let be cut up into rags, but her own failing eyesight and the poor condition of its once sumptuous and lovely fabric made her task a disheartening one. As she cut some thread with her teeth and poised her needle in midair, blinking, she spoke in a cool neutral voice:

"I know you do not drink, Eneas. Yet I have noticed the whiskey bottles are half empty these mornings . . ."

"I never touched it, ma'am, before my coming here . . . You know my father's views." He hung his head.

"Eneas, listen to me. You are everything and more than I could have ever hoped for. There could be nobody more valued here than you are!"

She put down the tablecloth, it fell from her lap to the floor; he rose, stooped down, and gathered it up for her, touching it as he did so with admiring fingers, and after a questioning look for permission from her, he began to fold it carefully and at a signal from her he put it on a great polished table.

"I believe everything you say, implicitly, Eneas." She motioned for him to sit down on a chair closer to her.

"I will give you all and anything, Eneas, if you will promise to remain with me."

"I had never considered once of leaving, ma'am," he countered. He looked into the palm of his right hand.

"I do not for one moment doubt you have seen *something* out there," she spoke with a sighing almost drowned voice. "And you say Aiken speaks to you now more . . . lengthily?"

"Yes, ma'am. A bit more." He had hesitated on saying this, and she looked out into the mottled colors of the lake.

"And does the whiskey help him?" she wondered.

"I think it warms him a little." Eneas spoke most painfully now, for he had been brought up, as he had indicated, never to touch it, and she knew if he touched it now he was very troubled.

"I will watch with you tonight," Lady Bythewaite said after a long interlude of silence. "But my poor eyes, Eneas! I am afraid

I will be a bad witness for you. But if I rest all day, perhaps I can see to help you . . . Oh, Eneas," she cried, going up to him, and as he rose, she held him to her very softly. "Promise me you will not leave me, pray do promise me. I am in my most desperate need . . ."

The first night Lady Bythewaite was to watch, the mist came in from the lake and the small hills and one could not see two feet away from one's hand, but as she waited she heard unaccustomed sounds, almost like small hailstones, and then despite her failing hearing, she swore she heard horse's hooves, and a whinnying. She rose from her lookout upstairs, and walked down the back staircase, which led to Eneas and Aiken's quarters. They were lying there asleep! Aiken in the big bed, Eneas in close proximity in the cot. She was about to go back upstairs again, having given them her blessing, muttering a few words of prayer, when she became aware of something, some movement coming in out of the mist. She turned, and distinctly saw the semblance there, light as thistledown, but palpable as flesh, the one hand, for it was indeed a hand, though paler than any she had ever glimpsed in this life, holding the horse's reins before her line of vision.

As she moved toward the figure, the mist came in, driven by some current of air unnoticed before from the lake, and she was staring with her tired imperfect eyes at mere billowing fog, and in the distance lemon-colored lights from, she supposed, moored boats, or fishing shacks, or a lighthouse, who knows? and everywhere an accusatory emptiness.

"Oh give me the clew!" She heard these words, though she did not recognize the voice, coming from one of the sleeping youths.

The speaker repeated his statement, and approaching close to Aiken's form, she saw it was he who was speaking in slumber.

"I wish I could give it to you," she bent over his face, and covered it with kisses. "I would give my life to do so."

His face, his lips relaxed under her caresses and her soft

speech, the twitching of his eyelids stopped, his breathing became more regular.

"Did you see aught?" Eneas' whisper came to her.

"Yes," she spoke, half-turning to him. "We'll talk in the morning."

Nora touched his shoulder lightly then and went out as noiselessly and imperceptibly to the mind of the new horsetender as the figure he had glimpsed in the mist.

Easter, the calendar informed her, was to be early that year, and it would come in snow and more mist, she supposed, with the air one breathed freezing one's lungs.

When the mist had come in from the lake one night more pronounced, whiter, more billowing than she had ever known it, rising from her watch, she had gone straight out into the wet pasture land. She heard Eneas' footsteps coming behind her, and turning slowly about she saw he stood, all duty and patience, almost touching her hand, and then they both looked together out into the invisible waters of the lake.

The mist moved now about their bodies, threatening to make them sightless to one another even in their close proximity.

"If there is any presence here," Lady Bythewaite began speaking into the fog which covered her mouth like some curious and sentient being of itself, "if some presence wishes us ill, depart, or if you cannot depart, keep yourself invisible and wrapped forever in the fog. Torment us no more."

She turned to look into a face almost filled with rapture.

"What is it, Eneas?" she exclaimed.

He pointed in the direction of the forest on the left of the house.

The two "watchers" were now both stricken into complete silence, immobility, little more than fog themselves. How could they doubt their eyes! *Yet the mist was so treacherous*, she whispered.

But they were looking at a horse, the same horse, and its nebulous rider, and then a moment more and it was disappeared.

"It was he, Eneas," Lady Bythewaite spoke now into a whirling damp as thick as oblivion itself. "I knew it could be no other than he, but all doubts are laid to rest by this visit. We recognized one another, Eneas. It was Owen, Owen."

They walked back toward the lights of the house then in silence.

And so the watch went on, the day seeming to absorb the quality of night, and both Eneas and Lady Bythewaite appeared in the morning haggard and spent, whilst Aiken now passed most of the time in a kind watchful slumber, that is, whenever they looked at him, his eyes were closed, but his eyelids trembled like an overburdened scholar's who reads late night after night and even in dreams sees the print swim across his vision.

"My eyes are strong and keen as those of eagles. I have never worn spectacles. When I heard your whispering and your confiding in Eneas, I knew something of course was afoot. Oh, your confounded love of the imagination! Is it not perhaps behind all our misfortunes and our fall?"

Nora Bythewaite was listening to the tail end of a long speech from the old maggot; how long he had been talking and scolding she had no idea. She had been "summoned" to his study like a truant, and he had delivered one lengthy speech or tirade after another.

Nora only smiled, she did not answer in her own defense, she disputed none of his charges. She would only say to his fury she had seen Owen, and Eneas had seen him. He demanded she deny this, and so she said nothing more.

The old maggot was struck by this change in her, did not like it, and was finally somewhat in awe of her silence, and he lapsed into less vociferous denunciations of those who believe in moonshine and self-induced visions. He spoke then again of religion, of which he claimed never to have been fond, and he warned of the palpable dangers of imagination and passion. He lectured to deaf ears and scolded on like one who has been sold a bad bill of goods.

"My eyesight certainly is poor," Lady Bythewaite finally rose to her own defense. "But I know, dear Mr. Skegg, what I have seen . . . And when did you watch, since you claim to know so much?"

"I have been watching from up here for three nights," he announced.

She gave him a sweeping look of interrogation.

"And if I saw nothing, how do you explain Eneas' vision?" she asked after long searching for the right words, a bit of her old vehemence coming into her voice.

Mr. Skegg shuffled some old slightly torn yellow sheets of paper which lay on his desk.

"I have known Eneas since he was no higher than a grass-hopper," he snapped.

Lady Bythewaite cleared her throat, perhaps in irritation at this homely figure of speech, perhaps at his looking through papers while haranguing her.

"Eneas has always been brighter and more susceptible at the same time than his older brothers, his father tells me," the old maggot spoke loftily. "But of course he *is* an expert horseman."

Nora Bythewaite had let the "argument" drop. She said nothing, she seemed to be not here, and her silence further disturbed and vexed him. *His* Lady Bythewaite was disappearing, as his Aiken Cusworth had disappeared.

"I must urge on you, however, one or two things," he began again in the face of her stony incommunicativeness. "I will insist that you close the doors to the pasture at night, Nora, and that you do not let Aiken rove about, whether in the company of Eneas or not . . . After all, how on earth do we know what Aiken *sees!*"

"And makes us see too!" She had stood up on these words, indicating that her "dressing down" was over so far as she was concerned, and she was free to leave chastened, humbled, corrected, and her information and observance set at naught.

"But just the same, Mr. Skegg, you caution me that the doors are to be locked against this *nothing!*"

She stood there, having thrown these words at him while closing the door, and her accusatory look recalled to him not so much the old Lady Bythewaite as her dead son Owen Haskins when he had upbraided his father for not listening to his own sorrow.

Lady Bythewaite had walked out of his study bowed and chastened, put in her place forever, told indeed which way the wind blew.

But nobody had ever been more unsatisfied with his victory or with himself than Mr. Skegg, and nobody was to remember the evening and the night that were about to follow more than he would, for he would remember it and its events again and ever again. He would remember indeed perhaps only this last evening and night which were now about to take place and shape in all their finality and dreadfulness.

Thus, plunged in those meditations that come only with extreme old age, half-aware of the "final" unfolding of events which were to come in larger-than-life presentation as in the world of the photoplay which he detested, he was unaware that Eneas Harmond had knocked many times, and at last, in alarmed hesitation, had entered the room and stood before him.

"Ah, it's only you, my dear fellow, thank God!" the old maggot exclaimed. "Yes, thank God it is you."

The old man then listened to Eneas' plea to be allowed to visit his family that evening. When Mr. Skegg did not give his permission but sat, with the kind of grim grin on his mouth which always betokened refusal, and certainly meditating too long for the request being put to him, Eneas finally spoke up:

"I won't go then, sir, if you feel I am needed for this evening, and for the watch."

"The *watch!*" the old man spoke now with all his usual turn of sarcasm and impatience and contempt, but then catching himself: "No, you are right to speak of it as *watch*, Eneas. You are always right . . . But go indeed home to your family. I insist. This is a night for me and for Lady Bythewaite."

"I will not go if it will cause you any more anxiety, sir. I'll stay gladly."

"I *am* most distressed, Eneas," Mr. Skegg confessed. "But—"

"Then I'll remain, sir, for I hope to stay with you here so long as you wish me to. For all time if you wish it."

"You have made quite a hit with my—" Mr. Skegg had almost said *wife*, and then corrected himself severely by slamming a drawer of a bureau shut which he had left, so unlike himself, unaccountably open. "You have greatly impressed Lady Bythewaite, Eneas, I mean. I do not know, in point of fact, what we would do without you. And *he*," here Mr. Skegg tried to find some part of the room where his eyes might light, "your charge, I am sure, is more than appreciative. You are more than anybody could ever have hoped for all around."

"I feel, sir, then I should remain tonight."

"I will not hear to it. I have promised Lady Bythewaite, as a matter of fact, that I will watch tonight." He became suddenly embarrassed by the word again, and changed his thought to: "I will sit up with Lady Bythewaite in case anything is needed."

Dusk fell, Eneas had gone, Mr. Skegg rattled his papers, lifted paperweights, cleared his throat again and again, and then dimly remembered his ancestors who had looked upon liquor as the direct and immediate entrance to hell, an opinion Mr. Skegg shared, in a way more intimately perhaps than they since he had seen what it had brought Clarence to. Nonetheless feeling both ill and trembling with an icy cold in his veins, and aware that even his sternest Calvinist ancestors had approved spirits as medicine, he opened the little desk which lay to his right, and fumbled with his chain for a tiny key, placed this in another little drawer, opened it, and took out a small bottle of bonded bourbon, a gift to him many years gone by, presented by some great Wall Street figure who had never heard of there being teetotalers. He cut the stopper free with a penknife, but before drinking direct from the bottle—he had no time to find a glass—he stared a long moment at the knife itself, for it was an expensive one, and it bore the words engraved upon its steely back:

To Owen, from Aiken,
Ever, faithfully,
Christmas, 1920

How long then he sat there was never clear to him. It was not true as some have said that he drank all the bottle. He drank almost none. A tablespoonful perhaps? An ounce? Two ounces? Certainly no more. For a strange peace all by itself had come over him, his life was settling down at last, time was settling down, the evening sky had long since slipped into the lake, the very trees and moon were asleep, and the earth was one great shadow.

Two young men stood before him in this peaceful penumbra, both horsemen, and as he now looked at them, dearer to him than life, as he stretched out his amazed hands to them, calling *Aiken! Owen!* he saw they were only children of some unknown light, they had however given him their look, which was like a blessing, before they went out of eyeshot forever, out of touch, hearing, human knowledge. "Yes!" Mr. Skegg called after them. "I do know you both, indeed I do!"

Then from below, now rousing him stark awake, he had heard Nora Bythewaite's agonized cries, cries that should have leveled the house, sent it crashing through the forest, and into the waters of the lake, but cries that no longer summoned help, but were final, some awful *Amen* uttered outside the hearing of or appeal to humanity.

But Mr. Skegg stirred, he rose, he went indeed like a drunk man falling and wheeling and twisting and even plunging downward past all those steps until he stood there in the great room where she kneeled at the deathbed of her only son, Aiken.

Near the bed fluttered some dark-feathered bird, injured, it would seem, in flight. Mr. Skegg's whole attention unaccountably strayed to this woodland creature, but his inattentiveness was lost on her, for she did not even hear him enter the room. He stooped down to look at it, and recognized it as a whippoorwill which had somehow in its injured state come through the door or down the chimney.

The bird had wakened Aiken, Lady Bythewaite told of her son's death. He did not look so much puzzled or alarmed, as awakened from his long slumber since Owen's death. He became alert, he said, *I must get ready.*

"Where will you go, dearest Aiken?" she had thought she had answered. He had looked at her this time in the eyes so that she thought perhaps he heard what she had said, for he did not look merely at her mouth, which had been his way since his sickness.

"I must be ready," he repeated, and he looked about the room.

Lady Bythewaite had stared at the afflicted wings of the whippoorwill, but she had no time for this wild winged creature. Falling into his mood, she began looking about also, helping him on his journey, helping him pack.

Then as he appeared to see something beyond the room, pushing past her, indeed knocking her out of the way so that she fell against a great rosewood commode, the blow stunning her for a few moments, he was gone.

She had only time to look out the window. She saw him on the horse made of mist, with its mist rider, but as she called out, she must have frightened the beast, if beast it was, for it reared, and threw one of its two riders.

Could she then have done what she knew she did? People about the region of the lake in Prince's Crossing wondered, but she was sure she had done this great thing, though there were no witnesses. As Aiken lay there on the ground, she had picked him up, though he weighed like all the sand of the shore, and she carried him to his bed. There was some little life left in him yet, she was sure, yes, for he had spoken to her when she questioned him, of this she was surer than anything which had ever happened in all the unclear and shifting hours and minutes of her lifetime.

"Do you forgive me, Aiken?" Her own voice had come to her out of the fog. She was wringing out the cloths sopped in warm water which was itself stained almost black with blood.

He had replied, just as in the old days, but already from so considerable a distance, "Whatever for, Mother . . ."

"Just to know you have forgiven me."

"Whatever for, whatever for" was all he would say.

"If you only know how much I . . . how it is you whom . . ." she had begun again, and she was sure, yes she should stake her own poor life on this, Aiken had said, "*I know it.*"

"It was the bird which frightened him," Lady Bythewaite kept telling Mr. Skegg over and again, and she studied his own face then most carefully, studiously, for there was not one look of doubt on all its worn lineaments.

"I do believe, Mr. Skegg, that for once in your life you understand and do not contradict anything I say . . . I do believe you know what I am talking about at last . . ."

The last reel had been filled with words, had stopped, Lady Bythewaite had risen, and was on her way upstairs, a climb of some ambition, the great-nephew was fastening the rolls containing her voice so that they would not come apart, and so that the words which had been pouring out all these evenings, so it seemed to me, Eneas Harmond, would not rush out into the world and stupefy its inhabitants.

But even before she began the long climb up the countless steps of the staircase to her same old great room, I had been looking about me, for I felt all the space peopled with voices, with sounds, but all that had been fifty years ago and more, yet all the while she was going poke-poke up the stairs, I had heard someone knocking at the front part of the house, no, banging—there was no one main door one could knock at so far as Lady Bythewaite's house was concerned. And who would dare to knock? Who had knocked here indeed in fifty years?

And did she hear it? No, she was nearly stone deaf. She had heard her words on the reels, the spools, sounds telling us of the fifty years ago, but she did not hear the bang-bang of someone's fist knocking against the crumbling wood. And as I looked at the nephew—but I should say here my own eyes are not of the best, as I looked at the nephew, but then my main attention was carried away by the fist knocking, and so at last I got up and made for the front entrance, but most pokily, like Lady Bythewaite going up the innumerable stairs, stopping at every other carpeted step, like a man who has been asleep half the night, and not being able to find a flashlight anywhere, and since the front corridors were no longer wired for electricity, if they ever had been, I lit a candle.

It was the sheriff from several counties away. He stared at the candle.

"Good evening, Eneas. I'm sorry to come over at this hour. How is Lady Bythewaite?"

"Best to tell me your business, Marcus, for I have to lock up and get home myself," I responded, watching the guttering candle, and then so uneasy myself, I pretended to yawn.

I heard what he said next as if his words too came out of the fifty-year midnight.

"We're looking for a deserter from the U. S. Army, Eneas," the sheriff was speaking to me in distant near-confidential tones, and he then made a motion to invite himself in, but I put my arm up in the direction of the lintel piece, which seemed to puzzle more than stop him.

"He wouldn't be here now, would he, Eneas?"

I was listening to his heavy difficult breathing almost more than his words. He breathed like a man with heart trouble or asthma.

"Eneas!"

"Nobody here such as you describe, Sheriff," I answered him, starting.

"I know Lady Bythewaite of course hires a good many young fellows to do her chores," the sheriff was going on under his distressful breathing. "The man they are looking for, Eneas, is—"

"Her great-nephew was here, Sheriff," I raised my voice now, "but he's gone of course quite a bit back." I wondered why I had said that.

"How long has he been gone, would you say?" the sheriff edged just a bit closer to me, and his heavy breathing stopped.

"Why, fifty years," I began and then laughed, and the candle sputtered, and went out, "fifty minutes or so, Sheriff, I'd say."

I couldn't see his look of dissatisfaction at that answer, but I felt it.

He talked on about a few other unrelated matters, but had I been going to be shot at sunrise I could not remember what it was he did talk about, the front steps needed fixing, perhaps.

"Well, much obliged, Eneas, for your trouble . . . Give my kind wishes to Lady Bythewaite . . ."

Had he gone, then, without any more to-do? Yes, I put my hand on the lintel piece, and saw his retreating form down that longest path to a house in the world. I bent down to pick up the box of kitchen matches lying there on a little low table, and I lit the candle again.

Then I walked slow-slow back into the big room where all those words had been pouring out, words that had changed everything for me, for here I had been a "bailiff" to her since the long-ago days just chronicled by her voice, and Eneas Harmond seemed long dead with the rest of the voices, but her words had made everything alive and new for me all over again, or different, or strange, or revealed, her words had done away with time, somehow, so that it came to me that everything that had ever happened from the beginning of the world was going on now and at the same time, and there were no dead or living, but all were together in some steady, if often flickering, band of light.

The lamp was on in the room again now, where all those whirling words had poured forth, but there was nobody there. The nephew had gone, just like I had told the sheriff he had. The spools were still there, though, tied neatly. The back door was open. I believe I had left it so, but I went and touched it.

Then I went through every room of the house that night, calling softly, *Corliss Vallant! Corliss!*

But he was gone of course, and what's more he would never come back. I would stake my life on that.

I walked down the long long unending path that leads to the road, and it was so different a path tonight, even longer, among the shifting summer shadows. I stopped to rest every few feet, breathing as hard as the sheriff. At the edge of the property I stopped again, and then slowly turned and looked back at the great house.

"*Fifty years,*" I said aloud, and then I started, my heart beating violently. It was the sound of horses' hooves! Somewhere on some back road! I leant against one of the great elms, waiting to get quiet. But then I had heard horses' hooves before, and at this time of night, and I was not perturbed. And this is a rural area, or so the Government and outsiders call it, or it was so this morning. And then also coming from the thicket I heard them, though I had heard them before and never cried out like this, a grown man weeping against an elm tree, the whippoorwills calling once and again, one call after another, and then at long last I heard my own footsteps in the prolonged silence the country night bestows on a late walker, trudging home.